THE WIDOW OF ROSE HOUSE

The Widow of Rose House

Diana Biller

St. Martin's Griffin
New York

This is a work of fiction. All of the characters, organizations, and events portrayed in this novel are either products of the author's imagination or are used fictitiously.

First published in the United States by St. Martin's Griffin, an imprint of St. Martin's Publishing Group

For information, address St. Martin's Publishing Group, 120 Broadway, New York, NY 10271.

www.stmartins.com

Designed by Devan Norman

The Library of Congress Cataloging-in-Publication Data is available upon request.

ISBN 978-1-250-29785-3 (trade paperback)
ISBN 978-1-250-29786-0 (ebook)

Our books may be purchased in bulk for promotional, educational, or business use. Please contact your local bookseller or the Macmillan Corporate and Premium Sales Department at 1-800-221-7945, extension 5442, or by email at MacmillanSpecialMarkets@macmillan.com.

First Edition: October 2019

10 9 8 7 6 5 4 3 2 1

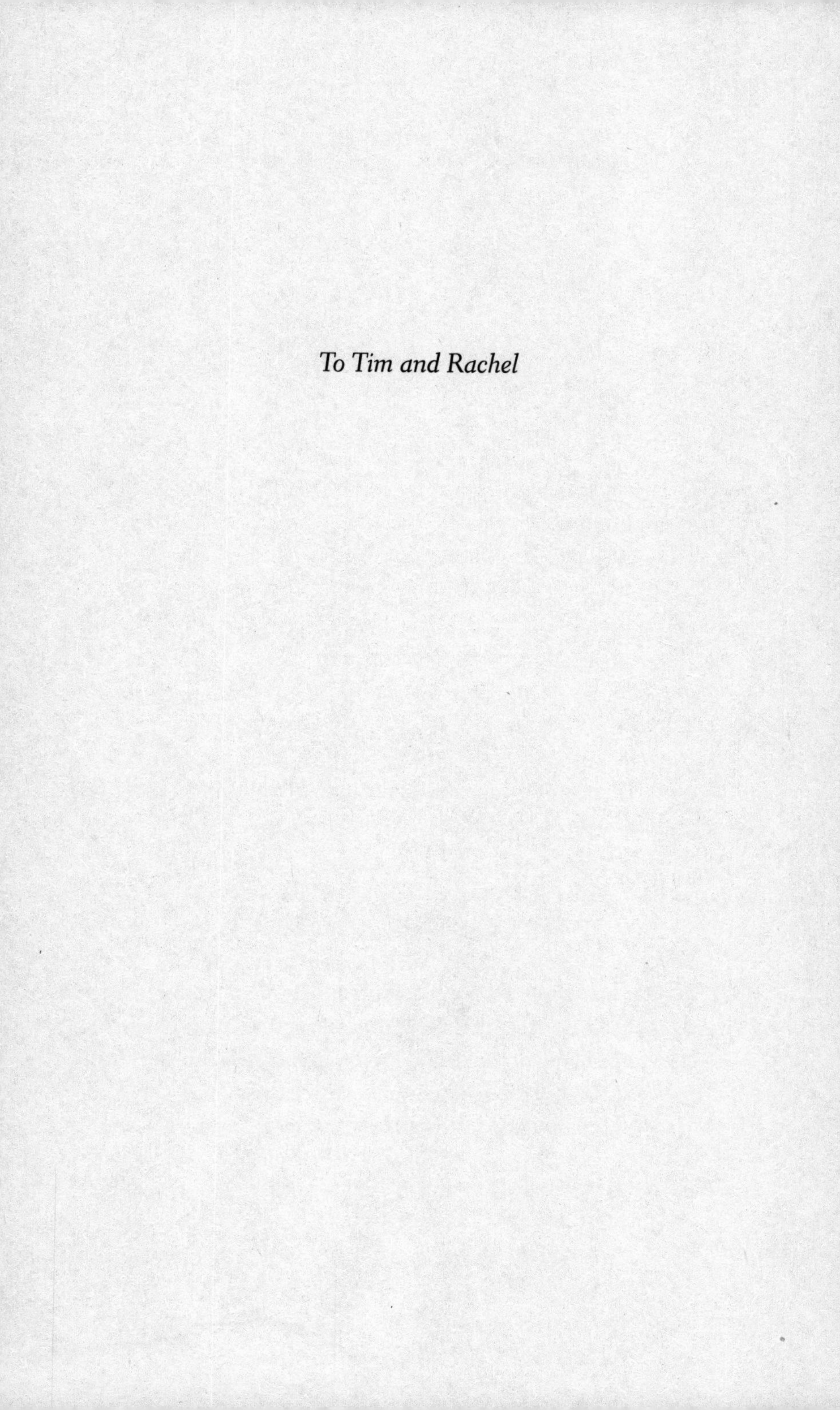

To Tim and Rachel

ACKNOWLEDGMENTS

I am surrounded by people of many magics. Without them, this book would not exist.

Patty, Tim, Brianna, and Bonnie Billings have never, in the two decades they've known me, wavered in their belief that I am a good thing to have around. Their magic is the Moore family's magic—they are profoundly good at loving.

Rachel Paxton has been my steady companion on this journey since NaNoWriMo 2013. So much has happened in those six years: so many book drafts and blog posts and cross-country moves and hours and hours and *hours* on the telephone talking about writing and men and books and friends and whatever CW show we're currently in love with or disappointed by. Here is her magic: no matter how good she was before, she'll always be better the next time you look. Underestimate her at your peril.

Rose and Bill Savard, my in-laws, always amazed me with their ability to simply love me as I am. Bill, who passed away several years ago, had the magic of a dreamer—he thought big and loved emphatically. In recent years Rose has been one of my biggest cheerleaders: she gloats on my behalf and makes me stop, once in a while, to appreciate the present. That is, perhaps, her magic—she brings out the beauty of the moment better than anyone I know.

My beloved grandparents, Jack and Marjorie Biller, built so much of the foundation I stand upon. My grandfather was another dreamer: once he loaded two thousand pounds of lead into the garage to prove a theory about gravity. He called Berkeley regularly with updates. My grandmother, I think, was the most magical person I will ever meet, because I loved her with the magic of childhood. She taught me how to work by paying me a penny for every rock I dug out of her horse pasture; she taught me the power of place through the stories she told, the trails she built, and the birds she watched; and she taught me how to love books simply by loving them so much herself.

My friends have all listened to so many confused ramblings about writing and *in addition* allow me to address them as "Aunt" and "Uncle" when speaking to my dog (I am that kind of monster). To all of you, thank you for your patience and your good humor.

Isaac Skibinski's magic is clarity of vision, which is a particularly dangerous kind of magic to have. Together we dissect the world.

Morgan Smalley once gave me very sound advice about my heroine; she also burst into tears of joy when I got the email telling me I had an agent. Her magic is that she loves selectively and deeply—I am honored to have made the cut.

Hilary Richardson has been on my side for many years. I moved a lot growing up, so it is a constant joy to me that I am now old enough to have old friends. Hilary's magic is that she enchants her surroundings, rendering the mundane comfortable and the absurd delightful.

All three of these people also make excellent houseguests.

It is impossible to fully express the debt I owe to Martha

Reynolds, who in the four years I have known her has brought incalculable grace into my life. She is a guide and a guardian, and that is her magic.

This book could not have had a better friend than my brilliant and charming agent, Amy Elizabeth Bishop. Amy's magic is that of story—I've never met someone who loves books more or understands them better. Without her vision, faith, and incredible effort, I would not be writing these acknowledgments today. I'd also like to thank my agent "siblings," whose support has brightened so many anxious days.

Vicki Lame, my editor, possesses the extraordinary magic of the sculptor: she can see the finished piece inside the uncut stone. She has shaped and championed and guided this book, and I could not be more grateful to her. Thanks are also due to the other remarkable people at St. Martin's Press, including Jennifer Enderlin, Anne Marie Tallberg, Jennie Conway, Barbara Wild, Naureen Nashid, Kerri Resnick, Marissa Sangiacomo, Sarah Schoof, Elizabeth Curione, Cheryl Mamaril, Devan Norman, and Brant Janeway.

As for my husband, Timothy Savard, giver of hugs, wiper of tears, champion orderer of Postmates, words will be insufficient. He is Sam's inspiration, and like Sam, his magic is his kindness and his brilliance and his laughter.

Finally, I've read one is not supposed to thank animals in acknowledgments, to which I respond: Thank you to my dog, Valentino "Trouble" Biller-Savard, who sleeps next to my desk, and whose magic is love and ears and singing.

THE WIDOW OF ROSE HOUSE

CHAPTER ONE

New York City, February 1, 1875

Alva Penrose Rensselaer Webster had been inside Delmonico's for nine seconds before Mrs. Henry Biddington asked the maître d'hôtel to throw her out. Alva knew because she'd counted them out: *one*, no one had noticed her yet; *two*, casual glances to see who had just come in sharpened; *three*, people began to nudge their neighbors; *four*, the whispers started; *five*, they turned angry; *six*, Mrs. Biddington, gray-haired battle-axe and leader of society, flagged her waiter down; *eight*, the maître d'hôtel crossed to her table; *nine*, Mrs. Biddington made an outraged gesture towards Alva and began to complain in a voice piercing enough to be heard clear across the room.

The restaurant waitstaff looked at Alva with increasing distress, but she just lifted her chin a little higher and followed the waiter to her table. She trusted her family name (or one of them, at least) still counted enough that she wasn't going to get tossed out of Delmonico's just yet. Even black sheep get to retain some of their perks.

The white-mustached man waiting at the table looked distinctly uncomfortable, but he stood politely when she arrived.

His fine wool suit mimicked the attire of the men around him, but no one in the restaurant would need to look at the slightly ill-fitting cut or the too-ostentatious buttons to know he was not one of them. They would know, because New York's upper crust kept track of their own.

"Mr. Smithson?" Alva held out her hand. After an almost imperceptible hesitation, he took it.

"Mrs. Webster," he said.

"It's so nice to meet you in person."

He waited until she was seated before he sat down again, clearing his throat and adjusting the crystal water glass in front of him. Echoes of his discomfort registered in the tightness of her chest and stomach, but she forced herself to ignore the feeling that hundreds of daggers were sailing towards her back. She could have told him this was how it would be, but he had insisted they meet at a restaurant instead of at his offices, and she wanted to meet him badly enough to agree.

The waiter appeared again, hovering at Smithson's right elbow, and her companion recovered himself enough to discuss the evening's menu. Alva occupied herself by scanning the room, noticing the restaurant had been redecorated sometime in the last twelve years. Green brocade paper now covered every inch of the walls, coordinating oppressively with the dark green velvet curtains. Crystal glinted in the low lamplight, and the air was hazy with smoke. An enormous painting of a ship being tossed on stormy seas dominated one end of the room.

"Well, Mrs. Webster," Smithson said, clearing his throat again. "I hope your journey was pleasant?"

"Very smooth," she said. Her ship had docked two days ago, and in a few days more it would return to France without her. Not for the first time, she wondered what on earth she thought she was doing.

"You must be pleased to be home?" he said, continuing without waiting for a response. "We—Braeburn and Smithson, that is—were very flattered you chose our publishing house to direct your query to."

It was a gracious thing to say, considering the general mood in the room, and her smile became a little easier. "I was very impressed with your firm's work on *The Principles of Interior Decoration*," she said, taking a delicate sip of water intended to show the rest of the room how at ease she was. The angry whispers were still buzzing around her. "I thought the photographs you included were especially helpful. You were an obvious choice for my own work."

The waiter returned to pour their wine, and Alva saw Mrs. Henry Biddington sail from the room in fury, her sister and two daughters trailing meekly behind. One of the girls snuck a glance in Alva's direction as she left, as though she wanted one last look at the tiger before she had to leave the zoo.

"Yes," Smithson said. "I must tell you, though, we're not convinced the market will bear another home decoration book, so soon after Mrs. Bellingham's. Your angle, though . . . it's interesting, at least. You've concluded the purchase of the house?"

"I signed the papers yesterday," she said. Smithson's shoulders had relaxed slightly since they'd started talking about business. She thought, overall, that she could have done worse with her choice of publisher. Now she just had to convince him to feel the same about her. "Work should start there next week."

The house was the basis upon which the whole mad project rested. The plan was to take a house that was on the cusp of being torn down, turn it into a showpiece of modern design ideas, and document the entire process in a book, along with photographs, illustrations, and general design principles that anyone could follow. Even now she could picture the keys to her new house sitting on her desk at the hotel, a certain imagined sheen glowing around them. They were extremely metaphorical keys.

"*The Principles of Interior Decoration* is an excellent book," she said, "but it's directed almost entirely to a very small, very wealthy portion of society. This must, by necessity, limit its sales. My book would attempt to distill my experience refitting Liefdehuis—that's the name of the house—into ideas the middle class could apply as well. There are a lot more people in that category than in the upper class, and they still have money to spare on books and home decoration schemes."

"We have been looking for titles for that audience," he said. He looked over her shoulder again, but this time with an appraising gleam.

The gleam was what she'd counted on when she'd sent the letter proposing her book, that the publisher would realize exactly how many people were likely to buy a book—any book, even one on the tasteful decoration of houses—written by the infamous Mrs. Webster. She just had to hope that once they had the book, some of them would keep reading even after they realized it was unlikely to contain any titillating revelations. After that . . . if even a handful liked what she had to say, respected the content of the book, if not its author, she thought she'd be content.

She decided to give him a little extra push. "And, as you know, my recent . . . exposure in the press . . . will ensure the book receives more than the usual amount of attention."

"Exposure" was a faint word to describe the two years she'd spent being pilloried in the newspapers, but "crucifixion" seemed a touch dramatic.

Smithson's eyes narrowed. "Not particularly positive attention," he said. "Boycotts, protests, maybe even some burnings. We have the other books on our title list to consider."

Alva took a deep breath. He wanted to publish it; she just had to get him over this last hill. "There will probably be some fuss, yes," she said. "But the more people are outraged, the more they'll talk about it, and the more people will want to buy a copy to see what the fuss is about. After all, think how many books it takes to make a bonfire."

His lips twitched, just a little, and she knew she almost had him. He stroked his mustache thoughtfully while the waiter laid the first course—molded fish pâté—in front of them. She took a small bite and let him think.

"You're not what I expected," he said abruptly. "I hope I don't offend you if I tell you that I mostly agreed to this meeting out of curiosity. But now . . . now I think I'm very glad I did."

There. Her smile widened, and she leaned forward, conspiratorially. "I'm glad you did, too, Mr. Smithson. I think we'll make a great deal of money together."

"My favorite amount," he said, lifting his glass. "To *Mrs. Webster's Guide to Home Decoration.*"

"Oh," she said as he touched his glass to hers. "I was thinking—I had proposed—the book be called *A Ladies' Guide*—"

Fully in his element now, he took a large forkful of the pâté. "Too restrained," he said. "If we're going to trade on your notoriety, there's no reason to be tactful about it. We should be slapping your name on every surface we can."

Of course, it was Alain's name, not really hers. Perhaps—

"Could it be *Alva Webster's Guide*?" she asked.

He shook his head, taking a long draught of wine. "People know you as Mrs. Webster," he explained. "Alva Webster could be anybody, but Mrs. Webster, the scandalous widow, everybody knows her. Now, the details . . ."

It didn't matter, she told herself. It might be Alain's name on the outside, but it would still be her work on the inside.

The restaurant was hot, the air smelled bad, and Sam's tie was choking him. He never would have put the damn thing on if Henry, his lawyer and business partner, hadn't bullied him into it, and now he was regretting it. Looking wistfully out the heavily becurtained windows at the New York lights beyond, he sighed. Somewhere out there was his laboratory, which had windows, excellent air circulation, and a casual dress code. He took an experimental sip of the whiskey someone had put in front of him and grimaced. Alcohol had many interesting properties; he wasn't sure taste was one of them.

It wasn't an opinion shared by the men he and Henry were dining with, a white-haired, red-faced, round-stomached man whose name Sam had already forgotten and his son, who would look exactly like his father in twenty years. If he lasted that long, which wasn't a sure thing going by the number of cocktails the man had tossed back since the beginning of the meal.

Ah, the beginning of the meal. Sam remembered it fondly, like the memory of a long-distant summer holiday. In his naïveté, he'd thought the whole business would be over in an hour. He'd thought that a generous estimate, actually—how much time could people spend eating? When he was back at the lab he could get the whole meal done in about fifteen minutes, and that was when he didn't just gobble down some cold meat and bread.

This meal was entering its fourth hour. It was agonizing. Inhumane.

"I think you'll find that if you go with my company, young man, this will just be the beginning of the perks." The old man's mustache had . . . things . . . in it. "Parties! Supper at Delmonico's every night! Balls! We can offer you something more than just sordid lucre, you know. We can offer you an entree into society itself!"

"And we appreciate that, Mr. Denton," Henry said, "but I'm afraid we must also discuss the investment itself. . . ."

Sam withdrew his attention from the discussion. There was no need for him to be involved in the money talks, and he'd just had an interesting idea about a lamp containing linked carbon blocks. He settled back in his chair and idly scanned the opulent room, feeling vaguely smothered by the dark green surroundings. The trick would be choosing the right material to sandwich between the blocks, he thought, patting his jacket idly for his notebook and looking down in confusion when the familiar lump failed to appear. It obviously hadn't made the transition between his normal clothes and the ridiculous formal suit Henry had turned up with tonight.

"Henry," he said, interrupting some point the elder Denton was making about commodity trading. "Do you have a pen?"

Henry pulled out a pen from the inside of his jacket and handed it to Sam without missing a beat in the conversation. Sam looked around for his napkin, found it on the floor by his feet, smoothed it carefully out on the table, and began to sketch.

"Err—" Denton senior leaned across the table and lowered his voice, incorrectly assuming, like many before him, that Sam's lack of attention denoted a lack of hearing. "Is he always like this?"

"You know how genius operates," Henry said, falling into the practiced words with ease. "Their intellect engages with the world in a different way from our own. . . ."

Sam let the conversation fade again. Perhaps the blocks could be held vertically, *like so*, and the fuse wire attached there, *like that*. . . . He nodded to himself and leaned back, tipping his chair onto its hind legs and letting his eyes wander the room while he thought. There was really only one thing in the restaurant worth looking at, and he let his gaze travel there again.

He wasn't the only one looking at her, either, which Sam didn't find at all surprising. When she'd entered the restaurant an hour ago—an agonizing *three hours* into his own torturous meal—the whole room had started buzzing like someone had knocked over a hive of bees. It made sense. She was . . . magnetic.

Her hair was dark, pulled away from her face in a complicated, severe knot that made her look elegant yet somehow fierce. She was all contrasts, this woman—Sam amused himself by counting them. Her red velvet dress, simple and bold, against her pale skin. Her straight, almost rigid posture, against the light laughter that drifted towards him across the room. The determination of her chin and the softness of her mouth. He wondered what color her eyes were—

"Disgusting, isn't it?" the younger Denton said, leaning across the table. Sam looked back in confusion, but it seemed the man was indeed addressing him.

"What is?"

"The Webster woman," he said. "Should have stayed in Paris. They tolerate behavior like that over there, you know."

Sam frowned, wondering how important it was to try to catch the threads of this conversation or if he could simply ignore it and go back to looking at the woman in red. Just as he had decided to do so, Denton the elder joined in.

"I'm sorry you've had to see that, gentlemen," he said, but his eyes, glued on the woman they were apparently discussing, didn't look sorry at all. They looked hungry. Sam's frown deepened as he wondered whether his own expression looked like that.

"Err, what's this?" Henry asked, in his best cat-herding voice.

"Mrs. Webster," the son said. "Over there, in the red."

Henry looked over blankly. "Who?"

"Surely you've heard of Alva Webster," the old man said. "Even in Indiana—"

"Ohio," Henry said.

"You must get the papers. She's been plastered all over them for the last eighteen months, at least—"

"Longer, I'd say—"

"Orgies, affairs, all kinds of goings-on, and that was *before* her husband died. God knows what she's been doing since. I heard—"

"We don't really have much time to read the newspapers," Henry explained hurriedly, cutting Sam off before he could say anything and sending him a sideways look that aspired to be both stern and soothing. "Now about those municipal contracts—"

"I heard she bought the de Boers' old estate," the son said, "the one up the river."

Denton senior paused in the midst of taking a drink, setting his glass back down and frowning. "Liefdehuis?"

His son nodded. "Sounds like she means to stay in the States," he said. "Who knows why. She can't imagine anyone will acknowledge her."

"You're acknowledging her enough right now," Sam said.

"What?" Denton junior said.

"Right now. She's all you can talk about. Seems to me you're getting a fair amount of pleasure out of it, too." He felt protective of the woman in red. She didn't deserve to have the Dentons of the world salivating over her, no matter who she was.

"Mr. Denton, the municipal contracts," Henry said, smoothing over the jagged silence that followed.

"Err, yes," Denton the elder said, turning away from Sam in puzzlement. "We have excellent contacts in New York, Philadelphia—"

"I heard it's haunted," Denton the younger said.

Sam's gathering indignation paused. "Haunted?"

"Oh lord," Henry muttered. "Mr. Denton, you were saying that you have business relationships in—"

"Shh," Sam said, flapping his hand in Henry's general direction.

Denton senior seemed to waver between wanting to focus on the money talk and wanting to tell a juicy story, and the juicy story won. "It's a pretty gory tale, actually," he said.

Henry smiled brightly. "I really think we should finish talking about the contracts—"

Sam stared Henry down and then nodded across the table. "Go on."

"Umm." The old man looked at Henry again, his face confused. Henry sighed.

"Professor Moore is very interested in folklore," he said, apparently resigning himself. That wasn't an accurate description *at all*, but it seemed to clear up Denton's confusion, so Sam let it go.

"Well, I don't know all the details," Denton began. "It was a bit before my time—although I'll bet it's hard for you youngsters to believe that there ever was a time before my time!"

"Yes, yes," Sam said. "The story."

"Well, the rumor is that sometime in the twenties—this was still when the de Boers owned the house, you understand—the family was having an enormous house party. At the time they were *very* well connected—of course, the next generation lost everything, had it all in Ohio Life, more fools they, but that wasn't until '57—so they invited the cream of New York society up to the house for the weekend. It was going to be the party of the decade."

He paused as their waiter set new drinks down on the table and made gentle inquiries about the state of the meal. Sam flipped his napkin over and started writing down the details of the story.

Denton took a long draught of his whiskey. "Where was I?"

"Party of the decade," Sam repeated.

"Right. So Friday night, after everyone had arrived and gathered downstairs for the opening party, suddenly they discover all the doors of the house have been locked. They're trapped. They can't get out."

"There being no windows on the entire floor," Henry murmured into his glass of water. Sam scowled at him.

"So they're panicking, and before they know it, smoke starts to come down from the top floor, and a man appears, wielding an axe. Turns out he was a radical from one of the nearby towns and he'd gotten it into his head to behead the aristocracy, just like they did in France a few decades earlier."

He took another drink and set his glass down dramatically on the table. "Murdered three people that night," he said. "Before the fire got him. The servants got the family out through the basement, see, and locked the doors behind them, so he was the one that was trapped. Burned himself alive, in the end. They say he walks the halls of Liefdehuis still, looking for more aristocrats to murder."

Sam nodded as he finished writing down the story. "Classic," he said. "Follows a lot of traditional story points. A dead murderer, hungry for blood. Excellent."

"Wonderful," Henry said. "What a delightful tale, Mr. Denton. Now that we've all had such a nice break, I wonder if we could turn back to—"

"You said it's this Mrs. Webster who owns the house?" Sam said, standing. "What a fortuitous circumstance."

"Yes," the old man agreed. "Although no one's kept it for more than—I say, Professor Moore—"

Sam was already several strides away from the table by the time Henry caught up.

"Sam, don't do it. Not right now."

"But that doesn't make any sense," Sam pointed out, quite reasonably. Henry could be a little shortsighted from time to time, but his willingness to handle the entirety of the business and administrative tasks more than made up for that. "We're here, she's here, and she just bought a house with a surprisingly modern ghost story—when was the last time you heard one that originated in the last fifty years? It sounds like the perfect test case for my theories."

"A letter," Henry said, leading him back to the table. "That's the way to do it. A letter, introducing yourself, laying out your proposal, discussing how much you'd be willing to pay. You can't accost the poor woman in the middle of a restaurant. It's not done."

Sam looked at the woman again and was forced to admit his scientific theories about the afterlife were only half the reason he wanted to approach her. He was just preparing to acquiesce when she and her companion stood up from the table and turned to leave.

"There," he said, breaking away. "She's not in the middle of the restaurant anymore."

He hurried after her.

Alva stood on the city sidewalk and sucked in a deep, triumphant gulp of air. The clock had just struck ten—the middle of the evening by New York City standards—and she was surrounded by elegantly dressed men escorting women dripping diamonds and rolled up tightly in furs. A few feet from her, the street was busy with carriages. She could smell the city: The damp fog, the sharp tang of refuse, the high floral notes of perfumed women. Horse dung.

Had she missed it? She wasn't sure, although she knew she missed the steep, tangled streets of Montmartre already. But it was America that held her future now, even as it held her past. For a second her triumph was tempered by the remembrance of the thin envelope in her pocket, a few brief lines from her mother's secretary, thanking her for her interest in visiting and regretting that Mrs. Rensselaer would be unable to see her. Alva knew her mother, likely even now sitting down to a stiff dinner with her husband and twelve of their closest friends fifty blocks away, did indeed feel regret. She just suspected it was about giving birth to her at all.

The restaurant door opened behind her, and, recalled to the moment, she signaled to the boy hailing cabs to find her one.

"Excuse me," a deep voice said. "Mrs. Webster?"

Oh, for heaven's sake. Couldn't she stand outside for *one minute* without some intrepid lothario assuming she must be waiting for him? In the less than seventy-two hours she'd been back in the States, she'd been propositioned eleven times. Twice by friends of her father's.

She glanced over her shoulder at the man, receiving an instant impression of *big,* though he stood mostly in the shadows. "I don't know you," she said, her voice flat. "Go home to your wife."

"But I don't have a wife," the man said. He took a hesitant step towards her, leaving the shadows, and her eyebrows lifted. He looked more like a laborer than a man finishing a dinner at Delmonico's, for all he was dressed in a suit and tie. *Sort of dressed,* she amended; the suit looked like it had been made for someone two inches shorter and two inches narrower across the shoulders. "Do I need a wife to talk to you? Is it a chaperone sort of thing? I have a mother, but she's in Ohio."

Alva blinked. "You're not very good at this," she observed. "I'm not a man, but I don't think it's standard behavior to invoke one's mother at a time like this."

They stared at each other in puzzlement. He was attractive in the sort of way she'd always imagined the heroes of western folktales to be: tall, broad shouldered, with a strong nose and a square jaw. He could stand to add barber to the list of people he needed to see, though, the one that started with tailor. Actually, looking at the way his dark blond hair fell into his eyes, she thought he'd better have it start with barber and go from there.

"There's been a misunderstanding," he said finally. "Perhaps if I introduce myself—my name is Professor Samuel Moore."

He held out his hand. She looked at it, looked up at him, and did not extend her own. Bafflingly, he smiled at her, as though she'd done something rather clever.

Was he really a professor? He certainly didn't look like one, not that it mattered, because she made it a policy, these days, never to talk to strange men—

"A professor of what?" she heard herself saying, although she was pleased it at least came out with a nice air of sarcasm and disbelief.

"This and that," he said, still smiling. "Engineering, mostly."

She looked at his rumpled clothes. Yes, she could see that, one of those men who always had a tool in one hand and a grease can in the other. She didn't know they were giving professorships out to men like that, but why not, after all? She was as appreciative of things like trains and working carriage wheels as the next person.

And now she'd gone and encouraged him. *Stupid.* "I see," she said as coldly as she could manage. "Well, I'm not interested, so I'll wish you good evening."

"But how can you know if you're not interested?" He shook his head in confusion, still smiling at her. The smile was . . . impressive. "I haven't even explained my proposition, yet."

"I find that if you've heard one proposition, you've heard them all," she replied. *Stop talking to him, you idiot.* "They're not as unique as men would like to believe."

"But—who else has approached you? Was it Langley, from Yale?" His tone turned plaintive. "How did *he* hear about this before me?"

"Langley—who?"

"Piers Langley," he said. "No? I can't think of anyone else reputable—look here, if you've been approached by anyone from that quack Santa Fe institute you should know they're absolute frauds."

"Institute?" Alva said faintly. "What *on earth* are you talking about?"

"Your house, of course. I hadn't realized I was so behind on the news." His face fell—*What must it be like to let all your emotions float freely on your face?*—but he nodded gravely. "If it's Langley, though, he's an excellent researcher, and a decent human, too."

"It's not Lang—what do you want with my *house*?" It was her turn to sound plaintive.

"But that's what—" He stared at her, his brows crunched together. "Oh god. I wasn't—I wouldn't—"

To her astonishment, a distinct touch of pink appeared in his cheeks. He cleared his throat.

"I beg your pardon, ma'am. Henry warned me—that is, I shouldn't have; my proposition is not of an intimate nature."

"I'm coming to understand that," she said.

"You thought . . . do men . . . they must—*good lord.*"

She began to feel in charity with this befuddled giant. "Indeed," she said. "I quite agree. But I must ask again—what is it you want with Liefdehuis?"

"To study it," he said. "One of my personal interests is in metaphysical energies, you see, and from what I've heard, your house may prove a most interesting case. Your ghost story is so recent, you know. I hardly ever hear one claiming to be that new—"

He broke off as she shook her head. "You almost had me convinced that you were unlike the majority of your sex," she said. "And now I see you are. I'm just not sure insanity is much of an improvement."

To her surprise, he smiled again. "You're not the only one who thinks so," he said. The embarrassment had left his face; he was quite relaxed once more. *A man who apologizes for a proposition and grins at an insult,* Alva thought. *Where did you come from, Professor Moore?*

"And I'll admit there's no conclusive evidence yet," he continued, "but what I have collected looks extremely promising. Certainly promising enough to warrant extensive study."

A hint of cold pierced her thoughts. Firmly, she banished it.

"You're talking about ghosts," she said.

"Maybe," he replied. "Or I could be studying some kind of alien intelligence that just happens to concentrate in areas corresponding to local folklore."

"Alien intelligence."

"*Invisible* alien intelligence," he clarified. "At least invisible to the naked human eye. But 'ghost' is probably the easiest term."

"Really."

"People tend to go a bit strange when you talk to them about invisible alien intelligences," he confided. "Which is odd, when you think about it, because why are the shades of one's dead ancestors any less unsettling?"

She found herself nodding before the rest of her wits caught up with her. "No," she said, not because the word corresponded with any particular question, but because she had the feeling the only way to survive here was to stick to very black-and-white words. His nuances were both compelling and sticky. "I'm afraid I won't give you access. I don't believe in ghosts, and I'm about to start several months' worth of building work."

"Don't decide yet," he begged. "I'm willing to pay you for the privilege, and I promise I won't be in the way . . . although there *is* rather a lot of equipment, so I suppose—"

The boy hailing cabs caught her eye and gestured as a hansom pulled up beside him.

"That's mine," she said. "I'm sorry I can't help you. Good evening."

"Wait!" he said. "I'll—I'll send you a letter. Henry *said* that was the way to do it—I'll write you and explain more."

"It won't help," she said as the cab boy helped her into the carriage. "I'm sorry. Good-bye, Professor Moore."

Finally, he sighed acceptance and raised his hand. "Good evening, Mrs. Webster."

As the cab pulled away from the sidewalk, though, she looked back at him, to find him staring after her with his hands shoved in his pockets and that apparently irrepressible grin back in place. An uncomfortable lightness expanded in her chest as she watched him standing head-and-shoulders taller than the passersby around him, looking back at her as though he would be perfectly happy never to look at anything else ever again.

What couldn't I get, if I could look at people like that? she thought, and settled grumpily back against her seat.

CHAPTER TWO

New York City, February 17, 1875

Sam took one look at the tidy brownstone, with its immaculate steps and delicate lace curtains, and retreated to the bottom of the stairs to scrape his boots more carefully. The mud clung, so he shrugged and sat down on the first step to unlace them.

His thoughts wandered to his most recent fascination: the scandalous Mrs. Webster. She hadn't seemed particularly scandalous when he'd met her—she'd seemed smart, and strong, and . . . wary. He'd discovered why the next morning when he'd started into the newspaper archives at the Astor Library. He'd meant to focus on her house, but his curiosity about the woman had overwhelmed him, and it wasn't as though she was hard to find.

Two years ago, with no instigating incident Sam could find, Alva Webster had jumped from the society column of the Parisian papers ("Mr. and Mrs. Webster hosted several American friends at a select dinner party . . .") to the pages of scandal sheets across Europe. Her name was dragged from salacious headline to salacious headline; thinly sourced stories about extravagant orgies and titillating affairs. Ten months later, her husband, whom she had not been living with at the time, had been murdered by ruffians in Monte Carlo. This poured oil onto an already roaring fire, and Mrs. Webster was promoted again, from scandal sheets to front page news. The papers had even breathlessly reported when she'd begun wearing lavender three months after the murder, a sartorial decision which was apparently very shocking for reasons Sam didn't quite grasp.

He got one boot unlaced and frowned down at it. Did it always take that long to unlace a shoe? He removed his watch and set it on the step next to him before he began the next one.

The stories were awful and almost certainly libelous. They would have flattened a weaker person. That Alva Webster still stood, with her back ramrod straight and her jaw set firmly against the world, only intrigued him more.

He'd researched the Rensselaers, the wealthy banking family she came from, and discovered her father was a member of one of the consortiums that had recently approached him about the same municipal lighting project the Dentons were interested in. Curiously, there was hardly any mention of them in the newspaper stories, a fact that nagged at him. He wondered how they'd been able to restrain themselves during the worst of it. He wouldn't have been able to, if it had been a member of his family.

Once he'd been able to tear himself away from the woman, he'd begun gathering data about the house. The project had occupied every spare moment of the last three weeks—well, perhaps not every spare moment; there was the prototype of the carbon lantern that had popped into his head that night, which he'd quickly knocked together, as well as the three iterations that had come after—but otherwise he'd been devoted to the Webster project.

He'd started in the libraries and government offices, simply gathering as much data as he could on the former occupants of the house, who had been born there, who had worked there, who had died there. This was surprisingly difficult information to obtain: property records, tax records, and census reports accounted for some years and some classes, but in between census years it was very difficult find out who the servants had been, let alone what their lives there had been like. He'd come across the woman he was about to visit, one Magda Kay, in the 1840 census listed as a scullery maid.

The second boot came off, and he looked down at his watch. Twenty-three seconds! That was forty-six seconds per pair of boots. Assuming it would take approximately the same amount of time to lace them up—an assumption he only barely restrained himself from testing *right then*—and only one cycle per day, which was conservative, since there were plenty of days in which you'd need to take your shoes off in the middle of the day for some reason, that amounted to *over four and a half hours a year.* Sam blinked down at the offending boots and took out his notebook. Perhaps a device that did the lacing and unlacing for you . . . or perhaps it would be better to simply redesign the shoe itself. . . .

"Professor Moore?" the voice came from above him, a little hesitant.

"Hmm?"

"Begging your pardon, sir, but Mrs. Kay wondered whether you might like to come inside, it being so cold out here."

Was it cold? Sam wiggled his sock-clad toes and realized they were slightly numb. "All right," he said, pushing his muddy boots neatly to the side before standing.

The voice belonged to a young maid, her arms crossed over her chest as if to trap her remaining warmth. Realizing he was the reason she was standing out in the cold, he quickly ducked through the open door, smiling apologetically at her as he went. Her cheeks went a little pink, and she let out a small sigh, no doubt pleased to be back inside.

She led him to a room right off the narrow hall they'd entered, a sitting room so tidy it looked as though it were only barely tolerating human occupancy. A plump woman in her early fifties stood as he entered, smiling at him cheerfully.

"Professor Moore," she said, her brown eyes sparkling up at him. "What an honor. I'll be the queen of the neighborhood for the next six months."

He grinned at her. "Mrs. Kay, if you're not already the queen of your neighborhood, I'll profess myself shocked."

"Hah! A flirt, too. Sit, sit." She waved him into a chair by the fire and turned to her maid. "Alice, we'll have tea, the cookies as well."

There was a bustle while refreshments were wheeled in, and Mrs. Kay made herself busy pouring tea while Sam enjoyed the crackle of the fire and four excellent butter cookies.

"Now," she said, handing him a cup of tea and settling herself into her chair. "I'll admit I was surprised to receive your letter. I haven't thought about Liefdehuis . . . oh, in years, probably. It seems on the other side of the world from me, now."

"You worked there in '40, right?"

"Thirty-five years ago," Mrs. Kay sighed. "From 1838 to 1840, that's right. I was sixteen when I started, and eighteen when I went to visit my sister in the city and met Mr. Kay; just a dockworker then, he was, but he did well for himself later. He was a fine-looking young man, you understand, and my head was fairly turned, but in hindsight, never having to go back to that house was a powerful incentive for marriage, too."

Sam wrote as she spoke. "That bad?"

"Mr. de Boer, that's the younger one, his father having passed a couple years before I started, he was one of those types that has to be making someone else feel bad before he can feel good. I read he committed suicide, a few years after the crash, and though I can't say I shed any tears, it made me wonder how bad it must have been for him, that he needed everyone around him to feel worse." She sighed and shook her head, as if to dismiss such dark thoughts. "Is he who you're researching? I admit I don't quite see what interest a famous inventor could have in the de Boers."

He hesitated, wondering how to lead into his subject. Henry would have finessed the conversation so it just sort of flowed in the right way, but Henry was boycotting this project. Maybe if he sidled up to it, delicate-like . . . "Actually, I'm researching the ghost," he said.

"The ghost!" Mrs. Kay set her teacup down in its saucer with a decided clink. "I don't think you'll be finding any world-changing inventions there, young man."

He laughed, too used to skepticism to mind her reaction. "I'm not looking for any," he said. "Just interested in the story. Call it a hobby."

"Hmm." She looked over at him, her lips pursed but her eyes still merry. "Well, which story?"

"You heard more than one?"

"It was quite a topic of discussion in the servants' hall, your ghost. A few of the maids swore up and down they'd seen it, that they knew the whole sad tale." Mrs. Kay snorted. "*Not* that they could ever agree on what they'd seen, of course, and it was my suspicion half the stories were made up, for attention."

"Only half?" Sam looked up from his notebook. "You mean you believed some of them?"

"Not exactly believed," she said. "Well, I couldn't *believe* in them, when the stories didn't even agree with each other, but let's say there were a couple of maids whose hysterics seemed less theater and more fear. I don't know if they hoaxed themselves into seeing something, or if someone was tormenting them on purpose. For all I know there were two ghosts wandering the halls instead of one."

Ghost infestation? Sam wrote on the page, briefly imagining ghostly rats fleeing before a ghostly terrier.

"Do you remember the stories? The ones you found more credible?"

"Oh yes," she said, beaming with the joy of a true gossip and storyteller. "They were both quite sad, of course. The first one was about a beggar, a village man who'd lost his family the year before, going door to door in the winter asking for food. Only the winter was uncommonly cold, and one night he crept up to the back door at Liefdehuis and asked to come in, just for a minute, to warm himself. But the servants were under strict orders about tramps, so they closed the door in his face and went up to their beds. When they came down the next morning, they found him where they'd left him, curled up on the back porch and frozen to death."

"You're sure it was a man?" He'd heard stories like that before, but they were almost always about older women.

Mrs. Kay tilted her head, thinking. "As sure as I can be after almost four decades," she said, nodding, and then chuckled. "Which is to say, more sure than not, but by no means without doubts."

Sam smiled back at her. "And the other?"

"Well," she said, and looked over her shoulder at the door. Putting her finger to her lips, she rose and crept stealthily across the room. When she reached the sitting room door she paused, pressing her ear against the wood, and then in one sudden gesture yanked it open, nearly toppling the young maid on the other side.

"Alice," Mrs. Kay said, "won't you go fetch Professor Moore some of those lemon cookies Cook made yesterday? He'll like them."

"Y-y-yes'm," Alice stammered, her face bright red, and almost ran from the room.

Mrs. Kay gave a satisfied nod and sat down. "It's not a story for maiden ears," she explained, pouring herself a second cup of tea. "But it's a familiar one, for all that. The tale goes that the ghost was a young servant girl who was seduced by the son of the house. She found herself . . . in a certain situation, you know, and went to him to tell him she was, and he looked her in the face and told her that he'd never been with her and if she was in such a situation it must be by one of the countless other men she'd slept with. She drowned herself in the pond the very next night."

Mrs. Kay added two cubes of sugar, stirring them in with a thoughtful air. "Maybe I should have let Alice hear it, after all. She won't always live in a house like this one."

Sam lingered another thirty minutes, but there was little more Mrs. Kay could tell him, at least until he had better-formulated questions to ask her. He took his leave, along with two more cookies for the road, and strode back down the tree- and brownstone-lined street deep in contemplation. Three different ghost stories, all collected within a three-week time span—how many more were there? Was it possible there was more than one ghost at the site?

He needed to visit Liefdehuis, and soon.

Hearing the rattle of the elevated railway as he approached the 30th Street Station, he jogged up the iron staircase and caught the train just as it pulled up. Making his way towards an empty bench near the back, he wondered idly how long it would be before passenger trains like this would be run electrically—the small locomotives this line used were an improvement over the stationary steam engines it had first relied on, but not ideal for either long-distance or long-term use. He pulled out his notebook and jotted down a few musings on the matter and then turned the page, smoothed it carefully, and started his third letter to Mrs. Webster.

Dear Mrs. Webster, he wrote—a pleasurable action in itself, to write the name of a beautiful woman—*I have just left the house of a woman formerly employed as a scullery maid by the de Boers at Liefdehuis. . . .*

He summarized the stories Mrs. Kay had told him, including a few of his own observations and thoughts, before renewing his plea for access. The first two letters had not received a reply, but as he wrote, Sam was filled with confidence. She had reason to be cautious, but how could she resist a possible ghost infestation?

Absorbed in his writing, he missed his stop and had to double back on foot. The sun was already setting, though it wasn't much past four, casting pale, watery light over the city and the suited men heading home for their evening meal. The gas lamps lining the street turned on, reminding Sam of his own lamp, and he spent most of the walk wondering how he could lengthen the lit time of the third prototype.

He was staying in a small boardinghouse a few blocks away from the burgeoning financial district, tucked into a quiet eddy of small streets and alleys that hadn't yet been absorbed into Wall

Street's moneyed frenzy. Deciding he would post the letter and then go to dinner at the tiny Italian restaurant he visited five nights out of seven, he started up the stairs to his room two at a time.

When he opened the door, though, all his plans went out of his head. A tall, dark-haired man lounged in the desk chair, glasses perched at the end of his nose, perusing the thin pages of a scientific journal.

"Benedict!" Sam cried, tossing his bag onto the bed. "What the hell are you doing here?"

His brother held up a finger, finished his sentence, looked up, and grinned. "Escorting you by royal decree," he said. "You've been summoned to dinner."

"To dinner! Then that means—"

"Yes, we're all here, descended upon you like locusts."

"Damned welcome locusts," Sam said, pulling Benedict to his feet and into a hug.

"This excess of emotion," Benedict drawled, even as he returned the embrace. "Really, Sam. I had hoped the sophistication of the city might rub off on you—"

"Oh shut it," Sam advised, squeezing a little tighter before releasing him. "You said everybody? Even Maggie?"

"Yes, the pest is here, too." At the mention of their younger sister, Benedict dropped his affectations in favor of a scowl. "I'm never traveling en famille again, Brother, I swear it. They met me in Philadelphia—you remember, that conference?—which means I've spent the last day listening to nothing but '*This is the latest style out of Paris*' and '*Don't you think this hairstyle is simply elegant?*'" His voice lifted in the universal tone of an older brother exasperated by a younger sister. "My knowledge of the latest fashions now rivals my knowledge of medicine."

"Well, it's always good to have a fallback career," Sam said, vaguely looking around for his coat before remembering he was already wearing it.

"It's better than ghost hunting," Benedict said as they walked out of the room.

"I don't hunt ghosts," Sam protested. "I bear them no ill will at all. I just want to make their acquaintance."

"Ghost social climber, then."

"Much closer."

Night had fallen while the brothers had talked, as much as night ever fell in the city. The air had turned sharp and cold, and Sam wondered where he'd left his scarf.

"We're staying at some fancy new hotel on East Twenty-ninth," Benedict said, turning left at the next street. "Maggie talked Mother into staying there. Something out of her magazines."

"I don't even know where East Twenty-ninth is," Sam said cheerfully. "As long as they have a decent kitchen and can produce me some dinner, I'll love it."

"Maggie says they're famous for some French dish," Benedict said. The brothers shared a concerned look.

"Maybe it'll be steak," Sam said, after a pause.

"It's probably fish jelly," Benedict said. "It's always fish jelly, with the French."

"They wouldn't," Sam said, shooting his brother a horrified look.

"They might," Benedict said. "It's that kind of place."

After a second of daunted silence, during which Sam made up his mind to be courageous in the face of possible fish jelly, he recalled himself to the moment.

"How was the conference?" Benedict had been a featured speaker at the meeting in Philadelphia, attended by doctors and scientists working in the rapidly expanding field of brain research.

“Would you believe we were protested?” Benedict said, pulling his coat tighter. “Some local church decided we were digging up graveyards to cut people’s heads apart. I even went out to explain we only use cadavers with correct legal permission, but it didn’t help. They threw a potato at me.”

Sam winced in sympathy. “Ow.”

“Oh, I caught it. Still, I told them in the future they should stick to rotten fruit, unless they wanted to do real injury.”

“Did Caton make it?”

“He did, and it’s a good thing those protestors didn’t get a look at his work. . . .”

CHAPTER THREE

When they reached the seventh floor of Gilsey House, a scene of carnage greeted them. Black-coated waiters scurried back and forth, a thick cloud of smoke hung in the air, and two maids were crying in a corner. The double doors of the suite were open, one hanging drunkenly off its hinges. Sam and Benedict exchanged a look and entered the room.

Inside was not much better. The long silk curtains framing one window had fallen to the floor, and the desk below was charred and smoldering. A large gray puddle had formed where the water used to extinguish the fire mingled with ash and soot. Sam quickly scanned his family, and once he was assured everyone was both alive and uninjured (mostly; Maggie had a bandage on her hand), he announced their presence.

"You could have saved the explosions until after dinner," he said. "Now the chef probably won't even serve us."

"That was just the one time," his mother said, launching herself towards him. "Oh, Sam!"

He caught her in his arms and squeezed her tight, grinning

at his family over the top of her head. Behind her stood his sister, seventeen-year-old Maggie, a younger copy of their mother, with curly red-brown hair and sweet brown eyes, and his father, gray haired and sporting an absurdly large mustache that he insisted upon keeping even over his family's protests.

Sam's mother stepped back, still holding his hands. "Not a letter," she said, "not one letter."

"That's not even a little bit true," he said. "I sent you a telegram when I arrived."

"'Arrived safe stop,'" his mother said, putting her hands on her hips. "'Write more soon stop.' And then not a word! Henry's written me every week—"

"Not that he could tear himself away from his precious business meetings today," Maggie muttered.

"And if it wasn't for that, I wouldn't know a single thing. You could be *dead* for all I'd know—"

"Oh, leave off him, Winn dear." His father stepped in for an embrace. "The truth is we missed you and the girls wanted an excuse to come to the city."

Sam looked at his mother and tried to conjure a sufficiently penitent expression. "Dearest Mater," he said, "I am terribly sorry I failed in my duties as your oldest, and, let's face it, favorite child . . ."—here he paused for the necessary insults from Benedict and Maggie—"and I promise to never do so again. Won't you forgive me, dearest, kindest Mother?"

"Such silliness. And you wanted to come, too, John," she said to her husband, "as you seem to have forgotten so quickly."

"So who's responsible for the fire crew?" Benedict asked, flopping down on a couch far enough from the explosion site to still be dry. Sam joined him.

"The girls," John said. Winn and Maggie gave identical shrugs.

"Ah," Sam said. "The alloy."

"We're making excellent strides," Winn said. "We tested it with water today, and I don't think either of us were expecting such a pleasing result."

"I wouldn't have worn my new dress if I had," Maggie said, futilely trying to brush some soot off the cream fabric.

"No," Winn said. "It's a shame, that."

"How are you producing it now?" Sam asked, leaning forward.

"A still Mags designed. We just finished the new version yesterday." Winn sighed. "Of course now we'll have to build a new one."

"It's based on the designs you sent me?"

Maggie nodded. "More refined, obviously."

"Well done, Rags," he said, rubbing his hand over her head and mussing her curls. She batted his hand away.

"I don't answer to that name anymore," she replied with great dignity.

"Oh yes, dear Margaret has become quite grand in our absence," Benedict said. "And she's sparking after Curtis Edwards, according to a letter I had from Lily Parrish last week."

"I am not!" she squealed. "And Lily Parrish is just trying to get you to notice her, anyway. She'd probably say I was engaged to the cheese on the moon if she thought it would get you to pay attention to her."

"I think Lily's nice," Sam said mildly. "It's not her fault Benedict's an ass. Are you really interested in Curtis, Maggie?"

"No! And you think everyone's nice."

"Lily said she saw them out walking together," Benedict said, grinning maliciously. "A couple of Sundays back."

"We were simply discussing the new agricultural taxation proposals," Maggie replied, sticking her nose into the air. "He's very well informed."

"Oh, I'm sure," Benedict said, dodging quickly to the right to avoid a pillow. "Why are people always throwing things at me?"

"Which one's Curtis?" Sam heard his mother say to his father.

"Hell if I know," he said. "Which family's Edwards?"

"Isn't that the postmaster?"

"I thought it was the family who owned the dry goods."

"His father's a senator," Benedict said, covering his quick retreat by lounging casually again the back of a chair. "Louis Edwards. Balding. Ugly, but with a pretty wife. Wanted you to support him in the last election."

"Oh, not the one who wants to break the railroad brotherhoods," John said with an expression of horror. "Talked to me for three hours last year about it. I thought I'd have to jump in the well to get away from him. I would have, but we were testing that new whatsit in it and I didn't want to damage it."

"I hope the son takes after the wife," Winn said, equally shocked. "The father's a horrible little toad."

"I hope he didn't inherit his father's politics," John said.

"I'm not sparking after him!" Maggie shouted. "It was one walk! And for the record, he thinks his father's politics are *quite* outdated!"

"Our charming family," Benedict murmured to Sam, a smile lurking at the corner of his mouth.

"I've missed this," Sam said, unable to stop grinning. "But we're going to have to move it along. I'm starving." He stood up and, putting two fingers in his mouth, let out a loud whistle. "Family," he said, "may I propose we continue this in the restaurant?"

"Always thinking of your stomach," Benedict said, but he straightened quickly enough.

"An excellent idea," his father said, standing as well. "Let us go at once."

"Daddy, you're wearing your slippers," Maggie said. "You have to go put on proper shoes."

"Eh? Oh, so I am." John shuffled off towards one of the bedrooms.

"And I have to change," Maggie continued. "I can't go down looking like this."

"Look here," Sam said in concern. "If I don't get food within the next fifteen minutes I'm likely to drop away in a dead faint."

"Fifteen minutes!" Maggie said, running out of the room like her dress was still on fire. Sam collapsed back onto the couch and shook his head.

"You'll have to carry me downstairs," he said. "I'll be too weak by then."

She didn't know why she'd gone, Alva thought as she swung through the grand front doors of Gilsey House. Her parents had made it more than clear they weren't interested in seeing her, and if one thing was absolutely true about Edna and Thomas Rensselaer, it was that they didn't change their minds.

Perhaps Alva had thought that if they knew she was standing only a few feet away they'd experience some sort of parental compulsion to see her. Which was really quite stupid, given that she'd lived a few floors away from them for a large part of her life and they'd never felt the need to see her then. Still, she'd gone, and she'd waited on the stoop in the snow for fifteen agonizing minutes while the poor red-faced maid who'd answered the door had gone to discover whether Alva was to be admitted.

She hadn't even been allowed to wait in one of the receiving rooms. Apparently her mother had foreseen that an impromptu visit was a possibility and had instructed the maids not to admit her without express permission.

Of course, waiting on the stoop had been far more pleasant than what had come next: the young maid, visibly distressed, returning to inform her that her mistress had already communicated her wishes regarding Mrs. Webster's visit and wished to inform her that a repeat attempt would be ill-advised and would, indeed, merely embarrass both parties. The girl had stumbled a bit on the word "embarrass," and momentarily Alva hadn't been sure if she'd manage to complete the message. She had, though, which Alva thought showed quite a bit of courage.

The hotel lobby was crowded with guests already changed into evening wear and preparing for a night out in the big city. One particularly rowdy group stood outside the entrance to the restaurant, and Alva let her eyes rest on them. A family, roughhousing and arguing and enjoying one another. The familiar envy cut through her: a quick pain, replaced almost immediately by weary acceptance. She steered a path well clear of them and headed for the stairs.

She was almost to the foot of them when someone called her name. A very particular someone whom she'd thought about more than she cared to admit in the last three weeks. It was because of the damned letters. The man didn't know how to give up.

She shouldn't recognize his voice already, she mused as Sam strode towards her, a head taller than the people he passed. It was deep, and a little slow, like he had all the time in the world to say what he wanted to. There was a bedrock of humor underneath it, which came out in the letters he'd written, too. He wrote like he spoke—warm and welcoming, inviting you to share in the fun.

Of course, fun wasn't for people like her.

"Professor Moore," she said, her own voice coming out strict and flat. "Are you following me now? If your letters haven't convinced me, this certainly won't."

"Ah," he said, smiling down at her. He looked . . . delighted to see her. Which was discomfiting, since the only people who had looked delighted to see her since she'd landed in New York were journalists. "But there's an even more convincing one in the mail. And I'm not following you; I'm here for dinner. Is this where you're staying?"

She looked at him in bemusement. "You have my address. I don't know how you got it—"

"Oh, Henry found it," he said. "Although I have to tell you, I don't think he had to work hard to get it, so if you were hoping to be incognito—"

"The point is," she continued, determined not to lose track of it, "you have it, so how can you not know this is where I'm staying?"

"Oh, very easily," he said. "I have no idea where I am."

"How can you—" She closed her eyes. "Never mind. Now if you'll excuse me, my shoes are quite damp, so—"

He looked at her shoes. "Those are ridiculous," he said.

She sighed and followed his gaze. They were ridiculous, of course: embroidered half boots in black suede, now quite destroyed by the slush and general grime and muck of New York, and uncomfortable on top of it all. She hated them. "They're perfectly ordinary footwear," she said. "Now if you please—"

"How long do you spend lacing those?" he asked, crouching down to get a better look. "It must take . . . good lord, it must take up to a minute. And then another thirty seconds to unlace them."

In truth, it took longer. The laces were tiny, and they went all the way up the boot. "I simply don't see—"

"And don't you women change during the day?" he said,

looking up at her in horror. “My sister does, and I think it’s general behavior.”

“I’m sure I don’t—”

“Why, it must take you . . . it could take you almost twenty hours a year to lace and unlace your footwear! That’ll teach Henry,” he said with savage pleasure. “He said no one would want a shoe-lacing device. We’ll just need to develop it for women. It’ll change the design a bit, of course—”

“I don’t think that sum’s right at all,” Alva said after a few seconds of furious thought. “That assumes doing the whole rigmarole twice a day—”

“Yes—”

“But with the same pair of shoes. These are extreme examples. Sometimes I wear slippers.”

“The kind you wear to bed?”

She almost laughed but managed to suppress it in time. “No, the kind you wear to go dancing.”

“Ah, and they don’t have laces?”

“No,” she said. “Although I suppose sometimes other shoes worn during the day do.”

“I see,” he said, rummaging inside his jacket and producing a notebook and a stub of pencil. “Now,” he said, “on an average day, how many changes of shoe would you say you go through?”

“Well,” she said, scrunching her brow. “Average is hard, because each day is—Oh, look here, I don’t have time for this sort of nonsense. I really must be going.”

She started to brush past him.

“Wait!”

“Really,” she sighed. “It’s always ‘wait!’ with you.”

“You only say that because you haven’t met my sister,” he said confidingly. “I’m quite the most prompt person in my family.

Well, except for Benedict. And maybe my mother. The third most prompt person."

"Yet again, you simply fascinate me. Good—"

"Wait! That's the point, you see. I want you to meet my family."

"I don't think—"

But he was already gently leading her by her elbow. Alva huffed in exasperation and tried not to focus on the new information his proximity revealed: that he smelled of peppermint and man, that the muscles underneath his coat sleeve were large enough to throw off the cut of the garment, that he'd nicked himself at least three times during his morning shave. At least he *had* shaved, she reasoned. That, at least, was an improvement over their last meeting.

"Mother, I want you to meet someone," he said, stopping in front of the rowdy family she'd seen earlier. A short, rounded woman with a chaotic tumble of reddish-brown curls turned around and greeted them with an enormous smile.

"Hello," she said.

"Hello," Alva replied, unable to keep from smiling back.

"Sam, release this poor girl at once," she said, her eyes landing on where he had grasped Alva's elbow. "I don't think people like to be hauled about."

"They don't," Alva put in, pleased to find an understanding spirit. She yanked her arm away.

"I wasn't hauling her about," Sam protested. "I just wanted you to meet her. This is Alva Webster."

"The woman with the house?" This was from a younger, slimmer version of Sam's mother, a girl no more than sixteen or seventeen. "With the ghost?"

This got the attention of the remaining two family members, and suddenly Alva found herself surrounded. There were a lot of them, she thought, trying to orient herself, and they were, every single one of them, beautiful. She blinked, as if they might fade a bit as she acclimated to them.

They didn't.

All three of the men were enormous. There was an older version of Sam, his father, she assumed, and a darker, leaner man around Sam's age. They all shared the same sparkling blue eyes and wide shoulders, and as she was being introduced a begrudging appreciation of their overwhelming masculine beauty overcame her.

"And this is my mother and father, John and Winn Moore," Sam was saying.

"It's nice to meet you," Alva said, smiling as politely as her shocked state would allow. There was something tugging at the edge of her brain, a feeling that she was being reminded of something she had long forgotten, and it was distracting her.

"Are you going to let Sam study your ghost?" Maggie asked.

"I don't have a ghost," Alva replied, which ignited a brief and passionate argument about whether one could indeed own ghosts. A consensus emerged that one could not, as they still possessed some human agency.

"Fine," Maggie said, rolling her eyes. "Are you going to let Sam study your house, which is currently inhabited by a ghost?" She looked at her brothers. "Better?"

Alva opened her mouth to deny any existence of a ghost, a task that looked fairly Sisyphean from this perspective, but was thankfully cut off by Winn.

"Let's not swarm the girl," she said. "She doesn't even know us and you lot can't wait to get your hands on her ghost." There was a general outcry. "Sorry, *the* ghost. Won't you take dinner with us, Mrs. Webster?"

"Oh, I couldn't—"

"Oh please," Winn said. "You look like you know all about New York, and we'd love to know everything we should do and see while we're here."

"Where are you from?" Alva asked.

"Ohio," Sam said from right by her shoulder. She hadn't forgotten he was there—that would have been more than even her concentration could have managed—but hearing his voice so close startled her a bit.

Ohio. The thing tugging at her attention increased. Something about Ohio, and something she'd heard once . . .

"I'm so sorry," she said, mustering up another smile, and because she found she quite liked Winn Moore, this one was warmer. "But I really can't. It was lovely to meet you all, though."

Maggie protested, but Winn shushed her and simply smiled back. "It was lovely to meet you as well, Mrs. Webster."

As she turned away, she found Sam had turned with her. "I really am leaving," she murmured. "I won't be distracted by insane inventions, or ghosts, or even conveniently placed mothers."

"Well, now you've gone and hurt my feelings," he said, grinning again. "And I was going to give you a prototype of my ladies' shoe lacer-upper, too."

"How shall I survive without it?" Alva replied, unable to keep herself from grinning back.

And because she couldn't, it was time to go.

"I hope your family enjoys their stay," she said, setting a foot on the stair. "Good-bye."

"Until we meet again," she heard him say, but she didn't turn around, and as she climbed she thought that she'd better make very sure they didn't.

CHAPTER FOUR

Hyde Park, March 2, 1875

As her barouche bounced up Liefdehuis's pitted drive, Alva reread the letter she'd received that morning. After scanning the three terse sentences for what must have been the twelfth time, she crumpled it tightly and threw it on the floor, where it failed to make any kind of satisfactory bang. She eyed it coldly.

Howard Miller, who had the only available building crew in town, was withdrawing his crew, effective immediately, and would not be returning. Furthermore, he had the gall, after a mere week on the job, to declare that the advance deposit was already depleted and "payment in full" for the remainder would be expected by the fifteenth of the month.

The letter had been waiting for her when she'd arrived at her Hyde Park rental house, rumpled and tired from the early morning train. She'd barely had time to meet her new staff, all hired by letter, and splash some water on her face before turning around and leaving for Liefdehuis. Something was fishy about Miller's sudden reversal, and she intended to find out what it was before she did anything about it. The first step was to see what, if any, work had been completed.

The carriage came to a rough stop in front of the house, and her new coachman-cum-footman, a local lad with barely fading acne scars on his cheeks, helped her alight. Alva gazed up at the house that had brought her back to America.

It loomed over her, surrounded by overgrown grounds that had probably once been the height of elegance. Here and there one could make out a vestige of former grandeur: the tall trees they'd passed on the way; the long-dry fountain sitting in the middle of the circular front drive; the wild forest of brambles that had once been a formal rose garden. The building itself was an uninspired gray stone rectangle, three stories high and crumbling around the edges. Save for its condition, there was nothing particularly distinctive about the property—it had been built with size in mind, rather than elegance, to impress rather than please. When it had been first built it would have been perfectly average; now, after decades of emptiness and rejection, its broken and boarded windows gave it a fragile, whipped expression, like an ugly dog who's come to expect the kick.

It was this expression that had popped into her mind, ten months ago, from her beautiful newfound safety in Montmartre. That had made her ask her lawyer to inquire after it, had inspired the book idea, had brought her across an ocean. . . .

Every summer, Thomas and Edna Rensselaer rented a house in the Hudson Valley, a habit not at all affected by their mutual distaste of the countryside. (The important thing, after all, was not whether you enjoyed doing something. It was whether somebody even wealthier and more powerful than you saw you doing it.) Alva didn't look forward to these summers—it was harder to stay indoors and be quiet and good when there were acres of green lawns inviting her to run over them, and servant children who looked at her curiously when they passed her in the hall, like they'd be willing to talk to her if she gave them a nod.

But she never did. And she never ran over the lawn. She stayed inside and learned her lessons and embroidered in her room after an early dinner, just like she did in the city.

But one afternoon when she was eleven, her parents had gone back to Manhattan for a night. And by luck, her governess had come down with a sudden, severe cold shortly after they'd left—in hindsight Alva supposed the governess hadn't thought it very lucky. And some of the staff had gone to the village to see their families for the day, given that Alva's parents were going to be gone, and in the end, the only person who could be found to watch Alva was a housemaid who couldn't have been more than five years older than she was. And so, for the first time in eleven years, Alva found herself with an opportunity.

The plan had appeared in her mind with perfect clarity, every detail already arranged. The housemaid wouldn't rat her out if she disappeared for an hour—she'd be let go or at least severely reprimanded if the housekeeper knew she'd let the daughter of the house go missing. She left the girl a note, telling her she'd only be gone an hour, to spare her unnecessary worry—and then she'd simply slipped out the French windows in the library into the side garden and, from there, into the woods beyond.

It was a perfect afternoon. The green-gold light hung heavily around her, dappled by bright pockets of unfiltered sunshine. She ate three dark berries from a thorny bush, thrilled by her daring—they could be poisonous, after all. She waited in delicious agony for five minutes, daring the poison to seep through her blood and into her heart, before two squirrels jolted her from her reverie by running up a very tall tree. They argued exactly like her parents did when they thought no one was around, only louder. Her parents liked to argue in whispers.

She decided to be Beauty, walking through the woods to the Beast's castle. Of course, Red Riding Hood was better suited to the circumstances, but Alva didn't want to be attacked by a wolf and she didn't want one to eat her surviving grandmother, either, even if she did barely know the woman. So she was Beauty, creeping though the forest with quickened breath, darting from tree to tree, imagining herself with a long, romantic green velvet cloak and hair so blond as to resemble moonlight, and without any warning there it was—the haunted castle.

She walked towards it, her feet kicking up puffs of dust. The sky was still blue, the sun was still golden, but it didn't seem to matter here, like the house wasn't allowed to be warm. Alva's breath quickened in earnest as she approached the front door, dark and dusty, pockmarked where a handful of daring souls had carved their initials. She felt sad and scared at the same time, the way she did when one of her nannies brought out the ruler or when she made too much noise at dinner, like she wanted to start crying in little gasps. But eleven was too old for that kind of behavior; thus she was rigidly composed when she touched the door, flattening her palm against it.

It was cold and clammy, far too cold and far too moist for a dry summer day with the smell of sun-warmed dirt in the air. Alva quickly seized her hand away, disgusted and terrified. That's what came of being childish, she told herself, backing away. She'd allowed her imagination to get the better of her—she'd probably overheated her brain. It was time to go back anyway; in fact, she'd have to run to be there before her hour was up.

She was shivering as she turned away, but she couldn't stop herself from looking back as she stepped into the woods, and she couldn't shake the feeling the house didn't want her to go.

Twenty years later, a few yards from where her eleven-year-old self had stood, the reality of what she'd just done crashed into her.

She'd bought a house because she felt sorry for it. A house no one had lived in for thirty years, a house that had changed ownership eight times in those three decades. Why in god's name did she think she'd have better luck? She'd made three major decisions in her life: her marriage, her escape, and this house, and didn't this one have all the elements of that first, disastrous choice? It was foolish, impulsive, recklessly optimistic, emotional, all the things that had trapped her in violence and despair for a decade, and only two years after she'd left Alain she was doing it again—

She closed her eyes and focused on the feeling of the coach side under her hand. Smooth. Cold. A little damp, the morning frost melting under her fingers. The sound of the stones under feet, crunchy. Too quiet, indicating the drive needed fresh gravel. She already knew that—she had eyes, after all—but the reminder soothed her. Fresh gravel for the drive. That was an achievable goal. That was something she could do.

She'd have better luck because she couldn't afford not to. Maybe the decision had been emotional, but the book idea was solid—she'd sold it to a publisher, after all. This wasn't like her marriage. This was her, standing on her own. Betting on herself, just as she had when she'd run from Alain and weathered the resulting scandal. She'd survived that, and she was better off for it. This would be the same.

Besides, this time the damage was sitting in plain sight. If you knew where the rot was, you could simply step around it.

"Ma'am? You all right?" Her coachman—really just a boy—looked worried.

"Yes, thank you," she said, squaring her shoulders. "There's nowhere to stable the horses here. You'd better drive back to the house and collect me in a couple of hours."

He looked doubtfully at the mansion, seeming to debate whether to speak again. "Ma'am," he said again, his conscience apparently winning out over what must have been very brief training, "I don't know if you've heard the stories, but everyone round here knows the place is haunted."

It seemed everyone she met, round here or not, had heard those stories. She thought about the cold door and the way Liefdehuis always seemed just outside the sunshine. Of course, it was obvious now that the thick trees pressing up against the house were blocking the sun and creating the unwholesome atmosphere of damp—those trees would have to be cut down, immediately—but to a bunch of villagers inclined to superstition, a ghost would be a natural explanation. She mustered a smile. "I'm sure I'll be fine. Please return at . . ."—she paused to look at her watch—"half past eleven."

He nodded doubtfully, visibly consigning her to the category of "city people who think they know better but don't," and clucked to the horses. As the coach crunched away over the remaining stones, Alva picked her way carefully over the cratered ground, breathing steadily. These panics still came upon her suddenly, although they were better than they had been. The trick to controlling them was to think very firmly about very mundane things: gravel, or the taste of different kinds of tea, or the recent quotes for window manufacturing.

The door had been replaced since the last time she'd touched it, but it was still cold and unhealthily damp. More important, it was unlocked, meaning the crew hadn't bothered to lock up before abandoning the job. Alva frowned, took out the notebook she'd brought with her for just this purpose, and made a note. Then she stepped inside.

The front windows had been broken for years, perhaps decades. The crew had taken down some of the boards covering them, so the cold winter sunshine could seep in, but the meager light barely permeated the darkness within. Alva stopped in the doorway, feeling blind and strangely vulnerable while her eyes adjusted. Slowly shapes appeared, lumps in stygian shades of gray and brown. The crew had apparently been in the process of knocking a wall down when they'd left—Alva squinted at her paper and made another note. She wasn't going to pay them a single dime they hadn't earned.

The house smelled of rot and mold—those damp trees again. She made her way cautiously towards the lumps, and frowned when she realized they were tools.

"At least I'll have hostages for good behavior," she murmured, but as she peered around the room her confusion grew. What kind of crew left their tools behind when they abandoned a job? She saw several hammers, three different kinds of saw, and at least five different tools she didn't know the name for. It was as though they'd just dropped everything right in the middle of the workday and rushed off, leaving their equipment to lie where it fell.

The smell of rotting fruit wafted from an open lunch pail—they'd been gone for several days at least, then. She pulled her cloak tighter around her shoulders. It was very cold in the house, somehow even colder than it had been outside. It was the damp, she told herself; it made it seem that way. Cold enough the fruit in the pail should have frozen instead of rotting . . .

Well, obviously it *had* rotted, so that was a silly thing to think. She was letting those letters from Professor Moore go to her head. Ridiculous how he seemed to not only believe in ghosts but also think they were a wonderful thing to have. Or not to have, she thought, remembering the Moores' rambunctious debate about ghost ownership.

The point was that the only unhealthy spirit in this house was the spirit of dampness and mold. And this spirit could be vanquished rather more simply than the undead variety—

Something flashed in the darkness. Alva dropped her notebook and froze.

There was nothing there. She took a deep breath and dropped her shoulders. There was only the dim light around her, the slight sounds of an old house settling. Nothing to be afraid of. She shook her head at herself—

There. Again.

She stood absolutely rigid, the distance between her and the door suddenly enormous, the distance between her and the darkness impossibly short. It had been a metallic flash, like light brushing over bright golden hair—

Her throat closed and for several moments her mind was completely, stunningly empty, the sound of her heart rushing hot in her ears. Something was watching her, waiting for her to make a mistake, something—

"He's dead," she whispered.

Alain wasn't standing in an old rotting house waiting for her. He was dead, dead and buried, six feet of earth weighting him down in his final resting place. She forced one foot in front of the other, cold nausea trickling into her stomach. It was only a bit of sunshine, reflecting off something shiny . . . never mind that there wasn't any sunshine, never mind that everything in the house sat under a blanket of dust. . . .

She closed a trembling hand over a nearby hammer. What if he'd followed her? What if his hatred could extend beyond the grave, across continents, over an ocean?

"There's no such thing as ghosts," she told herself, creeping slowly into the darkness, feeling it closing thickly behind her. She wasn't going to run out of her own house because she was afraid of something that didn't even exist, even if her spine was frozen in terror and the shaking from her hand had traveled into her whole body. Fear wasn't her way of life anymore.

The only sounds were her breathing and the tap of her footsteps as they fell hesitantly in the black. Her eyes strained to see—there was nothing there, nothing, ah! There it was again, only a few feet ahead—

Barely breathing, she took two firm steps forward, raising the hammer, and brought it crashing down—

And stopped two inches from shattering her reflection.

The mirror was splotchy and black with age, covered with a sheet that had half fallen off, leaving the top right corner exposed. Caught in that corner's reflection was Alva's own hat, a silly confection covered in gold velvet.

Her weak limbs collapsed into a crouch, and she dropped her forehead to her hands and laughed, catching her breath in hysterical gasps. She'd always had too much imagination for her own good. What a ridiculous way to act—she'd really almost believed the shade of her dead husband had found a way to cross the Atlantic to haunt her. What would he have done, taken an ocean liner? It would have been hard for him—she couldn't imagine they let ghosts into first class, and Alain had always been a strictly upper decks sort of person. Well, there were legends about ghostly pirate ships, weren't there? Perhaps there was also a thriving industry in ghostly luxury ocean liners, for the wealthy and discriminating shade.

"Now don't you start," she told her reflection as she straightened. "There's no such thing as ghosts."

"Actually," a voice said from behind her, "that's a matter of opinion."

Alva threw the hammer and screamed.

CHAPTER FIVE

It's all right; it's just me," Sam said, dropping the package he'd brought in and pulling Alva into his arms. "I'm sorry, I didn't mean to scare you."

"Didn't mean to—didn't mean to—" Alva pushed away from him furiously, her face completely drained of color and her breath still short and panicked. "So you thought, 'Ah, there's a woman in there, I'll creep up behind her *extremely quietly* and then shout at her, but not to scare her, just as a friendly gesture,' did you?"

"I didn't shout," he said. He'd knocked, too, but it didn't seem precisely safe to mention.

"You most certainly did," she said, crossing her arms. "They probably heard you all the way back in town."

"You're right," he said. "I'm sorry I frightened you."

She shrugged, glaring at him. "I wouldn't say 'frightened,'" she said. "'Startled,' perhaps."

But a slight tremble of her lips told him the truth. He stepped towards her again, intending to do some undefined but comforting thing that would seem clearer once he was closer, but she stepped back and put a shaky hand up. "Quite close enough, thank you."

She closed her eyes and took two deep breaths before opening them again. "All right." She shook her head. "All right. Serves me right for getting worked up."

"Why were you? Worked up, that is. Did you see something?" He tried to keep his enthusiasm from his voice. He didn't want to seem insensitive.

She shook her head, walking past him to pick up the hammer she'd thrown. It had missed him by about four feet. "Don't be ridiculous," she said. "I simply allowed the emptiness of the house to affect me."

"Was there a feeling of dread? A certainty something was just behind you? Perhaps a chill in the air?"

She looked over her shoulder at him, her expression dripping with condescension. He grinned back. "It's March," she said. "Of course there's a chill in the air."

"Good point," Sam said, noting she hadn't responded to the other two questions. He walked over to the lunch pail someone had left behind, grimacing when he peered inside. "What happened here?"

"Why should anything have happened?"

He looked pointedly around the room.

"Fine," she said, deflating. "My crew has abandoned ship, leaving all their possessions behind. I don't know very much about building work, but I can't imagine that's common behavior."

"I wouldn't think so," Sam said, crouching to examine a large saw propped up against one wall. He ran one finger over its teeth. "I'd guess some of these are the equivalent of a month's pay for a builder. They didn't tell you what happened?"

"Only that they were leaving." Alva rolled her eyes. "And I

don't know why I'm telling you this; it doesn't concern you. Come to think of it, why are you here?"

"I brought you something," Sam said, accepting the change of subject with good grace. "Which I definitely brought in with me . . . Ah, there it is." He retrieved the parcel from the doorway and held it out to her.

She stared down at it with suspicion. "You came all the way from New York City to give me a present."

"Oh no," he said. "I came all the way from New York City to convince you to change your mind about the house. The present is merely an excuse."

There! The side of her mouth twitched. She wanted to smile but was restraining herself. She'd smiled at him once before, the night she'd met his family. He wondered what he could do to provoke another one.

"I see," she said. "Well, since you did scare me out of my wits—"

"I thought I merely startled you."

"Since you crept up behind me and shouted at me like a lunatic"—here she broke off to glare at him—"I suppose I'll accept this present as recompense." She took the parcel, wrapped in brown butcher paper and tied with twine, and began carefully picking at the knotted twine.

"Why, Mrs. Webster, I never would have thought it," Sam said, leaning against the wall while he watched her. "You like getting presents."

"Everyone likes getting presents," she said, apparently giving up on the knot and deciding to shimmy the twine off the package.

"No one hates getting a present," Sam said. "But you're barely restraining yourself from ripping the wrapping off with your nails. You adore them."

"No more than anyone else. Do you have a knife?"

"Somewhere." He rooted through his pockets, producing several feathers, a coil of wire, and an interesting rock before he found his knife. He passed it to her.

"Thank you." She cut the twine neatly and meticulously unwrapped the brown paper, obviously intending her neatness to demonstrate her indifference. She lifted the small book out, letting the paper drift to the floor, forgotten. "It's a . . . journal?"

"An inventory, from about ten years after this house was built. I thought it might interest you." He looked around the room. "Although it looks like most of the furnishings have been removed."

"There are still a few pieces, here and there," she said absently, opening the book and scanning the first page. "Where did you find this?"

"During my preliminary research. I interviewed the grandson of the man who bought the house from the de Boers—oh, you probably haven't gotten that letter yet, he says his grandfather told him the ghost is a young man, an indentured servant who poisoned his master and was disemboweled by a local mob for the crime—and he found this tucked away in the family library."

She shut the book sharply. "I wish you weren't doing any research on this house, preliminary or otherwise, but I suppose there's nothing I can do about it."

"If it helps, think of the inventory as hush money."

"I'm not that cheap to bribe," she said. "Well. Thank you. I'm happy to accept your gift, so long as you understand this in no way constitutes permission to turn my house into a ghost-hunting laboratory."

"I suspect a laboratory would be too stationary for ghost observation purposes," he said. "Perhaps something on wheels. Hmm. You raise a very interesting point—"

"I absolutely did not. Now, if there is nothing else, I need to go find and possibly murder a foreman."

She looked at him expectantly, her face a mask of restrained politeness. It was funny how much people relied on etiquette to order behavior—like manners were as immutable as Newton's Laws of Motion. He smiled back at her and stayed exactly where he was. She narrowed her eyes. He smiled more. She huffed and crossed her arms again.

"Oh, for heaven's sake. You're the most impossible man I've ever met."

"I'm not in the least impossible," he said. "I'm not even improbable. What *is* improbable, though, is you miraculously appearing in town without a vehicle to take you there." He'd noticed the lack of carriages when he'd pulled up in front. It was only the open front door that had hinted someone might be present.

Her glower told him she hadn't considered that problem. "My coachman will be returning momentarily." He doubted it. "And anyway, it's hardly your concern."

"But it would be my pleasure to escort you to town," he said, prudently not mentioning his burning curiosity about why the workmen had abandoned their post. *One step at a time*, he thought.

She pursed her lips into a little frown, clearly wanting to confront her foreman as quickly as possible. Sam pitied the man, who could have had no idea what he was getting himself into when he so rashly angered her.

"You could leave a note here, for your driver," Sam coaxed. "You could be in town and yelling at the man inside of twenty minutes."

"I have no intention of yelling," she told him, very much on her dignity.

“Informing him, then,” Sam said.

“Oh, fine,” she said, and, frowning even more, continued with gritted teeth. “I mean, I thank you for your kind offer, and will gladly accept it.”

“Think nothing of it, my dear Mrs. Webster,” Sam said, chuckling. The day was turning out even better than he’d hoped.

Alva didn’t know what had possessed her, getting into the man’s buggy. A tiny voice told her it knew exactly why she’d gotten in; she suppressed it violently. She’d seen everything she needed to at Liefdehuis; he offered her a faster way back into town. That was all. It was . . . efficient.

There had been an instant, when he handed her up and she’d come within inches of his broad, broad chest, that hadn’t been efficient at all, of course, but she had gotten through it just fine. Physical reactions had betrayed her once; she’d since come to realize they were harmless, so long as one kept them carefully controlled and, most important, separate from one’s emotions.

It wasn’t the flicker of heat that worried her. It was that she . . . liked him. When they spoke she wanted to linger, to say one more thing, to hear what he would say in response. He made her want to laugh. That made him dangerous.

So why, *why*, had she gotten into the buggy? It wasn’t efficient. It was foolhardy.

She sidled a little farther away from him, although the bench wasn’t very wide and she couldn’t manage more than about a foot’s separation.

“I asked my maid where he lived,” she said, keeping her voice polite and impersonal. “She said to look at the Blue Stag Inn during the day.”

"Drunk?" The word was free of judgment, simply the question of a scientist gathering information.

"I don't think so," Alva said, and the memory tugged at her sense of humor. "Apparently his wife kicks him out of the house every morning, whether he's got work lined up or not. Says he gets in her way."

Sam chuckled. "Ought to build himself a laboratory," he said. "That's where my mother sends my father when he's irritated her."

She knew she shouldn't ask. Why was she so *interested*? She wasn't going to ask. She wouldn't—"Your father's a scientist, too?"

He looked at her with a little crinkle between his brows. "I assumed you knew," he said.

"Knew wha—oh." Mortification turned her cheeks hot; she only barely stopped her hands from flying up to cover her face. "Oh no. No, no, no. Moore. Ohio. The Moore family."

Of course she knew who the Moores were—they were practically the first family of American science. Why she hadn't made the connection sooner . . . she was an idiot. It was the only explanation. "You're Samuel Moore."

"Now you definitely knew that," Sam said, staring at her like she had taken leave of her senses. "I remember very clearly. I said I was Professor Samuel Moore, and you asked me what I was a professor of, and I told you, and then you told me you weren't interested in going to bed with me."

"I—" Oh, if her cheeks got any hotter they'd burn her face off. Maybe she could fling herself off the side of the buggy. Sure, she might break a bone or two, but actual physical pain might overwhelm her embarrassment. She took a deep breath and decided she could simply ignore his last sentence. "I've been in Europe for the last twelve years," she said. "I read American news while I was there, but it's not always in the front of my mind.

You're *the* Samuel Moore. The Moore Conduit. The Moore Rail System. The Moore lantern."

"Actually, I only invented two of the Moore lanterns," Sam said. "There are four. My parents have one apiece."

"And your parents! I met them! John Moore!"

Sam grimaced. "Yes, it's a shame he's so much more famous than she is. It's a travesty, actually—she's every bit as important, but no one seems to care. Does this mean you'll let me look at your house?"

"Oh, I—" Alva looked down at her hands, the question bringing her back to herself. Did it change anything? She still didn't have the time. She still didn't believe in ghosts—couldn't afford to believe in ghosts. And getting even closer to Sam still seemed like a very, very bad idea. "No," she said. "I'm sorry, but my answer hasn't changed."

She stiffened her spine and grimaced, waiting for his anger to come. She'd refused him before, but never after he'd come several hours to see her, and never without a crowd of people around her.

"Why are you looking like that?"

She glanced at him from under her lashes. His voice hadn't *seemed* angry, but she barely knew the man. She reminded herself she was no longer in the habit of bowing to other people's fury. "I'm sorry if that frustrates you," she said, testing the waters.

A small dog ran across the road, followed by three children and a hoop, and for a minute Sam was occupied in slowing the horses. When she looked at him once more, his expression was strangely sharp and considering, as though the cheerful professor had momentarily stepped out, leaving only the genius behind. "Let me be clear," he said. "I do want to use your house. I'm hopeful I can either convince you or irritate you or charm you into letting me do so. But whether you do so or not is entirely your decision, and I'm not going to fly off the handle if you refuse me. Even if you never let me in that house again, I'll continue to think you're a charming, funny, intelligent woman whom I like and respect very much."

"Sometimes you're not vague at all," she said, blinking.

"Not when something's important," he said, and clucked to the horses. The buggy started rolling towards town once more.

Alva didn't know what she was supposed to say. She was suddenly ashamed of her fear, embarrassed by its weakness and its unfair assumptions. Of course not all men were like Alain. The problem was you couldn't know right away which ones were and which ones weren't.

"I'm not funny," she said.

"Of course you are," he said, and seemed so convinced that she let the matter drop.

They sat in silence as they drove into town. The sun was breaking hesitantly through the clouds, and a few children took advantage of the sudden springlike weather to play a rowdy game of tag on the side of the street. Alva pulled her coat closer around her neck and reflected that only children could interpret slightly-above-freezing temperatures as playing-outside weather.

Sam eased the buggy to the side of the road, jumping down and tying the horses before he helped Alva descend. They stood in front of a dank little tavern, the kind of dark hole one can walk by a dozen times and never really notice. It was no more than a dozen feet wide, painted a blue that looked like it had survived the last war and possibly the one before, and had a stoop spattered dark with tobacco spit and dirt and other things Alva preferred not to speculate on.

"Thank you for bringing me," she said, hoping the tentative smile she offered would be taken as an apology.

"You're welcome," he said, smiling back. "But if you think I'm leaving before the fireworks you're insane. Shall we?"

Oh, right. For a few beats, she'd forgotten how infuriating the man was. A welcome trickle of irritation squared her shoulders.

"Again, I thank you for your escort," she said, using her very firmest tone. "Although I might also note you practically bullied me into accepting it. But I assure you, I no longer require your . . . kind services."

"Nothing kind about it," he said, with an outrageous twinkle in his eye. "You're going to go in there and yell at that man, and I'm going to gawk shamelessly. Wild horses couldn't drag me away."

She scowled. There was a little relief mixed in with her frustration—she wasn't really accustomed to storming unfamiliar taverns, and having someone, particularly a someone who looked like a long-lost Viking warrior, at her side might be nice. Perversely, this realization only irritated her more.

"I don't need your protection," she said.

"Of course you don't," he replied. He took her arm and walked towards the entrance. "I shall be exactly like those fools who picnicked at Bull Run. Spectating only."

And with that she found herself drawn through the entrance, a full battalion masquerading as a man by her side.

CHAPTER SIX

It might as well have been night, for all the light there was in the smelly, close little room. There were candles on the tables, tallow candles by the smell, and they let off a weak, wavering light utterly defeated by the general griminess of the establishment. Alva stopped inside the doorway, blinking in the darkness as she scanned the room. Her maid had described Miller as short, fat, and in possession of a bushy red beard, and there couldn't be too many men in town answering to that description. . . . Ah, there he was, sitting near the back of the room, a fresh, frothy pint in front of him.

She weaved through the tables, aware every eye in the place was on them. Well, she had plenty of experience with that, lately. Miller looked startled as they drew close to him, and even more so when she drew up the chair across from him and sat down.

"Howard Miller, I believe?"

He looked up blankly, taking in her appearance with confusion. She saw the instant recognition hit him. His slack jaw clenched close, and his shoulders stiffened. "Mrs. Webster," he said, and she nodded.

"I arrived in town this morning, and found this on my entry table." She placed the letter between them. "I thought I'd give you the opportunity to explain."

He stared at the letter, his Adam's apple working up and down. "Nothing to explain," he said, glancing nervously at Sam. "Put it all in there."

"Ah, my mistake," Alva said, picking the letter up again and snapping it open. "'Dear Mrs. Webster. My crew has discontinued work on your property. As the stoppage was caused by circumstances you had prior knowledge of, I require you to pay in full for all work above your original deposit, in the amount of one hundred dollars. Payment in full is requested by March fifteenth. Sincerely, Howard Miller.'"

Miller nodded, his discomfort slowly fading in favor of outrage. "That's right," he said. "Don't know why you came all the way down here to read my letter to me; I know what I wrote. This ain't a place for a woman, anyhow."

Alva thought this wasn't much of a place for anyone, but she kept that to herself. "Passing over this letter's transparent attempt at extortion—"

"Extortion! Lady, you've got some nerve coming into my place and—"

"Passing over that," she said firmly, "you agreed to do a certain job for me, Mr. Miller, and as recompense for that job, I agreed to pay you a large sum of money. We committed this agreement to paper, which we both signed, and which I have in my possession. In short, you are contractually obligated to return to work, and not only am I not going to release you from your contract; I'm going to require you to make up the money that has been lost by the stoppage in work."

"Contract's broken," he replied. "You got me to agree under

false . . . under false . . . can't remember what the word is right now, but the point is you lied—"

"What nonsense," Alva said. "You knew the house was in terrible condition. For one thing, I told you it was, and for another, if you live here you must have known—"

"S'not the physical condition that's the problem," he muttered into his pint.

"Oh lord," she said, putting her fingers to her temple. "Not you too. Tell me you're not talking about the ghost."

He took a long draught of beer and apparently found some courage in the bottom, because when he slammed it down he had a new look of determined belligerence. "Well, what if I am?"

"Aside from the fact that ghosts don't exist? I have it on very good authority everyone around this area knew about the house's reputation. You certainly knew about the rumors before you agreed to take the job."

"Rumors! Stories! Sure, I heard those, but there's a big difference between people saying a thing and it actually being true, see?"

"No," she said. "I don't see. What are you saying, Mr. Miller? Don't tell me you're a convert to these silly tales."

"Ain't anything silly about it," he growled, taking another gulp of his beer. Sam stood up and walked away, returning swiftly with a small glass of golden liquid.

"Here," he said, pushing the glass across the table. "Why don't you tell us what happened?"

Miller looked at Sam, unpleasant speculation in his eyes. "Who are you, then?"

"Sam Moore," Sam said, oblivious to the man's obvious assumption that he was Alva's lover.

"Professor Moore is interested in folklore," Alva said, despising herself for the justification. She owed Miller no explanations, but three decades of societal conditioning couldn't be overcome so quickly.

"Is he," Miller said, picking up the glass and tossing its contents down. "Won't be interested in this, then, because it ain't 'folklore' that's in the house, that's for damn sure."

Sam leaned forward. "What is, then?"

"You wouldn't believe me if I told you."

"I assure you I would," Sam said, causing Alva to roll her eyes discreetly. Still, it was obvious Miller was spooked and wasn't going back to work until whatever foolish idea he had in his head had been dislodged. She'd find out what had frightened him and deal with it.

Miller shook his head slowly, sighing. "Don't rightfully know," he said. "There were four of us there, and all four of us swearing we saw something different. If you ask me, there's a nest of them holed up in that house."

Alva opened her mouth to say something blighting, but a look from Sam stopped her. She settled for another eye roll.

"What did you see?" Sam's voice was soft, convincing. *I'll believe you*, it said. *You're not crazy*, it said. For a man who barely seemed to function on an earthly plane, he could certainly be competent when he wanted to be.

"It was getting on lunch," Miller said. "We'd been there since sunup, taking down some of those walls you wanted gone. Well, I say sunup, but it was one of those days where the light never properly comes, and there'd been some rain and snow off and on. It was dark enough inside we'd had to bring in some lanterns." He paused and looked pointedly at the small glass. Alva sighed and picked it up, shoving her chair away from the table with a distinct lack of grace.

"Another of whatever was in it before," she told the man

behind the bar, who goggled at her for several seconds before pulling a dirty bottle out from under the bar and filling the glass. She carried it back and set it crisply on the table. "Go on," she said. "I believe you were at 'it was a dark and stormy night.'"

He glared at her but took the glass. "As *I was saying*, it was lunchtime. And we were sitting down to eat, and sort of talking and joking, like we do, when a great gust of wind comes shooting through the house, icy-like, and it blows out all the lanterns, so we're just sitting in darkness."

"And you all felt the wind?" Sam had taken his notebook out and was writing furiously. "Everybody agrees on this part?"

Miller nodded. "At first, we thought it was the storm picking up, and Little Harry Stentler says something about it being the ghost, just joking around, and we're all looking for matches and running into each other and thinking it was all pretty funny, and we got the lanterns relit." He picked up the glass, saw it was empty, and switched back to the pint. "Then the wind came back and blew them all out again."

Alva glanced sideways at Sam. This whole scene was getting out of hand—she'd come to demand her crew return to work immediately, not to listen to ghost stories. Really, people's obsession with the supernatural was ridiculous. Did they have so little terror in their everyday lives that they had to invent some? "So it was windy that day," she said. "What does this have to do with you refusing to return to work?"

"I thought it was wind, too," Miller said. "Maybe not entirely, maybe my imagination was starting to fire up, but I didn't want to spook my crew, so I just laughed again and relit the one I was holding. And as the light flared up—" He took a sharp breath in and drained his pint.

"What did you see?" Sam's words were gentle, the smallest push.

“A hand,” Miller said, his voice almost a whisper. “A lady’s hand, white and long. It just sort of reached past me, over my shoulder, real delicately.” He swallowed. “It opened the glass, and pressed one finger down on the flame. Tamped it right out.”

“Someone was playing a joke on you,” Alva said. “One of your men—”

“Lady, I could see through it,” Miller said. “I could see right through the damn thing. ’Twasn’t no joke.”

“Classic manifestation,” Sam murmured, scribbling away. “And your crew? They didn’t see the hand?”

Miller shook his head. “If you ask me, they were playing with us, the ghosts. A whole pack of ’em. Harry, he swears up and down he heard footsteps behind him, but every time he turned around they started coming in a different direction. Jeb saw a little boy, pale as could be, with his hair wet and . . . and water coming out of his mouth, like he was drowning. Ed, now, he swears he saw a . . . a noose. Coming down from the ceiling like a snake, coming right at him—”

He broke off, clutching the empty glass in front of him. “There are bad things living in that place,” he rasped, looking straight at Alva. “You should go back to the city and pretend you never heard of it.”

She held his gaze, feeling the weight of the dark walls pressing against her lungs. It was ridiculous, his story—this whole meeting was ridiculous, a farce. She needed to breathe; she couldn’t breathe in this horrible dark, dirty place—

She pushed her chair away and stood up. “I need a breath of fresh air,” she said, enunciating each word so no one would notice something was wrong. “Excuse me.”

Sam pushed through the door into the glare and grayness of the winter afternoon, looking for Alva.

She couldn't have gotten far . . . there. The lot next to the Blue Stag was empty and overgrown, but it fronted a pasture, and there she was, looking over the fence at a pair of bedraggled sheep. He walked towards her.

She stood bolt upright, as he was beginning to realize she always did. Shoulders squared like a soldier's, arms folded in front of her. She looked dismayed and confounded, a general who's just seen his entire army routed by vastly inferior forces.

He leaned on the fence next to her.

"I loathe sheep," Alva said.

Sam digested this. "I see," he said, feeling his way. It didn't *seem* like sheep were what she was upset about, but he was willing to wait for the connection.

"Stupid animals. Always in a herd. Goats are better. I met a goat once. He belonged to a painter I knew in Paris, and he went to parties and salons and everything. He once ate the ruffle off a dress I was wearing, but the dress looked much better afterwards."

This was a pretty arbitrary distinction between species, but Sam wasn't about to get into an argument about the comparative intelligence of barnyard animals, or even party-going animals, so he settled for an encouraging nod.

"He died a few weeks before I sailed," Alva said. "Drank himself to death."

Sam frowned. "The goat?"

"The painter," Alva said, still staring at the sheep. They were great fluffy things, gray from the mud, with little wooly curls poking out in all directions. "Maybe the goat too. I don't know what happened to him. Listen here, you don't believe this nonsense, do you?"

"That a goat could drink himself to death?" He was fully at sea now.

Alva let out an impatient huff. "The stuff Miller said. About ghosts. Plural! Ghosts!"

"I believe he and his men think they saw something," Sam said.

She sighed. "Yes. Or *he* does, at least. He wasn't faking. But his men could have been playing a joke on him. They could all be in on it together."

"It's put them out of work," Sam said. "They'd have to be abnormally committed to it."

"So, children from the village, maybe."

"Could be," Sam said, turning to watch her profile. "Could also be they saw what they said they saw."

"No," she said, her lips compressed in a firm, thin line. "There's no such thing as ghosts."

"Why are you so determined that there not be?"

Alva was silent for several beats, staring out at the dead winter pasture. "For one thing, I can't afford them," she said. "If my house was actually haunted, that could be the end of my whole project. No one would come to do the work on the house, my designs would never be implemented or photographed, I wouldn't make my deadlines, and there'd be no book. I have . . . everything resting on this."

"All right," Sam said. "I understand that."

"And—" She broke off, looking away.

"And?"

She shrugged. "And it would be too horrible," she said, her voice rigidly composed. "That a person who tormented you in life could come back to torment you after death. If I—if people believed that, they wouldn't be able to go on."

Sam thought back to his research and came up with a pretty

good idea as to whom she was referring to. His skin went cold. All the scandal in the newspapers—what had it been covering up?

"No one's going to hurt you," he heard himself say. "I'll see to it."

She laughed, but it sounded empty and mean, as if she was mocking herself. "I've been rescuing myself for a while, Professor Moore. It's just . . . I'd rather not add ghostly specters to my enemies."

He felt a little dizzy. Why had he said that? Of course it wasn't his right to protect her. Except she was standing rather close to him and she really was very beautiful, all dark eyes and bravado.

"Is it such a long enemies list?"

"It's shorter now," she said.

"And do you never have help with these foes? Even Queen Elizabeth had knights, you know."

She turned to look at him, one elegant eyebrow winging up. "Who mostly wanted to marry her and steal her throne," she said.

"I would never steal your throne," he said, and immediately felt ridiculous. He was talking like a sixteen-year-old boy. He was feeling like one, too, every second tight with anticipation and yearning. He needed to take a step back, calm down. This was not how you wooed women. You waited for them patiently, and eventually they would probably come to you. And if they didn't, well, it wasn't the end of the world.

But she wasn't looking at him like he was ridiculous. There was something there—sadness? Longing? Wistfulness, he thought. Like she was looking at something she couldn't have.

Suddenly the most important thing in the world was to tell her she could have it. Him. Whatever she wanted, really. He lifted his hand and ran two fingers gently across her cheek. "You have such a delicate face," he murmured. "But strong, too.

Delicate skin and strong bones. I seem to find the combination almost irresistible."

She stood absolutely still, tension radiating from her skin into his fingers. She cleared her throat, and when she spoke her voice was hoarse, as though she hadn't used it for a long time. "Do you?"

"I find almost every damn thing about you irresistible, Mrs. Webster," he said, his arms aching to come around her.

"Don't call me that," she said. "Don't call me by his name."

"Alva, then," he said, and pulled her close.

When his lips first touched hers, there was only joy, and a feeling akin to homecoming. She was in his arms, and kissing him, and it was somehow both an event of monumental importance and exactly as it should be. Her muscles were tense underneath his hands, but she was kissing him back, and if some part of him wondered why her body was poised to flee, the rest of him was too overjoyed to care. At first she was tentative, almost questioning. Sam let her lead, blessing the control that let him do so when the sixteen-year-old inside him wanted desperately to push her against the rough wooden fence and maul her. He was swamped with new knowledge: the way her breasts molded against his chest, that she smelled ever so slightly of sandalwood, the exact taper of her waist, the precise angle of the flare of her hips. These facts were the things his universe was made of. Suddenly she kissed him more deeply, more enthusiastically, a low groan in her throat that shot all the way down his body, and then, just as quickly, pushed herself away. She took a step away, turning back towards the sheep and gripping the fence.

"Alva—"

"I can't believe I did that," she said, her hand creeping up to her lips. "Why did I do that?"

"Hopefully because I'm irresistible," he said.

She shook her head. "I'm sorry to have—to have given you the wrong impression. I can't do this. I don't have room for romance, or for . . . whatever this is."

Sam blew out a breath and pushed his hair out of his eyes. "It's romance," he said.

"I can't do that," she said.

"I see," he said, even though the only thing he saw was how absolutely muddled he was.

"I really should be going," she said, her voice formal. "Thank you for escorting me to town."

"May I see you to your house?"

"I took a rental house only a few minutes away," she said, shaking her head. "Good day."

She turned and started to walk down the street, stopping after only a few steps. "It would be best if we didn't see each other again," she said over her shoulder. "I don't want to be rude, especially since you're obviously a very nice man, but I'm not going to change my mind about the romance, and I'm not going to change my mind about the house."

She turned decisively and left him standing in front of a sheep paddock in perfect bewilderment.

Alva walked quickly down the street, the exertion steadying her, forcing her to breathe steadily. A few townspeople watched her as she passed, but their regard was more curious than hostile. Since most of the stories about her had run in European papers, read widely by New York society and hardly at all by people in small towns several hours north, she hoped she'd simply be less shocking here.

That was what she needed to focus on: her new life. Her

goals: Settle into Hyde Park. Finish the renovations. Finish the book. Get another book contract. Start a life that relied on only her.

Professor Samuel Moore was not on that list. So why had she let herself act as though he were today? She'd laughed at his jokes. She'd gotten in his buggy. She'd told him her problems. She'd almost told him about Alain, for heaven's sake.

And when he'd told her he wouldn't let anyone hurt her, she had simply stepped into his arms without a second thought. The idea someone wanted to protect her, to stand beside her, to face her problems with her . . .

And that kiss. She hadn't been kissed in many years—perhaps that was why it had felt so extraordinary, like spending forty years in the desert and stumbling, out of nowhere, into an oasis. Of course, for all she knew, kisses were like that in general. It wasn't like she had a great library of them to pull from. Alain's kisses, so long ago it was like thinking about something that had happened to a different person, had been thrilling more in their illicitness than in their technique or passion. Not that she could have known the difference at sixteen.

The familiar stabbing began in her stomach and she forced herself to speed up, concentrating on the warmth in her muscles and the slight perspiration on her skin. Her corset made it impossible to take a deep breath; by the time she reached the edge of her rental property there were little gray dots at the edge of her vision.

There was a buggy in front of her house.

The man didn't listen, Alva thought, trying to catch her breath and hurry at the same time. He was absolutely impossible. And the deep, sudden pleasure that was erasing all memory of pain in her stomach was misguided and traitorous. Pain was an honest emotion. It told you when something was wrong, kept you safe. Pleasure, on the other hand . . . pleasure was deceiving. She had to remember that. Still, she almost ran up the front steps and into the house. The banging door startled her maid, a stout blond girl named Liza, who was in the process of hanging a coat in the front closet.

"Ma'am," she said. "We didn't expect you back so soon. Rob hasn't even gone to put the horses to yet—"

"Someone drove me back," Alva said, casting her own coat off. "There's a visitor here to see me?"

"A man," Liza said, lowering her voice as though she was imparting a great confidence. "Ever so sophisticated, too."

Calling Sam sophisticated seemed like a stretch, but she supposed he did have a certain polish. "What room?"

"The front parlor. He—"

"Thank you." Alva strode to the door and opened it, preparing to tell Sam exactly what she thought about men who refused to take a hint, and froze.

Her dead husband was sitting by the window.

CHAPTER SEVEN

Alva," the sleek, handsome blond man said. "So gratifying of you, rushing to see me like this."

His voice released her. "What are you doing here, Alfred?" she said, her voice distant in her ears. Alain and his brother had always hated each other, Alain because he couldn't stand that there was someone else who looked like him and Alfred because he'd been done out of a family inheritance by a matter of eight minutes.

"I was in the area," he said, tossing the newspaper he'd been reading onto a nearby table. "I could hardly leave without seeing you, dear sister."

"I'm not your sister."

He shrugged, an elegant, boneless motion that made her breath stop again, it mirrored a gesture of his brother's so exactly. "Death may have parted you from my brother, but we're *family*. No funeral can change that. You'll always be a Webster."

Funny, that—how a name could structure your entire life. When she'd been a girl the Rensselaer name had made all her decisions for her: where she lived, who she knew, who came courting her when she turned sixteen. It was the same name that had attracted Alain; it stood for conservatism and money, both things he had needed very much. And now he lived on through his name's attachment to her, putting his mark on every contract she signed, every letter she wrote. On the book marking her new beginning. And now, apparently, on her sitting room.

She remembered the uncomplicated happiness in Sam's face when he'd talked about his family this morning. Obviously being a Moore was a different affair.

She tugged her gloves off and tossed them on a nearby end table. "I'll ask you again. Why are you here?"

"I can't come see my late brother's wife? I was worried about you. You didn't tell anyone you were coming back—I had to find out about it from the papers! Imagine my surprise to learn my own sister-in-law hadn't seen fit to tell her family she was returning home. And to discover she'd already bought a house, and not even in the city! What are you up to, my dear?"

"Nothing that concerns you or your father," Alva said. She remained standing, some primitive part of her brain insisting she stay ready to flee. Alain had been a perfect predator—a poisonous Prince Charming, with golden hair and white teeth and brilliant, flashing eyes, a textbook hero with the bite of an asp. She didn't know Alfred as well, but she knew him well enough to imagine the inside matched Alain's as much as the outside did.

"But everything you do concerns me," he said, his voice gentle. "After all, we're all you have left. I know your parents have been cold since your return—so sad they've let the scandal taint your relationship. I would *never* let that happen to us. Come home, dear Alva."

Well. She hadn't expected *that.* "Are you actually asking me to go live with you and your father?"

"But why not? Think what it would do for your reputation.

After all, how much of a whore can you be if your husband's family is willing to take you in after his death? Maybe your parents would even come around. If you were willing to live very quietly, that is."

"Alfred," she said, slightly hysterical laughter rising in her chest, "I can honestly say I would rather take up residence in Dante's Ninth Circle of Hell."

His muscles tensed, so subtly no one who hadn't seen it before would recognize it, but enough that Alva took two steps back, until she was in front of the unlit fireplace. There was a heavy candlestick on the mantel; she knew where convenient weapons were in every room. Her skin was cold and clammy.

He stayed seated, though. The blow would come in some other way. "An interesting choice, the Ninth Circle," he said softly. "The one for treachery, wasn't it?"

She didn't say anything.

"Ah, now you become biddable. Yes, 'treacherous' is an accurate word for you. You weren't a very good wife to my poor brother. And of course, I said death parted you, but that's not quite the truth, is it?"

Her voice was hoarse. "Unless you know something the Monte Carlo police don't."

He smiled, as though she'd pleased him. "An excellent way to put it," he said. "Sit down, Alva. We have so much to discuss."

"If you have something to say, say it. If not, it's time for you to leave," she said. They were in her house. The servants here were in her employ. They would come if she screamed. Not like before.

"Such hostility," he said, chuckling indulgently. His body was still taut, ready to spring. "All right. To be precise, I know two things the police do not. I know you were in Monte Carlo that day, and I know you were attempting to get a divorce."

The world froze.

"I don't know what you're talking about," she said. "I've been to Monte Carlo several times, and divorce? I won't pretend I was shattered by his death, but I'm not so ignorant I don't know how the law looks on women who want to divorce their husbands."

"Don't dissemble, Sister; it's not attractive in a woman. More important, it makes conversation more difficult. These facts are not in dispute."

"I'm sure I have no—"

He sighed. "Fine, if you insist on a sordid recitation. Several months before Alain died, you visited a lawyer in Paris, using your maiden name. One of the clerks recalls being assigned research on your behalf—he was to look into both choice of law for divorce cases, given the international nature of your marriage, and, provisionally, recent divorce actions brought by women in New York State. I don't know what came of this research, but I do know that two days before Alain's death you checked into the Hotel de Beauchamps, in Monte Carlo, again using your maiden name. If you'll permit a small criticism, my dear, Rensselaer is not a particularly common name in that part of the world. Perhaps something like Brun, or Bernard."

"Alain wrote me," Alva began. "He wanted—"

"I admit, I am not particularly interested in whatever story you choose to weave right now. Do you know, it never bothered me, his death. I think we can agree he wasn't a very nice man; he certainly wasn't a very good brother to me. I don't mind that he's dead. When the telegram came from my father—'Alain killed stop Apparent robbery stop'—I was almost happy. It left me as the only remaining child, after all, and even if there's not much left in the family pots, some inheritance is better than no inheritance at all. The problem, of course, is my father insists upon enjoying such extreme good health."

"I'm very sorry to hear your father is unlikely to die soon," Alva said. "But I'm afraid I don't see what it has to do with me. We are no longer related."

"That notion again," he said, gently reprimanding. "I wish you would put it out of your head. It has no bearing on our conversation."

"I—"

"How much money did you save with his death, Alva? I'm informed that in the case of a divorce he would have taken almost all of your original fortune."

"I didn't have anything to do with it," Alva whispered. She'd wondered if this day would ever come, if anyone would ever call on her to account for her whereabouts that warm May evening. No one had thought to look for enemies, or for wives staying under their maiden names.

"Once more you seem to be assuming interest where there is none," Alfred said. "I don't really care if you had him killed. Alain seemed rather to live and breathe reasons to kill him, actually. The thing is, I don't think the rest of the world is quite as broad-minded as I am."

"Are you threatening me?" Alva laughed, a strange titter that was all panic and no humor. "Unwise, if you believe me to be a murderess."

"You'll find it somewhat harder to dispose of me," Alfred said, smiling apologetically.

She swallowed. She was so cold, cold and stiff. "What do you want?"

"Ah, I knew you'd see reason. You always were the most practical little soul. Let's start with six hundred dollars a month and see how we do."

"*Six hundred dollars a month?* That's more than most people make in a year!"

"And neither you nor I are most people. Don't pretend it's too much for you, Sister. You can part with twice that and barely feel the pinch."

"And if I don't agree?"

"Oh, Alva, of course you're going to agree. But if you insist that we descend to the level of crude threats I suppose I must oblige you. . . . If you don't agree to my very reasonable request I will do three things. First, I will contact the Monte Carlo police, although I doubt they would do much. Next, I will contact the New York papers and give them the proof I have collected of your visits to the lawyer and your whereabouts last May fifteenth. Finally, I will send the resulting articles to your publishers—oh yes, don't think I don't know about that scheme, my dear—on the off chance they have somehow crawled underneath a rock and missed the enormous scandal that will result. They may be happy to publish a book by a ruined woman, but I imagine they have no desire to publish one by a murderess. They'll end your contract immediately, and you'll have no friends, no family, and no publishing contract. Your life, in any form you would wish to continue living it, will be over."

Alva stood and walked to the small writing desk along the back wall. Without speaking she removed her chequebook from one of the cubbies, filled one out for six hundred dollars, tore it loose, and walked back to Alfred.

"Here," she said. "Don't come back."

"My dear," Alfred said, standing and coming close to her. She fought the instinct to take a step back as he leaned towards her ear. "Never presume to tell me what to do."

She didn't answer, merely looked past him, willing her spine to hold her straight. She remained there, unmoving, while he bowed with a sickening little smirk, while he stepped into the hallway, while she heard Liza handing him his hat and coat, while his steps sounded lightly out the front door, and, finally, while the door clicked softly shut behind him.

She'd never be rid of them. Alain was dead, but there he was, in his brother's face and in his darkness, in the color of her hat and in the gossip that had followed her across an ocean, in the dwindling funds of her bank account. In the way her stomach clenched at the smell of lavender. In how she could only look at Sam Moore's face for a few seconds at a time, for fear of a crack in the wall keeping all this at bay, but here it was, cracking anyway, cracking, cracking, cracking, and the memories were coming through and now the only thing to do was get to her bedroom, to the cool darkness and the heavy wooden door—

There. The door closed behind her and she was alone. She sank against it, sliding to the floor, and let it come.

She could smell her mother's thick, spicy perfume—no silly florals for a woman like Edna Rensselaer—and feel the strong hand clasped painfully around her wrist as she was bundled unceremoniously into the carriage. She'd landed heavily against the seat, the thick upholstery scraping against her face as she righted herself.

"You'll mind your manners tonight, girl," Edna said, settling her skirts around her. Alva's father climbed in last, not looking at either of them. "I don't want any of your attitude."

"Of course, Mother," Alva said.

"'Of course, Mother,'" Edna mimicked, her voice high and cruel. "You'd better stay that way, you understand? You're lucky he

offered for you at all. Thank god you'll be married soon, and I won't have to look at you anymore."

Her seventeenth birthday had been three days prior, and they were on their way to her engagement party. She knew why her mother was angry—it made her stomach tight and painful to think about. But truly she wouldn't do anything to mess up the engagement. Alain was everything she'd ever wanted. He'd kept her guessing for months, all attention at one party, ignoring her completely at the next. She'd been desperate for him to notice her, to really see her, and finally, on her birthday, he had. Now she knew for sure he loved her, and passionately. She wasn't going to do anything to change his mind.

"There will be talk," her father said to her mother. He hadn't spoken to Alva since that night. "Happening so fast."

"It can't be helped," Edna said. "We'll say it was a long-standing engagement. And then they'll leave for Europe, and everyone will forget."

Silence settled in the carriage. Alva wanted to look out the window, but the curtains were drawn, as usual. The world outside the carriage was dirty and dangerous—soldiers crowded the city, especially after the attack on Fort Sumter the previous year; and the poor, always pitiful, seemed to be ever increasing. Alva's access to news was sharply restricted—her parents firmly believed newspapers were inappropriate reading for a young woman—but sometimes, when she was alone with her governess, she'd lift the edge of the curtain and peek out the bottom, just to catch a glimpse at the world outside her small corner of it.

But tonight was not the night to risk that. Instead she sat straight up, feeling the weight of her parents' shame around her shoulders and in her stomach but unable to regret the actions that had led her here. She loved him. As he'd said himself, what did a piece of paper matter when it came to love?

They swayed to a stop, and the door opened. It was already dark, though barely past five, and the path to the house was dimly lit. Alva hadn't been here before. Alain's mother was an invalid and didn't entertain, although his father was a fixture of New York society.

Alva had a vague impression that the house was older than her family's, which fit with what she knew of the Websters. In a world of new money and newer money (not that she'd ever let her parents hear her say such a thing) the Websters had about a generation on the Rensselaers. She caught a glimpse of an intricate carving as she passed through the entrance, but before she could admire it the wooden door shut heavily behind them.

Briefly, Alva found herself nervous. It was almost as dark inside as it had been outside, wavering candles reflected weakly in mirrors, highlighting dark, ornate wall hangings and glinting off gold accents. There was only the butler in the hall with them, a large, middle-aged man with an impassive face, who took their coats and hats before ushering them farther into the darkness.

Her nervousness lifted as soon as they walked into the dining room. There he was, next to his brother, burning somehow brighter than his twin. He rose when she entered, but didn't move. He didn't exactly look at her, either. Her stomach twinged again, but he was probably nervous, too.

Alain's father walked towards them, larger and darker than his sons. "Thomas," he said heartily, clasping her father's hand. "Edna. You look beautiful. And here's little Alva, all grown up and ready to be married." He appraised her for several beats too long. Her cheeks heated. Of course he knew what she'd done. When his eyes drifted downwards, she tried to take a step back, but her mother's iron grip held her in place.

"And this is my wife," he said. The woman was pale, wraithlike, her long golden hair seeming too heavy for her head. Her eyes

were the same pale blue as her sons'—Alva had wondered whom the boys took after, they looked so unlike their father. Mrs. Webster was a pale reflection of the twins, like looking back at them through deep water.

"I'm so happy to meet you," Mrs. Webster breathed, extending her hand. When Alva took it in her own it was cold and thin, hesitant, as though she wasn't sure what to do with it. Alva shook it cautiously. "Pleased to meet you, ma'am."

Alain's mother was rumored to have some sort of rare blood disease, and looking at her, Alva could easily believe it. She didn't look well enough even to be entertaining in her own home. When her husband spoke again, the woman flinched, as if he could bowl her over with the strength of his voice alone.

"Well, come along then," he said, steering them to their seats. "Nothing fancy tonight, my wife tells me, a simple family meal."

"It seemed nicer," Mrs. Webster whispered after a silence. "Since you'll be part of our family soon, my dear." She nodded at Alva, or possibly her head had become too much for her neck to support.

"How lovely," Alva's mother said, exchanging a quick glance with her husband. It was unusual to eat almost immediately after arrival, but perhaps this was the Websters' way of welcoming them. It occurred to Alva this might be the only time she saw Alain before the wedding—her family wouldn't be hosting his, because of his mother's condition.

Alva was seated between her father and Mrs. Webster, forced to crane her head to see her fiancé. When she caught his gaze, he looked away, leaving a little ball of dread growing in her stomach. Across the table, his brother watched her, a little smirk in his gaze. She ignored him—everybody knew Alfred was jealous of Alain.

Service began promptly, and Alva turned to her future mother-in-law, determined to make a good impression. No indication of judgment had come from the woman, which, considering the circumstances for the hasty wedding, would have been understandable. Come to think of it, Alva hadn't felt much of anything from her—she seemed drained, faded. Undoubtedly from her long illness.

"You have a lovely home, Mrs. Webster," Alva began, although, in all honesty, she thought it too opulent and heavy, the dim lighting only adding to the vague oppressiveness of the decor.

"Thank you," she replied after a delay. "I must admit, however, I rely heavily on my husband. He has such wonderful taste, you see, and I—" She raised her hand slightly off the table and gave a wobbly little flutter. "I'm afraid such decisions are beyond me."

Well, that made sense. It was hard to imagine the pale woman beside her choosing anything, let alone that embossed burgundy wallpaper. It was so . . . aggressive. This woman should live in a house with open windows and fluttering white curtains, the smell of flowers drifting in—Alva's mother caught her gaze sharply across the table, recalling her to the moment. As she racked her brain for other conversational topics, she saw Mrs. Webster's cuff had resettled slightly askew, revealing a dark bruise at her wrist. Almost as soon as Alva saw it, the other woman flicked the lace back in place. Alva looked down in chagrin—bruising must be a symptom of the blood disease. It had been terribly rude to stare, and she could only hope she hadn't embarrassed her.

Alva wished Alain were next to her. He always knew what to say—sometimes she felt so naïve and gauche next to him. She wished he would look at her.

It seemed impolite to ask about hobbies, given his mother's illness. Even the weather was a fraught subject—did she even go outside? Alva hoped she did. There was something about her that reminded Alva of some of the animals at the menagerie in Central Park, those that had been caged too long and had lost their spark. Like they'd simply given up.

Alva didn't like to go to the menagerie.

Her mother caught her eye again and frowned. This was not minding her manners.

With an internal sigh, Alva turned to the one truly safe topic of New York female society. "Your dress is beautiful," she said. "Is it French?"

"Yes," she replied after another strange pause. It was as if the sound was traveling an enormous distance to meet her. "Mr. Webster helps me choose all my dresses, and the French designs are the best."

They were *the best, but it was odd Mr. Webster would have so much input in his wife's wardrobe. Or perhaps not; she was an invalid, after all. "I'm so looking forward to seeing Paris," Alva said. "I* know *Alain loves it, but I've never been."*

Mrs. Webster nodded, her eyes flickering to Alain and back, an unnatural emptiness in them. Alva shifted in her seat, uncomfortable without knowing why—

"Mrs. Webster? Ma'am?" Liza's voice was muffled through the door.

Alva blinked, disoriented. "Yes, Liza?"

"Can I bring you some tea? Only you looked a bit pale—"

"Yes," Alva said, her voice steadier. "Please. Thank you."

Now she was the one with the pause. At least she no longer had the bruises.

The Hyde Park railroad station, located on the edge of the Hudson River, was a small one-story wooden building that had more in common with a schoolhouse than the grand stations going up in New York City. Sam stood on the platform and watched the train from the city grow larger in the distance. It was another wintry, muddy day, and the puffs of breath from the people on the platform were small versions of the steam from the train.

There were a few other people waiting, a handful of chauffeurs from the big houses standing around in a cluster and smoking, an elderly couple sitting patiently on a wooden bench, two men with duffels tossed over their shoulders. As the train pulled up, in a crescendo of screaming metal and whistles and smoke, station employees swarmed over the platform, opening doors, tossing luggage, shouting at people to herd them into place. Sam watched the employees work, trying to understand each movement, each tool they relied upon. There was always something that could be made better, more efficient, safer. He made some notes in his book.

Henry was one of seven people disembarking. He grabbed a suitcase from the luggage pile and walked crisply over.

"I have ten different contracts in my bag needing signatures," he said, by way of greeting, "and Winchester upped the offer for a rifle design."

Sam grinned. It was good to have Henry back. "I don't design guns in peacetime," he said as they started walking towards town.

Henry wasn't paying attention. "Obviously I declined, but you should know the amount mentioned was *truly* flattering. How's the new lamp coming?"

"It's promising. I'm experimenting with plaster of Paris—so far I like it."

"Good. Why the hell are we here, Sam?"

"I'm doing research," Sam replied reproachfully. "You know that."

"I know you were looking into the Webster woman's house,

but you've already been here a week. I thought this was an overnight, not a bloody trip down the Amazon."

"Don't call her 'the Webster woman.' She doesn't like it."

"Oh, she doesn't, does she?" Henry eyed him. "What should I call her, then?"

Sam knew he couldn't very well say, *Alva*, Alva with the firm chin and the snapping dark eyes. "I don't know. But not 'the Webster woman.' And as for why I've been staying longer than expected—"

"I retract the question," Henry said. "I understand completely. I once stayed in an awful town in Florida for much the same reason." His eyes turned uncharacteristically soft. "Her name was Mrs. Burns."

"I had no idea," Sam said, much struck. "What happened?"

"I never had much of a chance, I'm afraid. In addition to having the sweetest smile, and the merriest blue eyes, she was the widowed daughter of a senator. We had four weeks before her father intervened and engaged her to some awful little junior legislator." Henry grimaced, shrugging. "She wasn't terribly distraught, it must be said."

"Poor fellow," Sam said, clapping a hand to Henry's shoulder and accidentally causing the slighter man to stumble. "And now you live as a monk, abjuring all female companionship, hollow inside and impervious to the charms of the fairer sex. . . ." He shook his head. "Tragic, really."

"Yes, it's but a pale reflection of life," Henry sighed.

"So how's the chorus girl then?"

"In fine voice."

They laughed companionably and turned onto the street leading to Sam's rented house. It was a tidy two-story stone house, surrounded by a little yard and fronted by a bright blue door.

"What should I expect to see?" Henry said as they walked up the path to the door. "On a scale of messy to natural disaster?"

"It's as neat as if my own mother were here."

"So well past natural disaster and into the apocalypse, then?"

Sam pushed open the door and they walked into the house. He waited patiently while Henry shrieked and pulled his hair in horror. It wasn't that bad, Sam thought, surveying the room. After all, what was furniture for if not to provide surface space? Sure, chairs were supposed to be sat in, but that was a narrow and inefficient view. One person, even two people, didn't need ten chairs hanging around unused. And, all right, if he didn't currently have even one chair available, he knew which one was easiest to clear off. It was the uncomfortable wooden one, over by the window.

Maybe Henry would like it better if he had a place to sit down. Obligingly, Sam walked over to the chair and began to clear it, moving the metal sheets he had definitely needed for something to the floor.

"Here," he said. "Would you like to sit down?"

Henry turned, his face a rictus of horror, his light brown hair sticking up wildly. "I may faint," he said. "It's only been a week, Sam. How?"

Sam hunched his shoulders. "It's clean," he pointed out. "Just messy. Messy's okay."

"Messy!"

"You're shrieking again."

"This isn't messy; it's a bloody tornado strike zone!"

"But a clean one," Sam pointed out hastily. "The maid, Sally May, she dusts. I've seen her."

"Recently? Because it's not impossible that one of these piles collapsed on her and she's just been slowly rotting here for days."

"Of course I have," Sam retorted, and then crumpled his brow. "I think."

Henry blinked.

"I mean, definitely a few days ago."

The two men stared at each other, Henry's eyes still wide, Sam shifting uncomfortably from foot to foot.

"Shall we go to the garden?" Sam said.

"Yes." Henry picked up his case and headed towards the back of the house without another word.

Fortunately, the small garden area was mostly tidy (the weather had been very uncertain, and few of Sam's materials played well with water). There were even a couple of wooden chairs. Miraculously, as they sat down, Sally May appeared. Sam shot a triumphant glance in Henry's direction.

"Would you like some refreshment, sir?" she asked, smiling.

"Would I like some—" Sam frowned. "You've never asked before." Usually Sam got along well with his staff, but there had been an accident involving a fire—a very minor one!—and a new dress on his first day there. Of course he'd paid for the dress, but ever since then she had visibly categorized him as a dangerous madman.

"Ah, you will have your joke, sir," she said, shooting him a quick glare before blinking sweetly in Henry's direction. Ah. Now matters became clear—women were always fawning over Henry. He supposed it was the soulful brown eyes.

"I almost dread the answer," Henry began, once she'd hurried back into the house to retrieve some tea, "but how is the ghost research going?"

Sam shrugged. "I'm having trouble getting access."

"If you're flirting with the woman, surely you can convince her to let you in her house," Henry said, frowning. "After all, isn't access the point of flirtation?"

"Only if you take a somewhat joyless view of the matter," Sam said, evading the question.

"You don't mean she's turned you down? Well, imagine that, the handsome Professor Moore, rejected."

Sam didn't really want to talk about it. In the two days since Alva had, indeed, rejected him, he'd found himself thinking too much about her, about the protectiveness that had swamped him when she'd looked so scared, and the way she'd looked when she'd walked away from him. "There was an interesting development with the house a few days ago," he said. "Some laborers say they saw something, although what exactly they saw remains a little confused."

"Something supernatural?" Henry leaned back in his chair, looking skeptical.

"Why does everyone think I've gone mad? And I don't think I like that word, 'supernatural.' Unstudied, perhaps, but not beyond nature."

"Unstudied, then. And I've never said I thought you were going mad. But ghosts, Sam? You must admit the evidence points towards superstition and old wives' tales."

"I don't know why people think so little of old wives," Sam protested. "Most of the old wives I've met are quite sensible."

"Not the point."

"All right. Yes, I believe they saw something, and I think—no, I know—whatever they saw scared them, badly. What's interesting, though, is all four witnesses describe totally different incidents."

"So? They didn't really see anything and invented a story, whether knowingly or not."

Sam nodded. "It's possible. But in my experience, people in situations like that quickly gather around a central narrative. They want to have seen the same thing everybody else did. These workmen are sticking to their stories. When I questioned them yesterday they even argued with each other about it. And they're not the only ones who can't agree," he said, warming to his topic. "I've had five different stories already from people who used to live in the house, and every one of them claims to know how the ghost became ghostly. Had a letter last night from the son of a former groom there, says the ghost was the wife of a local merchant. She fell in love with another man and one day they decided to run away together. They planned to meet in the woods behind Liefdehuis, but her husband followed her and—"

"I can fill in the blanks," Henry said. "They aren't pretty, these stories of yours."

Sally May returned with the tea tray. They waited while she bustled about, dropping things, bending slowly to pick them up, Henry watching appreciatively, Sam tapping his fingers in impatience. Finally, after what seemed like hours, she left.

"All right," Henry said, taking a sip of his tea. Sam eyed it—he couldn't help noticing Henry had been given the only unbroken cup in the house. His own had a chip approximately the size of India in it. "You think what? There's a family of ghosts living in the house? The family that haunts together stays together?"

"Wouldn't that be something," Sam said, this enchanting notion driving both teacup grievances and deeper pangs temporarily from his mind. Could a ghost have a family structure?

Henry rolled his eyes. "Fine. I can see you're not going to be lured back to the city just yet. I'll make the necessary postponements. And I'm going to see about hiring a second maid, because I absolutely refuse to stay in this pigsty."

Sam grinned and leaned back, happy Henry would be staying, just as a thought burst into his mind and pushed everything else to the side. "Kaolin," he said. "I should try kaolin in between the carbon." He pushed off the chair and rummaged for his notebook. “Glad you’re back, Henry,” he said as he hurried back into the house, already wondering whether he had something suitable to use lying around or if he’d have to order it.

“Glad to be back,” he heard Henry say as the back door closed between them.

CHAPTER EIGHT

Howard Miller's house sat on a narrow road, little more than a cattle trail, off the main thoroughfare. Months of rain and snow had turned it into a muddy mire Alva's carriage was unable to manage, so she picked her way up it by foot. By the smell it *had* been a cattle trail recently, and for the hundredth time in the last month she reminded herself to buy some sensible boots.

It was just after nine o'clock in the morning and most of the street's inhabitants had already gone about their days, but there were two children playing in one of the yards, trying doggedly to have a snowball fight using the thin layer of snow clinging to the ground. Mostly it was a mudball fight—Alva remembered the cattle and shuddered—but they paused hostilities long enough to watch her walk by, smothering giggles when her foot slipped and she had to throw her arms out for balance.

Pride goeth before destruction, and a haughty spirit before a fall. She'd never cared for that particular verse, but it was certainly the theme of the day. She was there to beg.

After Alfred had left, she'd slept for sixteen hours. Then she'd gone looking for her account books.

Cold reality: she couldn't afford to bring in an out-of-town crew *and* be blackmailed. Losing six hundred dollars a month left her with barely enough to pay even a local crew, and she'd have to let the rental house go as soon as rooms at Liefdehuis were even vaguely habitable. Another day of rapid inquiry had left her with the information that there were no available work crews anywhere in the surrounding area, and there weren't likely to be, for her project, anytime in the near future. No one actually *said* it was because her house was haunted, but it was clear the story was out.

It was convince Howard Miller to come back or . . . nothing. This wasn't a life-or-death situation. She wouldn't starve; she wouldn't even be uncomfortable. She had so many more options than most people—she might not have enough income to simultaneously bring in an out-of-town crew, renovate a house, and be blackmailed, but Alfred had been right about one thing. Alain's death *had* meant she'd retained the small bit of her personal wealth he hadn't managed to spend. More than enough to take a comfortable flat, anywhere she wanted. She could go back to Montmartre. She could go anywhere. So why didn't she?

The uncomfortable truth was she wasn't sure she could. Oh, there were all kinds of rational reasons: the book would provide her with an income stream, which was always better than living on principal; it might even help restore her reputation somewhat. But it wasn't the money, and it certainly wasn't the reputation—lose one once and you suddenly realized how flimsy they were in the first place. The truth was selfish. She wanted something for herself. She wanted to *do* something herself, something big, to show herself she could. To show the world she could.

She stopped in front of a neat white house with lace curtains in the windows, consulted the directions Liza had written down for her, and walked up the steps onto the small wooden porch. Adopting an expression of unthreatening feminine contrition—or at least that's what she was hoping for—she knocked on the door.

Miller answered the door as she raised her hand to knock for a second time. His eyes were red and bleary, his beard unkempt and overgrown. He smelled of alcohol, but when he spoke his voice was sober enough.

"I don't have anything more to say to you," he said, watching her warily. "You can shout at me all you want, you can even get the lawyers on me about it"—here his expression grew even more anxious—"but you ain't getting me back in that house. You might as well save your breath."

"I don't want to shout at you," Alva said, although she certainly did. "In fact, I want to apologize for the things I said at the tavern. I shouldn't have talked to you like that; it wasn't respectful."

"Oh," he said, scrunching his eyebrows together. "Well, then."

He shifted uncomfortably, and Alva sighed internally. "After all, you're the foreman," she said. "You know your own business much more than I do. I should have listened to you."

"Right," he said.

"The problem is," she said, lowering her eyelashes, "I really have no one to guide me in these matters." She tried to say *since my husband died*, but that was a falsehood too far. She peeked back up at him and was pleased to see the nonsense was having its desired effect. Miller's face had softened.

"Well, I don't mind saying, I've regretted some of my own words, ma'am. Truth is, I was a few sheets to the wind already. It was quite a shock, you know, seeing that. Can't get it out of my mind; every time I close my eyes there's that hand, creeping forward ever so dainty-like, and me thinking it'd look the same reaching for my throat."

"How awful," Alva said, and this time she spoke the truth.

"It is, ma'am. But it was no excuse to talk to you that way neither. My wife near took my head off when she heard how I'd spoken to you. You can just ignore what I said in that letter, about payment beyond the deposit. We can call it even."

A frown tugged at her mouth and she forced herself to hold a pleasant expression. This was not the direction she was aiming for. "That's very generous of you," she said, sighing. "I don't suppose—no, of course not. I'm simply going to have to make up my mind to give up on the project. It's just . . . oh, here I am going on and on, Mr. Miller, and you're being so kind, listening to my prattle."

"It's no hardship talking to you, ma'am. If you'll forgive me, I'm confused as to why you're so set on the project. There are other houses, nicer ones, even setting aside the—the ghost." His voice weakened on the last word.

It was a good question, and she didn't have a good answer. Liefdehuis *was* ugly, and inhospitable, and sometimes, if she was perfectly honest with herself, and this *did not* mean she was entertaining the possibility of a ghost, it frightened her. *It's also alone, and afraid, and you know what that's like,* said an unwelcome whisper in the back of her head.

She had to force herself not to frown. This was not the time to start anthropomorphizing.

"It was the last wish of my grandfather," she said, inventing wildly. "He'd had such good memories of the house as a boy, you see, and it haun . . ."—bad choice of words—"bothered him so to see the house fall into such disrepair." And if that wasn't the thinnest story ever told, she'd eat Howard Miller's beard. Obviously a career on the stage was not in her future.

But Miller was nodding. "I know how that is," he said. "I had a grandfather, too. Took me fishing with him every summer, up the river a bit to this spot only he and his friends knew about. Just tucked into the trees, sweet as you like, and you couldn't put your line in without having three fish jump on it before you'd even settled in. Few years back, we had a bad flood season. Took the whole bank out, trees and all. Now it's only rocks and a little bit of sand. First time I saw it, I don't mind telling you I welled up a bit."

Firmly, Alva suppressed her guilt. There would be time to be a nice person later. "You *do* know how it is," she said. "And now . . . I suppose it's all over."

"I'm sorry, Mrs. Webster, I truly am, but even if I went back to the site, my crew wouldn't, not if their own mothers' lives depended on it."

And that, it seemed, was that. "Is there anything I can do?"

Miller shook his head regretfully. "Ma'am, unless you're able to get rid of the ghost somehow, there isn't a man in the county who'll so much as set foot there."

An idea began to stir in Alva's mind, sticking tentative green shoots up through the soil.

"What if I could? Get rid of it, I mean?"

Miller looked at her doubtfully. "Like an exorcism or something?"

"Yes," she said, thinking an exorcism certainly couldn't do any harm and perhaps simply knowing a priest had blessed the house—or whatever it was priests did; Alva hadn't set foot in a church in years—would reassure the men and make them less likely to imagine horrors around every corner.

Miller shifted his weight from one foot to another. "It's not that I don't believe in that sort of thing," he said, speaking cautiously. "I go to church every Sunday, like the next man. It's this ghost . . . well, I don't think a little splash of holy water is going to scare it."

"I see," Alva said. What would convince him, if not a priest? A bishop, perhaps? "Well, if I could find a way, do you think the men would come back?"

There was a pause while the man thought, pursing his lips like he was trying to force his mouth to say something it didn't want to say.

"The men, they're real scared, see," he began. "Not me, I'd go back. But the men, well, I'm not sure they would—"

A large redheaded woman loomed into view behind him, her arms crossed over her chest. "Howard Miller," she said, "are you a man or a mouse? This lady is here offering you *work* and you stand here quivering like a virgin on her wedding night. I'm Mrs. Miller," she said to Alva. "Pardon my intrusion, but I couldn't help but overhear."

"I'm very pleased to meet you," Alva said, and meant it.

"Now Penny," Miller began, his face turning a sweaty shade of red.

"Don't you 'now Penny' me, you coward. You let a little ghost story scare you off the best job you've gotten in years, and she's here to kindly accommodate you, and all you can say is no? I don't think so, my good man; I don't think so at all." She turned to Alva. "If you're still willing to have him, and willing to find something to placate these idiot men, you can rest assured he'll be there the first day back, even if I have to hog-tie him to get him there."

Alva tried not to smile, but a little bit crept out against her will. "Mr. Miller, won't you come back? If I can find some way to get rid of the ghost?"

Miller looked from one woman to the other, clearly feeling like he'd stepped into a trap. "I suppose," he said, his words coming slowly. "If you can get rid of it, and if I hear that from a person who knows their business."

Alva let the challenge to her honor slide. "I'm very grateful to you both," she said, sending a particularly warm smile in Mrs. Miller's direction. "I'll get news to you as soon as I can."

As she walked away from the house, her feeling of victory deflated. Who could she find that would be willing to get rid of a ghost that didn't even exist? Perhaps a priest could convince them, but Miller hadn't sounded like he had much faith in that option. Someone higher up in the church, perhaps? Two priests? A team of priests?

She didn't need a priest, Alva realized, stopping in the middle of the street and closing her eyes. She needed an expert. And unfortunately for her, that's exactly what she already had.

She felt like a damn fool. It had only been the work of an hour to return home, ask Liza where the famous scientist who'd come to town had taken lodgings, and make her way back there. That had been the easy part. Now that she was standing on his stoop, staring at his door . . . she remembered exactly what she had said to him the last time they had spoken. And why she had said it.

"This isn't personal," she murmured to herself, flexing her right hand in her glove. "It's business." She nodded firmly and knocked on the door.

The door opened swiftly, revealing a trim, handsome man in a brown tweed suit.

"Hello," he said, smiling politely. "May I help you?"

"I'm looking for Professor Moore."

"Please come in," he said, standing aside to allow her to enter. "I'm Henry Van de Berg, Professor Moore's man of business."

"Alva Webster," she replied, walking past him into the front room.

"Oh," he said, with a slight quirk of his mouth. "I see."

Alva registered the smirk, but more pressing observations were crowding her mind. "My god," she said, standing stock still in the middle of the room. "It's like someone took apart a train."

"Only if the train was filled with deadly chemicals and wires that could burn a house down," Henry said, sighing as he too looked around. "But if you think this is bad, you should see the family home. It's the whole railroad yard."

"Goodness," she said weakly.

"Indeed," Henry said smoothly as he removed a pile of books and something that looked like an inside-out clock from a chair. "If you would care to wait for him here, I'll have him out to you shortly."

"Thank you." Alva sat gingerly, realized there was something poking her, delicately removed a slide rule that had become wedged between the seat cushion and the chair back, and prepared to wait.

A few seconds later, she heard voices through the wall.

"The problem is once the fuse wire has been extinguished, the candle can't be relit."

"Sam—"

"Yes, of course you're right; it's not practical. We'll have to figure out a way to preserve the partially burnt ones, maybe a spare fuse or something. . . ."

"Sam—"

"Or not a fuse, but something that could serve as a fuse. . . ."

"Alva Webster's here."

There was a pause. Alva noted she should not be eavesdropping and shrugged. There was absolutely no chance she was going to stop.

"She is?" Sam said. "She's here? You saw her?"

"I even did more than see her," Henry replied. "I spoke to her. She's in the sitting room."

"Well, why didn't you say so!"

"I did. And you can't go out there in shirtsleeves. Where's your coat?"

Another long silence, during which Alva struggled with a reluctant smile.

"Did you put one on this morning?"

She was surprised by a giggle and clamped her hand over her mouth to prevent further slips. The man was ridiculous.

"I think so," Sam said. There were some rustling noises, and then—"Ah! There it is."

She heard him walk out of the room, and soon he was in front of her. "Alva," he said, grinning. "You came back."

Any impulse to laugh faded as she looked up at him. When she wasn't around him she tended only to remember how he made her laugh, the funny, clever, nonsensical things he said. He became, if not safe, at least safer, in absence. She forgot—perhaps she made herself forget—the sheer power of his physical presence.

My god, he's beautiful, she thought, a little sigh escaping her before she came back to herself. Her cheeks warmed a little in embarrassment. "Professor Moore, thank you for seeing me."

"I wish you'd call me Sam," he said, shoving some metal sheeting off a love seat and dragging it—she tried not to watch the play of his thigh muscles through his pants—across the room to face her.

"I'd be more comfortable with Professor Moore," she said, and stopped, wondering if she was about to make a terrible mistake.

His grin faded as he watched her. "Something's wrong. Tell me."

She shook her head briefly. There was no point in arguing with herself. She was committed to the course she was on. "There's nothing wrong. I've merely had time to reconsider your request to study my house, and I'd like to hear more about your proposal."

"I see," Sam said, leaning back against the love seat and resting one ankle on his knee. "I'm surprised."

"Yes," she said, fighting the urge to shift in her seat. "I can understand why you would be. And I want to be clear this doesn't affect the other . . . issue . . . at all."

"All right," he said, still watching her carefully. She had obviously failed to convince him everything was fine. "What do you want to know?"

"Two things only. First, if you fail to find any evidence of a haunting, will you be willing to make a public statement to that effect?"

"I will," he said without hesitation. "And second?"

She nodded. "Second, if indeed you do find such evidence, although obviously you won't, is it within your power to remove the ghost?"

"Remove the ghost?"

"Help it pass on. Cross over. Get rid of it."

Sam considered the question. "I don't know. It's an interesting question, but I hadn't considered it."

"You hadn't—then Professor Moore, what is the point of all this?"

"I told you," he said, a small smile returning to his face. "Scientific inquiry."

"Oh good lord."

"I can't promise you that I'd be able to help the apparition cross over, because I don't know if that's how it works. But I *can* promise you that if it's within ethical bounds, and it's scientifically possible, I'll do whatever is in my power to help it move on. And you won't find better than that, because I'm already the foremost expert in the field."

"Some field," Alva said, standing. "But I suppose it's the only offer on the table. If you're willing to sign a document putting all this in writing, I'll guarantee you my full cooperation. You can start tomorrow morning, if you like."

"It's that easy?"

"It's that easy."

He watched her. "Sometime, I hope, you'll tell me what's wrong."

"There's nothing wrong," she repeated. "I've simply changed my mind. Do we have an agreement?"

"Yes," Sam said, the smile spreading. "Just let me find a pen. . . . I'm sure there's one around here somewhere. . . . I had it in my hand just a few minutes ago. . . ."

CHAPTER NINE

The next morning Sam woke up with a happy lightness in his chest, a Christmas morning kind of feeling. He was going to study Liefdehuis—he already had a dozen ideas for new methods of measurement. And he was going to get to spend more time around Alva Webster.

He sprang out of bed—it was freezing; the architects of the rental house hadn't considered the preservation of heat in their design—and began the usual morning hunt for clothing. Pants he discovered over a chair, underneath a half-built prototype of a rather ingenious new device for measuring infinitesimal changes in sound. What if, his reasoning went, ghosts *could* talk, but they did so very, very quietly? Socks were under the bed, undershirt on the bottom-left bedpost, and, most confusingly, shirts were in a neatly folded pile in the armoire.

Also a mystery: Why had Alva (because he couldn't stop calling her by her first name, even if he knew he should) changed her mind?

He'd hoped she would, of course. He'd even been fairly confident about it—surely no one could withstand such a tantalizingly intriguing question for long. But he'd bungled things with that kiss, and he'd thought it would take bit longer to coax her back.

The kiss. He'd rushed it—he'd rushed her—and he didn't know why. Sam was hardly unfamiliar with the fairer sex. He liked women enormously, both as people and as lovers, but mostly, they came to him. They indicated their interest, they set the terms of the engagement, and when the time came for them to part there were no tears and no recriminations. It occurred to him that he mostly associated with the same kind of woman: they were usually a little older, experienced, and the only thing they wanted from him . . .

He frowned. If he thought about it, he supposed the only thing they wanted from him was to have relations with a famous inventor. And he liked them because they made it easy. It wasn't the most flattering thing to realize about yourself, but Sam's priorities had always been his family, followed by his work. There wasn't much left over for other people.

He didn't pursue. He didn't push. He didn't rush. But with Alva Webster, he'd done all three.

And he was having trouble regretting it. She had tasted of strength and passion, of meticulously banked fire and fury, and when he remembered holding her all he wanted to do was find out what would happen if she decided she trusted him enough to release it. There may also have been the odd fantasy about wooden fences.

The truth was he didn't know what to do with himself around her. And now he'd spent ten minutes dwelling on a woman when he should be getting dressed and loading his equipment onto the wagon he'd rented the night before. He didn't know why she'd changed her mind, but he was glad she had. And if he couldn't shake the feeling she needed help somehow, well, he could begin by doing what she'd asked him to do: find out if a ghost was haunting her property.

And if he happened to find out what else was upsetting her while he was doing it, he would simply find a way to fix that, too. After all, it's what he did. He figured out questions, and he answered them.

It was barely past first light when he and Henry (whom he'd pestered into coming with him so he could take the cart back) pulled up in front of Liefdehuis. Henry, who'd been dozing grumpily in his corner during the short drive, blinked his eyes open and squinted at the house.

"It's ugly," he said.

Sam hopped into the back and started untying the ropes holding his equipment down. "She'll make it pretty," he said, which caused Henry to squint at him instead.

"Will she?" he said, but apparently decided to leave it there. "Sam, why couldn't we have done this at a proper hour? For example, after breakfast?"

"The early bird—"

"If you finish that sentence," Henry said, "I will have *you* for breakfast."

Sam grinned. Irritating Henry before breakfast was one of life's true joys. "The faster you help me unload, the faster you can leave," he said instead.

This seemed to be a convincing argument, and for the next fifteen minutes they quickly unloaded the cart, leaving Sam's equipment in a pile in front of the door.

"And that's it," he said, putting the last box of wire and assorted helpful bits on the ground. "You and the horses can return to warmth."

"Not a moment too soon," Henry said, but he didn't immediately move. Instead he frowned and paused, like he was debating whether to speak. "Sam, be careful."

"And here I thought you didn't care," Sam said, making a silly face before shrugging. "It's highly unlikely the ghost is capable of physical violence."

"I wasn't talking about the ghost," Henry said, and climbed back up into the cart.

This was odd—Henry's warnings usually came with words like "liability" and "jurisdiction" and "three years in jail and a fine of up to two thousand dollars," but Sam trusted if it was important the meaning would eventually become clear, or at the very least Henry would bail him out of jail. He picked up the box again and carried it into the house.

It was dark inside, and dusty. He hadn't considered what dust might do to some of his instruments—the last time he'd been inside he'd been more interested in the house's owner than its condition. Still, once he brought some lanterns in and took down the rest of the boards over the windows, the place would be perfectly comfortable. He crossed to the nearest window, intending to pull the boards down immediately, and paused.

"I hope you won't mind if I take this down, so I can see better. Although," he added hopefully, "if you do mind, please don't hesitate to let me know."

As he pulled the boards away from the window he tensed in anticipation, waiting for a ghostly hand to reach out and stop him, but all he saw was a window with a broken pane and a rather extravagant cobweb.

"Thank you," he said, politely concealing his disappointment. "My name's Samuel Moore, by the way. I'm going to be here for a little while, and I'd very much like to meet you."

Still nothing. He shrugged and headed outside to find his lanterns.

And there, bending over enchantingly to examine his new sound-detection prototype, was Alva Webster.

"You're here!" he exclaimed, and immediately kicked himself mentally. Of course she knew she was here. It seemed even looking at her made his brain act strangely. Benedict would probably know why, not that he planned on asking him. He would never let Sam forget it. "I mean, good morning."

"Good morning," she said, straightening and turning. "I had planned to meet you, but I see you've already been here a while."

"Henry dropped me off," he said, wondering even as he said it why he thought it was an interesting thing to say. He cleared his throat. "I'm glad you're here."

"Mmm," Alva said, walking around his equipment pile. "I suppose I wanted to keep an eye on you."

"We scientists are pretty suspicious characters," he said. "You should probably use both eyes."

"Don't flirt with me, Professor Moore," she said, frowning at him. He loved when she frowned at him. "Now, this stuff needs to go inside?"

"Yes," he said. "I'm putting it in the large front room, if that's all right."

"There's nothing else happening in it," she said, and picked up an electrometer. "Lead the way."

"Alv—look here, what should I call you? Because you seem to be back to 'Professor Moore,' which would indicate I should call you Mrs. Webster instead of Alva, but earlier you specifically requested I not call you that—"

"'Mrs. Webster' is fine," Alva said quickly.

"Right. Mrs. Webster, please put down the electrometer."

"You can't very well carry this all in yourself," she said, "and there's no one else around. I'm perfectly capable of helping you. Why do men always assume women are so weak?"

"I don't think you're weak," Sam said. "I have two very good reasons you shouldn't help me. First, it's a very delicate piece of equipment and I'd feel more confident handling it myself. Second, you're wearing an extremely fetching dress this morning, and if it were damaged in some way, it could impact my enjoyment of it."

"Your enjoyment!"

"So you see, it's a purely selfish request, not one based in antiquated and easily disprovable notions about female strength."

"Because you want to continue looking at my undamaged dress."

"It's a very appealing shade of red. You wear a lot of red. I like it."

Alva opened her mouth to respond, looked at him, and shut it. "I don't know whether you're incredibly complicated or exactly as simple as you seem to be," she murmured, but she handed him the device.

"Simple," he said, turning towards the house. She fell into step beside him. "Practically simpleminded, or so Henry tells me."

"I wonder." She stopped a few feet short of the front door, staring at it. "I assume the mythical ghost has yet to appear."

Her tone was deliberately light, but Sam thought he heard an undercurrent of tension. "It's been perfectly quiet," he said. "Although I did startle a spider earlier."

She nodded, a little stiffly, and started walking again. She didn't pause as she opened the door, like she was daring herself to enter.

Inside, she blinked in the darkness and looked around, seeming to relax as she took in the dust and the newly taken-down board. The lunch pail was still sitting where an unnamed worker had left it, and Alva glared at it severely, as though it could convey her displeasure back to its owner.

"What does all this stuff do?" she asked, poking at the box he'd brought in earlier.

"A lot of it measures energy in different ways," he said. "I'm not sure what the best way to measure an apparition's appearance is yet, so I'm erring on the side of too much data rather than too little."

"Why are you so certain they exist? I thought you were mad at first. I still do, actually, but not in the completely off your head sense."

He leaned against a wall, watching her. "I believe in things I can measure. I also believe that what most people take for granted as reality is simply the top layer of a much more interesting truth. It's like looking at a lake and thinking it's only a flat blue surface because you can't see into the water. You can think it all you want, but fish are swimming under there all the same."

"And you think ghosts are the fish."

"I think they're *a* fish, or that they might be. It's worth checking to see if they are or aren't."

"And have you found any evidence that they are?"

"Yes," he said. "Enough that I've made it my priority for over six months, upsetting Henry greatly and angering any number of important people who apparently want my designs."

"Your family didn't seem to think it was unusual."

"No, they wouldn't. My parents have discovered plenty of things no one believed in before."

She nodded vaguely, still looking at the box, as if she didn't want to look at him directly. "May I ask why were you so set on Liefdehuis particularly?"

"Partially because there are so many different versions of the story," Sam said. "It's all over the place. Sometimes people think they see a murder, or a suicide, the ghost's origin story, if you will. Other times it's a lady's hand, or a noose unspooling from the ceiling—classic stuff, the kind you'd find in a Dickens story. It's fantastic. Other ghost stories, they may vary a little, but they're all basically about the same thing. A woman drowned herself, and now she haunts the road along the lake, her white dress dripping. Maybe she has long black hair trailing down her back, or maybe it's up in a bun, but everyone agrees it's a drowned woman. And there's you."

Alva blinked. "Me?"

"It's a factor. I like you. I'd like you even if you weren't the most beautiful woman I've ever seen, but I'm sure that's a factor, too."

"You shouldn't say things like that," she said. "We've already discussed it. Nothing is going to happen with regards to . . . to that."

"And I accept your decision, even though I hope you change it," he said. "But you asked me why I was interested in Liefdehuis, and you're part of the answer."

"I have to go," she said, looking up at him. "You can settle in on your own?"

"Of course," he said. "I'll let you know if anything interesting happens."

"Yes. Do so."

She was staring at his mouth, he realized, with a jolt of delight. "I will," he said, and feeling mischievous, he moved a bit closer.

She swallowed, nodded, and after a delicious half second turned and hurried from the room, like the ghost itself was chasing her.

"That wasn't very well done of me," he said. "But it was *very* fun."

Alva crumpled the piece of paper in front of her, heavily hatched with crossed-out words and scribbles, and threw it onto the floor, where it joined several of its peers. She drew out a clean sheet, put it in front of her, and stared at it.

And stared at it some more.

The book she had agreed to write for Braeburn and Smithson was to discuss general principles of good design, interspersed with photographs and small essays using the renovated Liefdehuis as an example of those principles. Those sections would have to wait until the house was completed (and she couldn't allow herself to contemplate the house *not* being completed), but work on the more general chapters could begin immediately. She had already accumulated extensive notes on a chapter about the ideal layout of rooms, and for the last day, since her cowardly retreat from Liefdehuis, she had been attempting to write it.

It wasn't like she didn't have opinions on the proper layout of rooms or about their relationship to one another. She had dozens of opinions. She even had an outline. No, the problem was every time she started a sentence, a memory of Sam Moore popped into her head and made all the words scatter like gazelles on a savannah.

The sitting room door banged open and Liza sailed through it, weighed down with a tray.

"Here's your lunch, ma'am, and the post as well, which was a surprise, let me tell you, what with Tompkins seeing Thomas the postman in the Blue Stag until well past midnight, if you take my meaning."

Alva paused, unsure what meaning she was supposed to take, other than the clearly stated one. She settled for a vaguely encouraging response. "Oh?"

"It's on account of his engagement with Sally May Reardon falling through, you see, although if you ask Sally May she'd say the engagement fell through on account of his drinking, so it's a proper mess either way you look at it." Liza busied herself setting the contents of the tray out on the desk, ruthlessly pushing the blank page out of the way and replacing it with a pot of tea, an empty cup, and a plate of delicate sandwiches. "And then there's the contingent saying it's because of Sally May's old beau Roger Pepper coming home on furlough, and looking so very fine in his uniform. He's in the Navy, you see, ma'am, and it can't be denied he looked awful nice in his whites, and there's something about a military man besides, wouldn't you say?"

"Mmm," Alva said, picking up the stack of mail.

"But of course he left, and so one way or another Sally May doesn't have any beaus at the moment, having broken it off with one and had the other leave. It's a proper kettle of fish, is what it is. Is everything all right, ma'am?"

"Hmm?" Alva stared at the delicate blue envelope in her hand, addressed to Mrs. Alva Webster. The return address announced that it came from Alfred Webster; the postmark informed her it had been mailed from Hyde Park yesterday, the morning after he'd visited her.

"Only you've gone awful pale, which I hope isn't on account of you receiving bad news, although how you could have received any without opening a single envelope I don't know. Maybe you'd like a splash of brandy in your tea?"

Alva put the letter down and forced herself to respond calmly. She knew better than anyone how gossip traveled, and she had no desire for Hyde Park to learn all about her family problems. "No, nothing like that, Liza. I'm just a little light-headed. No doubt Cook's excellent sandwiches will fix me up immediately."

"I'm sure they will, ma'am," Liza said, looking at the plate of thin sandwiches doubtfully. "Although if I might suggest it, perhaps a bit of red meat to put the blood back into you—"

"No, thank you."

"All right. I'll just go and see how young Jimmy's coming along with the stove, then, only it caught fire this morning—"

"Yes, thank you, Liza, please go do that."

As the maid bustled out of the room, her firm tread shaking the floors, Alva closed her eyes and filed the revelation of a kitchen fire that morning away for later perusal. Squaring her shoulders, she opened her eyes and sliced open the envelope. A single page fell out, crossed with delicate, spidery writing almost identical to her husband's.

My Dearest Sister,

It was delightful beyond words to see you on Wednesday—well worth the tedious journey from the city to look upon your lovely face. Indeed, I was so lost in the pleasure of your company I neglected to share with you the important details of our arrangement. You may send the agreed-upon sum to my bankers at Drexel, Morgan & Co. (the institution you likely remember as Dabney, Morgan & Co.) on the first of every month, and if you do so regularly and promptly I see no reason why our cozy familial relationship should not continue unabated. I know how much you would abhor the unpleasantness that must result if these guidelines are not followed with the utmost strictness, and I only seek to protect you from the hurt and embarrassment that would follow.

With my everlasting regard,
Your loving brother, Alfred

Carefully, precisely, she folded the thin, fine paper in thirds, the way it had come, and placed it back in the envelope. Breathing shallowly but perfectly regularly, she walked stiffly to the fire and placed it on top. Only once it had erupted in flames, the name *Alfred* briefly illuminated in the burning, did she allow the anger and shaking to come.

She'd never be rid of them, Alfred, Alain, all the others who had thought it their right to control her.

She had thought she was so terribly brave and bold, leaving Alain. He hadn't seen it coming, had simply come home one day to their large Parisian apartment to find her gone. She hadn't planned on filing for divorce at first. It was far from certain a court would even grant such a petition, and she'd assumed he'd be happy enough to still have her money that he wouldn't mind her living without him. That maybe, if she didn't enrage him further, he would let her go. After all, her money was the whole reason he'd married her—been forced to marry her, he would say.

But she'd been wrong. Oh, he hadn't minded at first. But when the rumors about why she'd left him had started—too many people had seen the occasional visible bruising; too many servants had overheard their raised voices—he'd had to retaliate.

The articles started appearing about three weeks after her escape. They whispered of scandalous doings, of lovers and orgies and drunkenness, of having multiple men simultaneously, of opium addictions and tawdry quarrels. She knew who had planted them. Who was a more reliable source than her own husband?

Thus society had an alternate version of their separation, one that was far more interesting. Alain became the pitied husband, a man trying to cling to his honor in the face of a woman trying to drag him down. Alva became some cross between a witch and a whore, a sexual deviant of mammoth and terrifying proportions.

When she decided she had nothing left to lose, she met with a lawyer to discuss options for divorce. Two days later, he'd—*no.*

She walked to the sitting room window and opened it, letting the cold air fill her lungs. There was plenty of it, she told herself. She could breathe the rest of her life and never run out. She could be greedy with it; she could even take more than her share.

She never needed to think of that night again, of gold buttons with dragons on them, emerald wallpaper fading to gray—*no, she would not think of it.* She pressed her hand against the bottom of the window frame, letting the sharp metal push into her skin until the discomfort cleared her mind. She wasn't going back there. She didn't have to; no one could make her.

It had been almost exactly ten months later that Alain had been killed, dying alone in a refuse-filled alley behind one of the casinos he had loved. She remembered reading about it in the evening paper the next day, eating alone at the table in her hotel room. She remembered pouring herself a glass of wine, and how different it had tasted. The taste of a prison wall that had suddenly vanished. Of freedom.

A false promise, it turned out. She hadn't escaped him.

Why did it feel like he was pulling at her? It was worse since she'd come here, actually. First New York City, where everyone had stared at her, reminding her that she was the infamous Mrs. Webster. Then at Liefdehuis, where for a handful of seconds she'd actually thought he was lurking in the shadows, waiting for her.

The hat was sitting in the back of her armoire currently, where it was going to stay. How had she come to buy a hat the exact color of her dead husband's hair? Gold wasn't even her color.

And now Alfred, who looked like him in every way. Who acted like him, too—money first, but if you could combine money and pain, or money and humiliation, that was best, the juiciest.

Yesterday she hadn't wanted to go in the house. It was her

house, her hope, and she'd balked at the door. Of course there hadn't been anything inside—no trace of the sinister feeling of earlier. Only dust, and Sam, and the strange lightness that seemed to follow in his wake. No Alain, waiting to pull her down with him.

He wasn't going to take this from her. It didn't matter if Alfred siphoned the last of her fortune; it didn't matter if she was afraid of the darkness; it didn't matter if her imagination conjured up horrifying fantasies. It didn't matter if she screamed and fainted every time she walked through the damn front door. Liefdehuis needed her, and she needed it.

It was hers, damn it, and dead or alive, no golden-haired snake was going to take it from her.

CHAPTER TEN

Sam's parents had been famous scientists since before he was born. While his mother had been pregnant with him, she'd filed no fewer than five patents, four of which were still in popular use today. His father was one of the foremost scientific names of the last century. Sam knew even his own name was recognizable in most of the nation's households, attached to brilliant discovery after brilliant discovery.

But what didn't make it into the newspapers' breathless reporting was the work that went into each achievement, the days and weeks and months spent simply monitoring experiments, tinkering with them, failing, and starting over. Or the backbreaking work that went into simply setting up a project, like he was doing now.

It was his favorite part. The moments of lightning discovery, he cherished those. But scientific life was one of small adjustments and constant work, and he loved it.

And so he whistled as he hauled equipment from room to room, making notes in each location about temperature, electrical readings, and environmental factors. If a room had a window, he wrote down the direction it faced. If there was a large patch of mold in the corner of the floor, he took a sample for later analysis. If there was a hole in the wall, he drew a simple diagram of its location.

Anything could affect the results.

As he worked, he let the part of his mind not necessary to the task at hand wander. Normally, his brain would flit playfully through dozens of ideas, some ridiculous, some important, some both. Today, though, there was only one thought—or, rather, one image.

Alva Webster.

Her face followed him, and he made no effort to banish it. He thought of the way she smiled, often as though humor or pleasure had taken her by surprise or had forced its way through against her better judgment. He thought of her eyes, watchful and wary, dark and passionate. He wondered why she guarded herself so carefully against even a hint of happiness, and an uncharacteristic surge of anger spiked in him at the person or persons who had taught her to do so.

Was her husband the one who had put caution into her eyes? Something had driven her to leave him, bringing scandal and ostracization upon herself. The papers had talked about other men, illicit lovers, but she hadn't married any of them, and there was certainly no sign of them here.

A polite chiming noise yanked him back to the present. He looked around in confusion for the source of the noise, frowning when he saw it coming from a machine designed to measure nearby electrical fluctuations. Crouching in front of the elaborate contraption, he studied the settings he had adjusted only minutes before. Wondering if he had accidentally entered the wrong values, he compared his notes to the machine and, when the numbers were identical, quickly ran through the equations again.

The values were correct. Which meant either something in the machine's wiring was faulty or it had picked up an increased amount of electricity in a room that, to Sam's naked eye, contained only himself.

He began to feel curls of excitement twisting through his body and forced himself to remain slow and calm as he wrote down the readings the machine was producing. It was almost certainly a problem with the machine; if there really was something else there he couldn't see, he would expect at least some of the other machines to pick it up—

The large device that measured changes in the magnetic field began to chime as well.

Sam sprang up, his notebook temporarily forgotten on the floor. Observation of the room showed no changes, just a moldy, dark room with a bunch of equipment in it. He saw no ripples in the air, felt no changes in temperature.

"Hello?" he said, his voice clear and loud. "My name is Samuel Moore. I intend you no harm. If you're there and you can understand me, a sign of some kind would be invaluable."

Nothing happened. The room remained still and quiet, except for the dual chimes of his machines. Slowly, Sam reached down for his notebook.

After two alerts, attempted to make contact. No response from first attempt. Possibly the ghost can't hear me—do ghosts have a way to receive sound?

He took a piece of chalk from his supply box and began to write on the floor in bold, large letters. *My name is Samuel*

Moore, he wrote. *I intend you no harm. If you understand this, please signal.*

He waited two minutes and made another note:

No response from second attempt—written communication. Can they see? Can they read?

He eyed the two machines, still happily chirping. Electricity was the key here. If they were measurable in terms of electricity, maybe they were reachable with electricity. . . .

Sam seized one of the unresponsive boxes and quickly opened the back of it. If he could cut and restore the power from the battery in some sort of pattern they could understand, a code of some kind. . . . He tested different patterns in his head, quickly rejecting those based on language, since he couldn't be sure what language, if any, the entity spoke or read. Numbers were the most universal method of communication.

He cut and restored the power once, waited two seconds, did it twice, waited two seconds, did it three times, waited two seconds, and so on to five. He stopped, cutting the power entirely and stepping away from it.

The machines stayed silent. It was as though nothing had ever happened.

"Damn it," he said, and repeated the process. "Come on. If you're there, if you can respond . . ."

But there was only the whistle of the winter wind far in the distance, and the sound of an old, decaying house settling and rotting around him.

He sat back on his heels, wiping his dusty hands on his pants, and made a face. "Well, that was a lot of fuss for nothing," he said, and started the process of measuring all over again. Such was the glamorous life of a scientist.

It was almost dark when Alva arrived at Liefdehuis—she'd timed it so Sam would be gone for the day. Her coachman—coach boy?—grimaced when she told him to come back in an hour, but he seemed to foresee how the argument would end, and so she was left alone under slowly drifting snow.

She was going to walk through the door. On her own, as many times as she needed to, in order to remind herself she could. The plans for the renovation were tucked under her arm for motivation.

The dull gray twilight made the house seem so dark, so lonely. And those trees—really, it was amazing, how the smell of mold and damp could survive even freezing temperatures. The minute she got her crew back that whole copse was going to be firewood. Honestly, how hard could it be to cut down a tree? Surely there was an axe somewhere in the pile of tools that had been left behind. Maybe she'd do it herself.

The cold was creeping through her coat while she stood there procrastinating. She sighed, strode towards the door, the frozen ground crunching under her boots, and in one great motion wrenched it open and stepped through.

She stopped just inside, her hand clutching the doorknob behind her. Sam had taken down the window boards, but the dying winter light didn't permeate the grime of the remaining panes. The blackness inside brought back the days after she'd left Alain, when she simply hadn't bothered to open the heavy velvet curtains in her flat. The stories in the papers had gotten fairly awful by then, and the bright sun of the Paris summertime had seemed only to tease her with impossibilities. She could almost feel the heavy oppression of the darkened rooms, the apartment swaddled as though in mourning.

Alva shook her head. The strength of the memories had been worse since she'd returned to America, seemingly waiting for her at every turn. Right now she could have sworn she'd caught a hint of Alain's cologne, lavender and rose, custom blended for him by the House of Guerlain. The sickly sweetness of it had clung to her clothes and possessions for weeks after leaving, haunting her where once it had been part of the fabric of her existence.

Enough of all that. Alva lit the lantern she'd brought, froze briefly while she waited for a ghostly hand to snuff it out, and stepped briskly into the room.

Sam had moved his equipment, so the only things left in the room were the covered mirror and the pile of lumber. He'd taken the lunch pail away, she noticed. She gave the mirror a wide berth—after all, she'd already walked through the front door. She didn't need to prove her bravery further.

The temperature dropped as she moved deeper into the house. She held her coat together at her neck as she walked, the sound of her steps strangely muffled in the empty building. It was probably having so many walls—the front of the house resembled a rabbit warren. There were no open spaces, no clear views, only walls, pressing in on her, and shadows, shadows that seemed wet and dark and deep, like they could hide any number of sins and secrets. She caught the hint of lavender again and stopped short—not a memory, then. Alva made herself take a breath, but it came into her chest short and shuddery. Someone had left a sachet somewhere or set dried lavender in one of the closets—

She flinched as a sharp gust from one of the broken windows cut across the back of her neck. The lavender was gone; only the smell of dust and rot and frost remained. The lantern barely illuminated her path. She needed to move. She needed to leave this hallway. But the shadows were getting longer as the light faded, and it *had* smelled like lavender, and—

"Pull yourself together," she whispered. "It's just a house. Any house would seem sinister after being empty so long." The wind sobbed around the old stone walls, and she hugged her arms over her chest as she thought about just how long Leifdehuis had been left empty, alone and forgotten. Abandoned to the fate of a monster.

Fear gave way to sadness as she walked, a whole-body kind of sorrow, one that started in the pit of her stomach and went across her clavicle and into her throat. Had anyone ever loved this house? Or had they only built it because it was expected of them, to show off?

Had anyone missed it, after they'd left?

Probably not, she thought, moving into one of the three long rooms that formed the back of the house. They'd simply packed up and gone, scared off by the dust and mold and their own disordered superstitions. No one had thought about what would happen to it, abandoned to the wild and the elements and the cruel passage of time. No one had given a damn.

She set the lantern down onto an old, battered table, left over from who knows how many owners, and stared out the cloudy windows at the Hudson River. The banks were muddy and barren, only a few spindly, warped trees clinging to life along the edge. Some teetered precariously over the water, nothing below them to break their fall when their roots finally lost their hold on the loose earth.

In summer the river would move slowly, a lazy blue thing that would delight with promises of languorous nights and days free from responsibility. Now, though, now it tore through the land, muddy water and white, frothy chop: turbulent and frenzied. If a person were to slip and fall in, there would be no question of rescue—it would already be too late.

No one wanted to stay around for this part. People only wanted the sunshine and the parasols and the charming picnic lunches. No one cared about the flood that came after.

Well, let them be fools; it was no matter to her. And how was she supposed to see how her designs translated to reality if this ugly table was squatting in the middle of everything? She took off her gloves and pushed hard against it, shoving all her sudden rage into the action. It protested at first, but another furious push got it moving, its legs scraping angrily across the uneven floor. Finally, it slammed into the far corner, and Alva leaned against it, panting.

"Alv—Mrs. Webster?" Sam's voice said from the doorway, and she came back to herself abruptly. What was coming over her lately? One minute she was terrified, the next almost in tears, and the next she wanted to scream. She couldn't even trust her own thoughts anymore.

"Professor Moore," she said, hating how wobbly her voice sounded. "Good evening."

He was leaning against the doorframe, his large, solidly built bulk filling almost the whole opening. There was a slight smile playing on his lips, not the full-on dazzling Moore Smile, but one of its playful predecessors. And it was as though the house calmed with her; it got a little lighter, suddenly more dust than rot.

"Ah, I see," he said. "You had a sudden urge to rearrange the furniture. My mother has those, too. It's why my parents can't share a lab."

"I was—" She looked at the table behind her, wondering how much he'd seen. Thinking quickly, she gestured towards the rolled-up plans she'd dropped on the table. "I needed to see the whole room, to make sure my designs will work here."

Sam made an excited murmuring sound and strode towards them, for all the world like a small boy headed towards a Christmas tree. She snatched them away.

"No," she said.

"But—"

"No."

"But—"

"Absolutely not."

"Mrs. Webster, you cannot actually be so cruel as to stand there with *schematics* and not let me see them."

"They're just blueprints. You know, blue paper, white lines, that sort of thing."

"Uh-huh. Did you design them yourself?"

"Yes."

"Then they're not just blueprints," he said. "Maggie corresponds with him, you know."

Alva blinked. "Who?"

"Poitevin." When she merely stared, he continued. "The man who invented blueprints? It's quite a clever technique. One I will explain to you in painful, tedious, exacting detail unless you hand over the plans."

How did he do it? One minute her world was blackmail and anger and skeletons in dark, shadowed corners, and then Sam Moore walked into the room. It was as though he walked in an almost imperceptible beam of light, which rendered the terrifying ordinary, and the ordinary beautiful.

She didn't realize she'd held the plans out until he took them from her.

CHAPTER ELEVEN

As he smoothed the plans out on the table, he watched her out of the corner of his eye. Tension was written in every line of her body—her shoulders were so square she could probably hold a pencil between her shoulder blades. She wouldn't tell him what was wrong if he asked, so he was going to sidle up to the problem instead.

"It's beautiful," he said, studying the design of the ground floor. "Unexpected, this elliptical center hall, but . . . airy, and open, and when combined with the symmetry of the rooms, lovely. You're very good at this, aren't you?"

She shrugged. "I have some experience."

"I don't know much about architecture and interior design, but I'd imagine it takes more than experience to envision something like this. You're an artist."

"I'm not an artist," Alva said, staring at him as though he'd grown a second head.

"A strange thing to say when I'm holding the proof in my hand. Aren't you writing a book on the subject, too? That's what I heard."

"I am, but it doesn't make me an artist. I've done it a lot, decorating houses and so forth, and I've developed opinions on the matter. That's all."

"And all I do is tinker around with bits and bobs of metal, but I'm still a scientist."

"That's different."

"Why?"

She made a confused gesture, as if there were too many things she wanted to say at once. "I don't know, because you're a certified genius? A rather famous one, at that."

"There are lots of different kinds of genius, and I'm looking at one kind right here." He gestured to the plans. "Tell me about the book."

She gave a defeated sigh. "It's going to be divided into chapters on general principles of design, with the renovation of Liefdehuis as a sort of case study. We'll use photographs reproduced throughout the text. Hopefully it will appeal not only to the society women in big cities but to middle-class women as well—the idea is to explain our design philosophy in a way that's accessible to people living in more limited spaces. That's been an ongoing struggle, to find the things that hold true no matter what kind of house one is working with."

"The search for underlying principles," he murmured. "I know it well. Show me how the plans will be?"

"You're like a puppy with a bone. You can't possibly care about this."

"I care about everything," he said, placing the floor plans into her hands and steering her out of the room. "And especially about things that are excellent. So walk me through it."

He didn't need to be walked through it, of course—as soon as he'd skimmed the plans he'd known exactly how they would fit into every part of the existing structure. But this time when she huffed there was a little bit of a chuckle along with the eye roll, and he knew his plan to cheer her up was starting to work. And when it did, he could start to weasel out what was bothering her.

"Fine," she said, walking briskly towards the front entry. "This hall will open out from here. The rooms will be arrayed around the ellipses. There will be a seating area in the middle. The whole central hall will be open to the second floor."

He peered up at the moldy ceiling. "Sometimes I get invited to fancy houses. Usually Henry gets me out of it, but sometimes I have to go because some politician or rich client wants to meet me, that sort of thing. One thing I've always noticed is that for all the space, there's no freedom inside it. Just a bunch of little rooms, one after the other. Suffocating."

Looking back down at Alva, he saw her staring at him with an arrested expression. "I wouldn't have expected you to understand."

"I promise to buy your book anyway," he said, warming to the core when she laughed.

"It's nice to have at least one copy spoken for." She fell into step beside him, leading them towards the side of the house. "Sweeping stairs over here, leading to the second-floor bedrooms. The roof over the central hall will have an elliptical glass section mirroring the hall itself."

"Really? You must have had a time with the engineering."

"I'm still working it out," she admitted. "But it'll be worth it."

"Yes," he said, looking around. "I believe it will. And the outside?"

"Oh, just the usual."

"No, I meant, will you show me?"

"Professor Moore, you're really very kind to take an interest, but it must be below freezing outside."

"You're wearing a coat," he said.

"I am," she agreed, slowly, "but you're not."

"Oh," he said, looking down in some surprise. "No, I'm always losing it. Can't be helped. Shall we?"

"But—"

Before she could protest, he pulled her out into the fresh winter air. Snow had begun to drift down, almost invisible in the end-of-dusk light.

"You'll freeze," she said.

"We'd better not waste time arguing then," he said, linking his arm with hers and guiding her around the back of the house. "So, the outside?"

"Gardens," she said. "Down there. Formal. Woodlands around the edges. Can we go back inside now?"

"Have you seen the summerhouse?"

"When I toured the place. Not since."

"I visited it this afternoon. It's charming."

"I'm sure it is."

"Let's go visit it."

"You know, when I first met you, I was convinced you were mad," Alva said, her teeth starting to chatter. Sam pressed her a little closer. "There was the whole ghost thing, and the bit with the shoelaces—"

"Ah yes! I'm glad you brought that up. I've revised my calculations, but I'm going to have to create a test group—"

"Then, for a while, I thought I misjudged you. Perhaps you were brilliant and the things I thought were crazy were simply all the bits I didn't understand—"

"Oh, I'm quite sure most of them were just mad," Sam said complacently.

"But now, now I'm absolutely, completely, sure of it, because only a madman would haul me out into below-freezing temperatures to go look at some patches of mud that may, at some point in the future, be gardens, and insist upon continuing to a house specifically designated as being appropriate only in the summertime. Without even wearing his coat."

"You know what they say about madmen," he said, mounting the rickety, frosty steps of the summerhouse.

"I can't even begin to imagine."

"You should humor them." He smiled at her and opened the door. "After you."

"All right, we're inside," she said. "Can we leave now?"

"You're very impatient," Sam said, pulling a chair away from the wall and crouching down. "I want to show you something."

"And this something just *couldn't wait* until warmer weather, I suppose," she grumbled, but she moved nearer nonetheless.

"Here." Sam pointed to a place on the wall, gesturing her even closer. He'd found the carving in his initial tour of the property and been charmed by it. *EdB + MS*, the worn markings declared. *Forever and a day.*

Alva's fingers traced the shallow cuts. "When do you think it's from?"

"If the dB is de Boer, then it must be sometime between 1789 and 1840."

"A long time ago," she said, her fingers still on the carving. "They would have been young."

"Why young?"

"To believe so passionately in love's permanence that you'd carve it into a building? Only youth possesses such blind naïveté."

Sam considered her. "Here," he said, pulling a dusty, motheaten blanket down from a high shelf and draping it around her shoulders. "Do you know how my parents met?"

"Your mother was his secretary or something, wasn't she? I remember reading a feature on them in a newspaper."

"She was. He had recently announced the first of his really big discoveries—arc lighting in the first of the Moore tubes, although in the end Geissler beat him out there—and she applied for the job because she'd read about it. Her family was livid that she'd run off to Columbus and gotten a job, since she was the last of her siblings left unmarried and they had all pretty much decided she was going to be the eccentric spinster aunt who took care of her parents and her nieces and nephews, but she went off anyway, because she figured, if she couldn't be a scientist herself, she could at least help one."

As he told the tale he'd heard a hundred times, the usual warmth bloomed in his chest, the feeling of love and happiness that always accompanied thoughts of his parents' marriage. His mother was quicksilver, funny and brilliant; his father was like the Mississippi River, slow and deep and powerful. They couldn't have been more different, or more perfect together. They were two sides of the same story.

That's what he'd been waiting for, he realized. The other side of his story.

And now he very much thought he might have found her. The sudden epiphany threw him off-balance, and he forgot what he'd been saying.

"She worked for him for three months," he said, slowly, letting himself fall back into the familiar recitation. He was moving too fast again—a habit, with her. He needed to slow down, to think. "Taking his dictation and writing his letters and picking up his laundry, and on Christmas Eve he came back to the laboratory unexpectedly and found her sketching an improvement to the gas discharge tube. She assumed he'd be furious, and was bracing herself to be let go, but all he did was pick up the sketch and look at it for, according to her, the longest five minutes of her life. After, he put it down, nodded, and told her they'd take it to the glassblowers as soon as they opened up after Christmas. He said she was fired as his secretary, of course, and that they'd have to expand the laboratory so she could have her own space. And finally, he said he was damned glad he'd discovered this, because now that she was his partner instead of his employee, he could ask her to dinner without feeling like he was abusing his position."

Alva's smile was reluctant. "It's a sweet story," she said.

"They were married the next month. And they've been madly in love for the last thirty-five years, every child they've raised and every discovery they've made together a promise and a testament to that love. Just like this carving. Love isn't naïve, Alva. It's hope, and it's faith, and it can outlast buildings and wars and empires."

She looked at the floor. "We should go back in."

"Something's upsetting you," he said. He didn't know what to do with all the feelings fermenting inside his chest, but this was easy. She was in trouble, and he wanted to fix it. "Tell me what it is."

"Professor Moore—"

"Tell me."

"It's nothing. Merely a—a slight irritation."

"More than, I think. Let me be your friend. I think you might need one."

"You couldn't possibly understand," she said, with a hint of frustration. "With your perfect family, and your parents who've been in love for four decades, and your general goodness. It would be like trying to explain capitalism to someone who's never seen money before. The concepts wouldn't make sense."

"Try me."

"Love isn't always like that, you know. Good and lasting and true. It isn't even usually like that. Sometimes it's an illusion that baits a trap."

"Were you caught in a trap, Alva?"

"I still am," she said, standing. "And I don't know why I told you that, but we need to go back now."

"Let me help you," he said, standing as well. He moved towards her, taking her gently by the arms. "Please. Let me fix it."

"You assume all problems have solutions," she said.

"We can't know they don't unless we try," he said, pulling her closer. "Let me try."

Briefly, she relaxed against him. Her body fit against his like they had been formed at the same time; he rested his chin on her head.

Then she stepped away.

"No." One word, but it was like ten tons of wall landing between them.

"Alva—"

"It's not your problem to solve." She took a deep breath, dropping her shoulders. "We should go back. It really is freezing out here."

Sam had pushed her today, more than he'd meant to. He'd wanted to cheer her up, and he was afraid he'd only reopened wounds she hadn't wanted to consider.

He gestured towards the door. "As you wish."

It was fully dark when they stepped back outside, lit solely by the reflection of the moon on the thin layer of snow. Snowflakes twisted in lazy twirls before landing softly on the ground. The only sound was the crunching of their footsteps.

Alva walked stiffly, every sense open to the man next to her—his smell, peppermint and leather and Sam, the heat radiating through his shirtsleeves into the space between them. He made her feel awkward without trying to. His vision of the world was such a positive one, powerful. Why couldn't her world be the same? Why couldn't she be the sort of person who trusted others, who could risk openness and not fear pain?

Was he angry she wasn't that person? She peeked up at him through her lashes, trying to gauge his mood, and realized his attention wasn't on her at all. He was staring intently at the black bulk of Liefdehuis, a slight smile on his face.

"In a few years, you'll be able to light this electrically."

"What?"

"Imagine it, coming home on a cold, snowy night like this, every window filled with bright pure light, accessible at the push of a button." His expression was almost dreamy, and Alva wondered whether this was how he would look at a woman he was about to make love to. "Harnessed lightning, available in every room, to be called whenever you want it."

"It sounds almost blasphemous."

He smiled wider. "Are you worried Zeus will descend Mount Olympus and smite us for our effrontery?"

"Something like that."

"Wouldn't that be a red-letter day for science," he said.

Alva rolled her eyes, the tightness in her stomach easing. "You have a unique and frequently disturbing outlook on life."

"Oh, come now. The discovery Zeus is not a mythical figure but does in fact exist? Think of the questions that could be answered. For example, what does it feel like to have your daughter born from your own skull?"

"Is Hera as horrible as the stories make her out to be, or is it classic scandalmongering?"

"How, exactly, do you transform heroes into celestial constellations? And does it hurt when you turn them into a series of stars spread over hundreds of light-years?"

"Where exactly does one find ambrosia? Is it suitable for dinner parties?"

"See? You have just as many questions as I do, so you must cede the point. If angering the gods resulted in their appearance on the scene, it could only be counted as a good thing."

"Only if they didn't kill you with a lightning bolt first."

"Oh no," he said, quite sincerely. "Then I would die in the name of scientific discovery. Think of the things my fellow scientists could discover from my body!"

Alva waved her hands. "I cede entirely, if only to leave this conversation as far away from me as possible."

He chuckled, and they walked a few steps together in silence.

"Did you mean it, though? That electrical lighting will be available for houses within a few years?"

"At the rate of progress we're currently experiencing? Yes. Within five."

Alva looked at the huge, dark house in front of her and tried to imagine it.

"I was going to put gas lighting in."

"It's certainly a popular choice."

"But you think electricity will be better."

"It'll be safer, for one thing. No more noxious fumes, no more explosions caused by faulty installation. It'll be cleaner, too."

She glanced up at him again. "But that's not why you love it," she said. "That's how you justify it. You love it because it's harnessed lightning."

His grin was sudden and adorable, the moonlight glinting off his straight, white teeth. "I told you I was easy to understand."

"Lightning in Liefdehuis," she mused, thinking of twinkling white light and sharp, pure air. "That would be something indeed."

CHAPTER TWELVE

There was no public library in Hyde Park, but there was an informal lending arrangement run out of St. James' Chapel on East Market Street, and so eleven o'clock the next morning found Alva already ensconced in the church's reading room. The space was little more than a small sitting room: a few chairs scattered in front of a large stone fireplace; three glass-fronted bookshelves lining the walls. Only a handful of the three hundred–plus books were available for loan, so Alva sat in one of the chairs with a short pile of books from the church's permanent collection in front of her.

Perhaps unsurprisingly, the library collection of St. James' leaned more towards sermons than ghosts. The few references she'd been able to locate insisted, quite firmly, that although ghosts—as in the spirits of people who had died—did not exist, demons and possessions did.

"Just what I need," Alva muttered, closing the third book to make this point. "If it turns out to be a demon, it can have the damned place."

An angry intake of breath behind her informed her that the

local volunteer, a plump woman with a face all hitched up around her nose, had overheard her and wished to make clear she approved of neither swearing nor demons. Or possibly found it a criminal extravagance to allow such a creature to live rent free.

Alva ignored her, reaching for the one book on local history the collection contained. It was a handwritten text, written by a Mrs. D. E. Clarke twenty-five years before in light, graceful script. The pages showed signs of slight water damage, but most of the writing was easily legible.

In recent years, the text began, *our little town has drawn significant attention from the richest and greatest members of our fine State. It seems only suitable then, in accordance with our newfound prestige, that we should boast our own written history. Some readers will no doubt be inclined to discount this attempt because of its feminine authorship; to them, I can only say, Have you ever met a man with any good memory for gossip at all? And after all, what is local history but local gossip?*

The small settlement that eventually became Hyde Park was probably founded near the beginning of the last century, although even the oldest of our residents cannot stretch their mind back far enough to be sure. There was certainly settlement by 1742, by which time—

"Mrs. Webster?" The voice was low and polite, and when Alva looked up she met a pair of smiling brown eyes.

"Hello, Mr. Van de Berg," she replied, smiling back at him. There was something about Sam's man of business that made one feel calm and secure. He was the sort of person you wanted to be able to send for if you were suddenly clapped into jail or if your house burned down, because he would almost certainly know what you should do next. "Are you browsing for business or pleasure? Because if it's for your employer, I'm fairly certain I've already got the only relevant text."

"Ah, Mrs. D. E. Clarke," he said, sitting smoothly in the chair next to her. "You may currently be in possession of the only copy, but I'm afraid I have the trump card."

"A warrant for its immediate arrest?"

"Better." He leaned forward slightly, dropping his voice as though imparting a precious secret. "Permission to take it from the premises."

Alva pretended to gasp. "Surely not. I was told very sternly it was not to leave the room!"

"Ah, but that's only the rule for you common people. For the brilliant Professor Moore and his terribly charming associate, rules must be bent."

"I see what happened," Alva said. "He came in here and smiled, in a perfectly harmless, genial sort of way, and before they knew it the poor women who volunteer here were putty in his hands. And then, if I understand the relationship the two of you have correctly, you swooped in while they were still puddles on the floor and maneuvered things exactly how you wanted them."

Henry beamed. "You understand matters perfectly. And as this establishment is closing in fifteen minutes, I have come to collect my ill-gotten gains."

"Fifteen minutes!" Alva looked at her watch, pinned low on her bodice.

"They close early in the winter," Henry said, standing politely as Alva rose. "It occurs to me that I face a certain difficulty."

"I can't imagine it's anything the combined forces of Moore and Van de Berg can't leave crushed and mewling in the dirt."

"Ah, even we are helpless to resist the forces of chivalry, ma'am. You see, I can't very well seize the book out of your hands, can I? Were you a man, it would pose no difficulty at all. I would simply insist the book was by rights mine and abscond with it before a reasoned argument occurred to you."

"Reasoned arguments occur to me very quickly," Alva protested. "Although perhaps, were I a man, my intellectual capacity would be somewhat reduced."

"A hit, a hit!" Henry exclaimed, staggering slightly and clutching a hand to his chest. "Here is what I propose: we shall divide custody of the book between the houses of Moore and Webster."

"That's a very kind proposal, Mr. Van de Berg. Are you certain you have Professor Moore's blessing for such generosity?"

"My dear Mrs. Webster, we both know Professor Moore would give you whole custody of this book at the slightest flutter of your admittedly lovely eyes, along with the patents to his five most recent inventions and the keys to his entire kingdom."

"I'm sure that's not the case," Alva said, after a pause.

"No?" Henry watched her with eyes that measured as they smiled, and she had the distinct sense she was being issued a warning, the most charmingly delivered warning anyone had ever experienced. Finally, he shrugged, and the tension was gone. "Then you'll have to rely on my word alone, and I say you shall have equal share of the book."

Alva had forgotten they were talking about a book. "Oh. Well, I'm certainly not going to turn you down," she said, struggling to regain her flippant tone. "But you must have the first crack at it."

"I'll have it delivered to your house in a few days," he said. "May I escort you home?"

"Thank you," she said, and gathered her things as he arranged matters with the volunteer—who, Alva noticed with some cynicism, bore no trace of the sourness she had previously displayed.

The streets outside were still covered with a crisp layer of snow, mocking the bright blue sky above it. Only a few people were about, huddled close as they went about their days.

"Have you worked with Professor Moore long?"

"Since I graduated from law school," Henry replied. "But I practically grew up with him. The Moores were like a second family to me as a child."

"I met them in New York. They seemed like wonderful people."

"There's nothing like them," Henry said, a softer smile than she had seen before creeping across his face. "Going to a Moore family dinner is like trying to sit down and eat right in the middle of a circus. You'll never get through the first course without an explosion of some kind, and the only question is whether they'll stop talking long enough to notice it."

"How fortunate you are, to have grown up in that environment."

"More fortunate than you can possibly imagine," he agreed, smoothly guiding her across the street. "And still more so to be able to work with them now."

"It must be fascinating." They stopped in front of her house. "It was nice to run into you, Mr. Van de Berg."

"And you, Mrs. Webster." Henry tipped his hat. "I'll send you the book, as promised."

As he bowed and walked away, Alva wished that the words he'd said earlier weren't running through her mind. She wasn't some gawky girl, ready to swoon when someone told her a boy liked her. Still, it would take a harder woman than her not to experience a little flutter at the words "and the keys to his entire kingdom."

It was all nonsense. The whole thing. Henry warning her (about what? She hadn't mistaken the look, but what was she being told not to do?); her silly flutters; Professor Samuel Moore as a whole. She was a sensible woman, and because she was a sensible woman, she was going to go back in her house and do something . . . oh, something terribly sensible. Setting her chin, Alva marched inside.

"I brought food," Henry said, walking into Sam's lair at Liefdehuis.

Sam grunted and sat back on his heels. His eyes were tired from hours spent disemboweling and examining the machines that had registered something earlier, until he was positive they hadn't malfunctioned. He had an ache the size of a mountain between his shoulders, his brain mushy from thoughts of hauntings and Alva Webster, and even after he'd spent yet more hours reassembling the machines, his ghost (because despite the official position on owning a ghost, he had somehow slipped into the habit of thinking of the one his equipment had registered as his) had not made a second appearance.

"She didn't show up," he said, sounding a little pathetic even to his own ears. "I tried everything, and not a peep. I waited and waited."

"My good man, you can't wait around on a woman. It gives them terrible ideas. And since when is this ghost a she, anyway?"

"She just sort of . . . feels like one. Not a terribly accurate statement, I admit."

"The way a ship feels like one?"

Sam winced. "Yes. Maybe. Which goes to show it's a fairly stupid thing to say. Especially since it's perfectly possible that there's more than one. Or none. I'm tired."

Henry shrugged and set the bags he was carrying onto the cluttered worktable. "Take a break. When was the last time you ate?"

"When was the last time you fed me?"

"Last night."

"And what time is it now?" He pushed a hand through his hair, trying to move the tiredness aside along with it.

"Seven o'clock. In the evening."

"Good god." The tiredness wasn't shifting, but he attempted a smile anyway. "What are you trying to do, starve me to death?"

"You've found me out. I'd hoped to inherit your collection of useless metallic doodads, you see."

"Obviously," Sam said, helping Henry clear some of said collection out of the way. "It's the envy of every thinking person this side of the Mississippi. Ah, stew."

"And all the rolls I could wheedle out of the landlady."

"You're a jewel without price, my friend. A prince amongst men."

"A cactus without prickles," Henry added, gesturing widely and vaguely.

"A cat amongst pigeons."

"A moon made of cheese."

"Is there cheese, too?" Sam looked hopefully in one of the bags. "No. How many of these rolls do you want? They're a little puny."

"Let's say three and see how things develop."

Yawning, Sam reached into the bag and started to count the rolls out.

It had been a long twenty-four hours. Alva might have gone, but her presence remained; even the delicate perfume she wore lingered in the air. He'd needed to think and he thought best when he worked, so he'd flung himself into his research with abandon. He'd finished every baseline reading he could think of. He'd designed new equipment, knocked some prototypes together, disemboweled and reassembled three existing machines. He'd read math problems aloud in every room on the ground floor. He'd tapped patterns on the wall until his knuckles hurt. And he hadn't noticed it until now, but he was . . . exhausted. Spent. And not much clearer on, well, on any of his problems.

"Hey, I said three, not half a dozen."

"Sorry."

"Here's your stew." Henry handed the mounded plate across, and for a few minutes they sat in friendly silence, chewing and making the occasional appreciative grunt.

"I ran into Alva Webster at the reading room." There was a long pause. "Sam?"

"Huh?"

"You look like a sixteen-year-old thinking about his first girl."

He shrugged. "Sorry. You saw Alva?"

"When I went to pick up that book from St. James'. She was reading it when I got there."

"Hah! That's Alva Webster for you. She doesn't believe in ghosts, but she's damn well going to be prepared for them." He frowned. "You didn't take the book away from her, did you?"

"I arranged a shared custody agreement, but we get it first."

"How did she look?"

"Beautiful. She's a lovely woman."

"Oh lord. You flirted with her, didn't you?"

It was Henry's turn to shrug, an insouciant little gesture accompanied by the slightest hint of a smirk.

"You did. First my housemaid, then my . . . my . . . Alva. What next, my ghost?"

"So much whining. Are we or are we not getting hot tea regularly?"

"Only when you're in the house," Sam grumbled. "No more flirting with—"

"With your Alva?"

"With Alva. Who belongs entirely to herself."

"I wouldn't worry about the striking Mrs. Webster," Henry said, his grin spreading. "My read was that she's well able to take care of herself."

Sam sighed. "She's wonderful, isn't she?"

"You're doing it again."

"Doing what again?"

"Looking like a moonstruck idiot. It's putting me off my food."

"Sorry."

They cleared their plates, sitting back in their chairs with the air of men well contented.

"Are you working more tonight?" Henry asked, rooting into another bag and producing some cookies.

"A few more hours."

"You need to sleep."

"Yes, Mother."

"You're no good to me dead."

"True. I'm leaving my collection of useless metallic doodads to Maggie anyway."

"I shudder to think what your benighted sister would do with it. Explode something, obviously, but what?" He stood up, piling the plates and clearing the bags. "Don't work yourself into a state of nervous exhaustion, and if you can spare five minutes to finalize that streetlamp proposal, I'm sure the citizens of Montreal would be most grateful."

"Mmm," Sam said, biting into a cookie. "That's due the sixth?"

"The twenty-ninth."

"I'll make time. Night."

"Night."

Sam sat at the table a bit longer, yawning and turning over his next course of action in his mind. The ghost was determined not to come out and play, and he'd exhausted every trick he could think of to convince her . . . it . . . they to do so. With another yawn he turned to the designs for Montreal. He'd knock them out quickly, so he could go back to thinking about her. One of the hers, at least.

Right as he was calculating the number of streetlamps he was promising, it happened. He'd counted the number they'd proposed in the downtown area, fifty-four, and the ones a little farther up in one of the residential neighborhoods, twenty-seven, and added them together to get the total.

And made six.

He didn't even catch the error until he'd written it down on the form Henry had given him: *Downtown: 54 lamps. Residential: 27 lamps. Total lamps: 6.*

For a minute he wondered if he'd finally gone mad. Carefully he brought the two numbers together again and got eighty-one. The world righted itself enough to allow him to take a deep breath, and he sat very, very still and thought.

Samuel Moore did not make adding mistakes. Ever. He could not remember a time, not once in his entire life, when he had made any sort of mistake in either addition or subtraction. The numbers were simply there, whenever he called upon them. It was like looking at blue and thinking it was red.

And besides, surely this wasn't the sort of adding mistake people made? Eighty-one wasn't even close to six, except perhaps in a very relative sense. . . .

Six.

Six rolls instead of three. The sixth instead of the twenty-ninth. Six instead of eighty-one.

A pattern ending in five, where the answer was a six . . .

"I'm sorry," he said quietly. "You must think I'm very stupid.

Here you've been trying to get my attention and I haven't even noticed."

No one answered him, but he hadn't expected anyone to.

"Are you letting me know you're here? In case I wasn't sure? That was very thoughtful of you. I'm sure now." Excitement was crawling along his skin, his heart beating faster and faster in his chest. "My god, you can get into my head. You can influence my thoughts. How far, I wonder? Could you tell me to do something, or is it limited to sixes?"

He jumped up and shouted with glee and astonishment.

"Given that I meant to say 'simple ideas' instead of sixes, I'll take that as your answer, and also as a sign of a slightly cheeky sense of humor." He laughed, clapping his hands together. "Oh, you beauty! Sixes! Genius! Is it hard for you, I wonder? It'd be a miracle for a human, but who knows how different it is for you? Are you the only one like you? Are there others? Were you ever a human, or are you some intelligence I can't even conceive of?

"It must be difficult for you," he said, dropping his voice again and reaching for his notebook. "You'd have done it more if it wasn't. Even now, you could push in more, and you're not. Or maybe you're being polite, in which case, I assure you, I don't mind. One plus one is two! Two plus two is four! Four plus four is eight! No sixes? Yes, I must assume it's difficult."

He opened his notebook and starting scribbling madly, desperately trying to get down the entire incident, in case he'd missed something. He kept doing simple math problems aloud while he wrote, saying words that started with *s*, anything he could think of to give her another opportunity to jump in, but there was nothing more. He couldn't have said how long he sat there, but at the end his throat was hoarse, he'd filled his notebook, he'd tried every machine he had on hand, to no result, and he was certain the ghost wasn't planning on chatting anymore. He stood.

"Thank you," he said. "You've honored me tonight, and I won't forget it. I won't forget you, either. I think you may need my help, and you have my word I'll give it to you if I'm able."

He bowed gravely, feeling it was the right thing to do. "Good night, my friend."

CHAPTER THIRTEEN

Alva sat in bed, her writing desk balanced on her lap, the house quiet around her. The servants had long gone to their rooms; she was alone with only the night outside her windows for company. Frost formed delicately on the glass, a cold film between her and the clear black sky.

"Chapter ten, on the dining room," she murmured, glancing over the notes she'd made. *Overview on place of dining room in history*, she'd written. *Comment on changing role today—more people have them, differences in class.*

Nodding and muttering, she began to write. After a few minutes, she stood to pull a book out from a bookshelf by her bed, crawling with it back across the covers. "I know you have something on French dining rooms," she told the book, quickly flipping through it. "There."

Skimming the paragraph she'd been looking for, Alva allowed herself a brief moment of contentment. Yes, construction on the house had been indefinitely halted. Yes, she was having trouble being in her newly purchased house alone. Yes, she spent more time thinking about Samuel Moore than she wanted to.

Well, that wasn't really true. If she was honest, she enjoyed every minute she spent thinking about him.

The point was that all sorts of things were wrong, but there were a few things within her control and she had them well in hand.

Like chapter 10, for example. She'd known she'd been right about the dining rooms in French villas.

She'd almost told him everything in the summerhouse. Again. Apparently the slightest bit of sympathy made her want to pour out all her problems—actually, that wasn't right. It wasn't sympathy Sam offered. It was safety, and understanding, and vision. He saw her, more than he should.

What would her life have been like if she'd met him first?

It was a treacherous thought. What if she'd met him thirteen years before, at some grand gala of her parents? What if he'd come into the ballroom, broad shoulders clad in an elegant black jacket—

She laughed. That wasn't right at all. Give Sam five minutes at a fancy party and he'd have his jacket off, his tie askew, and be hip deep in some new brainchild that couldn't wait a second longer. She didn't want some pretend Sam, one who would have been acceptable to a callow heiress and her even more callow world. She wanted this Sam, the one of flesh and muscle and blood, the one who held her against him like she was the only thing he'd ever wanted to touch and looked at her like she was a sunset and a miracle and the whole advent of electricity balled up into one.

Thinking of him brought heat to her throat and face, making her aware of the thin fabric draped over her body. He had a way of making the complicated simple, or the simple complicated. What she wanted him to do to her was both.

"Stop it," she told herself. "Can't even focus on this for *five minutes* without daydreaming like a . . . like a—" She couldn't even complete the sentence.

"Get back to work," she hissed, and pulled the writing desk back towards her.

Five minutes into her discourse on the newfound importance of a separate chamber dedicated to eating, there was a rattle at her window. She jumped, but a quick glance reassured her no fearsome specter was looking in, and she looked back down at her page, trying to reclaim her thought. Five seconds later, something hit the window again, so she crossed over to it, her feet dragging a little bit as she contemplated the potential horrors lurking outside. Pushing her chin up and reminding herself that she'd never yet heard of a ghost who haunted the part of a lawn underneath a second-story window, she pushed the glass a few inches open and looked down.

"Oh, for heaven's sake," she said, and pushed it the rest of the way. "What on earth are you doing?"

"It's not polite to come calling after . . . some hour," Sam called up. "I'm not sure which one, but I'm positive one in the morning counts."

"You've missed a key point there," she said, furious with the smile she couldn't stop from spreading over her face.

"But this way I'm only disturbing you, and I knew you were still awake, because your light was on. I wouldn't have thrown the pebbles if it hadn't been." He wrinkled his brow. "Probably. Well, maybe."

"How did you know the light belonged to me?" And *be-damned* to her racing heart, and the giddy feeling in her chest that apparently thought they were all having a really excellent adventure.

"Servants don't sleep in the front of the house," he said simply. "Anyway, I'm coming up."

At this point, Alva knew, she should certainly say something like, *Oh no, you're not,* or possibly, *Help! A man is trying to sneak into my bedroom!*, or even a polite, *I wish you wouldn't*—basically anything but what did come out of her mouth, which was: "How? The door's locked, and I might wake the servants if I open it for you."

"I'll climb," he said, smiling up at her, and oh, if she didn't smile back. And then he took off his jacket, and at this point the voice that had been shouting, *You must shut the window and* lock it, *miss!* was shoved away into a tiny box in the back of her brain where it was promptly sat upon by all the other parts of her brain, who were much more fun and interesting anyway.

Besides, it was after midnight, and surely things that happened after midnight, under a clear, full winter's moon, and with no one else observing them didn't count?

The moonlight cut clearly across his magnificent shoulders, allowing Alva to see the way his muscles tensed and bulged even from fifteen feet above him. Was he really going to climb up the stonework?—He was. Even as she thought the words he pulled himself up off the ground, finding a foothold in the thick, bumpy stones that formed the front of the house. His arms bulged with every movement upwards, and Alva's mouth grew drier and drier and drier.

After a few minutes seemingly suspended in honey, he pulled himself over the edge of her windowsill, and suddenly she was faced with the reality of having approximately six feet and four inches of gorgeous, smiling man in her bedroom.

"Hi," he said, slowly surveying her nightgown.

She cleared her throat. "Um. Hello." She hurried to the armoire and looked for a dressing gown—possibly instead of ogling him as he'd climbed she should have been finding something to cover herself with. Something large and fluffy, preferably, instead of the light gauzy thing that seemed to be the only option hanging in front of her. Still, it was better than only her thin nightgown, so she quickly wrapped it around herself before turning back.

He hadn't moved. He stood frozen, with his hands firmly in his pockets and his eyes glued on her. "This might not have been a good idea," he said.

Heat rose into her cheeks as she tugged uselessly at the dressing gown. "I'm not the one who decided to pay his morning calls a few hours early."

"Hmm?"

She crossed her arms over her chest. "You came here for a reason?"

"Yes," he said.

"And it was?"

"Something very important." He cleared his throat. "Which I will remember at any moment."

"Oh, for the love of—listen, I'll get a blanket—"

"Mrs. Webster. Do *not* turn around again."

Alva froze, half-turned. "But I just want—"

"Your dress is very sheer," he said, half-strangled. "I don't think you intended—and that dressing gown doesn't look—"

Now her face was aflame. "Oh," she said. "Um. Yes, I see."

They stood there, staring at each other in silence.

"I know," he said. "We'll both turn around."

"Right." She waited, but he didn't move. "Well?"

"May I say—you're beautiful."

The thrill started from her toes and crept up her whole traitorous body. She wrapped her arms tighter around herself in protection. "You grow compliments like dandelions," she said, and frowned when he laughed. "Are you turning?"

He put his hands up in mock surrender. "I'm turning."

She waited until he was facing the window before scurrying to her bed, snatching the heavy woolen blanket off the top.

"There," she said, after she had thoroughly cocooned herself. "Now maybe you can tell me what you're doing here."

"It's the ghost," Sam said, pulling a chair over for her. It looked so fragile and delicate in his hands that she almost missed his next words.

"What did you say?"

"It made contact. Alva, it exists. At least one. And I know you were hoping it didn't, but I don't think it's violent; in fact, it seems to have the capacity for rational thought . . . or at least mathematical—"

She didn't realize she wasn't sitting down until she landed with a jaw-rattling thump.

"I've found fairly convincing evidence in the past, of course, but I've never made contact with one before. This is *proof*; even if I can't replicate it, I'll *know*—"

But it had just been her imagination, Alva thought numbly. It had been dark corners and mirrors and local superstitions. She was hot; it was terribly stuffy in here; she couldn't breathe—

She dashed to the window, pushing it open again and leaning out of it. The cold air tingled fresh against her face; she sucked it greedily into her lungs. Sam came up behind her, she heard him say something, but the ringing in her ears drowned him out.

There was no such thing as ghosts, she thought wildly. People couldn't follow you after death; they couldn't keep tormenting you. If there was something after death, it didn't happen here. Your body died, and at the very minimum, you *left*. Because if that wasn't true, there could never be an ending.

Sam's hands were on her shoulders: he was turning her around to face him. His arms were circling her—they were strong and offered comfort she couldn't afford. She tried to push him away, and he released her out to arm's length.

"What are you afraid of?" His voice was soft, warm. Confident that, whatever the problem was, he could fix it.

A simple question, with a simple answer: everything. She was afraid of the whole jagged-edged world, with its trapdoors and sticky webs and predators whose claws never released their prey.

She'd never get free of him. He'd followed her here; he was taunting her—

"Alva." Sam's eyes were sharp, like he knew what she was thinking. He couldn't, of course; no one knew what Alain had been capable of. "Remember, the stories about Liefdehuis go back five decades. Whatever's in there, it's been there a while."

And just like that, the rigidity left her body.

Of course. Alain wasn't haunting her. He couldn't be, not unless he'd somehow mastered time travel. The ghost in Liefdehuis had been dead at least fifty years.

She sagged into a chair. Suddenly she could hear the world around her—the tick of the clock on the mantel, the crack of the fire below it. It was snowing again, the light of her room reflected off the meandering flakes. And Sam was kneeling in front of her, concern etched in the lines of his face.

He was worried for her. This discovery was likely one of the most important of his entire career, and instead of celebrating he was here comforting her, because she was acting like a fool. She'd *been* acting like a fool—she hadn't even realized what she'd been afraid of, until tonight. If she'd been less afraid, more honest with herself, two seconds of rational thought would have calmed her down.

"I'm sorry," she said. Her throat was dry. "I—I was taken aback."

Sam lifted an eyebrow. "You were terrified," he said. "And now you're not anymore. Why?"

She looked away. She didn't tell people about Alain. When she'd left him people had turned on her so quickly—no one would have believed her.

Sam would. Alva realized she didn't question that at all. Which was why he of all people couldn't be told.

She'd pretend—it was something she'd gotten good at, over the years. "You *are* talking about a ghost," she said blandly. "I'm a delicately raised gentlewoman. I was actually supposed to faint just then."

"Ah," Sam said. "So the plan is still obfuscate, obfuscate, obfuscate."

"I don't know what you're talking about."

"Yes, you do," he said, his voice mild. "And I guess when you're ready to tell me, you will. But Alva—if you need help with something, come to me."

She swallowed. His expression was so earnest—he was like a knight, pledging his troth. Good and pure, brilliant but in some ways strangely innocent. What she wouldn't give to live, for a little while, in his sunshine.

Relief pumped through her, a gentle drug. Her muscles were warm and loose. Sam was watching her, a rueful smile tilting his lips.

He wasn't angry with her. Frustrated, perhaps. He was still . . . he was still her friend.

He stood up, apparently deciding he'd gotten as much out of her as he was going to, and started lazily prowling around the room. The sheer size of him amongst her belongings was overwhelming. Alva supposed she should ask him to leave—or at least be embarrassed when he started poking around her vanity—but somehow all she felt was . . . fascination.

He uncapped the secret pot of rouge she used on the mornings when she was particularly wan. "What is this?"

"Rouge," she said.

"What's it for?"

"None of your business," she said, but when he turned amused eyes on her she sighed. "You use it to tint the lips and cheeks."

"I don't think Maggie uses this," he said, smelling it.

"I should hope not," Alva said, rather scandalized. "What's appropriate for a disgraced thirtysomething widow is certainly *not* for a girl of seventeen."

"Ohh," he said, looking at the pot with interest. "It's something shocking. How can an oil-based dye be shocking?"

"Prostitutes use it," she said.

"And?"

"That's it."

"Huh," Sam said, setting the rouge back down. "I've learned many confusing things since I met you, Mrs. Webster."

Alva's mouth twitched. "You spent your evening chatting with a ghost and this is the thing that confuses you?"

"I'm a genius. I can be confused by many things at once."

His hair was long enough that it brushed the top of his collar. Alva found herself mesmerized by the way the gentle curls lapped at the cloth, both a little damp from his walk. The night air from the open window brought a wild crispness in, the smell of evergreens and smoke—and something indefinable, the promise of freedom.

He was still pawing at the pots and bottles on her vanity, his back bent slightly so he could reach them. He hadn't put his coat back on, and the shirt he was wearing had seen better days. The material was worn thin between his powerful shoulders—really, where did the man buy his shirts? They obviously weren't made for him, and with shoulders like that they needed to be. He probably tore through the backs of them with regularity. Alva gave a little internal shiver at that image.

Actually, she was quite warm, despite the chill from the window.

Any minute now she'd ask him to leave. Any minute now she'd stop watching him, noticing how small the perfume bottle looked in his hand, letting her eyes caress the line of his back. . . .

Why did he have to leave?

She almost gasped at the thought. It was shocking in its clarity, the first gulp of cold water on a hot day. Quickly she recited all the usual reasons—she didn't get involved with men, look at what had happened the last time. . . .

But Alain was dead.

And she remained so afraid of him that not ten minutes ago she'd been nauseous with fear.

He'd never really stopped dictating her decisions. Not when she'd left him. Not when he'd died. Not when she returned to America, not with an ocean between them. Had she left Paris because she'd wanted to? Or had it been because of the elegant gray tomb she'd chosen and paid for and never seen, which stood in Père Lachaise Cemetery a few yards from the wall where 147 Communards had met their bloody end four years earlier?

She'd escaped. She'd survived. Why was she living like she was the one who was dead?

Her hands were shaking as she stood, carefully smoothing her dressing gown. He was apparently absorbed in—Was he taking apart one of her new atomizers? She took a deep breath.

"Professor Moore—"

"If I just connect this more firmly it'll pull better—"

"Sam," she said, and he looked at her. "Would you like to make love to me?"

CHAPTER FOURTEEN

Sam stared at Alva. Then he stared at the little glass bottle. When that didn't offer any helpful suggestions, he stared at her again.

She was slowly turning pink. Her shoulders were flung back, her posture rigid. It was her belligerent stance, which he had come to adore. It did, however, make him wonder if he'd heard right.

"Sorry," he said, putting the bottle down. It made a small click in the suddenly silent room. "It's possible my wishful thinking has run away with me. Did you—"

"Yes," she said, her tone formal enough to sign contracts. "You've indicated in the past—or at least you've implied—"

"That I want to make love to you," Sam said. He leaned against the wooden desk she kept her cosmetics on and considered. "I hope that's not the only thing I've indicated."

She flushed a deeper shade of rose. "It's the only thing currently under discussion. Do you?"

"Yes," he said.

The quick little breath she took went straight to his manhood.

It was becoming difficult to think, and that was bad, because he had a nagging feeling thought was required.

"Alva," he said, gripping the edge of the desk so he wouldn't take two steps forward and pull her against him, "you've had a shock—"

She untied her robe and dropped it to the floor.

"Or possibly I've had a shock," he said faintly, staring at the thin, lacy nightgown. He hadn't really seen the front of it before. It was . . . not opaque. He could see the curves of her breasts, even the faint shadows of her nipples.

She lifted her hand to the first of the buttons running down the front of the dress, and his fingers dug so firmly into the wood he thought the whole edge might snap.

"Wait," he said, his voice sounding desperate even to himself. "This isn't—where is this coming from?"

She stopped, her hand frozen by her throat, her head tilted a little to the side. "You've read the newspaper stories," she said. "You're a kind person, so you haven't mentioned them, but you also wouldn't have come here without doing your research. You know what my reputation is."

The stories. It was hard to hold the ink-and-paper version of Alva in the same breath as the flesh-and-blood one—they were such different people. And not just when it came to the sexual exploits, although the ones described in the papers smacked more of imagination than reality. It was that the woman in those stories didn't hurt, didn't care, didn't bleed.

The one standing in front of him had scars. He knew where some of them came from; others were marks of wounds he could only guess at. She'd been hurt over and over again, and in response she'd only grown stronger.

"I researched you the week after I met you," he said. "I've read every story written about you that made it into papers with American distribution."

She nodded, dropping her hand. "Well, they're not true. Not a single one. Oh, I suppose the part about me leaving my husband, that's true enough. But everything else, the affairs, the orgies . . . nothing. I was faithful, god help me." She laughed, and the sound skittered down Sam's spine. "What a word, 'faithful.' Faithful to what? But for ten years, I was. Even after I left him . . . I—" She looked away, staring into the fire.

"Alva, it wouldn't matter to me if you weren't," he said, tentatively feeling his way. "And of course the stories aren't true. I never thought they were."

"You don't understand," she said. "Don't you see? I've paid the price, but I haven't done the crime. I haven't even *considered* doing the crime. Until I met you."

He kissed her.

There wasn't room for careful consideration; her words had pushed it away. There was only room for her—for the soft skin of her lips, the warmth of her body against his. He didn't even know how he had gotten there, only that her lips were meeting his with need and passion and that his blood was pounding in his body.

She pressed against him, her breath coming in little moans between the meeting of their lips. Her arms were wrapped firmly around his neck, as if she would pull him even farther towards her, merging them into one continually combusting ball of desire.

His hands traveled firmly down her sides, memorizing every inch they covered. The sides of her breasts, soft, tantalizingly sensitive. Her waist, deliciously curved. Her hips, flaring out with dark, womanly promise.

With his last ounce of self-control, he pulled away, his hands lingering on her hips. They stared at each other, breathing hard. "Alva—"

"Make me feel alive, Sam," she whispered.

And with that, his final tattered shred of willpower evaporated, like water under the sun. He was lost.

"Yes," he said, his voice hoarse and low. "God, yes."

She pressed against him again, and he was kissing her, and he didn't have to stop. Desire encircled them, shutting out the world, making him blind to anything but her, deaf to anything but her. He wasn't prepared for the quickness of the heat—like they held the molten center of a volcano suspended between them. It swamped him.

He pulled her up, needing her closer. She wrapped her legs around him, the fragile nightgown riding up to reveal smooth, ivory thighs stronger than he had expected. Deliciously stronger—they clamped around him, bringing him firmly against the astonishing heat radiating between them. His hands were on her gorgeously rounded bottom, every angle of that perfect curve burned forever into his memory.

Their mouths were frenzied, desperate. He didn't know what was ahead of them, only that they were here *now*, that they could be together *now*.

And if he didn't get himself under control, he'd be spending himself *now*, too.

He'd dreamed of this woman, fantasized about her for weeks. He wasn't about to rush this, now that he had her wrapped around him. Carefully, deliberately, he slowed his movements. She wanted to feel alive—he could give that to her. Thoroughly.

"What do you want?" he asked, tracing a lock of hair that had escaped from her braid. It curled gently over her clavicle, and as his finger brushed her skin she trembled.

She hesitated. "What do you mean?"

"I mean, you're in charge. What do you want me to do? To you?"

Another quick intake of breath, another jolt of heat and need shivering through him. This woman was going to be the death of him. She was blushing again, the pink traveling down her chest, and . . . and he needed to focus if he was going to last until dawn. And this *was* going to take until dawn.

She shrugged, trying to school her face into a nonchalant expression. "I suppose just the usual," she said.

"Interesting," he said, pulling out the vanity chair behind him and pulling her into it on top of him, so her luscious backside was settled delectably atop him. "What's *your* usual? Because I'm not sure I can say I have one. I mean, for example, if I were improvising, I'd be tempted mightily by your breasts, which have intrigued me for several weeks. But on the other hand, I've recently discovered you have a truly extraordinary posterior, which I had not previously had firsthand knowledge of, so that might lead me in a different direction—you see, already there are so many places from which to begin."

A shiver ran down her spine under his fingertips. God, even *talking* to this woman was delicious. She was perched atop him like a bird that at any moment might take flight—but she stayed where he'd put her.

She cleared her throat again. "I want—"

"Yes?"

"I want you to take your shirt off." Her face was bright red as she said it, but she got the whole sentence out. He grinned.

"Your wish is my command," he said, and leaned back to pull the bottom out of his trousers. Slowly, teasingly, he unbuttoned each button, watching her eyes track his every movement. His mouth was dry by the time he reached the last one—he'd meant to tease her, but in the process he'd frayed his own control. He sucked in a breath when she reached out and ran one tentative finger down his sternum, her touch agonizingly light on his skin. He forced himself to stay absolutely still, not even breathing until she lifted her hand away.

She was staring at him, seemingly mesmerized by the expanse of his chest. Surreptitiously he looked down, wondering what it was she found so fascinating. All he knew was he wanted her to keep looking like that at him. Forever.

She knew she was staring, but she couldn't help it. Even her fevered imagination had failed to conjure anything remotely accurate. He had *muscles* on his chest, where Alain had been all elegant smoothness. As soon as she made the comparison she rejected it. Alain had no place here. There was only Sam and Alva, no past, no ghosts. No last names. She'd decided on this, consequences be damned, and she wasn't going to waste a second of it.

She took a deep breath, calming the trembles racing through her limbs, and touched him. This time there was no hesitation; she let both of her hands flatten against him, his muscles contracting under her palms. He was holding his breath again, this enormous, strong, brilliant man brought absolutely still by her touch. Power rushed through her, an explosive reaction down her body, pooling in the tips of her breasts and between her thighs. She felt drunk on it.

His eyes were closed now, his head tipped slightly back. She let her hands trail down his stomach until they encountered a trail of dark blond hair that disappeared under the waistband of his pants.

She was really going to do this. She was going to . . . have relations with this man, like the scandalous woman everyone already thought she was. So far, she had to admit, she wasn't doing a very good job of being scandalous. That was going to have to change.

She let that woman, the daring one, take the reins. "Now the rest," she said, and even her voice sounded like the other woman now—husky and low and sensual. No trace of fear.

Sam opened his eyes and, without saying anything, lifted her up and stood. He settled her back in the chair and faced her, his hands on his waistband and his gaze never wavering from her. He pushed off his shoes, and with brisk, economical motions he undid the buttons of his trousers and let them fall, kicking them aside when they hit the floor. He stood before her in nothing but plain cotton drawers and a mismatched pair of socks, one black and one green. Alva smiled inside as well as out—was the man colorblind? It wasn't as though he had to do his own laundry; presumably his socks were returned to him from the laundrywoman already matched. It took more than a casual amount of absentmindedness to achieve this result.

But he was pulling off the socks, and now his hands were at the band of his drawers and the time for lighthearted amusement was gone. He was looking at her with a teasing question back in his eyes, and it was her turn to hold her breath. She nodded, a punch of power shimmering through her once more, and he slid the drawers down and off. Samuel Moore was standing stark naked in the middle of her bedroom.

He was all gold planes and dark shadows, his phallus standing stiff and straight. He was the most beautiful thing she'd ever seen in her life. And he was hers, if only for the night. She let her eyes linger, memorizing every inch of his body, so later, on the cold days and nights that lay ahead, she could pull out this memory and say, *I lived.*

Alva's breath was coming fast, so fast it made her dizzy. And he just stood there, watching her. Letting her look her fill, a mixture of heat and want and fun in his eyes. There was something predatory in his gaze—like having a lion in her bedroom, one currently content just to play.

A lion she had absolutely no idea what to do with—but she was absolutely sure she wanted to do *something* with him.

She crossed her legs, enjoying the sensation of silk shifting over skin. "I want to know my options," she said.

Sam grinned, and it turned out the only thing more alluring than a naked Samuel Moore was a naked and *grinning* Samuel Moore.

He *liked* her. Alva pushed the thought away, but it left an uncomfortable little glow in her chest. It wasn't important that he liked her. It was important that he was the most beautiful man she'd ever seen, and he was naked, and they were about to make love.

"Makes sense," he said. "With all this"—he gestured up and down his body—"on option, you naturally want to formulate a strategy."

She rolled her eyes. "Yes, that's it," she said. "Or perhaps I want to see if your sexual imagination is as prodigious as you implied."

"I assure you my 'imagination' is prodigious indeed—no, that's really too easy, isn't it?"

"Beneath you," she agreed. "You're stalling."

"I'm a genius," he said. "We don't stall. We consider."

"I don't think I have any circuits for you to engineer, Professor."

"Engineer, no. I can't improve on nature. But you certainly have circuits, darling."

The warmth rose up her chest into her cheeks.

"Option number one," he said. "I lay you down in front of the fire. I unbutton your shocking excuse for a nightgown; for a woman who's secretly obsessed with respectability you have incredibly erotic nightwear—"

"I'm not obsessed with—this is a perfectly ordinary nightgown—"

"You are, it's not, and I look forward to learning what other delightful concoctions reside in your armoire," he said. "Now do you want to hear your options or not?"

She nodded her head meekly.

"This will allow me to fulfill a long-term scientific interest of mine," he said, "namely, the exact shape and texture of your breasts, which I will determine using both my fingers and my mouth, because, my beautiful girl—and I'm sorry to dwell on the whole saucy nightgown issue, but that fabric is very sheer—I've wanted to set my tongue to your nipples since you dropped your robe."

His words were darts of sensation; she shivered as they landed, one by one. He moved towards her, kneeling before her and placing his hands on her knees. They were capable hands—strong and clever, with a light dusting of dark golden hair trailing up from his wrist. She thought about the times they'd touched her, and shivered again.

"I'd follow the buttons downwards," he said, and his voice had lost the amusement, and his eyes were dark and fervent. "Taking my time, until I came to the tuft of hair between your legs, and then, darling, I'd find out what you taste like, because that is another question that has come to occupy much of my time."

Alva swallowed.

"And frankly, we could be there a little while, because—"

"Option one," she croaked. "I want option one."

"Thank god," he said, and stood, pulling her up and kissing her in one smooth motion. He half-carried her the three steps to the fire, gently resting her on the rug in front of it. The warmth of the fire caressed her skin, but it paled in comparison to the heat building inside her. It wasn't the first time she'd experienced desire—it was partially desire that had so betrayed her twelve years before—but it was the first time she'd understood the full depth of an adult woman's passion, this furious, unholy maelstrom of lust and thirst and need.

He stretched his length next to her and looked down at her like she held the answer to every question he'd ever had or would have. "It's like I've wanted you forever," he whispered, and took her mouth, his lips demanding something she couldn't name but desperately wanted to give.

Those dexterous hands set to work, loosing each tiny, silk-covered button until the fabric simply slipped apart, revealing her to him. She felt more than heard his ragged intake of breath—felt it in the clench of her cunny and the tightening of her breasts. For a moment he simply looked at her, long enough to make a flicker of nerves spark, but finally, almost reverently, he touched her.

At first he used only the tips of his fingers, like he was mapping the curves of her body. Slow, agonizing waves of pleasure rolled through her, leaving only his touch and the sound of the fire next to her. He lingered on the undersides of her breasts, seemingly fascinated by the swell of them, before drawing slow, ever narrowing circles around her peaks. Finally, he took one nipple between thumb and forefinger, and, ever so gently, squeezed.

She came up off the floor.

"Yes," he murmured, and then he was everywhere, his hands caressing her, pinching there, until she was barely able to remember to muffle her own cries. She bucked next to him, wanting him closer, wanting more, more, more.

Her nipples were flushed and hard under his attention; she

barely recognized them as her own. They looked . . . wanton. He put his lips to them, sucking each one into his mouth until they were glistening, swollen buds.

One hand drifted downwards, continuing to loose the long line of buttons. Slowly his lips followed, while the other hand moved here and there, wherever he pleased, as if he couldn't bear to stop touching her. She was gradually melting into a state of hazy, delicious, squirming excitement.

When he reached the buttons that would bare her to him completely, he paused, focusing totally on the unbuttoning. Watching him study her—feeling his excitement—was so shockingly arousing she almost forgot what he was revealing.

That is, until he pressed his hand against her.

She cried out, a jagged exhalation that sounded alien to her ears.

"Yes," he said, watching her face with the pure, passionate concentration she associated solely with him. He pressed a little harder and she moaned again.

Just when she thought the feeling could be no more intense, his fingers moved.

"Holy god," she blurted, and the damn man had the audacity to chuckle.

"You, my love, are beautifully, beautifully sensitive," he said, and when she opened her mouth to say something tart and dignity saving he moved his fingers again and proved his point.

"Let's talk about this nightgown," he said.

Her eyes had drifted closed with his latest motions, but they snapped open. "You . . . have . . . a strange obsession," she said, struggling to speak.

"Ah," he said, doing a thing with his thumb that made her arch her back and wriggle. "But when will I have you pliant and under—"

"Do *not* say . . . under . . . your thumb."

". . . and obliging again? It seems like the perfect time to indulge said obsession."

Alva didn't respond immediately, because two of his fingers had slipped inside her and she needed all her wits to manage the tsunami of pleasure that had flooded her.

"We can start with the easy questions," he said generously. "How many of these enchanting garments do you possess?"

"Four," she said, because she had no sense left with which to lie.

"Mm-hmm," he said, and rewarded her appropriately. "And where did you purchase said items?"

"In Paris," she said. "Before . . . before I left."

"And tell me," he said. "How do you feel when you're wearing them?"

She didn't want to answer. She wanted to lie there and feel the wonderful things he was doing to her; she didn't want to think—

His fingers stopped.

She glared at him. He was . . . yes, he was absolutely smirking at her. "I feel entirely sensible," she said. "Silk is a very practical fabric—"

A small flicker of movement made her gasp.

"Try again," he said.

"Oh—" Faint, teasing stabs of pleasure tormented her. She wanted more. She needed more. "I suppose I like the way it feels against my skin."

"Better," he said, and began, very slowly, to move again. It wasn't enough. It was almost worse, as if there was some itch that desperately needed to be scratched and he was just barely missing it. "But I think there's a little more."

The bastard was doing it on purpose.

"How do they make you feel, Alva?"

Even her name on his tongue was arousing. He was drawing circles around her, light, painfully slow. She wanted to cry.

"How do they make you feel?"

"Wanton," she blurted. "A little debauched. Sensual."

"Good girl," he said, his voice soothing as he stopped touching her entirely. She almost cried out at the injustice, but he just smiled and moved down her body, settling himself between her legs.

CHAPTER FIFTEEN

One second she was opening her mouth to protest the removal of his fingers, and the next, with one touch of his tongue, she was being melted into pure sensation.

He lapped at her slowly, almost lazily, his eyes fluttering closed, his hands tight on her hips. Alva whispered his name, or at least hoped she whispered it, knowing as his tongue caressed her she was losing her connection to everything in the world except one small point between her legs.

She didn't care. The world was going to have to wait.

Gradually the pressure intensified. His tongue worked faster, his fingers joining him once more. He took her over mountainous peaks and long, teasing valleys, bringing her to the brink, over and over again, each time larger and higher than before.

When he finally let her fall, screaming his name and clinging to his shoulders, it was as though she would fall forever.

He held her as the last tremors passed, touching her lightly here, stroking her there, unable to take his hands from her.

"Now I know what all my friends were talking about," she murmured, his hands beginning to warm her again.

Sam chuckled, a low, masculine, intimate sound. "Is that what women talk about? It sounds much more interesting than male conversation."

"In Paris," she said, her breath catching as he brushed his fingers over her breasts. "My friends in Montmartre. They called it *brouter le cresson—*"

"To graze the—I don't know the word."

"Watercress," she said, with a small choked laugh that ended in a gasp as he leaned over and kissed one of her nipples. "It's not the most flattering translation, although far from the worst I've ever heard."

"To graze the watercress," he said, grinning. "I like it."

He kissed the other nipple, pulling it into his mouth and making her lose her train of thought.

"So you and your French lady friends talked about grazing the watercress, did you?" he asked, after a few seconds of delicate nibbling.

"They talked," she said. "I didn't believe them; eventually I chalked it up to charming French depravity. I take it all back."

Sam's eyebrows snapped together. "Do you mean that was, err, that you haven't—"

"It's not that shocking."

"It's a little shocking."

Alva laughed, refusing to let the past intrude on the lovely glow enveloping her. "Do you know, my friends in Paris had other outlandish stories," she said.

"They did?"

"Something called *fumer le cigare*," she said, rolling onto her side and trailing her fingers down his chest.

"Um . . . smoking the—Ah."

"Another story I didn't put much credence in," she said. "But presently I think perhaps it's unwise to dismiss something without a fair trial."

His breath caught. "A laudatory sentiment," he agreed. "But if I'm to survive this encounter, we'd best leave the trial to a later date."

"And here I believed you were a man of science," she said, feeling deliciously wanton as her hand found his length. He made a low moaning sound. "Where is your sense of experimentation?"

"Every man must keep something for himself," he said, pulling her against him and flipping her over, so he was above her. "Science cannot have it all. And in this case, sweet Alva, I've been thinking about burying myself inside of you for far too long to waste myself anywhere but here." He slipped two fingers inside of her, her entry too wet to pose any barrier.

Her hips rose towards him and her legs spread. Her eyes shuttered closed, already imagining him pushing inside of her. What would it feel like, to be filled with him?

"Alva," he said, his voice suddenly strained. She opened her eyes again. "I . . ."

"What?"

"I wasn't planning on this, you see." He removed his fingers, expression miserable.

"What on earth's the matter?"

"I didn't bring anything. Um. Any protection."

"Any—oh!" Understanding dawned upon her abruptly, and, just as abruptly, she blushed. "I have some."

She scrambled to her feet, hurrying to her armoire. "My friend Amelie gave them to me. It was a joke. I think. It's hard to tell with her, honestly."

She found the little envelope, tucked deep inside one of the back compartments, and turned around to find Sam right behind her.

"You have marvelous taste in friends."

"Oh," she said as his arms snaked around her. "Well."

"Indeed," he said. Lifting her up so his hands cupped her bottom, he carried her over to the bed.

Outside the window, the snow was falling heavier—large, fluffy flakes illuminated by the weak moonlight. It made her simple bedroom seem enchanted somehow, a room out of time, hidden from consequence. When he dropped her lightly on the bed, the plain bedclothes seemed as luxurious as the finest silks and velvets. The no-nonsense iron bedstead, its worn curves glowing gold in the firelight, creaked when he joined her.

He kissed her long and deep, his hard length pressing against her. His clever hands were bringing her banked flames roaring back to life with a simple stroke. She needed him. Her hands urged him to go faster, to *hurry*, and finally, when her whole body was vibrating, he rose to his knees and pulled one of the folded condoms out of the envelope. A purr of delicious warmth shivered through her as she watched him smooth it over his length, those strong fingers tying the silly pink ribbon at his root.

He was grinning again, the beautiful fool, and she was grinning back, even as he parted her legs with casual authority and pulled her closer.

He kissed her as he thrust into her, her first gasp muffled by his mouth. As he began to move she brought her hand up to stifle herself, but he caught it, pushing it to the pillow.

"I want to hear you," he said.

"The servants—"

"I want to hear you."

So she let her hand stay where he'd put it, and as he thrust inside her she forgot to censor her cries. He touched her as he fell into an easy rhythm, playing with her tightened nipples, stroking her between her legs. It was as though he was intent on absorbing her, collecting her every curve and gasp and tremor. Like there was no discovery more important to him than her.

Long waves of pleasure cascaded through her, each one washing her closer to something beautiful, something enormous. She closed her eyes, tilting her head back to absorb every sensation she could. He nibbled her collarbone, the stubble on his cheeks scraping pleasurably over her skin. He worked higher, until his lips were at her neck, and it was . . . all right. It was fine. Something men did. Women liked it.

So why did it suddenly feel like panicked birds were beating inside her rib cage? She wanted to lower her chin, protect her throat, but she forced herself to not move. He was inside her, for god's sake. If the man wanted to nibble at her neck she should try to enjoy it, like a normal woman would—or at least pretend long enough that he wouldn't notice—

Emerald green wallpaper, fading to gray. Bright gold buttons, whimsically embellished with fire-breathing dragons. Expensive cloth beneath her clawing fingers, as she fought for breath.

Those fingers weakening when it didn't come.

Not now, damn it. Alain didn't control her anymore—

His face, elegantly handsome, transformed in fury. His hair, always perfectly arranged, rumpled, one golden lock falling across his forehead. She wouldn't let it be the last thing she saw—she looked past him at the wallpaper—

No. She wasn't going to let him ruin this—

It took Sam a moment to notice something was wrong. One minute he was in heaven, wrapped in her glorious wetness, tracing a line of kisses up the beautiful curve of her neck, and the next . . . she wasn't there anymore. Oh, her body was present, but her muscles were rigid and her eyes blank. He stopped moving.

"Alva? Alva."

"It's fine," she said, from far away. "Keep going."

"Uh-huh," he said, pulling out. When she made a slight protesting sound, he lay down beside her, drawing her against his chest. "Just for a minute. What's wrong?"

"Nothing," she said, and the expression on her face sent a curl of horror into his stomach. "Please. I don't need to stop."

"Who said I was stopping because of you?" He made himself answer casually. "You take a lot out of a man. I need a rest."

She blinked, and he saw her come back to herself. "You do not," she said.

"Listen, sweetheart, it's not every day a man is confronted with the opportunity to swive the living embodiment of all his sexual fantasies. I felt faint."

"You did not!"

Color was slowly seeping back into her cheeks. He leaned back against the pillow, his cock desperately informing him it would like to return to what it had been doing. He tried to ignore it. "I assure you I did. Have you seen your breasts? They're enough to make a man dizzy."

She huffed, and a ripple of relief passed through his chest. If she was huffing, she was feeling better. He took a strand of her long, dark hair and coiled it around his fingers. "You know, for me, half the pleasure of intercourse is watching the woman."

She looked at him suspiciously. "It is?"

He nodded. "Don't get me wrong; the other half is important, too. There's nothing on earth that feels as good as sinking into a wet, willing woman. But watching her . . . seeing her pleasure mount, that's beautiful. And incredibly, incredibly arousing."

They lay in silence. He let the lock of hair uncoil, weaving it in amongst his fingers as he watched her think.

"I don't like my neck kissed," she said finally, her voice gruff.

"All right," he said. "What do you like?"

She glanced at him, the suspicion not completely gone.

"For example," he said, "do you like it when I do this?" He pinched her nipple gently. Which, if he was honest, wasn't totally fair. He already knew she did.

A slight smile—success. "Yes," she said.

"Hmm," he said. "And this?" The other nipple.

The smile grew a little. "Yes," she said.

"What else?"

The color was definitely back in her cheeks. "I suppose I liked it when you touched me down there," she said, a little embarrassed, a little wary, but he could hear the need coming back into her voice. She wanted a path to continue. That something bad had happened to her—well, he had suspected, and now he knew for sure. But wounds healed strange, sometimes, and his instincts said it was more important to give her that path forward than push her about something she wasn't ready to share.

"Uh-huh," he said. "Where was that?"

"You know where."

"Nope," he said. "You'll have to show me."

There it was, the full, unrestrained Alva smile. He wondered how many people got to see it.

"You're ridiculous," she said.

"So true," he said. "Show me."

"I don't—"

"You can't tell me you've never touched yourself there," he said, lowering his voice and watching the pink color her chest. "Not owning those nightgowns."

"I . . . why—"

"Show me, Alva. Show me how you touch yourself."

She didn't break eye contact. That's what he would remember, later, the way she held his gaze as her hand moved down her body.

"Here," she said, her fingers moving through the soft, dark hair covering her mons and into her slit, the tips of her fingers disappearing. The curls near her entrance were wet, and Sam was overcome with an urgent stab of desire. His cock sprang back to immediate, insistent, aching life.

"Oh," he said, torn between warring desires to touch her himself and to keep watching her. "There."

Ultimately she decided for him, opening her legs in invitation. "Come back, Sam."

He needed nothing else. In the blink of an eye he was above her, pushing inside her, closing his eyes in ecstasy as the warm tightness of her sheath closed around him.

This time there was nothing but surging carnal bliss. The sound of her breath hastening, his hands on the soft flesh of her hips. Her legs wrapping around his back, bringing him yet closer. His heart pounding against his chest, the roar of desire thrumming in his ears. Her hands clutching the bedclothes. Finally, the heaven of her muscles contracting around him, bringing him over that last, glorious edge.

He didn't know how long it took to return to his senses. Less time than it took Alva, he was pleased to discover: her eyes were almost shut, her mouth curved lazily and contentedly. It occurred to him that he was probably crushing her, so he rolled off to the side.

She was gorgeous after a tumble. Well, she was always gorgeous, but it turned out there was nothing more beautiful than Alva Webster right after he'd had her. A smug kind of joy welled up in his chest, like there was sunshine beaming directly out from his heart.

He was in love.

It wasn't a shocking statement; he didn't recoil in surprise. It was the answer to a question he hadn't been quite aware he was asking, and now that it was here, it was like it had always been true: a quiet, permanent underlying fact that made everything else in his life make sense. He saw it and acknowledged it, even with the whisper that told him being in love with a woman like Alva was going to complicate things. There was nothing to be done—he was in love with her, he always would be, and that was that. She was his person. If she was complicated, then he loved her complications, too.

She was the other side of his story.

Her eyes fluttered fully open, and she gazed at him with distinct satisfaction. He smiled, certain that the sunshine in his chest was going to split him open.

"You should be careful," he said, leaning closer.

She smiled hazily. "What should I be careful of?"

"Lying there naked with an expression like that on your face."

"And what sort of expression do I have on my face, oh learned one?"

He chuckled. "See, I was going to be polite and say it was a smug one. But now you've mocked me, and so I'll retaliate by saying it's the expression of a woman who's been well bedded, and who wouldn't be against giving it another go."

"And if I say that's exactly what my expression is intended to convey?"

"I'd say give me five minutes and I'll be happy to oblige," he said, and pulled her on top of him so her legs straddled his waist. "I haven't seen your breasts from this angle." He reached up to them, lazily playing with one, and then the other, until Alva closed her eyes and moaned.

"There's something about this part right here," he said, tracing the undersides with his fingers. "That makes me want to nibble at them until you scream. I wonder how long it would take?"

"An interesting question," she said, her voice already ragged.

He glanced out the window, noting only a glowing pile of embers remained of the fire. The sky was still dark outside, though—he had some night left. And he was going to use every minute of it.

"Let's find out," he said.

CHAPTER SIXTEEN

Alva watched the night sky turn gray through her frosted window, the first light falling gently on Sam's sleeping face. She was warm, enfolded in his embrace, and content to watch him sleep. She felt . . . safe. It was a curious word to use after the night she'd spent. She'd taken a dangerous risk, but somehow . . . somehow she knew it was going to work out all right.

Perhaps she'd been too extreme, earlier, refusing to even allow a hint of passion in her life. It had made sense after Alain's death; she'd been so raw then, so suspicious, though there'd been several men willing to engage in a discreet affair, in the traditional French style. She hadn't been ready. It had taken Sam to show her she was.

Of course, there would be no happy-ever-after here. She acknowledged the pain and let it pass. Eventually he would need to move on. He deserved a proper life, with every wonderful experience it could afford him. He would want to marry, to father children. Alva closed her eyes and took a deep, controlled breath. She would be happy for him, she told herself. But for now, why not enjoy what they had? This passion . . . she might not be very experienced, but she didn't think it came along every day. They'd enjoy it together, and when it was done they would part.

The rays of light grew stronger, turning Sam's skin a pale gold. Her lover, she thought, a ripple of anticipation moving through her body. How sophisticated and debauched she was this morning; she was almost drunk on it.

Finally, she was going to reap the benefits of ruin.

She pressed closer against him, feeling the hard stretch of his body all the way along hers. She arched her back, reveling in the sleepy groan he made and the way his hand traveled down to her hips. Closing her eyes, she did it again, feeling every inch of his hardness. She didn't think he'd mind waking up for this.

There was a brisk knock at her bedroom door, and as Alva opened her mouth in panic the door swung open, followed by a cheerful Liza.

"It's a bleak morning, ma'am, so I supposed you might like to have your tea in—*Aach!*"

The tray of tea things flew through the air, hitting the floor with a variety of crashing and banging sounds. Exploding shards of china scattered through the room. Liza turned the red of Alva's favorite crimson suit and stood, with her mouth open, rooted like a stock to the floor.

"Liza," Alva managed, her voice weak. Frantically she tried to think of something to say that would make the tableau seem other than what it was: a loose woman with a naked man in her bed. How could she have forgotten the time? It was dawn, past dawn, for god's sake; she'd been watching the light for the last ten minutes—

This was bad. She could lose her whole staff if the town started to gossip about her morals. No one wanted to work for a whore.

Sam shifted beside her, and she willed him to stay down—at least this way her body concealed his face.

Naturally, he did nothing of the sort.

"Good morning," he said, speaking to Liza. The girl turned even redder. "Do you mind me asking, is that the usual way you carry tea upstairs?"

Oh no.

Alva risked a sideways glance at him and almost closed her eyes again. She recognized that expression. It was the *I'm absorbed in an extremely interesting problem and nothing you say will derail me until I'm satisfied I've worked it all the way through* expression. How could that expression exist in this environment? And would it be too dramatic to simply throw herself out the window?

Liza was staring at him in horror, her mouth working as though it was trying to say something and failing. Alva had never seen her at a loss for words.

She finally managed to produce sound. "Sir?"

"The tray. Is that how you usually carry tea things?"

Liza's eyes darted frantically downwards, taking in the disaster on the floor, before nodding.

"But aren't cups and saucers and that sort of thing usually made out of china? China's quite a slick surface," he said, and *oh god no* he kicked his feet out of bed, casually wrapped one of the blankets around his waist, and walked over to the scene of the breakage. The two women simply watched him, both their faces frozen. He picked up the broken teapot and looked at it. "See, it's not as though it's got any traction. Someone's made an attempt here, and it's not a bad one, putting felt on the bottom to increase the cling. But it's obviously not enough."

"Here now," Liza said, obviously working something out.

"You're that inventor, aren't you? Samuel Moore? The famous one?"

"Mmm," Sam agreed, picking the tray up and examining it. "And this has to be quite heavy, too, with all the bits and bobs on top of it. And only one maid carrying it—"

"We heard you were in town," Liza continued, her face loosening and a new look dawning in her eye. "Sally May Reardon, the girl who does for you, she reckons you're mad as a hatter from the way you sleep at all hours and talk to yourself and burned a hole in her brand-new dress, but Cook, *she* says Sally May's a flibbertigibbet who wouldn't know a genius if he knocked her right on the nose, and that the dress was ugly anyway. It's because of the new gas stove you invented; see, Cook wants one desperately. She cut out the magazine story she saw it in and hung it right in the kitchen, so she can look at it every day."

Oh lord, Alva realized, feeling as though everything in the world had suddenly turned upside down. The girl was starstruck.

"Mmm," Sam said, nodding vaguely. "Now tell me about this tray."

"Well, sir, I use it to carry the tea and coffee service, and sometimes meals—and oh, ma'am, I'm so sorry I dropped it everywhere, I was just so surprised, not knowing that the gentleman was Professor Moore here—and it *is* heavy, sir; you're right about that. And I have to carry it so flat, because if I don't everything will just go skidding off the edge."

And they were off, engaged in a thorough and far-reaching discussion about the usage of the common tea tray and how it could be improved. Alva watched them from bed, bemused. Apparently finding a naked man in the bedchamber of an unmarried woman was perfectly fine, so long as the naked man in question was Professor Samuel Moore. He wasn't even clothed!

He was just standing there, listening to Liza talk, with a blanket wrapped around him! And the girl didn't seem to be flustered at all by it.

He had a magic about him, an utterly frustrating and impossible magic. No one who spent more than thirty seconds with him could fail to be lulled into calm, drawn into his ridiculous schemes.

It was because he thought they mattered, Alva realized. That was his magic. He thought every single person he met mattered, and because he thought so, the people he spoke to began to think so, too.

"No, sir," Liza said with a burst of explosive laughter. "Bless you, it was the goose the whole time!"

The liquid had been sopped up and the shards piled on the tray while they'd been talking, and Liza hefted it back up. "Now if I were you, ma'am, I'd have him go back out the window, and quick. We don't want everyone in the village gossiping about poor Professor Moore here, do we? He has a reputation to maintain."

"No," Alva said. "We wouldn't want that."

"I'll go back downstairs and tell them I tripped on the stairs, and no one need be the wiser. After all, I don't know if Cook could stand it that I met him before she did."

"But you will test the tray prototype for me, won't you?" Sam said, looking up from the sketches he was busily making on Alva's writing desk.

"Oh, sir, I'd be honored," Liza said, the blush returning to her cheeks. "Imagine you wanting me to test something for you. You just send it right along, and I'll think of something to tell the others."

Her smile threatening to overwhelm her whole face, Liza backed out of the room. Sam made a few final notes on the paper he'd been working on, folded it, patted his blanket as though searching for pockets, and looked up at Alva with a confused expression.

"I'm not wearing pants," he said, seemingly puzzled but unconcerned.

"No," she agreed.

He shrugged, let the blanket drop, and got back into bed. "Good morning," he said, grinning. "How much time do you think we have?"

"Unbelievable," Alva said, regarding him dryly. She grabbed his pants from their resting place at the foot of the bed and tossed them at his face.

He caught them one-handed. "What?"

"Remember the whole leaving by dawn thing? The idea was to *avoid* the servants, not mine their brains for new and exciting engineering dilemmas."

"I will grant you that," he said, setting the pants aside and sliding across the bed so he could put his arm around her. "But since we'd already failed to avoid them, it seemed a waste to ignore such an interesting problem. Besides, she had a very amusing goose story."

Alva narrowed her eyes.

He tipped her chin up and kissed her. "Did I mention you're beautiful?"

"Oh, for heaven's sake," she said, but she blushed. "Are you going to get dressed or not?"

"Is not an option?"

"No."

"Then I'm getting dressed," he said, smirking at her when she threw a pillow at him. He watched her as he tugged his pants on, delighted by the amusement playing around the corners of her mouth. She was happy—he'd *made* her happy, the woman he was in love with. All he wanted to do . . . was keep doing that. For the rest of his life.

He opened his mouth before he knew he meant to. "Let's get married," he said.

"Oh, Sam." Alva froze, one arm in her dressing gown. "No."

They stared at each other, the silence a pit between them.

What had he done?

"I . . . I didn't know I was going to ask you that," he said.

She put the other arm in the gown and tied the sash around her waist. "I knew you were good," she said, sitting down next to him. "I just didn't know you were this good. It seems I've just seduced an archangel. You can't marry me, Sam."

"Of course I can," he said. "You mean you don't want to marry me."

"I can honestly say I've never even considered it," she said. "It's . . . not a possibility."

He should stop pushing. He'd asked; she'd answered. There was no point arguing about it. "Why?"

She sighed. "Besides the fact that you'd be ruined along with me? Sam, last night was wonderful. It was probably the best night I've ever had. But I've told you all along, I can't . . . I can't do the romance thing."

"So nothing's changed, for you."

"Of course something's changed, but not—not that."

Sam shook his head. "You don't need to explain," he said. "You made it clear you weren't offering more. I don't know why—I don't know why I thought last night made a difference."

He was . . . stupid. Naïve. What had he thought, one night of lovemaking and she'd be ready to walk down the aisle? And when had marriage come into this, anyway? Not that it was such an insane thing to think about. Lots of people did it. If she'd been a virgin last night, it would have been required.

Why did he keep ending up in this position with her? He was always off-balance, always craving more, always rushing things. He wasn't like this with other women. He'd had plenty of nights like this; they'd never left him aching before.

He stood to pick up his shirt and straightened in frustration. "What does that mean?" he said. "You don't do romance? Because I've had meaningless relations before, sweetheart, and last night wasn't that."

She took a pause before responding, plucking one of his socks off the vanity chair and handing it to him. When she finally spoke, her voice was careful, composed. "I haven't," she said.

"What?"

"Had meaningless relations," she said. "Or any relations, really. This was my second relation."

"You mean I'm your second partner," he said. "You told me that already."

"No," she said. "I mean, last night was the second time I've had intercourse. Second, third, and fourth times technically, I suppose."

He sat down again. The ground kept shifting beneath him.

"I told you I wasn't the scandalous woman the papers made me out to be." The bed sank down as she sat next to him. "I'm telling you because I want you to understand. Last night was important to me. I didn't fall into bed with you casually. But I'm never going down that road again."

"Marriage."

"Yes."

"All right," he said, fumbling with his shirt buttons while he tried to understand what she'd told him. The anger and hurt in his chest were making it difficult to think. "Thank you for . . . breaking your fast with me? I'm not exactly sure what the polite thing to say here is."

"Oh, damn it, I'm making a mess of this, and it's supposed to be so sophisticated. My friends in Paris never had any difficulty."

"Maybe the problem is that we're not French, then." He needed to get out of there before he made even more of a fool of himself. He shoved one foot into the sock she'd found, while casting an eye around for the other before deciding it wasn't worth the extra time to find it. He grabbed his shoes and pushed the socked foot into one of them. "It's all right; I understand. You wanted a night of passion; I provided. It wasn't exactly a hardship."

"I'm trying to say that I want more than a night," she said.

"But—"

"We should have an affair."

"Oh," he said, and dropped the second shoe. He was utterly at sea. He'd been reacting instead of listening, he realized, finally looking at her face. What was she trying to tell him?

Last night had been the second time she'd had intercourse, but she'd been married for ten years.

Ten years. And he knew she'd been unhappy; he knew there was more wrong with that decade than the lack of lovemaking. He'd seen the fear in her eyes too many times.

"Alva," he said.

"It makes sense," she said, speaking quickly. "I'm attracted to you. You're attracted to me. Why do we have to make it more than that?"

"If it were merely physical attraction I could see your point," he said. "But you know that's not all we have between us."

"No, we like each other," she said. "Wouldn't that make such an arrangement better? We can be lovers for as long as it suits, and when it doesn't, we'll part like friends."

"Alva . . . It would be more complicated than that."

"Only if we let it," she said. "I was foolish to think I could resist you. This is . . . sensible."

"Sensible," he repeated. "Alva—"

"I can't get married again, Sam."

"This is about him," he said. "Your husband. Is he what scares you so?"

"I don't want to talk about him. This is about me."

The moment was familiar. He'd been here with her before—the closed expression on her face, the feeling a wall three feet thick had abruptly descended between them. This time, though, he wasn't going to go away as easily.

"Fine," he said. "Tell me about you."

"It's not—"

"If you're about to say it's not relevant, you can stuff it. You're the one proposing an affair. If I'm going to agree to such an arrangement, I deserve to know why."

She scowled, and he worried he'd overplayed his hand. The wall was too thick; whatever wound it was protecting was too deep. Yet, to his surprise, she nodded.

"You're right. You deserve to know why." She took a deep breath. He ached to lean over and put his arm around her.

"You know I was separated from my husband. I suspect you also know it wasn't a happy marriage. What you don't know is . . ." She broke off, grimacing. "There are only four people left alive who know this. What you don't know is this is how . . . why . . . my first marriage started. With intercourse."

"But you were a child when you married," Sam said. "I researched you."

That coaxed a small smile out of her. "Of course you did." She rolled her shoulders. "I was sixteen when I met Alain, and seventeen when I slept with him. Before marriage."

The anger began to trickle back, but this time it was directed at a dead man. "He must have been fifteen years older than you."

"Fourteen," she said. "It's not so unusual."

"It's damned unusual for a thirty-year-old man to seduce a child," Sam responded. "Or at least it should be."

"I wasn't so young that I didn't know better," she said. "But . . . Alain could be so charming, you see. He was handsome, in exactly the sort of way that appeals to a silly young girl, like a prince in a book of fairy tales. And he was far too good at the game. One party he'd lavish attention on me, send me longing looks, leave right after dancing with me, and other nights he'd ignore me entirely. I thought I was in love with him. One night, the night of my seventeenth birthday, he suggested we find a quiet room, and . . . my god, I'd never even been kissed. My parents found us. Later, I realized he'd arranged it that way, but at the time, I didn't regret it. To my mind, we were in love. And I kept believing it until we were married and on the boat to Paris. That night, my wedding night, I put on one of the beautiful negligees from my very hastily assembled trousseau, and I waited. And waited. And waited. When he hadn't come to me by midnight, I crept to his room, worried I misunderstood. He opened the door, stared at me in my robe, and laughed. Told me I was a bitch in heat and he didn't like to sleep with dogs. Slammed the door in my face."

"My god," Sam said, suddenly queasy. "Alva—"

"I later learned that his father had made a catastrophic investment, the most recent in a line of unwise business decisions, and the news was about to hit the markets. Nobody knew how depleted their accounts were—his father had been very careful to keep that quiet—but this loss was too big to hide. Alain couldn't afford to wait." She paused, and when she continued it was almost as if she was speaking to herself. "He never forgave me for that. He hated me for it, for having the money he didn't. I was some callow child from a family who'd barely been wealthy for two generations; it was intolerable that he'd had to lower himself to me just to live at the level he deserved."

"He was an evil man," Sam said, his voice quiet. It had to be quiet—if it weren't quiet it would be a roar.

"Yes," she said. "He was. Do you understand now? It's not about you. I know you're not him. I—you're probably the kindest man I've ever known. But I paid a very high price the first time, and I can't put myself in that position again, without rights, without recourse. Even for you."

Sam sat with her words in silence. "He's still hurting you," he said at last.

She took a breath, as if to deny it, but let out a long exhale. "Perhaps," she said. "But . . . this is the best I can do, Sam. This moment, right now. I can't give you a happy ending. Only the meantime."

"The meantime," he repeated slowly. "And if I don't want only the meantime?"

"There will be no hard feelings," she said. "And no regrets."

Could he do it? Could he have her now and bedamned to the future? His gaze ran over her, remembering the night before. He could still feel where her body had fit against his, hear her unguarded laughter.

"No," he said, standing. "You're using the wrong construct."

"What are you talking about?"

"The options, as you've laid them out. You've decided that lasting affection, lasting love, isn't in the cards for you. That the only thing you can have is fleeting physical connection, and you've only barely granted yourself that. Well, with all due respect, that's nonsense, and I'm not going to be made a party to it."

"That's not your decision to make," she said, standing too. "You can accept my proposal or decline it, nothing else."

"I decline it," he said. "I want to have more nights like last night, too, Alva. I could make love to you every night of my life and still not be satisfied. But I can't—I *won't*—do so with a bunch of ridiculous strictures hanging over my head. I won't be told what I can and can't feel for you."

She nodded, looking at the floor. "I understand," she said. "Then—This is it, I suppose."

Her expression almost broke his heart—lonely, bereft. "You can have more," he said softly. "It's all out there. But you have to reach out and take it."

"No," she said, and laughed a little. It wasn't a pleasant sound. "*You* can have more. Do you know what happened the last time I reached out and took something? It was two years ago, I left my husband, and within weeks I was a monster on the scale of Medea. I like you, Sam, but you don't know what you're talking about."

It hurt, those words. He wanted to defend himself; he wanted to take her in his arms until that horrible expression left her face; he wanted to show her how wonderful the world could be; he wanted to build her a tower she never had to leave.

"Maybe I don't," he said. "But I know you. I'm in love with you, damn it. And so I'm going to keep believing you'll get a happy ending, and maybe if I believe it long enough, you'll start to, too."

"You're—you're—"

"You shouldn't be shocked. I would hardly propose marriage to a woman I wasn't in love with. So the whole emotionless affair thing wouldn't really work, would it?"

"Sam—"

There was a muffled knock on the bedroom door, followed by Liza's voice.

"And in all the stories, this is my exit," he said, picking up the shoe he'd dropped and stuffing his foot into it. He grabbed the jacket from the chair, tied it around his neck, and opened the window. "Doesn't look like anyone's around yet. We should get away with it. Good-bye, Alva."

"Good-bye," she said, her voice stunned, and he was out the window and into the biting cold of dawn.

CHAPTER SEVENTEEN

Last night's snow lay crisp and flat under the gray overcast of the morning sky. Sam's boots made crunching sounds as he broke the first path through it. His jacket was too thin for the temperature—in his excitement the night before he'd forgotten to take his overcoat. Shoving his hands into his pockets—no gloves, either—he bent his head into the sharp wind and trudged onward.

He didn't know where he was going. Liefdehuis meant Alva, even if she wasn't there, and he was feeling surrounded enough by thoughts of her. None of the taverns were open yet. To the rental house, he supposed. Maybe he could lose himself for a while working on the lantern prototype . . . the lantern he'd thought of during the dinner where he'd first met her. Or the shoe lacer . . . the one he'd imagined while thinking about her on the steps of Mrs. Kay's brownstone. Or the tea tray . . . Were all his projects about Alva Webster?

He'd never felt like this before, hurt and frustrated and angry and generally tied up in knots over a woman. Then again, he'd never proposed marriage to one before, either.

Flashes of the night before briefly distracted him from the cold. Her hair, glowing red-brown in the firelight. Her skin, flushed pink with desire. Her laugh, her smile—

Her laugh turning bitter when she'd talked about the dreams of her youth. How she'd looked when she'd said good-bye.

Had he really believed her complications would be so easily dealt with? "Complications." What a stupid word for a pile of horrible experiences, all dating back to the piece of shit masquerading as a man that she'd called her husband.

Had he hit her?

That nasty little suspicion had been hidden in Sam's brain for a while, apparently, because it sprang easily and forcefully to life. He thought about the way Alva watched him sometimes, as if she wasn't sure how he was going to react. How brittle she seemed. How she could be pugnacious one minute and heartbreakingly fragile the next. What wound did that scar tissue correspond to?

A beast he hadn't known lay inside of him woke up and snarled.

It felt good. Damn good.

The rage spread out from his lungs, roaring into his ears and turning his hands into fists. *Alain Webster.* Too bad the son of a bitch was dead, leaving nothing behind upon which Sam could vent his fury.

Even if Alain hadn't hit her—and it sure as hell looked like he had—he'd left her with a goddamn warren of mental cuts and bruises. Seducing her, discarding her so cruelly—the man didn't deserve to be dead. He deserved to have his face pounded in. To be left in the gutter with every bone in his body broken. To be shot in the stomach and spend hours bleeding out in agony.

And where the hell had her parents been, exactly? Happily marrying her off to the scum who had preyed upon her?

Sam kicked the snow away as he stalked through it, the anger finally burning the cold away. His blood pounded in his chest, demanding satisfaction against a man long rotting.

She'd been sixteen when she'd met him. Younger than Maggie. She'd been younger than his goddamn sister, and when he imagined someone doing to Maggie what that bastard had done to Alva—

He'd tear him apart. And he'd laugh while he did it.

He was shaking when he reached the front door of his rental house, banging through it and slamming it behind him. Out of habit he turned towards his workshop.

Time to get himself back under control. He took a calming breath, and another, which did absolutely nothing. He wanted to hit something. How did Alva deal with it, knowing the man who'd hurt her was beyond punishment? Of course, he had been murdered. That was something.

It was an ugly enough thought to jar Sam. This was not him. He didn't think things like that. He turned the idea around in his head, but no matter how hard he looked, he couldn't find a damned thing wrong with it. He wasn't glad the man was dead, but only because it meant Sam couldn't kill him himself.

He sat down on the wooden stool in front of his worktable, blindly grabbing the first thing that came to hand. Some copper wire. *Fine.* He uncoiled it and promptly sliced his hand open.

"Goddamn it," he snarled, throwing the wire across the room.

"What the hell?" Henry's voice, sleepy and irritated, came from the doorway.

Sam scowled and glanced over his shoulder. "Sorry," he said curtly. Henry was still in his pajamas, and Sam hoped he would go back to bed and let him simmer.

"Please don't concern yourself," Henry said. "I love being woken up first thing in the morning after a midnight train journey and having coils of wire hurled at my head."

"Great," Sam said, and picked up a half-built prototype of a clock.

"You're cheery this morning."

"Yep."

"What the devil's wrong?"

"Nothing," Sam snarled. "The goddamn wire took a slice out of my goddamn hand. I'm fine. Go back to bed."

"Three 'goddamns' in as many minutes," Henry said, crossing to the chair they kept the medical supplies on and tossing Sam a bandage.

"I'm fine."

"Mm-hmm," Henry said. "I'll be right back."

"I don't need you to—"

But it was too late; Henry was gone. Sam wound the bandage around his hand with what even seemed to him like bad grace. He just wanted to be left alone with his anger—was that too much to ask? He looked at the clock and tried to remember what he'd been doing with it.

A bottle of whiskey landed in front of him, followed by a pair of boxing gloves.

"Pick," Henry said, now perfectly and neatly dressed.

"Listen, I don't need—"

"I'm not going to leave, so the faster you pick the faster you get to be alone."

Sam put the clock down and looked at his options. On one hand, he could drown his sorrows in alcohol. On the other, he could pound the shit out of something.

He picked up the boxing gloves. "Fine," he said. "But I'm not pulling my punches."

"Only matters if they land," Henry said.

For safety, they went to the backyard. Sam pulled the battered leather gloves on, the familiar shape of them engulfing his hands. He remembered when he'd bought them, a few months after the end of the war. He'd spent the last two years in a government-funded lab with his parents, designing rifles and artillery and other things that killed people. Benedict, eighteen months Sam's junior, had joined as a medic on his eighteenth birthday. When the war ended six months later, he'd returned to them extremely ill, and for several godforsaken weeks they hadn't known if he would live or die.

Sam hadn't known what to do, but before Benedict had left he'd been an avid boxing fan. So Sam ordered a sporting-goods catalogue, and he sent off for three pairs of gloves, and the first time Benedict walked around the yard he and Henry had brought out the packages and Benedict had smiled, just a crack of the lips really, but it was the first time Sam had seen his brother's smile in a year. And after they'd ogled over the gloves, Sam had gone into his lab and cried.

Maggie had been little then, just a girl, but she'd been furious they were getting to do something she wasn't, even after they had all explained the gloves were too big for her small hands. The tantrum had continued until Henry, all of fourteen himself, had figured out how to make half-size versions, cutting and sewing the leather himself. They'd looked awful, but she loved them. Naturally, she'd rewarded Henry by pounding on him every chance she got.

Sam squared off against Henry and put his hands up. They started circling, throwing out the occasional testing jab.

"So what's wrong?"

"Nothing." He took a swing; Henry ducked and pranced

backwards. This was how they fought—Sam was strong and Henry was fast.

"Uh-huh." A quick jab, Sam wove fast so it glanced off his cheek.

"Shut up and fight," Sam said, and this time when he swung he connected, pushing Henry back two steps.

Sam danced away instead of pressing his advantage, suddenly wanting to draw the fight out. Henry came back swinging, and for a few glorious moments the only things that mattered were absorbing Henry's hits and dealing out his own. Snow flew as they fought, landing icily in Sam's boots and dripping down his ankles, but the cold air was sharp and thrilling in his lungs, and he liked the way the snow muffled noise, so the only sounds he heard were their breaths and the thud of fists hitting flesh.

After a while, the fight degraded, as it always did. Henry used a left feint/right hook combination, giving Sam what would surely turn into a beautiful shiner the next day. Sam responded with a fierce undercut, knocking the smaller man over. Henry, who, though neatly buttoned-up in life, was rather wild in a fight, responded by throwing the Marquess of Queensberry's rules out the proverbial window and kicking Sam's legs out from beneath him. What followed was not a perfect exhibition of boxing style, being instead a fairly exact rendition of two ten-year-old boys fighting in a schoolyard. Finally, after an unfortunate bit of hair pulling (again, Henry, for whom the Marquess's rules had always been more limiting than inspirational), Sam maneuvered Henry into a headlock, pulling ruthlessly until Henry called truce.

They collapsed into the snow side by side, panting.

"You're a vicious little bastard," Sam said, rubbing his scalp.

"Yes," Henry wheezed. "I'll apologize as soon as air is traveling through my esophagus again."

They lay there a while longer. Sam could feel the snow melting through his shirt. He could think again, he realized.

"You spent the night with her," Henry said.

There was a long silence while Sam looked up at the gray clouds, far above him. "I'm in love with her."

"Ah." Henry's voice was gentle. "And she doesn't feel the same way?"

"Worse," he said. "I think she might, if she could let herself."

Henry sighed. "I understand that," he said.

"Do you? Because I'm trying to make myself understand it and all I can see is that bastard—that her past is stopping her from happiness. And she deserves happiness so much. Even—Even if it's not with me."

"I've read some of the stories about her," Henry said.

"Lies," Sam said, defensive.

"Don't take my head off; I wouldn't have cared if they weren't."

"Sorry."

"The point is, nothing in your history has prepared you for a woman with the kind of baggage Alva Webster has. No, don't interrupt me. You have a great life. You grew up with the most amazing parents, the best family in the world. God knows I'm not saying you haven't faced your own problems, but you don't know what it's like to not have people to hold you up when you need it most, parents who will pick you up when you fall down. Sometimes people who don't have that, who aren't used to that—sometimes it takes them longer to trust. And sometimes they aren't ever able to, no matter how much they want to."

"You always have us, you know," Sam said softly. "You *are* my parents' son. They think of you that way."

"And I'm so lucky they do," Henry said. "They've been there for me since I was ten years old, and still I struggle to trust people.

Now imagine if I'd never had them? Imagine if I was a woman, and didn't even have the protection of the law? You have to prepare yourself for the possibility that Mrs. Webster is never going to be able to give you what you want, even if she tries."

"I can't accept that," Sam said. "I understand what you're saying. But . . . it's not an option."

"Then you'll probably get hurt. No, you'll definitely be hurt, even if it swings your way in the end."

"Then I'll be hurt." He stood up, brushing the snow off as best he could, and held out a hand for Henry. "It's worth it, you know."

Henry took the hand and let Sam pull him up to standing. "I've warned you, and in classic Samuel Moore style you will now proceed to do exactly as you please." The words were tart, but he put a hand on Sam's shoulder. "Now *look* what you've done to my new shirt."

"Ma'am?"

Alva looked up from her work. Or rather, looked up from the two sentences the morning had produced. Thirty hours had passed since Sam had climbed out her window, and still her thoughts were mired in tar. "Yes, Liza?"

"Cook says to say she couldn't get the walleye for tonight and would perch be all right?"

"Oh," Alva said, struggling to remember what the menu for tonight was. "Yes, of course."

"And there's a package for you," Liza said, putting a small box wrapped in brown paper onto the desk.

"Thank you."

"And about the other thing," Liza said, lowering her voice

conspiratorially. "You may tell Professor Moore that I've been making notes about the tea tray question. I've dropped it into conversation with the girls in other houses, casual-like, and I think he'll be quite interested in what they had to say."

Alva stared at the girl before forcing a smile to her face. "I'm sure he will be," she said. "How clever of you to think of it. And you don't need to go through me, I'm sure he'd be happy for you to drop by."

Liza beamed. "Do you think so, ma'am? Imagine that, me calling on a famous inventor." She laughed. "Well, see if I don't. Would you like some tea while you work?"

"No, thank you, I'm fine."

"All right then," Liza said, hurrying away and leaving Alva to her thoughts.

Not that she wanted to be with them. The package caught her eye, and she pulled it towards her and absently began to unwrap it.

She hadn't slept the night before. The day had been bad enough, trying to pretend like everything was normal while she relived the morning. The proposal—her first, actually. Alain hadn't ever asked; it had been . . . assumed . . . after what her parents had witnessed. The argument. Sam's strange response.

She'd worried about the damage she'd done to their partnership, whether he'd still be willing to help her with Liefdehuis. She'd desperately tried to convince herself that was what she was worried about, losing his expertise, not about losing *him.*

Except the night had come and her sheets had still smelled like him.

She slid the elegant black box out of the paper and lifted the lid.

Inside was a beautiful blue silk scarf. Alva threw the lid on top of it and sprang back, as if she'd just picked up a snake.

It was the exact blue of Alain's eyes.

Her hands shook as she searched the packaging for the note. Finally, she found the small card, familiar black writing on the thick cream paper.

This made me think of you, the card said. *All my love, Alfred.*

Blindly she gathered everything up—box, scarf, packaging—all of it, and threw it in the fire. She wrapped her arms around herself while she watched it burn.

She needed to go to Liefdehuis. She needed to prove to herself there was something left to her, something Alain and Alfred couldn't take. She waited until the last of the evidence had burned, and rang the bell for Liza.

Sam wasn't at Liefdehuis.

Alva had known he wasn't there within the first three rooms, though she'd told herself not to be fanciful. The house was different when he was in it, lighter. That made sense; who wouldn't prefer Sam to her? Even the ghost liked him.

But when it was just her—she squeaked as a rat scuttled across the study floor and into the cobwebbed fireplace. A particularly elaborate pair of andirons watched it run: two iron dragons, their tongues pulled gruesomely out of their heads to bear a chain between them. The shadows stretched and waited for her, their damp, velvety depths promising hideous secrets.

She made herself walk through every room, even navigating the shaky stairs to the second floor she'd only seen once before, with the estate agent. The house hadn't been this . . . moody then, merely ugly, dusty, and falling apart. Waiting for her? Luring her in? What exactly could this ghost do, anyway?

The ghost (or ghosts; Sam would want her to remember that)

didn't seem very important just then, though. If it was trying to scare her, it wasn't working, because . . . well, because Sam was gone and that was much worse than shadows being wetter than they ought to. He wasn't in the summerhouse. He wasn't in the ramshackle old gardener's cottage. He wasn't in the gardens.

Of course he'd left. It was a good decision. She couldn't give him what he wanted. What he deserved.

As she entered the room he'd made into his lab, facing out grimy windows to the brown rush of the Hudson, she realized she hadn't *actually* thought he would leave. That had only been the fictional worst-case scenario, the kind of thought that haunted you even while you didn't believe it.

His equipment stood cold and abandoned in the room. Which of these machines had he designed? Which had he made with his own two hands?

She tried to tell herself it was all for the best, but that was so manifestly false she wasn't able to get very far with the idea. It was all for the worst, and that was obvious. She'd followed a stupid impulse, and now she'd been left behind, with only an empty haunted house to console her.

Next she tried to convince herself the only reason her stomach hurt was because she was worried about Liefdehuis and Alfred and the book, but even that wasn't very successful. So she compromised: she was sad she wouldn't see Sam again, because she liked him. She didn't need him as a lover or—god forbid—a husband, but he had been her friend, just for a little while. It was all right to miss friends. She missed her friends in Montmartre, too.

The equipment would have to be sent along to him, of course. She'd have to find out his business address in Ohio—it shouldn't be too hard, given the Moore Laboratories were so famous. She ran her hand over the tops of the machines. He must have been very angry with her, to leave them behind.

How could he have left her?

The pain in her stomach increased. He'd said he loved her. Did people just leave people they loved? Probably. No one had ever loved her before, so she wasn't sure. Or more likely he'd said that in the heat of the moment and, once he'd left, realized she was much too difficult to be worth the trouble. Perfectly sensible decision.

He'd left her. He was gone. Of course he was gone. He was light, and she was bruises and sharp edges and shadows, and people like her didn't get to have people like him.

She *wasn't* going to cry. Not standing in the middle of a haunted house. This wasn't a gothic novel, after all.

It was just that her stomach really hurt.

"Pull yourself together," she said sternly, and when that didn't work she took two deep breaths and looked around for something to distract herself. There, in the corner, some very ugly crumpling plasterwork. She thought it had been modeled on a Grecian frieze: unfortunately by someone who had never actually seen a Grecian frieze. Whoever had decorated the place really had the most appalling taste.

Another stabbing pain. And now her throat was seizing up. She was *not* going to cry. She was *not* going to fall down on this disgusting, dusty floor, curl up in a little ball, and sob.

Fresh air, maybe. Yes, that was the ticket. She was going to walk outside, ignoring the way the shadows seemed to be pressing in on her. "Go ahead," she said. "Pull out your tricks. I promise you, a little see-through noose isn't going to make my day any worse."

Her footsteps sounded loudly in the hallway, echoing off the narrow walls with their dark, peeling paper. He'd left, he'd left, he'd left. Would she ever see him again? Would he even want to see her?

Why would he? She'd behaved abominably. He'd had enough of her nonsense, and he'd gone back to New York, or Ohio, and she was going to *miss* him. Miss him horribly.

One hand on her stomach, she opened the front door, grimacing at the slight damp on the doorknob. She stepped onto the front steps and forced a deep breath of the cold air. It was . . . surprisingly cold. Bitingly cold. She was so distracted by it she barely even noticed stepping out onto the fresh snow.

The snow was high, higher than it had been going in, higher than it had been that winter. It was growing higher by the minute; snow poured down from the sky in angry, hard bullets, scraping the soft skin of her face.

She was in the woods. When had she come to the woods? The only light came from the half-moon above her, the weak, silvery light outlining barren trees with ever shifting branches, walling her off from the house she knew must be somewhere behind her.

It was the kind of cold that pulls at the blood, stealing its heat and setting ice crystals in the veins.

And there was someone behind her, someone who was terribly, terribly angry.

She ran, stumbling forward as the snow dragged at her ankles and numbed her feet. Branches stabbed her, drawing blood from her face, cutting through her thin coat. If he caught her, it was over.

This was what it meant to be prey.

If she could just find her way out of the woods, she thought, desperately. Someone at the big house would help her. All she needed was to find another person; he couldn't murder her in front of witnesses—

She could hear him behind her, calling out threats and promises. There'd never been a difference, with him. The only sounds in the woods were their footsteps, mingling with the strange, empty shrill of the snow-choked wind. There wasn't much time left. Her body was already giving up—in one final humiliation, her corset made it impossible to draw breath. She clawed at it as she ran, but its iron grip refused to loosen.

She fell once and kept running. She stumbled again and used the trunk of a tree to scramble back up. But when she fell a third time, her legs stopped and wouldn't support her anymore.

She'd been running for too long.

Instead she crawled, searching for handholds in the snow, her bloody palms leaving streaks of red in the white.

Suddenly he was in front of her, pulling her up by the neck, slamming her back against a tree. The dark shrouded him, the gold of his hair and the silver of the knife the only colors visible to her failing vision as he choked her. Her feet kicked desperately for some foothold in the snow, seeking solid ground they'd never feel again.

"I warned you," he said. "I told you not to try me. This is your fault."

When he brought the knife down, she didn't feel pain. There was only darkness.

CHAPTER EIGHTEEN

He was walking back from the forest at the edge of the property when he saw her fall.

For the rest of his life, he'd remember how small she looked when she crumpled, how far away he'd been. How long it took him to reach her—days.

When he finally pulled her into his arms, her body was stiff against him, her muscles tight and joints locked.

"Alva?" Panic, lightning fast, gripped him by the throat. She didn't respond, though her eyes were open. "Alva. Honey. Focus on me."

Her gaze stayed as it was: unblinking, unfocused, unresponsive. Fear raced through him, pounding through his heart as if the vessel had stopped moving blood and was pumping terror instead. He pushed the door open with his back, dragging her more than carrying her inside.

Resting her on the dusty floor, he checked her pulse. It ticked rabbit fast in her wrist, so frantic it vibrated the skin. It was the only motion in her entire body.

He ran through possibilities as he checked her breath. Never had he so bitterly regretted his lack of interest in the medical sciences. It was obviously a fit of some kind—an epileptic seizure? A stroke?

God, don't let it be a stroke.

She was breathing evenly, if swiftly. He needed to get her to a doctor.

Hands almost numb with panic, he was lifting her again, prepared to drag her to his horse, or all the way to town if necessary, when she coughed.

"Alva? Alva. Honey. Talk to me."

She coughed again, but her eyes focused on him, and her muscles began to loosen.

"Sam?" Her voice was little more than a croak. "You didn't leave."

"Oh god." The alarm rushed out of his body, leaving behind a hollow pit in his chest. "You're back."

"Your hands are shaking," she murmured, slumping against him as the stiffness left her. He lowered them both to the floor, holding her tight as he slid down the wall.

"That's because you scared the wits out of me," he said, closing his eyes and focusing on the warm pliancy of her body next to his. "It's going to be a few minutes before I fully recover my masculinity."

"But apparently the bad jokes return almost immediately," she said, a little more normally. "I . . . I think I met a ghost. Or I'm going completely mad and should be locked up at once."

He opened his eyes and looked down at her. "Explain."

She took a stabilizing breath, the air stuttering a little as she took it in. "I had . . . a vision, I guess you would call it. Except it didn't feel like a vision at all. It was as if I was trapped in someone else's skin, living their life instead of my own." Briefly, in short, simple sentences, she outlined what had happened. As she described running through the dark woods, knowing she only had minutes, seconds, left, Sam held her tighter and tighter. He'd been right next to her and he hadn't been able to do a damn thing to protect her. He hadn't even known.

"And then it was only blackness, and I could hear you talking to me—to *me,* Alva Webster—and I knew it was over. Because whoever that was, it wasn't me." She furrowed her brow. "Mostly, at least."

"I'll ask you what that means later," he said. "And don't think we won't discuss this *at length.* But right now, we're leaving."

"Aren't you listening? It was a ghost, Sam. I'm sure of it."

"It was definitely a ghost," he said, standing and reaching down to gather her in his arms. He'd heard the clatter of wheels coming down the drive. "Your driver is here."

"But—don't you want to run tests? Try to talk to it? Design some new machine?"

"No." He hoisted her easily, walking back through the open door and kicking it shut behind him. Her carriage came to a halt in front of them.

"I don't understand you. Aren't you happy? Excited?"

"Excited?" He paused midstep, frowning down at her. "I'm furious. I'm terrified. And I don't give a damn about anything except getting you somewhere warm and safe."

She opened her mouth, shut it, frowned, and tried again. "I can walk, you know."

"Good for you."

Her driver climbed down off the box, his expression concerned. "Is everything all right?" He looked from Alva to Sam. "Has something happened?"

"Mrs. Webster collapsed," Sam said. "Take us to her house, please, and then I'll trouble you to go for a doctor."

"I don't need a doctor," Alva said as he carefully laid her on the carriage seat and climbed in after her.

"You can walk and you don't need a doctor," Sam repeated, the carriage rocking into motion. "I don't care."

"I didn't collapse, either," she muttered, but in the tone of someone who knew her arguments would not be attended to. "A ghost commandeered my brain. It's completely different. Now people will think I'm delicate."

He didn't answer. A choking, directionless anger had filled the empty chasm the fear had left behind. He knew it was simply a response to the terror of the moment; he could easily explain it. Somehow, though, knowing the explanation did nothing to reduce the emotion. He was furious—furious at the house, furious at the ghost, furious at Alva, for no reason except that she'd put herself in a situation where something bad could happen to her.

Realizing that she too had lapsed into silence, he glanced over at her. It was hard to see her clearly in the dim light of the carriage, but he could make out the pallor of her face and the knotted hands in her lap. Wordlessly he put his arm around her, pulling her into his side and hanging on. She sank against him.

"What did you mean, I didn't leave?"

"Oh." She shrugged. "I came to find you, but you weren't there. I thought you'd left."

"You thought I'd left? As in vacated the premises?" He lifted his eyebrows. "May I ask why?"

"We had a fight. You weren't there. It was a perfectly reasonable assumption."

"Out of respect for your condition I won't comment on that," he said, tugging her closer. "But for future reference, I'm not going to just disappear on you."

"I was only concerned because of our partnership," she said, but she didn't move away.

"Uh-huh."

"I mean it. And it *was* reasonable. You were angry."

"All right," he said. "But, so you know, for our *partnership*, people can have fights and still like each other. I was angry. No one likes to have their heartfelt declarations of feeling rejected. But I'm a grown man and I can control my own damn feelings. That doesn't mean I agree with what you said, by the way, but something someone said to me made me see it comes down to trust. You need to trust me, and you don't yet. Which is perfectly reasonable. So here's what I'm going to do: I'm not going to get angry at you over things you can't control, or make you relive past hurts, or make you less than you want to be. Instead I'm going to be your friend. I'm going to support you. I'm going to flirt with you, and I'm going to do my damnedest not to hurt you. And when you trust me, if you decide you've changed your mind about the whole courting thing, you can let me know." He pulled the blanket up around her. "And if you're wondering, right now falls under friendship, support, flirtation, and one category I didn't mention, which is that you just scared about ten years off my life."

She didn't say anything. After a long pause, she nodded. And they stayed like that, silent but entwined, for the rest of the drive.

Night had descended by the time they arrived at her front door. Golden light spilled out her windows onto the white ground below, a cozy picture of winter that did nothing to replace the image of blood-streaked snow Alva had painted earlier. The driver opened the door and Sam climbed out, lifting Alva into his arms. She didn't complain, apparently having given up.

"I'll call for the doctor, sir," her driver said, and Sam nodded his thanks before climbing the front stairs.

"I suppose it's fruitless to argue," Alva murmured.

"Absolutely pointless," Sam agreed as Liza opened the front door.

"Ma'am! What—oh, what's happened? Did you fall? Did you hurt yourself?" They were both swept inside on a tide of Liza's concerned chatter. "It's that house! Maybe the local boys are right when they say it's cursed on top of being haunted, and I hope you'll take that into account and consider not pressing on with this fool project, because you can't fix a place what has that kind of darkness on it, ma'am, not with all the will in the world—"

The girl kept up a constant stream of words as she hurried them upstairs into Alva's room, pulling back the bedclothes and telling Sam—in between fully formed opinions—how to arrange her in bed. When Alva tried to break in, protesting that she was fine and didn't need any of this fuss, Liza simply refused to acknowledge she'd spoken. Respite finally came ten minutes later, when Liza left to organize some herbal tea she promised was a sure thing for inflammation.

Alva and Sam sat in stunned silence.

"I wonder what she thinks is inflamed," Alva said.

"It's hard to say," Sam replied. "But since it's a sure thing—"

"Oh yes," she agreed, a smile flickering on her mouth. "Since it's a sure thing."

He drew a chair to the side of the bed and sat in it.

"You know, I really don't need to be in here," she said.

"I wouldn't fight it, if I were you. I have backup now, and Liza's rather more formidable than I am."

"Well, obviously," she said, her smile lasting a little longer. "But we need to talk about this more, Sam."

"In the morning," he said. "After the doctor's seen you and assured me you didn't take any lasting damage. And after you've gotten some sleep."

"I do feel a bit tired," she said, yawning.

"Being murdered will do that to a person," he muttered, low enough she didn't hear him.

There was a knock on the door, signaling the doctor's arrival. The man looked sternly at him, going so far as to strongly hint his presence was inappropriate, but as Sam simply refused to get up from his chair, he had to eventually get on with his business. Fifteen minutes later, Alva was declared perfectly fine, if in need of some serious rest.

"I'll leave a sleeping draught," he said, speaking more to Liza than to Alva or Sam. "See that she takes it."

He sent one last disapproving glance at Sam and left. A few minutes later, Liza returned with a mug of something hot and sharp smelling, which she bullied Alva into drinking.

"You should leave," she said to Sam, speaking quietly. "She'll fall asleep soon and the whole house knows you're up here."

"I'll move my chair to the corner and stay there the whole time, but I'm not leaving tonight," he said.

Liza's mouth twitched up at the corners, but when she spoke her tone was no-nonsense. "What am I going to say to the others, if you please?"

"Tell them I'm eccentric. And tell your cook I'll give her a prototype of my new cooker before it's released."

She considered before shrugging. "Yes, that'll likely do it. I'll bring some blankets up. But you're to stay in your chair, mind—there'll probably be people in and out of here all night."

He nodded. "Oh, and—" He pulled his notebook out and wrote a brief message. "Have someone take this to the telegraph office. Get it out tonight, I don't care if you have to wake someone up to do it."

She lifted her eyebrows and hurried out, presumably to go relate the whole story to everyone in the kitchen.

"The doctor didn't like you very much," Alva said, her voice sleepy and a little slurred. "It's strange. Everyone likes you."

"You didn't," he said, smiling at her and pushing a stray lock of hair out of her face.

"Course I did," she said, and turning so her face snuggled firmly into her pillow, she drifted off to sleep.

The next morning, still sprawled in the chair next to Alva's bed, Sam woke to a knock downstairs. Rubbing the sleep out of his eyes, he leaned forward to check on her, anxiously noting that she was still too pale. He left the room and was closing the door behind him when his brother walked up the stairs, carrying his black medical bag.

"All right, damn it, I'm here," Benedict said, the purple under his eyes testifying to his own sleepless night. "What's so urgent I had to leave my bed at three this morning?"

"Mrs. Webster had an accident," Sam said, skipping the formalities. "I'm worried it may have affected her brain. I want you to check."

"Mrs. Webster? The one with the house?"

The one with the house, my future, my heart, everything that's at all important in the world, Sam thought, but settled for a nod.

Benedict gestured towards the door, obviously deciding to save his questions for later. "In there?"

Sam opened the door and followed him in. Alva was sitting up in bed, looking pale and a little confused.

"Sam?" she said, her eyebrows snapping together over eyes that looked bruised against her white skin. "What's going on?"

"You remember my brother, Benedict," he said, sitting next to her and taking her hand. "He's a doctor, specializing in the brain. I want him to examine you, to make sure you've taken no lasting injury."

"Only to my pride," she said, but it lacked her usual snap. "Really, Sam, there's no need."

"I disagree," Sam said, pleased when her eyes narrowed in response.

"I wasn't aware I required your agreement regarding my own medical treatment," she said, and probably would have gone forward from there if Benedict hadn't stepped forward.

"Mrs. Webster," he said, bowing smoothly. "I do apologize for my brother, but he does tend to get rather stubborn about things like these, and I'm afraid that if we pause to debate the point he'll keep us arguing in this room until nightfall. Perhaps, in this one instance, a strategic retreat?"

Alva's lips compressed, but she nodded. "Forgive me, Dr. Moore," she said. "Of course I'm honored you would come all the way up here to examine me. Unnecessary though it may have been."

"Perhaps you'll let me be the judge of that," Benedict said, ousting Sam from the chair and taking his place. "What was the nature of the accident?"

When no one answered him, he looked back at Sam. "If you expect me to be useful, you're going to have to give me the facts."

"I know," Sam said. "It's just . . . I don't think you'll believe me."

"Try me."

"Alva was haunted."

Benedict stared at him, no change in his dry expression. "I see," he said. "Are you concerned that she's hallucinating, or that the ghost has somehow addled her mind?"

"Neither," Alva said. "I'm perfectly sensible."

"The latter," Sam said, drawing an outraged gasp from the bed.

"In what way did this haunting manifest?"

"We were at the house," Sam said. "Alva collapsed. She was unconscious for at least two minutes, her muscles were rigid, and her eyes weren't tracking." An echo of panic came back at the memory, and he pushed it away. Alva didn't need panic; she needed someone with a clear head watching out for her. "When she came to, she reported visions that she was convinced were given to her by a ghost."

Benedict frowned. "Are you epileptic, ma'am?"

"No," she said. "And I know his story sounds bizarre. But it's . . . I do believe I was briefly possessed by a supernatural presence."

"You've never had seizures before today?"

"Never," she said. "Do you think . . . Could it be some disorder of the mind?"

Benedict held up a pen and passed it back and forth in front of her. "What do you think?"

She paused. "I was haunted."

"You don't strike me as a fanciful woman, Mrs. Webster."

"I'm not," she said, speaking slowly, and nodded. "I'm not."

He reached into his bag and removed a stethoscope. "Breathe in. Again. All right. My brother is the kind of person who holds fifteen different impossible ideas at any given time. In the thirty-some years I've known him, more of those impossible ideas have become possible than not. I'm not thrilled ghosts are one of the select."

"Me neither," Alva agreed emphatically.

"Look towards the light, please. The other way. Good. Can you move your feet for me?"

Alva wiggled her toes obligingly.

"Good. And how do you feel now?"

"Fine. A bit tired," she said.

"Well, I don't see any lingering effects of the encounter," he said, returning his tools to his bag. "Sam, I admit I don't exactly know what I'm looking for here, but she's returning sensible answers, her reflexes are all fine, and she doesn't have ongoing symptoms. If any of that changes—"

"I'll let you know."

Benedict nodded curtly and picked up his bag. "You might as well walk me out," he said. "Mrs. Webster, it was a delight to see you. Please contact me if you have any lingering concerns."

"I'm sorry to have put you to such trouble."

"It was no trouble at all," he replied as he left the room, Sam behind him.

He waited until the door was firmly closed before speaking. "You must understand, I'm very limited here," he said, walking down the stairs. "The family's staying in the city for another two weeks. If you bring her down, I can borrow equipment from one of the hospitals and give her a more thorough examination."

"Do you see any reason for concern?"

"A seizure like the one she had is always cause for concern, ghostly interference or no," Benedict said. "Keep an eye on her. And damn it, be careful. You're a nuisance, but you're the only brother I have. I don't want to have to bring Mother into this."

Sam laughed, feeling some of his fear dissipate. Benedict wouldn't lie to him. "Like she'd stop me," he said. "She's more likely to demand to see my notes and mount her own ghostly expedition."

"Saints preserve us," his brother said, and gestured up the stairs. "I like her. But mind yourself. She's a bit out of your experience, I think."

And on that enigmatic note, he clapped Sam on the shoulder and walked out the front door.

CHAPTER NINETEEN

Cold morning light pierced through her windows as Alva leaned back against her headboard, painting clean-cut lines over her bedsheets. She followed one line to Sam, stepping back inside the room and looking down at her in concern. In the uncompromising brightness his strong bones stood out fiercely, like he was a Viking warrior from long ago, back from battle, his full lips the only hint of softness in his face.

She smiled. A Viking warrior, if such warriors were kind and funny and gentle and brilliant. She couldn't really see Sam Moore brandishing a weapon and raiding neighboring villages—he'd be more likely to discuss more efficient crop rotation so everyone could have enough to eat, no raids necessary.

"He's headed back to the train station," he said, resettling in the chair.

"Oh, I should have offered him breakfast," Alva said. "One ghost possession and I completely lose my manners."

"I wouldn't worry about it. Benedict wouldn't know a manner if it hit him on the head."

"Well, if that's not the most egregious case of the pot calling the kettle black that I've heard in my entire life, I don't know what is."

"Just so long as we agree the pot is by far the better looking of the two."

"No woman should have to make such a choice," Alva said. "Did you really spend the entire night in that chair?"

He nodded, kicking his feet out so they rested on the edge of the bed. "It's not the worst place I've ever slept," he said, and eyes lingering on the neckline of her nightgown, he grinned. "Of course, I can think of better places."

"I see you've recovered already," she said.

He stood, his expression suddenly serious once more. "It's not my recovery I'm concerned about. Are you sure you feel no ill effects?"

"I'm sore," she admitted. "All over, as if I've climbed a mountain. But that's all. It feels like . . . like a bad dream I had. Not like something that really happened to me. I'd like to talk about it, but not here. I need to get dressed first."

The things she needed to say couldn't be discussed in a bedroom, while one was still soft and warm from sleep. They required the protection of layers, of careful hairstyles and formal rooms.

He nodded. "I need to go home, wash and change, and tell Henry what's happening. I'll come back afterwards and we can discuss it over breakfast."

He stood, stretched again, walked over to the bed, and kissed her firmly on the mouth. "Thank god you're all right," he said, and walked out.

She sat still, letting the feel of his lips echo against hers, and fell back against the pillows and closed her eyes.

It had been an eventful forty-eight hours.

Liza came in, ending her reverie and propelling her out of

bed. The time for reflection and wallowing was over. She washed and dressed quickly, eventually sitting down at her desk to record her memory of the . . . haunting? vision? in as much detail as she could.

After fifteen minutes she opened one of the desk drawers and pulled out the stack of letters Sam had sent her before she'd agreed to let him study the house. As she read them, the trickle of dread that had begun to drip through her swelled to a steady stream.

There was a terrible familiarity to the story she was recording—oh, not the setting, not the details, but the overarching structure of it, the theme. . . . It reminded her of the memory she most wanted to forget. And after reading the other stories Sam had recorded, she didn't think it was a coincidence.

Which meant the ghost hadn't just been in her head. It had been rooting around, looking for secrets it could turn into fodder for its terror.

And she was going to have to share this memory, this *thing* that she wished she could have buried with Alain's body, not because she felt safe doing so, but because she had to. Because something had made itself at home amongst her deepest terrors.

She closed her eyes against the weakness trembling through her, whispering that she could ignore the similarities. Maybe it *was* a coincidence. Maybe it didn't matter. . . .

No. It wasn't a coincidence. And she wasn't a coward. She'd tell Sam everything, open up her guts for him to look through, to see the grisly truth inside.

She just wasn't sure he'd ever be able to look at her the same again.

A few minutes after she finished writing she heard the knock at the door and came down the stairs as Liza admitted Sam into the house. He'd shaved and changed into less rumpled—

although, this being Sam, not entirely *un*rumpled—clothing, his eyes were bright again, and he was carrying a large stack of books.

"I stopped at Liefdehuis to get some of my research materials," he said, pushing his still-damp hair away from his eyes with one hand and almost losing the top part of the stack. "Where do you want to do this?"

"The dining room," she said as he stamped the rest of the snow from his boots and handed Liza his overcoat. His presence filled the entry hall.

They settled around the dining table, Sam stacking the books haphazardly in the middle of it.

"Are you sure you're feeling well enough for this?" he asked.

"I think I have to be," she replied.

"In that case, I'm ready whenever you are."

"You never told me how you confirmed its presence," she said. "Did you . . . did you see anything? When it made contact?"

"No," he said, sitting down at the table. "It did sums, in my head."

"What?"

"I had posed her—it—a mathematical problem, the day before. She sort of borrowed my brain to answer me."

Alva sat down across from him. "That's horrifying."

"I was in raptures at the time," he said.

She nodded. That conformed to one of her budding theories. "I think it preys on people's fears," she said. "I think . . . the more afraid you are, or upset, the more it has to work with."

Sam leaned back, a thoughtful frown on his face, and she hurried forward. She needed to get this all out. "I told you earlier it was like something that happened to someone else." She paused while he nodded. "But that's not—that's not exactly right. When I was in it, it was real. I just wasn't me."

"Who did you think you were?" He looked at her like he already knew the answer.

"Right afterwards? I thought I was living the ghost's story. That I had just experienced her death. I was so sure, Sam. I would have bet my entire fortune on it."

"And now?"

"Now . . . now I believe that's what I was supposed to think. All the hauntings, all the horrible visions you've recorded from people who lived here, they're all violent deaths, aren't they? We all think we know the truth of the ghost that's touched us, the reason they're lingering on. That's why we don't know how many there are. You called it an infestation."

Sam nodded, his eyes steady on hers. "Go on."

Alva took a deep breath. "All right. We all see different things. You've recorded what, five different encounters? But here's the thing: I don't think we have five different ghosts. I think we have one."

Sam stiffened, but he didn't interrupt. He kept watching her.

"We've been assuming the hauntings are basically random," she continued. "Or at least that there's no particular connection between the ghost and the person that's haunted. But what I saw . . ."

She trailed off, a dead, tired feeling blooming inside her chest.

"I'm going to tell you some things about my past," she began, dragging the words up through her throat. "I'm giving this information to you to use scientifically, but I need you to understand that I'm not ever going to want to discuss it again, or face your pity, or your sympathy. All right?"

"Alva—"

"No, Sam. All right?"

There was a long silence as they stared at each other across the table.

"All right," Sam said at last, inclining his head slightly.

"You know my marriage was unhappy. What you don't know is that it was violent. Alain hated me, and when he was angry, or threatened—which was often—he enjoyed reminding me of that. Physically."

"Oh, Alva." Sam's voice was soft, and she heard the lack of surprise, the forbidden pity. The pity could not be tolerated. It made it too real, not like a set of facts that had happened to someone else, but like something that had happened to her. Years that had happened to her.

She set her shoulders. "It's not uncommon for a husband to use . . . bodily coercion . . . upon his wife."

"It should be," Sam said gently. "It should be illegal."

"The law, perhaps, is going that way. My point is, even though it's not uncommon, even though it's still legal in many places . . . it's not a . . . it's not a tolerable state."

"No," Sam said. "Of course it's not."

Her throat closed up suddenly, and she looked away, trying to compose herself. He was threatening to shatter her walls with a handful of words and a tone in his voice, and she couldn't allow it.

"I won't go into the details," she said, once she could trust her voice. "Suffice it to say, he enjoyed having me in his power, having me as . . . as an outlet. Even today I wonder if I had just gone along . . . if I had just stopped fighting . . ."

Sam reached across the table for her hands, but she moved them away. He let her, but he didn't break his gaze. "There is nothing, *nothing*, you did to cause that," he said. "Do you understand me? There is nothing anyone can do to deserve that kind of violence in return."

She broke eye contact first, staring down at the table, at the smooth, dark wood that smelled like beeswax.

"How did you leave him?"

No one had ever asked her before. Her friends in Montmartre had met her after she had left, and they had simply taken her as she appeared. She suspected her friend Amelie had guessed something of the reality, but to the rest of them, it wouldn't have mattered if every word printed in the papers were true. There were so many scandals there on the fringes of Paris, up that steep hill Haussmann's grand improvements had been unable to climb, where the rent was cheap and there was dancing every night. She loved them for their incuriousness, their easy acceptance. It had been exactly what she needed, and after Alain had died it had allowed her time to heal. It had also allowed her to . . . not forget, but to bury.

"Alain's mother died, four years into our marriage," she said, the words pushing past her careful wall. "She was . . . The story was that she was an invalid and had a rare blood disease that kept her indoors. That made her bruise easily."

She glanced quickly up at Sam, saw the understanding in his eyes, before looking down again. "I only met her once. She . . . fell. That's what they said. She was weak, from her illness, and she fell, and hit her head."

"She didn't fall."

"She didn't fall," Alva said, the sentence heavy in her throat. "Alain must have known. But . . . that was the story, and the story was all that mattered. Maybe he made himself believe it. Maybe he didn't care. I don't know."

All those years, and she'd never been able to see inside him. Violence, intimate violence, was a kind of bond. He'd been the most important person in her life for so long, and still, she'd never understood him. She didn't know if he'd grieved his mother, if he'd been capable of such grief, and the love it demands. All she knew was his anger, and his fear.

"This will sound strange, but I'd never put the pieces together before. The way I was living then—that kind of stress slows you down, makes you miss things. When I heard how she'd died I understood. She was me. And I realized I'd never even known her first name. So I asked him."

Her lips were dry as she spoke. "He looked at me like it was the strangest question, like it . . . like it was irrelevant. And he shrugged. He stood there, holding the telegram in his hand, and he shrugged. He asked me what it mattered, and he put on his jacket, and went to his club like it was any other day. I don't know whether he remembered it or not. She looked like him, him and his brother, and I still don't know if he knew her first name. And I knew if I stayed, it would be me. And no one would remember my name."

She paused, trying to pull some of the necessary detachment back. "It took me another six years. Secretly I started writing for a small expat paper in Paris, a short column on design under a pen name. Alain liked his houses to be at the very height of fashion, so I'd become quite good at interior decoration, and to my surprise, I found I liked it—both the design itself and the writing. Eventually the little column became bigger, and I started writing for larger papers. I put the little bits I made from the columns away, and after a few years I had enough for my own apartment. And I left."

She looked up from the table, saw the grief and pain and rage in Sam's eyes, and for a half-second she lost herself in it.

"I know you don't want pity," he said. "So I won't offer it. But Alva, know this. The world is so much better with your name in it."

She gasped. She didn't see it coming. His words hit her in the stomach and simply robbed her of breath. When she held a hand up, it was trembling.

"No more, Sam. I can't."

He met her eyes and nodded.

She took one calming breath, another, and another. "This is the important part," she said, and she saw him open his mouth to protest and close it. *Good.* She needed this part to be clear and scientific. Unemotional. "I thought at first it was the money that mattered the most to him, and if I left him in control of it, he'd let me go. And I was right, for the first week or two. But he found out people were talking about why I had left him. And he started planting all those vile articles. . . ."

She shook her head. "After a few months of that, I met with a lawyer to find out if divorce was an option. Alain found out, and he came to my apartment. I was giving a party," she said. "Just a small one, for some of my new friends. They were mostly artists and . . . well, I suppose charming drunks pretending to be artists. But they didn't care about the rumors. I suppose everyone had their secrets and scandals there, so mine weren't as important. They were kind."

She'd been so proud to welcome them to her little flat, a sixth the size of any house she'd ever lived in but filled with her own choices. The furniture she'd cobbled together from the used markets, the deep emerald wallpaper that was so much bolder than Alain ever would have tolerated.

"I didn't want a scene, so I pulled him into a separate room. We argued, quietly. I didn't want them to hear. I told him to leave. I told him I knew who had given the papers those stories. That there was nothing more he could do to me. And he pushed me against the wall and choked me until I lost consciousness."

Her fingers scrabbling against his coat. Those buttons with their whimsical dragons, the buttons of a lighthearted man without a care in the world. The sound of her friends' happy chatter in the next room, knowing they couldn't hear her, knowing she'd die three yards from help.

"The last thing I remember is him saying it could get a lot worse and I should try him and see what he could do."

She stopped, staring down at the shine on the dining room table. There. It was out. She felt . . . nothing. Empty.

"The man in your vision, he said he'd warned you, that he'd told you not to try him," Sam said quietly. "And he choked you, against the tree."

"And his hair was golden, like Alain's. It *wasn't* Alain. But if someone were to tailor-make a nightmare for me, it wouldn't be so far off."

Sam swallowed. "That's it," he said, a fleet of emotions—rage, tenderness, sorrow—crossing his face as he spoke. "You've cracked it."

She looked fragile, sitting in front of him. Sam had to remind himself not to put his arms around her. She'd told him what she wanted—no pity, no sympathy—and now, of all times, he needed to respect that. He put all his rage, all his sorrow, to the back of his brain to be processed at a more appropriate time and did what she needed him to do. Put the pieces together.

"It's been the most puzzling aspect of the whole case," he said. "All the different stories. Even discounting the smaller hauntings, there were so many people who claimed to know the ghost's background, and not one of them agree. Now I see. I should have been focusing on the people who were haunted, not the ghost at all."

He saw the relief cross her face when she realized he wasn't going to press her further. "You really think it's the answer?"

"Have I ever told you how I heard the first story? It was at Delmonico's, the night I approached you. I was having the longest dinner of my life with this horrible old man and his son—"

"Harold Denton and Harry Denton junior," Alva said. "I saw you with them. You're right. They're horrible."

"And you came in, all red velvet and shiny hair, and they couldn't *wait* to talk about you, which obviously was a lot more interesting than what they had been talking about, not that I remember what it was, because I wasn't listening. And he—the older one; are they really both named Harry?—told me about the house." He kept his voice easy, but his eyes were trained on her. "He told me the story about the mad revolutionary who tried to burn a house party alive."

"The radical farmhand mass murderer," Alva said, and Sam was pleased to hear a touch of her old dryness in the statement. "It was in the first letter you wrote me."

"Now, old Harry had heard this story from someone else—he wasn't haunted himself, and who knows how many people it got filtered through first—but if we assume it came from someone's firsthand experience, who would that person likely be?"

"For the story to get to Harold Denton? Someone a lot like him. Older, probably. Rich. Male."

"Exactly. And what are those people afraid of?"

Alva's eyebrows snapped together. "People who want to take things from them. Losing their power."

"Losing their power," Sam repeated. "A good way to put it. The next ones I heard were from a former scullery maid, who'd worked at the house about thirty years ago. She said there was a lot of talk about the ghost, but two servants had stories she deemed . . . maybe not credible, exactly, but more so."

"The beggar who froze to death," she said. "And the pregnant servant girl who drowned herself. Rather different from the first story. More about the loss of safety, security, than about power. People who are living on the edges, where one catastrophe might be enough to ruin them."

"Which wouldn't be a surprising fear, for two servants dependent on their positions for their livelihood." He stood up and began pacing. "It's a theory with lots of holes. People's fears . . . we can only guess at them."

"The man who bought the house from the de Boers. That was another like Denton's story. An indentured servant who poisoned his master. Another one about the lower classes threatening those above them." She nodded. "You're right. It's a lot of guesswork. But it fits with what we know—and with my experience as well."

"Not mine, though," he said, frowning. "I didn't even see a vision. And . . . I mean, adding a sum wrong was extremely unsettling, but it's hardly my worst fear."

"I wonder what your worst fear would be," Alva mused, with an expression he couldn't quite interpret. "I don't think it was haunting you. Your experience isn't remotely similar to anyone else's. I'm wondering if it paid you a social call."

"But why me? Why am I different?"

She was still watching him with that odd look in her eyes. There was warmth there, but something like envy, too. "You wanted to meet it," she said. "You never brought fear into the house. I don't think it even occurred to you. The only things you brought in were curiosity, and . . . love." She shook her head. "I thought this was me being ridiculous, but . . . the house gets less scary when you're in it."

He blinked, startled. "It's true I wanted to meet it—"

"You're probably the only person who ever has, at least since it died. Maybe you didn't have enough fear for it to work with. Or maybe . . . maybe it just wanted to talk to you."

He stared back at her, disconcerted. She was right; it never occurred to him to be afraid. A month ago he would have cheerfully asked what there was to be afraid of. Now he knew he was simply incredibly lucky. Slowly, he nodded, acknowledging her point. "So if none of these stories are about the ghost itself—if they're all about the people experiencing the haunting—who's the ghost?" He pulled his notebook out and started scribbling. It didn't take him long to record what they knew, and when he was done he pushed it across the table. "A chart of the stories. Notice anything?"

She scanned it, slowly shaking her head. "It seems random. The ghost is any sex, all classes—wait." She frowned. "Not any class. There's no one from the upper class here. And no children."

"No old people, either. And if we assume these are intentional misdirections . . ."

"We should be looking for what's not there, rather than what is!"

Sam rifled through his stack of research, pulling out the large family tree he'd copied out and unrolling it on the table. "If we're looking for people in the upper class, it's most likely a member of the family. Someone who died either when they were, let's say, younger than eighteen or older than sixty."

Alva came around to his side, standing next to him, her arm brushing his. "There are a lot of people who lived long lives here," she said. "It looks like making it into one's sixties or seventies isn't so unusual for the de Boers."

"Most of these people I've already looked into, though," he replied. "It's somebody who didn't seem important on a first pass—someone who doesn't show up in the news articles, for good or ill, whose death at least wasn't recorded as violent—there.

Mary de Boer, 1775–1838. That roughly aligns with when the hauntings started. Or there was one who killed himself in his late fifties . . . but that would have been after the stories started. Maybe Edward de Boer; he died in 1831 at the age of seventeen. No cause of death mentioned. These are from the family Bible, so they aren't very complete."

"I heard about the suicide," Alva said, picking up the top book. "But that wasn't even very long ago. No more than fifteen or twenty years. This is the book Henry got from the reading room."

Sam looked over. "After all that, I haven't had a chance to look at it yet," he said. "See if she says anything on the de Boers. And do you think there's any chance of some food?"

She snorted as she sat back down, flipping the book open. "I'm quite certain if you asked Cook for some you'd make her entire year," she said.

"I wish your staff would talk to my housemaid," he said, walking towards the door. "She won't even bring me a cup of tea if Henry's not around."

After procuring a satisfyingly heavy tray from the kitchen—he was willing to bet Alva hadn't eaten at all that day, and he wanted to be sure he could tempt her—he walked back to the dining room, thinking about what she had told him. Alva's story, and all the other, unspoken stories living between the words, thrummed against the back of his mind in a constant rhythm. The bleak look on her face, the dispassionate tone of her voice as she related horrors to him, clung like spider webbing to his heart.

Sam had never spent much time ruminating on the nature of heaven and hell before today, either, but it occurred to him there were some people for whom eternal torture was a fitting end.

He paused in the doorway and watched her, the graceful arch

of her neck, head bent over the book. A rush of emotion, of love, tore through him. She'd walked through her own hell and escaped it . . . not unscathed, but tempered, like a metal alloy toughened in the heat. She could bend, but she wouldn't ever break.

"Find anything?" he asked, sliding the tray onto the table and placing a sandwich in front of her.

"Mmm," she said. "The locals really didn't like the de Boers, even back when they were building the place. Mrs. Clarke says here that '*while the people of the town and the people of the city have never mingled particularly well, local ire was especially enflamed around the building of the monstrously named Liefdehuis, meaning "Love House," in the late part of the last century. It appears that when Mr. de Boer was busy building his fortune on the stock exchange he was routinely underpaying the men who were building his mansion on the Hudson, men who included my own grandfather. . . .*'"

"Charming. Anything about the offspring?"

"Oh yes. Edward died of a fever. Mrs. Clarke doesn't have much to say about him, except he had a bit of a reputation amongst the local girls and they didn't miss him much after he was gone."

"Doesn't *feel* like our ghost," Sam said. "But the dates fit, so we should keep him on the list."

"There's also a bit about the de Boers selling up, but that's about when the book was written, so not much more." She closed it and put it gently back on the table while eyeing the sandwich. "That's enormous."

"It was constructed to my exact specifications," he said. "I'll be very wounded if you don't enjoy it."

"Hmm," she said, but she took a bite. "What next? Do you have any other research materials we can look at?"

"I can do one better," he said. "I have a source—Mrs. Kay, the former scullery maid. But I'll have to head back into the city for a couple days."

"I'll ask Liza to pack my bags," she said. "We can leave in the morning."

CHAPTER TWENTY

The city was black and grim underneath the remnants of a late-winter storm—the dark stone of the buildings and statues dusted lightly with bright crunchy snow. The cab they'd hailed at the train station was cold inside, making Alva particularly aware of the warmth radiating from the man next to her.

They'd spoken only of light things on the journey down, a courtesy on his part that she was grateful for. She'd shared things with him yesterday she'd never wanted to tell another soul, and his discretion and respect were more than she'd hoped for. Just being able to still talk this way with him, even laugh occasionally, was a grace she would never take for granted.

As she looked out the window, she was struck by how much the city of her birth had changed in the twelve years she'd been away. Whole neighborhoods had appeared where before there had only been fields, smashed right next to blocks that hadn't changed in a century. There was a vibrancy, a fast-paced thrumming aliveness, to the city that had surged up through the bottoms of her boots as soon as she'd stepped off the train. It made her aware of possibilities, of different lives waiting to be led.

They turned down a street she'd never been on before, lined with the small but respectable houses characteristic of a new, up-and-coming middle class, and stopped in front of a neat brick town house with lace curtains in the windows.

"Here we are," Sam said, handing money to the driver before helping Alva out of the cab. "I sent a telegram before we left, so she should be waiting—"

As he spoke, the front door opened, revealing a young maid, her face wreathed in blushes. Alva hid a smile. "Professor Moore," the girl said breathlessly. "Mrs. Kay is waiting for you, sir, if you'd come this way."

"Thank you," Sam said, smiling down at her, and the pink turned to red. "Come on, Alva."

They walked into a pleasant front hall—quite narrow, paneled in simple wood and obviously less than ten years old—and were met by a short, round, middle-aged woman, whose dress was perhaps a trifle too opulent for the occasion but whose smile was charming enough to make up for it.

"Professor Moore, you've come back to see me," she said, holding out a hand to him. "And you've brought a friend, as well."

"I thought I'd eat some more of your cookies," he said, grinning, and Alva found herself smiling along with him. "And maybe ask you a few questions. Oh, this is Mrs. Alva Webster. Mrs. Webster, Mrs. Kay."

"It's nice to meet you, ma'am," Alva said.

"And you," Mrs. Kay replied, with a measuring look that reminded Alva they were back in the city, where people knew exactly who she was and what she was supposed to have done. The scientist and the scandal, Alva thought ruefully. Mrs. Kay would be able to dine out for the rest of the year on the basis of this visit, but to her credit, she didn't appear to be letting her knowledge color her manner.

"I'm sure I don't know what more I could tell you," Mrs. Kay said. "But come on in. I had a fresh batch of those cookies made just for you, Professor Moore."

Alva and Sam followed her into a small sitting room completely fitted in the latest style, or rather the latest style as it was diluted to the masses through ladies' magazines. Choosing an armchair upholstered in brocade stiff with newness, Alva looked around the room, wishing she could take notes. This new class of working families who had enough money to furnish their houses in the latest style, to compete with their neighbors and accumulate status through interior decoration, had been so far out of her world the first time she'd lived in New York. Now they were her audience, and she needed to know them a lot better.

However, that would have to wait. Hauntings took priority.

"We've learned more about the Liefdehuis ghost," Sam was saying. "And we have some names to pass by you."

"Ooh," Mrs. Kay said. "You mean—Professor Moore, are you saying there really is a ghost?"

"We believe there is," he said.

"Oh my," she said, leaning back and placing a small, heavily ringed hand upon her generous bosom. "Well, my goodness. Imagine that. I worked in a haunted house!"

Change that to two years dining out.

"Mrs. Kay, do you remember a Mary de Boer? We think she was a daughter of the original builder, died in '38, right when you started working there."

"Mary de Boer," Mrs. Kay repeated. "It doesn't sound familiar. How did she die?"

"We don't really know. She would have been in her mid-sixties at the time, but she doesn't show up in any of the contemporary accounts of the family, and we haven't found any other records."

Alva and Mrs. Kay exchanged a look. Women were a lot easier to misplace than men, when it came to records. "If she never married," Mrs. Kay said, "there probably wouldn't be. You have a death certificate?"

"Just a notation in the family Bible," Sam said.

"Could be someone got the date wrong and she died earlier. I certainly never heard of her, so either she married and nobody bothered to write it down or she died before I started working there."

Sam nodded and made some notes in his little book. "What about Edward de Boer? Died in '31?"

"Now him I remember from my time before I worked there, because he got down to the village fairly regularly. I remember my mother warning my older sister off him. Handsome, he was, slender and fair. Pretty as a picture, you might say, but not as good as he ought to be on the inside." She made a wry little face. "Though how many are, one might ask."

Alva leaned forward. "Did he die in the house?"

"This *is* a morbid subject, isn't it?" Mrs. Kay laughed. "Yes. Scarlet fever, I believe, or something similar; they would have had him confined to his bedchamber. Do you think he's the ghost, then? Unpleasant in life and unpleasant in death, eh?"

"He might be," Sam said, his voice neutral. "Can you think of anyone else connected to the property who died during, oh, say from '30 to '38?"

"There might have been some staff," she said, her brow scrunching in concentration. "I think—the old housekeeper, the first one the house had, she might have died during that period. I tell you what, I'll stop in to the butler I worked under,

Mr. Hargedy. He's old, but he's still around. Lives with his son, just up the island. I'll see if he has any helpful recollections; maybe he even has some journals."

"We'd be grateful," Sam said, jotting something down and tearing the paper off to hand to her. "That's the hotel we'll be at while we're here. Just send us a note if you hear anything."

After a bit of quaint chat about their journey and the weather, Alva and Sam followed the blushing maid back through the hallway and into the bright early afternoon. Alva pulled her scarf closer around her neck as the cold nipped straight into her skin, and descended the steps gingerly, watching for ice. She was conscious of a sense of disappointment, tinged with panic. She hadn't realized how much she'd been counting on an answer. Everything since she'd received Alfred's horrible little present had been a blur of one thing after another, but in the background always was his threat, and the understanding that she needed to solve her ghost problem quickly. Somewhere inside, she'd thought this might be the day they did.

"She's a delight," she said, keeping the panic out of her voice. "But I admit I was hoping for some startling reveal."

Sam laughed, the sound startling a pigeon hopping nearby. "Such is the nature of research," he said. "Constant disappointment. Still, it wasn't a total loss."

"You don't really think Edward is the ghost," she said.

"Why are you so sure he's not?"

Alva considered it as they started to walk, his easy manner calming her, allowing her to push Alfred away. "I'm not sure," she admitted. "I feel like I have a sense of it, though. It was in my brain, after all, yours too. You can't tell me it felt like the person Mrs. Kay and that book described."

"It didn't," Sam agreed. "But are you sure that's not the point?

This ghost has done everything it can to throw us off the scent. Maybe this . . . conviction . . . we both have is part of that. For example, what gender would you say the ghost is?"

"Female," Alva said without pausing. "Although that might be because of the haunting I was shown."

"I'd say the same," Sam said. "Ever since we . . . conversed, if one can call it that, I keep calling it her and she. With no evidence whatsoever of a gender."

"I see your point," Alva said reluctantly. "But I still don't think it's Edward. Maybe Mrs. Kay will turn something up with the old butler."

"Let's hope. Change of subject—there's an official Moore family dinner tonight."

"That will be nice for you," Alva said. "I know you miss them."

"Ah, you misunderstand. You're included in the summons. Orders directly from my mother."

"Sorry. Your mother wants me to come to dinner?" Alva frowned up at him. "Sam, what have you told her?"

"Oh, only that I enjoyed our lovemaking like I've enjoyed no other and I hope to wear you down so you'll let me enjoy it again—Ouch! Ouch! Ouch! You know, for a fairly average-sized woman your fists have a surprising amount of strength behind them."

"Sam," Alva said, speaking slowly. "Please tell me you did not say that. I know your family is unconventional, but please tell me—"

"All right, all right, I didn't tell her anything," Sam said, twinkling at her in a very provoking way. "Just that we were both traveling down here. She likes you. She wants to see you."

The sudden panic faded, revealing a layer of unease below. She liked Winn Moore. She liked Sam's whole family. But if they were successful here in New York, she hoped this entire adventure would be concluded quickly and Sam would be going on his way. Going to dinner . . . getting attached . . . it could only end badly.

"I'm not sure that's a good idea," she said. "They'll want to catch up with you, and I don't want to horn in."

"You might as well give it up. Either you show up at Gilsey House, with me, at seven o'clock this evening or my mother will take herself and our entire family to your hotel room and invite herself in. I'm afraid you're stuck. There's no going against her."

And with that, Alva sighed and gave up.

It was drifting snowflakes when Alva and Sam walked up the sidewalk towards Gilsey House, the kind of snow that might simply be little gusts of wind playing in the snowbanks. Lamps burned in storefronts, and people, rich and poor and everything in between, jostled past one another in the street. Alva glanced at a dark window as they passed, trying to catch a glimpse of her reflection.

Getting ready for dinner had been a trial. At first she'd thought she should wear her most conservative dress, but they weren't a very conservative family, and so she'd waffled back and forth before settling on the red velvet dress Sam liked so much. It was just a coincidence that he liked it, or maybe it was a good indication the rest of the family would like it, too.

Not that it mattered if they liked it, of course. She wasn't trying to impress them. In fact, it was extremely unlikely she'd ever see any of them again after tonight.

On the other hand, it wasn't every day one took dinner with America's leading scientific family. If she was a little nervous, a little on edge and anxious to please, it was only to be expected.

Oh lord, what if all they talked about was science? She knew nothing scientific, not a single thing. Quickly she started to run through any half-remembered scientific facts or newspaper articles she'd read, but her brain was a muddle. If only she'd had time to do some studying before dinner! But she'd had a meeting with her publisher that afternoon, and of course it had run long, and by the time she'd gotten back her hair had completely collapsed, her boot lace had broken, and—maybe Sam really was on to something with that shoe lacer-upper, although goodness it would need a new name—

"You've met them before, you know," Sam said.

"What?"

"It's not like you have to impress them. They already like you."

"I—of course I'm not worried about impressing them."

"Uh-huh. So why are you nervous?"

"I'm not nervous. That's ridiculous."

"All right. So it's a coincidence you've examined your reflection in every shop window we've walked past."

"I haven't!"

There was a long pause. When she finally got up the nerve to look at him, he was smirking at her.

"Perhaps I'm just very vain," she said.

"All right," he agreed.

"I'm not—Oh!" She broke off in frustration and, she had to admit it, nervousness.

"You are," he said, and the smirk widened into a grin. "You're nervous about meeting my mother. Because you're wondering what she's going to think about us traveling together, and you're wondering what I've told her about you, and because, let's face it, you've fallen for me a bit and there's some part of you that's trying her on for mother-in-law status."

"Why, you—" Nervousness fled in the face of outrage. "That's the most arrogant—Samuel Moore, I swear on my *life*, I have never met anyone more outrageous than you."

"That's more like it," he said, and escorted her up the front steps and through the wide, ornate doors.

It was much warmer inside, and Sam paused to take off his coat and help Alva out of hers. Handing it to the girl behind the counter, he looked around appraisingly. "It's very fancy," he said. "I'm surprised they haven't gotten kicked out yet. Usually the shine of having the famous Moores to stay wears off after a week or so."

"It's because the manager's fallen in love with Mother," Benedict said, walking down the stairs into the lobby. "It was after the first explosion. He came up fussing and she sat him down and poured on the . . . *you know* . . . and now he's putty in her hands."

"Well, why she couldn't have done that the time we were kicked out of the one in Kansas at two in the morning—" Sam said.

"The first explosion?" Alva said.

"We've had three since then," Benedict said, a smile lighting up his grave face as he offered her his arm. "Only one big one, but *all three* caused by the women, Sam, which seriously makes me wonder why women don't have the entire weapons-design industry on lock-down."

"*Three?*" Sam said, falling into step on Alva's other side as they mounted the stairs. "The man must be completely besotted."

"Through and through," Benedict agreed. "He appears at our door three or four times a day, and when Father answers he turns bright red and stammers and looks like he's about to be pushed in front of a firing squad. Naturally Father has no idea what sins are being contemplated in the little man's mind. Here we are."

He pushed open the door to the suite, which bore no sign of

the many disasters that had befallen it. The hotel was obviously losing money on this proposition, with all the repairs it was shouldering.

"Sam!" Maggie hurtled across the room and into her brother's arms, hitting him with enough force that he took two staggering steps backwards.

"Hello, ragamuffin," he said, easily holding her off the floor and peering over her shoulder at his parents, who approached at a more restrained pace.

"Sam, darling," Winn said, kissing his cheek. "Mrs. Webster, I'm so glad you could come. You remember my husband, John, and my daughter, Maggie."

"Of course," Alva said, smiling politely even as the nerves enthusiastically returned to her stomach. "Thank you for inviting me."

"We're all looking forward to hearing about your ghostly progress," Winn said. "We've been able to talk of little else."

"If only that were true," Benedict muttered darkly. "I seem to recall *forty-five minutes* yesterday at dinner on the changing placement of bustles."

"Ignore him," Maggie said to Alva, drawing her towards a small sofa. "He's horrible, and he never says anything interesting. I love your dress; it's terribly elegant. Did you get it in France? I've never been to France, but I want to go just enormously, on account of all the beautiful fashions, and also obviously because it's where Lavoisier was from, although I suppose since it's also what killed him perhaps it's a mark *against* rather than for it, but even that aside, it *is* the birthplace of modern chemistry. Did you ever visit the Academy of Sciences? They don't allow women members, of course, but just to see?"

"I don't know where it's housed, I'm afraid," Alva said, feeling lost.

"Don't know that I'd say France is the birthplace of modern

chemistry," John said, his slow words rumbling over Maggie's quicksilver ones.

"But how could you disagree, Daddy? When one thinks about the Baron de Morveau, or Berthollet—"

"But then there's Boyle, Mags; he was Irish," Sam said from behind the sofa. Alva suddenly steadied, like she'd been tossing about on the high seas and someone had dragged her onto dry land. "Or Cavendish—"

"Oh, what do you know, you tinkerer—"

"Surely the country that executed the father of modern chemistry should lose the honor of being its birthplace—" Benedict interjected.

"And Priestley too, he was English, and Scheele, who was Swedish—"

"And then there's the Comte de Fourcroy—"

"Children, let us all agree that many countries contributed to the foundations of modern chemistry," Winn said, smoothly talking over the argument. "And let us eat, because dinner is served in the dining room."

The family moved en masse to the dining room, Benedict and Maggie still arguing under their breath.

"Obviously it was us who should have worried about making a good impression," Sam said quietly, his face alight with affection. "Rabble."

Alva smiled and shook her head, not sure what to say. She wondered whether she'd ever seen a family as happy with one another as this one, wondered if before she'd met them she would have believed such a family existed. Her nerves had faded during the argument, replaced entirely by the good humor and laughter that seemed to surround the Moores. They *liked* one another, she thought, and wondered whether anyone in her family had ever liked anybody at all.

They settled around the table, already set with dishes brought up from the hotel's kitchens. Two waiters stood at the ready, the wary looks on their faces testifying to the Moores' habitual chaos.

"Now tell us all about the ghost," Winn said after they had all been served.

Sam nodded at Alva. "You tell; I'm starved."

"Err—" Alva looked around the table at the waiting Moores. "Um. Well, it seems . . . It seems there is one. Just one, we think."

"Oh, I'm so sorry, my dears," Winn said. "I know you were hoping for a nest."

"Oh, Winn, one could be just as interesting as a nest," John said. "You always think in terms of quantity."

"I find you do as well, John," Winn said tartly, narrowing her eyes. "At least when it comes to the number of rolls on your plate."

"But it really is incredibly interesting," Alva said, discovering a need to defend their ghost. "It's been . . . putting hauntings in people's heads. Oh! And it possessed Sam once, and he talked to it!"

That set them buzzing with questions, and at least a minute passed before any one voice could be picked out of the noise.

"But how exciting," Winn was saying, with a charming disregard for the sanctity of her firstborn's brain. "And how clever of you, darling, to think of using a mathematical pattern to engage it."

"What did it feel like?" Maggie asked.

"Why didn't you tell me about this when I was up there?" Benedict demanded. "I should have given you both exams!"

John had been listening intently throughout and carefully finished chewing a piece of chicken before he spoke. "What I want to know is, how did you figure out it was only the one entity?"

"Alva solved it," Sam said, beaming across the table at her. *For all the world like I'm his prize cow,* she thought, but instead of rancor, pride filled her. "She was the first to see the hauntings were connected to the people being haunted."

"Was she," John said. "Clever, my girl, very clever of you."

Heat came into her face, and Alva covered her disarray by taking a sip of wine. The pride was growing, swelling within her until she was warm and happy all over. It was a dangerous suite of emotions, she knew, but maybe she could enjoy the glow for a night. . . .

"I should say it was," Winn said, looking impressed, and Benedict winked at her. "So tell us what you've found out on this trip. . . ."

CHAPTER TWENTY-ONE

The next morning Alva woke to a message from Sam requesting that she meet him in the lobby of their hotel. She hurried to get ready, still wrapped in the golden glow of the night before. She remembered she'd brought some fashion catalogues back from Paris with her and wondered if Maggie would enjoy them.

Not that she'd be seeing Maggie, Alva reminded herself. But she could always mail the catalogues, and Maggie would probably enjoy looking at all the beautiful illustrations. . . . Maybe they could even keep up a correspondence, in a small way. . . .

She put down the brush she was running through her hair and met her own eyes in the mirror. A correspondence would be nothing more than a series of tiny, painful paper cuts. Little dribs and drabs of information, the occasional, casual update about what Sam was doing, whom he was seeing, perhaps one day whom he was marrying—no. She picked the brush up again and started pulling it through her hair angrily, yanking at the tangles until her scalp burned. There could not be a correspondence between her and Maggie.

But she could still find the catalogues and send them.

Forty-five minutes after waking she walked into the lobby, scanning until she found Sam's shaggy blond head towering over everyone around him. He was leaning against a pillar, sketching something in his notebook, with a pencil smudge on his cheek and his hair already pulled into disarray.

"Good morning," she said.

"Mmmm," he said, continuing to scribble. An unwelcome smile threatened to disarrange her carefully neutral expression, so instead she rolled her eyes and sat down in a nearby chair to observe the lobby. He'd surface when he surfaced.

Two minutes later, he threw himself into the chair across from her.

"I've had a letter from Mrs. Kay," he began without preamble. "You look beautiful this morning, by the way. She visited the old butler last night, and she says she has something for us."

"God bless gossips," Alva said, a thrumming excitement building under her skin. Maybe this trip would produce answers after all.

"I wish all my research assistants were as efficient," Sam said. "Shall we?"

They took a cab to Mrs. Kay's. It was a dark morning, the kind where the sun hasn't fully decided whether to come up or not, but the streets were quick and loud and busy. Alva stared out the window as the driver navigated between horses and unloading vehicles and children darting out suddenly into the middle of the road, thinking how little of the city she'd known while she was growing up. For Alva, Manhattan was her bedroom at her parents' house, the small schoolroom on the same floor, the grand, quiet street that her parents and all their acquaintances lived on. The small, exclusive park a short walk away. Later, during her courtship with Alain, her world had expanded to the ballrooms and dining rooms of other people's houses. Boarding the ship for France the day of her wedding had been the first time she'd ever even visited New York Harbor.

There was so much more world here than she'd known.

The cab pulled in front of Mrs. Kay's tidy brownstone. Sam paid the driver and helped Alva down. There was a twitch in one of the lace curtains; the lady of the house had obviously been waiting. The door was opened by the same rosy maid as the day before.

"Morning, sir, ma'am," she said, staring at Sam as though he personally were responsible for the design of the sun and moon. "Mrs. Kay's in the sitting room."

"Waiting impatiently for you," Mrs. Kay said, appearing in the sitting room doorway. "I've expected you for an hour past."

"My apologies, ma'am," Sam said, his eyes twinkling.

"Never mind, you scoundrel," she said. "You can still have your cookies."

Sam made a direct line to the plate sitting on a low coffee table in the middle of the room and helped himself to two.

"I have news," Mrs. Kay said, in a low, thrumming voice that clearly indicated a missed opportunity in the theater. "Oh, sit, sit."

She ushered them into chairs.

"I went to see Mr. Hargedy yesterday afternoon, after you left. What he wanted to know is, is there a chance your Mary de Boer is old Rose de Boer?"

Sam frowned and pulled his notebook out, flipping through it until he came to a page with a tiny family tree drawn on it. "Mary Rose de Boer," he confirmed, looking up sharply. "So he did know her."

"I clean forgot about her," Mrs. Kay said. "Of course now I'm remembering a couple of quiet bits of gossip about it. She's not showing up in your research because they packed her off to an asylum when she was merely a child and, after, did their damnedest to pretend she never existed, poor thing. That was in . . . must have been my mother's time, but Mr. Hargedy's father, he was the first butler, and he knew Miss Rose as a child, so he never forgot."

"They put her in an asylum?" Alva repeated.

Mrs. Kay nodded. "She was a little different, apparently. Mr. Hargedy says his father never held with the asylum bit, though, says it never sat right with him. He never thought she had any harm in her, couldn't understand why they'd ship off their own daughter. You think she's the one haunting the place?"

"It's possible," Sam said, scribbling notes as he spoke. "Her death date roughly matches with the first accounts of hauntings."

"Rose de Boer," Mrs. Kay mused. "Well, I guess if ever there was a woman who was owed justice and didn't get it, it was her, but don't ghosts have to haunt the place they died? As far as Mr. Hargedy knows, she died in the same place she lived: the New York Hospital."

"She spent her whole life there?" Sam asked, his jaw tensing. "They just . . . left her? What cause had they to do so?"

"To hear Mr. Hargedy tell it, she was simply a frightened little rabbit when she was a child. But she'd have fits, see, screaming and carrying on, and it got so the family couldn't have guests in the house without them hearing. So off she went."

That was high society for you, Alva thought. *About as much caring as could be packed into a walnut shell.* Her parents would have done the same.

"The New York Hospital is on Broadway, a few blocks up from City Hall," she said to Sam. "We could walk there in fifteen minutes or so."

He nodded, his skin a little white around his mouth. "Write

us if you or Mr. Hargedy remember anything else," he said. "And thank you."

Silence hung between him and Alva as they walked out of the house. The air was cold, biting through Alva's coat and dress and seeping in with the snow through her boots. She glanced at Sam as they walked, his expression grim.

"What parent could do that?" he asked, and his tone broke her heart. He was genuinely shocked, she realized, and seeing his surprise and horror only made her understand how completely not shocked she was.

Suddenly the weight of her cynicism hung around her shoulders like an extra hundred years. "The families I grew up with could have," she said. "Some of them, at least. You don't . . . show your weaknesses, in that circle. A child who was odd, who had fits, who maybe scared people a little—and those kinds of people are easy to scare—is a weakness. They'd want to hide her, put her away where they didn't have to look at or think of her, not even remembering the weakness in question was a child."

Sam fell silent once more, staring at the pavement as he walked. They passed from the quiet residential streets to the bustle of Broadway, walking past small businesses and men in dark overcoats, hurrying along in the abruptly bright midday light. Carriages rolling past splashed dark, icy water onto the sidewalks as undernourished children with dirty faces looked for easy marks with poorly secured wallets. It was a normal winter day in the city, beauty and horror walking arm in arm and yet invisible to each other.

The New York Hospital was an imposing building of gray stone, stained darker by smoke and dirt. Alva looked at Sam's furious face, wondering if there was anything she should say, but there were no words that could—or, perhaps, even should—make this better.

She simply put her hand on his arm and nodded towards the large double doors. "Shall we?"

Ten minutes later, they stepped out.

"The Bloomingdale Insane Asylum," Sam said, biting out the words. "Do you think they even noticed she'd been transferred?"

"I doubt it very much," Alva said, a weary droopiness around her shoulders. He took a deep breath, closing his eyes and reminding himself that no amount of railing at the sky was going to help Rose de Boer. It took some doing—the piece in the *New York Tribune* three years prior exposing the horrific practices of the Bloomingdale asylum and resulting in the release of at least a dozen unjustly imprisoned inmates had been brought fresh to the front of his mind.

"I'm sorry," he said. "My outrage got the better of me. I shouldn't be placing it onto you." Especially given what he knew about her own past. Atrocities were not new to Alva Webster.

"There's no need to apologize," she replied, crisply straightening her hat and walking to the curb to hail a cab. "Your outrage is entirely reasonable, and I don't observe you placing it on me."

A cab pulled over, and after giving the driver the address and climbing in Alva let out a little huff of air. "You *should* be horrified, Sam. That I am not is, perhaps, only because I have seen so many similar crimes committed before." She laid her hand over his. "*Be outraged.* Maybe it can change something." He heard what she didn't say: if someone had been outraged for her, maybe she wouldn't have lived through the horror she did.

The cab lurched into traffic, beginning the long drive from the throngs of downtown Manhattan to the upper wilds of Bloomingdale.

She removed her hand, leaving an imprint of warmth behind. He stared at his own a moment longer, turning the new evidence over in his mind.

Mary Rose de Boer had been transferred to the Bloomingdale Insane Asylum immediately after its 1821 opening. The clerk at the desk had informed them, reluctantly at first, and then eagerly once Alva had casually mentioned who Sam was, that almost all the hospital patients labeled "insane" had been transferred to the new facility.

Mrs. Kay had described a sensitive, easily frightened child. Sam imagined this described children as a general population—certainly he'd never met the exception. To put a person of that description in an asylum, to close her up and forget about the key . . .

The pieces were beginning to come together. He could feel them sliding into place, feel the satisfaction of a puzzle solving itself even through his disgust.

"We're here," Alva said quietly, looking out the window as the cab came to a stop. He handed her out of the carriage and looked at the now-infamous building.

The Bloomingdale Insane Asylum was a pleasant three-story manor house, set in meticulously sculpted grounds. The wide drive split in two and curved around the building, creating a pretty, snow-covered garden island. A passerby could be forgiven for thinking it a charming country hotel or the home of somebody terribly wealthy and important.

In 1872, the journalist Julius Chambers had feigned insanity in order to be admitted. He was released ten days later, and the exposé that followed spoke of barbaric practices: patients slowly starved, surviving only on spoilt food; blind men being beaten; young children made to stand naked in the elements; the most basic tenets of the United States Constitution violated at every turn.

Nothing of this unpleasantness appeared on the outside. There was only a pretty, snow-covered house, and a white-clad nurse wheeling an elderly man inside.

Inside, too, there was little sign of squalor. The front room, obviously intended as a comfortable waiting room for well-to-do family and friends, was open and spacious, the furniture in good repair. Only the faint sound of screaming in the background informed visitors they were, in fact, standing in one of the most notorious asylums in the country.

Alva asked a woman at the front desk about Rose's records, and after a subtle exchange of money she hurried through the double doors at the back of the room and down a dark hallway. Alva and Sam sat down to wait on a settee near the large front window, Alva running her hands over the upholstery.

"It's not precisely what I imagined," she said, her tone dry. "I suppose I thought we'd drive up under a thunderstorm, hearing manacles clanking and the piteous wails of the damned."

Another cry sounded from behind the double doors, followed by a loud crash.

"Of course," she continued, her mouth compressing into a thin line, "one out of three isn't bad."

"It makes it worse," Sam said, staring at the room. "For us, at least. I can't imagine it makes much difference to the inmates."

"No," she agreed, and they lapsed into silence.

The woman returned, holding an old, dusty folder. "Here's all we have on her, ma'am."

Alva stood and took it from her. "That's it?"

"Doesn't look like she was one of the troublemakers," the woman replied, shrugging. "It's most likely just treatment plans."

"I see." Alva nodded, dismissing the woman, and turned to Sam. "Let's look at it after we leave."

He rose, not sorry to be leaving, and keenly aware of his freedom to do so. Once they were in the carriage he nodded towards the file. She propped it open across both their laps.

For fifty years of involuntary incarceration, Rose de Boer's file was pathetically thin—less than one page per year, Sam estimated. Most of it was a cornucopia of quackery, every discredited treatment of those five decades making an appearance somewhere in the file. As they quickly thumbed through page after page of changing treatments, Alva frowned.

"But what was she in for in the first place?" She flipped back to the beginning and started again. "I see what they did to her, and her yearly evaluations, but what exactly was she being treated *for*?"

"I see reference to nerves," Sam said. "And here: 'patient is inordinately terrified of her surroundings.'"

Alva's frown deepened. "Is it possible to be ordinately terrified of an insane asylum?"

"And there's something about occasional fits. But—no. I don't see anything in here that amounts to a good reason for someone to be imprisoned for her entire life. If I had to guess, I would say she was exactly what Mrs. Kay described, a sensitive child prone to frequent fits of extreme nerves." He sighed, shutting the file.

"You think it's her."

They were getting back into the city, and the sounds of a busy metropolis began to bleed through the windows.

"I think our ghost is fractured, desperate not to be seen, and deals almost entirely in fear. If we assume that ghosts in death retain some relation to their living selves, I cannot imagine a life more likely to result in those characteristics than that of a woman shunted off to a mental hospital as a child and basically just . . . forgotten . . . until her death. After her death, even. The life lines up; the dates line up." He nodded. "I think it's her."

"But she didn't die at Liefdehuis," Alva said. "Her death wasn't violent, either. Isn't that usually part of a ghost story? Rose died of pneumonia, it says here."

"The folklore on hauntings does usually focus on the death," he agreed. "It's always seemed strange to me. Why should a death be so much more important than a life? Rose spent fifty years in what we can assume, looking at these papers, was daily torment. If we set aside what we think we 'know' about ghosts, what could be more worthy of a haunting?"

"Liefdehuis too," she said. "That's where it all began."

The last of the pieces slid into place. "That's right. That's where everything went wrong, for Rose."

"So . . . what do we do?"

He closed the file. "I have no idea," he said. "The stories suggest naming the ghost can release it. Of course, so far the stories have been almost entirely wrong, but it's worth a shot. It's certainly worth finding out where she's buried, too."

As he turned the question over in his mind, the familiar pattern of investigation calmed him. "We do what scientists should always do," he said more surely. "We gather information and experiment."

"Somehow I knew you were going to say that," she replied, the little smile accompanying her words fading swiftly. "I was so eager for answers, this morning. All I could think was I might be able to finally solve my problems. It seems so selfish now."

He reached across and took her hand. "You didn't do this to her, Alva," he said. "And maybe these answers can help both of you."

CHAPTER TWENTY-TWO

They were almost back at the hotel when Sam suddenly leaned towards the window.

"Wait!"

Alva dropped the file onto her lap. "It really is always 'Wait!' with you. I don't want to wait. I'm not even sure how I can. I'm already sitting almost perfectly still, quietly reading. I'm a captive audience. I can't possibly be waiting any more than I am right now."

"I didn't mean you," he said, and leaned forward to open the window between passengers and driver. "Driver, could you let us out here?"

"We're still blocks from the hotel," she protested, thinking of a warm cup of tea and a crackling fire.

"But I've just remembered I have a terrible problem," he said as the driver swerved through traffic to bring them to the curb. "And, for once, I also have the perfect solution."

"Oh yes? What's this terrible problem and magical solution?"

"The problem, and I assure you it is indeed a critical, even life-threatening one, is that my sister's birthday is only three days away and I have yet to buy, or even consider buying, a single present for her. The solution, of course, is you." As he spoke he opened the door, bundling her out and quickly walking towards a large storefront with an elaborate window display.

"Me?" Alva said, or perhaps squawked, as he pushed her through the door. "I don't see what I have to do with it."

"You're going to be my savior," he said, helping her out of her coat and handing it to the coat check girl along with his own.

"I see. And do I get a choice in this?"

He pulled her to the side of the entrance and moved in front of her, his hands gently resting on the sides of her shoulders. He looked down at her, a woeful, singularly masculine expression on his face, his dark blond hair a little wet from the snow. Her legs went wobbly. "Of course you get a choice," he said. "It just depends on how much you currently want me to die. Because if my sister wakes up on the morning of her birthday and does not find a thoughtful, fashionable, and extremely expensive present from me waiting for her, she will travel all the way to Hyde Park to murder me. And it won't be a particularly clean murder, either." He pushed a curl out of her face. "Come on, Alva. It's been an ugly day. Let's put some joy back in it."

Alva clutched the folder, thinking of pretty snow-covered asylums and screams echoing in hallways, and, looking up at him, understood. He was trying to offer her something that wasn't covered in the sins of other people. Something he needed, too. "I've met your sister," she said. "She's about a foot shorter than you and half your body weight."

"And when she gets angry, the whole world runs and hides," he said. "At least if it has any sense, it does. Please? Save me?"

"Fine," she said, pretending to sigh. "I suppose I still have some use for you, after all."

The gleaming interior was a sharp contrast to the gray, slushy streets. Marble floors met glass counters so clean they winked in the gaslight, counters piled with luscious towers of goods so plentiful it was as though the entire store was one enormous cornucopia of plenty and delight. The effect was one of promise and comfort, a reassurance everything was right in the world, so long as there were beautiful stores stuffed with beautiful goods.

This particular store hadn't been here when she'd left. At least not in its current form—she thought she might remember a small dry goods sitting on this corner. Yet this wasn't merely a new store. It was a whole new way of shopping, emerging just as she was leaving New York, having all different kinds of goods crammed together under one roof, even ready-made clothing. She'd seen the new "department" stores springing up in Paris, but she'd never visited one—they'd been beneath her parents' notice, and Alain had been critical of anything that put one in contact with ordinary people.

She thought the store was wonderful.

"What sorts of things does your sister like?" she asked as they wandered deeper inside.

"Um. Well, she and my mother are collaborating on a fascinating potassium alloy—"

"Honestly, why did I even ask?" she muttered, turning and marching towards a nearby counter. "Perfume it is."

Sam laughed behind her, and the sound trickled into her blood like brandy, warming her from the inside out. The grim news of the morning, the leaden weight of the last several days, lifted a few inches, and she smiled. She hadn't been shopping in ages. This could be . . . fun.

And it was. They started at the perfume counter, where Alva selected one of the scents that had been all the rage in Paris when she'd left. From there they wandered past counters of jewelry and gloves, whole rooms of hats, entire stores of fabrics. She pointed him towards a pair of lusciously soft kid gloves, and he bought two pairs, one for Maggie and one for his mother. He selected a scarf in a bright blue pattern he liked for himself, and one he thought Benedict might like, and even a pair of slippers for his father. The man shopped like he thought—in all directions, but to great effect.

Eventually they collapsed, surrounded by parcels, at a table in the store's restaurant.

"Your sister is very lucky in her choice of brothers," Alva said, taking a welcome sip of delicately scented tea. "You've bought most of the store."

"She's a pretty good sister," he said, his expression turning fond. "She's a lot younger than Benedict and I—I was twelve when she was born. All lungs and hair. Not so different from now, come to think of it."

"She has you wrapped around her little finger," Alva said.

"Completely," Sam said, grinning back at her. "The little tyrant."

"What's it like?" Alva said, blurting out the words before she realized how desperate they sounded. She tried to cover. "I mean, having such a close-knit family."

"It's wonderful," he said, not even seeming to notice her awkwardness. "You should see us around Christmas. My father gets really excited about a month beforehand, right after Thanksgiving. He starts hauling in decorations, some of which he only took down about two months before, and my mother gets mad because he insists on decorating in the labs, too, and invariably ends up disturbing some *very important* pile of materials, and after, Maggie usually blows something up, although, to be fair, that's not actually a Christmas-specific activity." He chuckled to himself, obviously replaying holidays past.

"I'm starting to think you're lagging behind your family in terms of explosions," Alva said.

"Oh, the women are far and away the worst offenders," he said, a distinct tone of envy in his voice. "It's because they work with chemicals the most—my inventions are usually more likely to only start fires, without an exciting explosion."

"Tragic," she said. "A mere fire is nothing without an explosion."

He nodded vigorously, and even more vigorously began to apply himself to the large slab of chocolate cake a waitress placed in front of him.

"Did you even order that?" Alva turned to look at the young waitress, who was clustered with two other girls, giggling and staring at Sam.

"Didn't I?"

"Never mind," she said, chalking it up to the perks of being very handsome and very famous. "Tell me more about Christmas."

"Well, it's really a pagan holiday at bottom, but several centuries ago the Christians—"

"Hilarious."

He smiled and took another enormous bite of cake. "Oh, you know. Lots of food, lots of games, lots of presents. A toasty fire. Popcorn. A really big tree that my father and brother and I almost kill ourselves bringing in."

"It sounds perfect," she said.

"It is." A final bite cleared the plate, leaving Alva blinking in astonishment. "What about you? Any particularly lovely Christmas memories?"

She took another sip of tea, trying to remember. "I had a wonderful governess for a couple of years when I was a child. She was young, and pretty, and she liked me, which was fairly unusual. Her family lived in the city, so she'd go home for Christmas in the morning but be back by the afternoon, after our stuffy family Christmas was over, and she'd bring me leftovers from her family and we'd sit in the nursery and stuff ourselves. Sometimes I still think of her, and wonder what she's doing now."

"What happened to her?"

"She was dismissed. According to my parents, she was allowing me an unbecoming amount of freedom." *And enough reminiscing.* "They have a whole books section over there," Alva said. "Shall we?"

Sam looked at her with that disturbing focus he sometimes had, as if he knew she was changing the subject, and was allowing it, but also making a note of the exact date, time, and subject in question so he could return to the matter later. His scientist gaze, collating data. She forced herself to meet his eyes pleasantly and calmly, and soon he rose, coming around to her side and putting his hand on the small of her back. It was a polite gesture, but she swore she could feel the heat and strength of him through all her layers of silk and cotton.

She didn't want to talk about her family, but she felt almost a compulsion to know more about his. A craving. His love for them was a tangible thing, uncomplicated and unquestioning in its solidity. "Solidity" wasn't the right word; it was more than solid—unbreakable, water rather than rock. It was all around him, it held him up, flowing unendingly between them.

"What about Henry?" she asked. "He said you were like his second family, growing up."

"My mother says Henry is her fourth child," Sam said. "He—some of this is not really mine to talk about. But he came into our lives when he was ten, and he's my brother in every way that matters."

Alva could imagine a variety of circumstances leading to such an arrangement, and none of them were pleasant. "He's protective of you," she said. "It's lovely."

Sam grinned. "I guess we're all protective of one another," he said. "Henry's way of being protective involves a law degree, a significant amount of charm, and an ability to convince almost anybody of almost anything. Benedict, on the other hand, will wither his opponent with a look and a well-chosen word."

"I assume Maggie will simply blow her opponent up."

"Or talk to them about French fashions for two hours, which is significantly worse," Sam said broodingly, with the air of a man who had been subjected to this particular torture more times than he could count. "Or sometimes she pinches."

Alva snickered.

"Oh yes, laugh all you like," he said darkly. "But she *twists*, you see."

They reached the book section, an elegantly laid-out space with dark wooden shelves and a selection of beautiful tomes laid out on display. She crossed to a particularly lovely book, bound in embossed burgundy leather, and opened it. "*The Principles of Interior Decoration*," she said. "By Edna Bellingham. This was brought out by my publishing firm last year."

Sam looked over her shoulder. His nearness had all her senses singing. "Nice organization," he said.

"It is," she agreed. "It's why I inquired with them. But this is aimed at a fairly exclusive audience—it's geared towards society women, and the price matches it. This leather binding is beautiful, but middle-class women probably can't afford it. Or at least not easily. Mine's going to be brought out in cloth binding, with a paper cover over it."

"Less fancy, more accessible."

"Exactly."

He leaned against the shelves, facing her. "You know, you're the first published author I've ever met."

She looked at him skeptically. "Sam, everyone in your family is a published author. And I'm not published yet."

"You will be," he said. "And scientific papers in journals aren't the same. You're going to have a *binding*."

Alva rolled her eyes and closed the book. "It's amazing, the excuses you find to think well of me."

He looked at her like *she* was the odd one. "Alva, three days ago I proclaimed my undying love and devotion to you and asked you to marry me. I simply cannot fathom why you are so constantly surprised by the height of my esteem for you."

She opened her mouth. Shut it. Looked around the book section to make sure no one had overheard them. Opened her mouth again, and of all the things she should have said, the one to come out of her mouth was: "You never said undying."

"It was implied by the whole marriage thing. Oh, look, here's a whole book on trains!"

The sun was sinking towards the horizon when they stepped back out onto the sidewalk, a florid, hazy orange thing painting the Manhattan streets in delicate, wispy light. The packages—and there had been a lot of packages—had been sent on to the hotel.

"Cab or walk?" Sam asked.

She hadn't dressed for walking. She'd chosen a Worth silk day dress with a close-fitted jacket and full skirt. The fabric of the jacket was particularly exquisite—rich blue and gold in a pattern that reminded her of dragon scales, over a jade green skirt. She'd told herself at the time she wasn't dressing for Sam—after all, he preferred her in red—but of course the look of admiration he'd given her that morning in the hotel lobby had called her bluff. It *was* a rather flattering dress, but silk was far too delicate a fabric to be walking out on the dirty Manhattan streets and far too thin to be outside in the cold in, even under her coat. The sensible choice would be to return to the hotel by cab, after which they would go to their separate rooms and the evening would be over. . . .

"Walk," Alva said, even as she berated herself. He was becoming a drug to her—he brought light, even to her darkest moments. She craved this light, despite how dangerous it would be to depend on it. But the choice had already been made, and he'd taken her arm, the solid length of his body pressed to her side, and once more she allowed her rational side to be overruled.

Two blocks later and they were in yet another part of the city she didn't recognize. She let herself gawk, like a country mouse just off the train. In a way she was, she thought, smiling to herself. This city *was* new to her. For her whole life New York had been in a frantic state of creation and re-creation, and even putting aside the narrowness of her childhood world, twelve years was a long time to be away.

It was the beginning of the end of the day, and men were walking home to their families, and couples were walking arm in arm towards their evening plans. She luxuriated in the warmth of Sam's body next to hers and imagined she was one of those women, walking next to her sweetheart, marveling at this wonderful, terrible, ambitious city.

"Alva?" Sam's voice had a chuckle in it, and she realized it wasn't the first time he'd spoken.

"I beg your pardon," she said. "I didn't hear you."

"Out with the fairies, that's what my grandmother would say."

She smiled. "Fairies of iron and steel, then. I was thinking how much the city has changed, since I've been away. I suppose

I've been making us look like easy marks." She ran her eyes up and down his tall, solid body. "Or maybe not so easy."

Sam's expression was pure masculine satisfaction. "I can take off this coat if it would help you ogle me better."

"I wasn't *ogling*," she said, grateful he couldn't see the scenario jumping deliciously into her mind. "I was merely acknowledging that you're large enough to warn off any would-be muggers."

"Oh, my darling girl," he said, and she swore he was leering simply for the pure joy of it, "I'm large enough for all sorts of things."

She rolled her eyes. "Of course, if the robbers were to get close enough, they would eventually realize you're more likely to help them design new pickpocketing apparatus than fight them off."

"I would certainly fight them off—what do you mean, *new* pickpocketing apparatus? Do they really have existing apparatus? All right, I would fight them off *first*, and when they were lying helpless on the ground I would ask them about their apparatus. . . ." He paused. "And now I've said 'apparatus' so many times it sounds like I'm referring to something else entirely. I'll say 'equipment' instead. No, that has hidden depths as well. I think I'll just abandon the attempt. Why houses?"

"What?"

"Is what I was asking you while you were out with the fairies. Why decorating houses?"

She shrugged. "I'm good at it," she said. "And I needed the money."

"All right," he said.

She looked at him suspiciously, but he seemed content to let the subject drop. As they walked, the wrongness of her statement pressed against her, like a little betrayal. She didn't owe him her whole soul, she argued. It had been the truth, as far as it went.

She'd made a habit of not over-sharing, and this was such a tiny thing.

The omission wasn't a betrayal of him, she realized suddenly. It was a betrayal of herself.

"I like things to be beautiful. And . . . people's homes, where they live, they should . . . nurture. It doesn't mean they have to be fancy, or large. I've seen it in a set of curtains in a French cottage, or a flower box. My first flat in Montmartre, it was only a few rooms." She stopped, waiting for the pain that usually accompanied the memory of her little apartment. She'd left it shortly after the night of the ill-fated dinner party, unable to walk past the emerald wallpaper without remembering. But this time, she remembered the first buds of freedom she had planted there. How much she had liked that wallpaper. She'd chosen it with her friend Amelie, her neighbor and the first of the friends who had embraced her there so easily.

Amelie was a dancer at the Paris Opera Ballet, a tall, graceful woman with a mane of auburn hair, a kind smile, and eyes that turned wary when she thought no one was looking. There was a story there, as with so many of Montmartre's residents, but unlike many of her neighbors Amelie seemed to prefer to keep it to herself.

One evening, shortly after Alva had moved in, she'd simply arrived at Alva's door, a bottle of whiskey dangling from her elegant fingers. She'd crossed Alva's sitting room, pulled the heavy drapes apart to let in the soft light of the streetlamps, and sat down on a chair by the window. There she'd proceeded to stare into the night, apparently lost in thought, before speaking.

"It's bad," she'd said eventually. "But you're still here. Tonight we'll numb the pain. Tomorrow you'll go for a walk outside. And the next day, it will be a little better."

And for a few months, she'd been right.

"Different fairies, this time, I think."

Sam's warm voice brought her back. "Memories," she said, her lips curling. "Good ones." She shook her head, gently, not to throw the thoughts away but simply to settle them.

"You're talking about healing," he said, and there was that look in his eye again, the one that said he saw too much. "Restoration. Not just of houses. Of people."

Uncomfortable, she frowned. "You make too much of it."

"Alva," he said, and in his tone there was such a well of understanding she had to look away, a lump of threatening tears swelling in her throat. She took a deep breath, staring at the unfamiliar buildings lining the street.

"Where are we? I don't remember this on the way back to the hotel."

"I was following you," he said, and they stared at each other.

"Oh dear," she said, the tears vanishing in a burst of laughter. "We could be anywhere."

She looked around, trying to recognize something. They couldn't be so far from the hotel, they hadn't walked long, but everything was so new. . . . She saw the corner of a familiar building about a block away and crooked her head. "I might recognize that. Let's see."

The houses grew grander as they walked towards the building, all bearing an unmistakable sign of newness: they were clean. Alva was still trying to puzzle out where she and Sam might be when they reached the corner she'd seen and turned it—suddenly she knew.

She was home.

CHAPTER TWENTY-THREE

"Oh," Alva said, a breath more than a word. She'd stopped abruptly, one step behind him, although their arms were still entwined. They were surrounded by large, opulent houses, mostly brownstones, but a few newer ones in different materials.

"Alva?" Sam asked, not liking the sudden emptiness of her expression.

She cleared her throat. "We're on Thirty-fourth," she said. "That's Fifth Avenue, right there. I must have gotten turned around on our walk—I was here a few weeks ago, but we . . . we drove up Fifth. . . ."

She wandered away from him, turning slowly. "I didn't really look around," she said. "That marble thing across from the Astors', she must be furious. It looks more like a Napoleonic monument than a home."

"Alva, where are we?"

"This is where I grew up," she said absently. "See, Mrs. Astor built first, and the people who wanted to be like the Astors built as close to them as they could. My parents have always wanted to be like the Astors."

Sam didn't know who Mrs. Astor was, but he could fill in the blanks.

"You don't talk about your parents much," he said cautiously. "You visited them when you were in town?"

"Mmm," she said, which Sam took for a yes. There was still so much he didn't know about her, so much he had to guess at.

"Which one is theirs?"

"This one," she said, gesturing to a wide three-story brownstone with some sort of decorative white edging.

"And which was your window?"

"Second story, farthest to the right. But I don't think your habit of late-night calling would be quite so tolerated here." She smiled a little but slipped away, moving closer to the house. She stopped by a large tree, empty of leaves and dusted with snow. "This was only a sapling when we moved here. I was . . . ten, maybe. It grew up with me. I used to stare at it out of my window."

There was sweetness in the words but loneliness and wistfulness, too, and Sam pictured a ten-year-old girl, staring outside and wishing for something that didn't come. Alva may not have spoken much about her parents directly, but he remembered her comment about families who would discard their children rather than lose social standing, and he thought about the kind of parents who would let a monster like Alain Webster marry their seventeen-year-old daughter and take her an ocean away, and the anger that had been sweeping over him ever since the night in Alva's bedroom poked its head up again and growled.

The door to the brownstone opened, and Alva froze. A footman walked out, followed by a man and woman, dressed in layers of finery. The man was of medium height, with thin hair on the sides showing underneath his hat and a belly even his heavy coat couldn't disguise. The woman . . . the woman looked like Alva.

Sam heard Alva's intake of breath, saw her take one quick step forward, as well as the second her mother noticed her. The woman paused, a perfect statue of Alva in twenty years, but with none of Alva's warmth or humor or intelligence. Just the features, with nothing familiar or kind underneath. Alva had stopped breathing next to him.

The moment froze in time. The two women staring at each other, years of things Sam didn't understand moving between them. The look on the older woman's face: surprise, disgust, anger, and, underlying all of it, fear. He thought of his own mother, warm and loving and brilliant and funny, and his stomach soured. Today was a day for knowing things he'd been too lucky to know of before.

It was probably less than a second before the woman moved, gesturing a maid towards her. She spoke briefly into the girl's ear and, without looking at her daughter again, followed her husband into the waiting carriage.

Alva let out a rush of breath as the maid walked towards them. Sam frowned, staring at the carriage, which had yet to move. Were they not going to greet their own daughter?

The maid was young, probably only sixteen. She was red-faced with embarrassment, her blond hair tucked neatly away.

"Here we go," Alva whispered, but there was no outward emotion on her face.

"Mrs. Webster," the girl began when she reached them, her words coming out flat and separate, like she wanted them as far away from herself as possible. "Mrs. Rensselaer wishes me to remind you that she has no interest in seeing you and your repeated attempts to contact her only embarrass yourself and her."

Sam's jaw dropped.

"I wasn't . . ." Alva paused and took a breath. "It doesn't matter. Tell Mrs. Rensselaer I won't embarrass her in this way again."

The maid curtsied and turned to leave.

"Now wait just a minute," Sam said, his simmering anger bursting to a boil. "That woman is your mother, right?"

Alva nodded curtly.

"Like hell she's going to talk to you this way," he said, and started towards the carriage.

"Sam!" Alva hurried after him, yanking on his arm. The maid stood stock still, with her mouth open. "Sam, no."

"*You*, embarrass *her*? No. It's enough." He pulled on his arm to free it, but she clung on stubbornly.

"Sam, you'll make it worse," she said, a pleading note in her voice that brought a sick, nauseous edge to his fury. "It is how it is. I'm sorry you had to see it, but please don't involve yourself."

"Alva," he said, turning fully to face her. "It's already worse. She has no right to say that to you—to anyone, but especially not to you." He wanted to say because she was the woman's flesh and blood, but it was so much more. No one had a right to treat the woman he loved this way, and they had. But he was damned if he was going to sit by and let them continue.

"It won't make any difference," she said. "You can't . . . you can't yell her into loving me, Sam. I wish you could, but you can't."

That made him pause. Because underneath all Alva's firmness and strength and matter-of-factness, he heard the ten-year-old girl who was looking out her window and wishing.

"I don't want a scene," she pleaded. "Please."

He looked down at her and saw her distress and realized his fury, no matter how righteous, would only hurt her more. He closed his eyes, unused to what to do with so much anger, but rigidly drawing it back inside. "Your father is Thomas Rensselaer," he said, opening his eyes. "He's part of the Rensselaer Johnson De Vries investment consortium."

Alva's eyebrows drew together in confusion. "How on earth do you know that?"

"Research. And sometimes I listen to Henry more than he thinks I do. The Rensselaer Johnson De Vries investment consortium wants very much to invest in several of our new municipal lighting projects."

"Sam . . ."

He nodded to himself. It wasn't as good as yelling at someone, but it was better than nothing. It was the sort of thing Henry would do, and Henry was as vicious as a ferret when provoked. Sam turned to the maid.

"My name is Professor Samuel Moore," he said, and judging by the girl's startled expression, she knew who he was. "Please convey my greetings to Mr. and Mrs. Rensselaer, and say that until I witnessed their appalling behavior towards their only daughter I was inclined to favor Mr. Rensselaer's interest in my latest project. Not because I care one way or another about their proposal, mind, but because I have a great respect for Mrs. Webster. Now, however, I have decided to reject their offer, and all others that follow." He paused and thought some more. "For that matter, they probably shouldn't bother trying with any of my family. Or my family's friends in the scientific community. And we have a *lot* of friends." He frowned. "That's rather a lot; do you think you can remember it all?"

The maid gave a tiny, tiny smile, so small he wouldn't have been able to see it if he hadn't been within a few feet of her. "Oh yes," she said. "I have a very good memory." She turned to walk away.

Alva stared at him. "Wait!" she said, still watching him.

"Now who's yelling wait?" he murmured.

The maid turned around.

"What's your name?" Alva asked.

"Ingrid," she said, giving a small bob.

"Ingrid, do you like working for my mother?" When the girl hesitated, Alva's lips curled into a rueful smile. "I wouldn't worry about me tattling to her," she said.

Ingrid nodded. "No," she said. "She's difficult to please, she refuses our half days, and when she's mad she's cruel. But I have a younger sister and our parents are dead, so . . ."

"Any job is better than an almshouse or worse," Alva finished.

"Yes."

"How old is your sister?

"Nine years old, ma'am."

"And are you particularly attached to the city, or do you think your sister could grow accustomed to country air?"

Ingrid blinked, and a sort of terrified excitement began to steal over her face. "We could both become very accustomed, ma'am," she said, her voice hoarse.

"It's settled, then. Give your proper notice here and come to Hyde Park to work for me."

"You'd do that, after the messages I've had to give to you?"

"On the contrary, it shows you have quite a bit of backbone." The girl straightened, as if Alva noticing reminded her it might be true. "Sam, I need your notebook. And a pen."

He produced both after a bit of searching—Alva didn't even flinch when he put the snail shell he'd found earlier into her palm for safekeeping—and she wrote down her address and tore the page out, adding to it a bill she pulled from her wallet. "In case she lets you go earlier than expected, or withholds your final wages," she said. "And to help with the travel. I'll expect to see you in about a month?"

Ingrid nodded quickly, slipping the paper and money into her apron. "I don't know what to say. Thank you. Now I'll really enjoy giving the message to them." She turned and walked back to the carriage.

Alva laughed, and the sound warmed Sam's very bones. "That was . . . surprisingly fun," she said.

"You've given her hope," he said.

She rolled her eyes. "She's smart and she deserved it," she said. "And . . . you inspired me." She slipped her arm in his and they began to stroll towards Fifth Avenue, away from the still-waiting carriage and the people within.

"What do you mean?"

"I mean, you wanted to fight for me. You *did* fight for me. But you reminded me that I could fight for myself, too."

He started to grin. "So what you're saying is, yes, you're giving the girl a better life, and yes, it's because she's smart and you like her, but *also* you're stealing her from your mother, thus . . . giving her a sort of metaphorical black eye."

"Good help is hard to find," Alva said.

"And I thought I was being strategic," he said. "I'm in awe."

She chuckled again, but as they walked through the twilight, the traffic and noise of Fifth Avenue racketing about them, her face lost some of its humor. "I wish you hadn't seen that," she said. "Obviously, the relationship between me and my parents is complicated."

"It doesn't seem complicated," he said. "Of all the children on this earth, they got you, and instead of realizing they've experienced a fucking miracle they decide to throw you out with the refuse. Seems simple, actually. Horrifying, appalling, dumb as rocks, but simple."

"I strongly doubt they would think of me as a miracle," Alva said. "A curse, perhaps. The scandal after my separation was truly enormous, you know. They managed to cover up the reality behind my sudden wedding, but if they hadn't distanced themselves after Paris they probably would have been cast out of society, too."

He stopped and stared. "And?"

"And . . . what do you mean?"

"I mean, what would have been so terrible about that? If it's a choice between your child and a bunch of rich people throwing parties . . ." He shook his head. "No. That's not a choice. There's no choice there. You pick your child."

"You know, for someone who must be quite wealthy himself, you certainly don't think much of the rich."

"Don't change the subject, and don't defend them. *You're* the wronged party here, can't you see? You are brilliant, and warm, and kind, and funny, and god knows brave, and they are fools if they can't see it. And I know that can't make up for how they've treated you, but I want you to know . . . I want you to know, you aren't how they see you. You *are* a miracle. And I'm not the only person who knows that."

Her eyes flew to his. "You—I—you overwhelm me. I don't know what to say. Thank you, for all you've said and done today."

Her gratitude sat poorly, but she seemed incredibly tired next to him, like the weight of the whole day had suddenly landed on her shoulders. Instead he lightened the mood. "Well, let's not forget you saved me from being murdered by my sister today," he said.

It took a beat, but thank the stars, she laughed. "We'll call it even, then."

"We'll call it even."

CHAPTER TWENTY-FOUR

Alva stood in the hallway—thick, lush carpeting at odds with the pattern of the wallpaper, gilt and crystal sconces, the overpowering smell of too many lilies taken out of season—and stared at the door. It was, in one sense, an insignificant door: pine, painted white, with a doorknob that could doubtless be seen on any one of a thousand doors in New York City. In another, more personal and dramatic sense, it was one of the most important doors Alva had ever encountered.

If she knocked on it, Sam would answer. And if Sam answered, the same overwhelming emotion that had propelled her out of her room and down two floors to stand in this particular hallway would propel her into his room, and into his arms, and almost certainly into his bed.

She definitely shouldn't knock. She'd made her position regarding a romantic relationship very clear, and to knock on this door would only muddy the waters.

The problem was . . . The problem was he was wonderful.

There was a thrilling, sickening feeling in her chest, as though her core was trying to hurl itself towards him, held back only by bone and muscle.

Why shouldn't she knock on the door? Why couldn't she have this, when she wanted it—him—so badly?

Oh, she wasn't thinking straight. On the one hand, there were any number of good reasons she shouldn't—but, on the other hand, there were good reasons she should. His actions earlier in the afternoon, for one: the way he'd stood up for her, tried to protect her. The things he'd said on the way home, the way he'd deftly shifted from sincerity to absurdity to make her laugh. He'd been . . . on her side.

That wasn't something she could take for granted.

There was his righteous anger, too, the way he'd railed that morning against an unkind and unjust world, because by doing so he thought he could make it a little bit better. She loved his kindness and his fury, and the way they weren't two separate emotions at all.

She loved . . .

She knocked on the door.

Several heartbeats passed before he answered, his jacket off and his white shirt unbuttoned at the throat. His hands were ink stained and his expression slightly absent.

"You're working," Alva said. She hadn't considered that he might be busy, and the doubt pried open a large enough crack for a trickle of embarrassment.

"Mmm," he agreed, and pulled her into the room. "The question is, would water be a more elegant cooling solution?"

He sat her down on the edge of his bed, which was covered entirely by clothing and the mysterious bits and bobs that always floated in his orbit.

"I'll come back," she said, standing, but he waved an impatient hand at her, clearly instructing her to *sit back down and stop making noise,* so she shrugged and did.

After two days of being inhabited by Sam, the room had begun to look like one of Maggie's explosions, which wasn't really any worse than its original design, given that the hotel had apparently been decorated by a tapestry-addicted toddler with a Midas delusion. Alva played her mental editing game, subtracting this and that, adding architectural detailing around the windows to highlight the beautiful Manhattan view.

Once she had rearranged the room to, if not her satisfaction, at least the best she could do with the materials she'd been given, her gaze drifted back to Sam. His hair curled over the back of his collar, the lack of coat highlighting the broadness of his shoulders and the strength of his back. She thought about running her hands over the muscles there, playing with the fringe of hair where it skimmed his neck, moving lower to investigate the narrowness of his waist and the strength of his thighs. . . .

She took a calming gulp of air and reached for her reticule, rummaging through it until she found her notebook. There was no telling when he would surface, and during her mental edit she'd come up with a couple clever quips she thought would work well in the book. Perhaps it was a little unusual, to come to a man's room and end up getting some work done, but the atmosphere was cozy, the bed was really quite comfortable, and the room provided plenty of grist for her mill. She took off her hat, removed her jacket, scooted up to the pillows, and began to write.

The next time she looked up, the city outside was dark, with twinkling, wavering lights forming constellations of avenues and neighborhoods. There was a fire in the small cast-iron fireplace—one of the few details she'd allowed to stay—and Sam was sprawled in his desk chair, watching her.

She closed her notebook. "Hello."

"Hello," he said, his lips twitching upwards. "You're beautiful."

"You're going to wear that compliment out," she said, but inside she preened.

"You're beautiful, and you're in my room."

"I am," she agreed.

"On my bed."

"You put me here."

"Did I? What a terribly clever fellow I am."

She opened her mouth to say something rude like *You're terrible, at least*, or maybe *You're certainly terribly something*, but nothing came out except a little puff of air. He was looking at her as though she were the most interesting and wonderful person in the entire world. As though he liked her, through and through.

He was the only person who had ever looked at her that way.

If she was going to go through with this, though, there was something she had to establish first.

"You said I had to trust you. Last time we—after we were intimate. I said we should have an affair, and you said you would just wait until I trusted you."

"I remember the battle lines," Sam said, his grin turning a little wry around the edges. "Although now that you're sitting on my bed with an entire article of clothing already off, I'm having trouble remembering why I was so damned adamant about it."

A little bubble of laughter rose in her throat, which made it a lot easier to continue. "I guess I'm here to say that you weren't wrong. I still don't know if I can offer you everything you want, Sam, but I trust you. As much as I can trust anybody, I trust you."

He stared at her for a long while and nodded. "Good enough," he said, standing and swiftly crossing the room to her in two long strides. "Good enough."

Sam pulled her to her feet and kissed her, and it was as though she'd been crossing a desert for days and weeks and *months* and finally he was giving her a drink of water. She sank into his lips like she was coming home, and for a few moments their embrace was about nothing more than meeting those basic needs: nourishing each other, sheltering each other.

"I missed you," she heard herself say, surprised to discover it was true.

"Thank god," Sam said, his hands busying themselves with her blouse. "It would have been depressing if I was the only one."

She laughed, and when he pushed her blouse off her shoulders, picked her up, and tossed her with more haste than style onto the bed her laugh rang out even more, throaty and bright and reckless.

"Mock me all you like, madam," he said, stripping his shirt off with inelegant speed. "You're at my mercy now."

"Oh, I don't know," she said, pushing herself to her knees and trailing one dainty finger down the middle of his bare chest. "It seems to me it's the other way around."

He closed his eyes and groaned as she made her slow progress downwards, until finally her hand was loosening his trousers. "You're right. I admit it. The statement was entirely bravado."

"I thought as much," she said, pulling him onto the bed with her and then pushing him back, straddling his waist with her legs as her skirts pooled around them. "Since we have that established, let me show you what I'm going to do with you."

With one confident motion, she freed him from his trousers, rose up above him, and sank down upon him through the slit in her drawers. He hissed a breath in through his teeth, his eyes going wide and blank. Power surged through her. *She* affected him this way. *She* brought him this pleasure.

Slowly she rose up, lingering at the top of his penis before sinking down once more. "I've thought about doing this," she said, speaking carefully through her own pleasure as she continued the slow, aching rhythm. "Riding you until your completion. Feeling you spasm inside of me."

"When?" His voice was rough, his words choked, and she smiled wider.

"Hmm?"

"When. Did you. Think about it?"

"Oh, lots of times. And it wasn't just this particular position, either." She leaned forward, allowing his hands to free her breasts from her corset, and gasped as he found her nipples.

"Details," he growled.

"Yesterday," she said, closing her eyes to allow more room for sensation. "On the train."

There was a silence, punctuated only by the sound of their breathing. "Alva," Sam said, his voice thick with outrage. "It was a private car. Are you telling me there were *three hours* in which I could have been experiencing this and I didn't even *know*?"

She laughed, breathlessly. "Yes."

"We discussed irrigation," he said.

"Yes."

"And drank tea."

"Yes."

"And played *bridge*."

"Oh yes," she said.

"And the whole time—oh god yes—you were thinking about *this*?"

"Yes! Just there, Sam, oh yes!"

She came around him, her muscles contracting over and over again in a dizzying fall. She'd heard the phrase "seeing stars" before; she hadn't realized it was meant literally.

"Darling," Sam whispered, letting his fingers play over Alva's cheekbones before she leaned down and kissed him, a deep, gorgeous kiss that did nothing for his restraint. "My darling girl, if I don't put protection on this second—"

"Oh, I did bring some," she said, blinking unfocused eyes. "Somewhere."

"You'll think I'm presumptuous," he said, reaching into his trouser pocket and pulling out an envelope. "But I've become rather more prepared in the last week."

"Thank god for men who come prepared," she said, lifting up just long enough for him to roll on a rubber. Wrapping an arm around her waist, he shifted them both so she was on her back, her full skirt bunched up around her. Quickly he pulled down her drawers, hoping she'd forgive his lack of finesse, and plunged inside her.

He took her almost desperately, possessing her without elegance or restraint. They moved in a frenzy, hands everywhere, mouths everywhere, in a sweaty, frantic tangle. When he came inside of her, his body coming apart in a mind-erasing explosion, it could have been a minute or an hour later.

He made to move off of her, but she tightened her legs around him and pulled him close.

"I'm going to crush you," he mumbled, and when her legs showed no sign of loosening he rolled them both over, so she was resting on his chest.

As the sensual haze cleared from his mind, it was replaced by a giddy, sparkling feeling, like sunshine on fresh snow. Suddenly life had never been so good. Everything was going to work out—it had to.

He shifted underneath Alva, grinning when she muttered angrily and resettled firmly atop him.

"Alva," he whispered.

"Mmm."

"Alva!"

"You can't possibly be ready again," she said, her voice muffled by his chest.

"I absolutely could be," he said, defending his masculine pride, "but that's not what this is about."

"Uh-huh."

"Not everything's about that," he said in angelic tones. "You have a particularly filthy mind."

"How lovely that must be for you." She opened one eye. "Sam?"

"Yes?"

"Why are we talking?"

"Because we have to get up."

The eye shut, and she resettled once more. "You're having one of your brain fevers," she said. "Rest quietly and it'll go away."

He squinted down at her, but she seemed to have gone back to sleep.

"All right," he said, "but remember, you left me no choice."

"Wha—Sam! Put me down!"

"In a minute," he said, scooping her fully into his arms, swinging his legs out of bed, and standing up. "There, now you can go down."

She narrowed her eyes at him, her breasts still unconfined, her hair long and loose, and he took time to simply drink her in. A hint of worry shivered into his mind; he pushed it away. Everything was going to be fine. She trusted him—it was already so much more than they'd had before. He loved her, and he thought she loved him. What more could they need?

"We got up." She shoved her hair out of her eyes and put her hands at her waist. "Why did we get up?"

"Ah." He smiled at her. "Because this is too perfect to waste.

We must celebrate! We must dance and revel! We must howl at the moon!"

She lifted her eyebrows, biting her bottom lip as though she could stop it from curving. "Because we're pagans? Or possibly wolves?"

"Because we like each other," he said, drawing her close to him and looking in her eyes. "And that's worth all the celebrations in the world."

She looked back at him, and if he was being optimistic, which he almost always was, he would have said her expression softened. "All right," she said. "What are we going to do?"

"What are we going to do," he repeated. "What are we going to—Ah-hah! We are going out to dinner."

He looked around for her blouse, finding it crumpled on the floor by the fireplace, and retrieved it. "There's a place not far from here," he said, opening the garment and placing Alva's arms into it. "I went there while I was staying here researching Liefdehuis. It's run by this Italian grandmother—"

She batted his hands away from the blouse and turned around to arrange herself. "I've never had Italian food," she said.

"You never visited Italy while you were on the Continent?" he asked, searching for his shirt.

"Alain despised the Italians," she said. "'A bunch of layabouts who want something for nothing,' according to him. We were mostly in Paris, although we relocated to London during the Siege and the Commune."

Sam was getting used to the sudden rage that arose every time she let drop some detail of her married life. "I am nearly certain you'll like it," he said. "And if you don't, we'll simply go from restaurant to restaurant until we find something you do."

She smiled at him while she buttoned her jacket. "How extravagant," she said. "But you'll find I'm in a terribly easy-to-please mood."

Because she was charming, and because she was beautiful, and because he loved her, he kissed her—a happy kiss, with both parties smiling. As he pulled away he touched her nose gently with his finger and grabbed her hand.

"Come on!" he said, pulling her towards the door. "We have to hurry. There's a whole city out there we need to see!"

"My hair's a mess," she said, laughing as he pushed her into the hallway and closed the door behind them.

"We don't have time for hair-related quibbles," he said, pretending impatience. "You must simply learn to transcend these narrow, societally imposed standards of beauty."

"Ah, as you have," she said as they hurried down the stairs.

"Precisely."

He strode through the lobby without letting go of her hand, conscious of nothing but the thrill of her skin touching his and the glistening headiness of the moment. When they reached the double doors, pushing them open together, the sharp winter air filled his lungs. He took a deep breath, reveling in the feeling of health and rightness that pervaded him, and kissed her. It was getting to be a habit, this kissing Alva business. The little worry flickered in and out.

The restaurant was only a few blocks away, but in a far less fashionable and far more comfortable part of town. It was squashed cozily between a cobbler and a bakery, no more than ten feet wide, its lights spilling merrily onto the sidewalk. Judging by the full tables at the windows, dinner was already in full swing, and they could hear snatches of conversation and laughter as they approached.

Inside was warm and loud and very busy, which was especially wonderful because it meant Alva had to stand very close to him. He put an arm around her waist and snugged her even closer.

"Professor!" Mrs. Russo had spied him from across the restaurant and was making her way with expert haste through the crowd. She was a plump, dark-haired woman, well into her sixties and quite handsome. "You have returned to us."

"I've been out of town," he said, kissing the hand she held out to him. "Mrs. Russo, this is Mrs. Alva Webster."

If Mrs. Russo recognized the name, she gave no sign of it, simply smiling at Alva and shaking her hand. "Welcome, welcome. You shall follow me, and we shall give you a magnificent meal."

"She will, too," Sam said in Alva's ear as they weaved through the tables behind Mrs. Russo.

"I imagine that woman can do anything she says she can," Alva whispered back as they arrived at a small corner table occupied by two darkly handsome youths. Mrs. Russo burst forth in Italian, and after significant finger-pointing and back-and-forth the two young men shoved away from the table and slouched towards the kitchens.

"Two of my grandsons," Mrs. Russo explained. "I've sent them to work in the kitchens, where they will pretend to work and flirt with the girl doing dishes. Youth." While she spoke, she cleared the table of the unfortunate grandsons' half-eaten plates of food. "There, sit and enjoy."

"The woman kept me alive when I was staying in New York before," Sam said, reaching across the table to play delicately with Alva's hand. "I would have starved to death without her lasagna."

"It seems to me you have an entire army of women trying to feed you," Alva said. "I can't go anywhere with you but you're having cookies or cake or sandwiches thrust in front of you."

"I live on the kindness of others," he said, adopting a woebegone expression.

"Uh-huh," she said, raising an eyebrow as Mrs. Russo returned with some buttery, crusty bread and a bottle of earthy red wine.

"This is delicious," Alva said blissfully. "It may be the best bread I've ever eaten."

"It's the garlic," Sam said. "I swear I dream about this bread sometimes."

She smiled at him, and he thought he'd dream about this now, too.

"Tell me more about your family," she said.

"Surely you're sick of hearing about them," he replied, grinning at her.

"I don't know if I ever could be," she said. "They're like . . . they're like a fairy tale, to me."

"Don't tell them that," he said, affecting horror. "They'll be insufferable. All right. You know Benedict's a doctor? He's starting this new institute, for government-funded brain research. Not even thirty years old yet, and they picked him out of all the other medical scientists to head it."

"You're proud of him," she said, and he wondered if he'd ever seen her look happier.

"Very, but again, don't tell him."

"And your sister? Does she want to be like your mother when she grows up? It's so uncommon, to hear about a woman scientist."

"I didn't really understand that until I left home," he said. "Growing up it seemed perfectly normal. Experimentation was just . . . what we did, all of us. It wasn't until I started traveling on my own that I realized how prejudiced people are. I don't think Maggie knows what she wants to do yet, though. Right now it vacillates between being a famous chemist and being the head of a famous fashion house."

"So long as it involves fame," Alva said.

"It does seem to be an important factor," Sam admitted, and they both laughed.

Mrs. Russo returned with a full platter of heavenly-smelling dishes, placing them on the table so there was barely an inch left anywhere on the surface. "Enjoy," she said, and hurried away to scold a nearby waiter.

"I don't understand what this is," Alva said, staring down at a plate of spaghetti. "How do I eat it?"

"You twirl it," he said, picking up his fork and demonstrating.

"It seems very risky," she said.

"Ah, but what is life without risk?"

She rolled her eyes towards the ceiling, a classic Alva gesture he was beginning to treasure, but she twirled the spaghetti anyway. He could see the instant the sauce touched her tongue.

"It's heaven," she said.

Staring back at her glowing face, he had to agree.

CHAPTER TWENTY-FIVE

Alva looked out her window as the train pulled into the Hyde Park station. The sky was a dull gray, the ground muddy underneath a spotty layer of churned snow—a dreary scene that made her loath to leave the cozy train car. Beyond the window lay ghosts and a vindictive brother-in-law and money problems and looming publishing deadlines; but in here, at least for a few more minutes, she was in a world that allowed her to sit quietly in the arms of her lover, leaning back against his chest while he played with a tendril of her hair.

The train came to a full stop, a final jolt marking the end of her delicious bubble. They were back, and she didn't know what came next.

"We didn't talk about what the plan was for the ghost—for Rose," she corrected herself. "We should decide our next step."

"I've been thinking about it," Sam said, standing and pulling down their luggage. "We should try talking to her, since we know who she is. She's been hidden away, in one way or another, for almost her entire existence. Let's try treating her like a person, and see what comes of it."

"A very Sam-like plan," Alva said, smiling at him as they made their way off the train. "All right. Shall we try this afternoon? I need to stop at the house for an hour or so to freshen up, but I could meet you at Liefdehuis after."

"Excellent. That'll give me time to make a few adjustments to some of my equipment—I had a few ideas for improvements while we were in the city."

They stepped down onto the train platform, and the uncertainty in Alva's chest intensified. She could see Liza waiting for her a few yards away, flirting with one of the local boys to pass the time. Suddenly the words in her head seemed clumsy; her very stride became awkward.

"All right," she said again. "Till this afternoon."

She made to turn away, but Sam grabbed her hand. "I know we're in public," he said, pulling her closer. "And I know I probably can't kiss you the way I'd like to. But—if I remember social protocol correctly—I'm allowed to do this."

He brought her hand to his lips, his gaze never leaving hers, and even though the kiss was perfectly ordinary and polite, the expression in his eyes was anything but. She swallowed, heat flooding her cheeks and chest.

"Yes," she said, her voice a little breathy. She cleared her throat. "Quite right."

He grinned at her and nodded. "Until this afternoon, then."

"Yes." She turned around and walked to Liza, not daring to look back at him, since, unlike Sam, she was quite familiar with social protocol and fairly certain that leaping into a man's arms and kissing him until he had no choice but to take you on the spot was not acceptable behavior in a train depot.

"Mrs. Webster," Liza said, straightening from her position leaning against a wall and shooing her companion away with a look.

"Thanks for meeting me," Alva said, forcing herself to concentrate and not to notice Liza's knowing and *extremely* impertinent smirk. "Did everything go well in my absence?"

"Oh, it's been fine, ma'am, just fine," Liza said, taking Alva's bag and leading her to a waiting carriage. "Only Maisie's gone and ended it with Fred—the butcher's boy, ma'am, you remember—and now the butcher's been mysteriously out of the best cuts for the last two days, which means Cook's in a right stew about what she's supposed to cook tonight, and shouting at Maisie to go make it right with Fred, even if she is casting her eye on the new farmhand out at Foster's farm, because Cook says what's a farmhand got to do with supper? Which there ain't much of an answer to, it has to be said, except that he has a lot less to do with it than a butcher's boy does, only Maisie said love was more important than food, and Cook screamed and threw a pan at her, which missed but upset the cat, and then the cat tore up onto the counter and knocked off the sauce Cook'd just finished, and so they were all in a right fuss when I left, ma'am."

Liza took a deep breath, and Alva eyed her with respect. She'd only counted three stops in the entire monologue, which might be a new record.

"Will Cook be able to provide supper tonight?"

"Don't see why not, ma'am," Liza said, her eyes wide. "It's nothing unusual."

Alva tilted her head to one side and tried, very hard, not to laugh. "Good," she said. "I hope the cat has recovered from her shock."

"She was faking, if you ask me," Liza said darkly. "Lickin' her paws when I left, ma'am, lickin' the sauce right off her paws."

The carriage pulled up in front of the house, and as Alva descended she noticed another carriage stopped across the street. Sighing to herself, she straightened her hat, smoothed her skirts, and hoped the caller wasn't for her.

The door opened as they approached, revealing Maisie, the scullery maid of recent fame, looking very nervous. "Ma'am," she whispered, looking fearfully at Liza. "There's a man inside who wants to see you."

"You shouldn't have let anyone in," Liza said, her voice suddenly stern. "Mrs. Webster's only arrived; she'll be wanting rest and a cup of tea, not to deal with some man."

"I'm sorry," Maisie said. "I told him you weren't here, but he insisted on waiting, and pushed his way in and sat down. I didn't know how to stop him."

"It's all right," Alva said, familiar dread beginning to trickle through her veins. "I'll take care of him. Liza, take my case up to my room, please."

Handing her hat to Maisie, Alva patted her hair into place and pulled the sitting room door open.

Alfred lounged gracefully in a chair, one impeccably clad leg crossed over the other. Quickly Alva closed the door behind her.

"What are you doing here?" she demanded, her stomach one tight, painful fist.

"My dear sister," Alfred said, not rising from his chair. "I knew if I only waited a few minutes you'd arrive. Of course, had you informed me you were in the city, you could have spared me a journey."

"I don't owe you any information about my whereabouts," Alva said, slowly taking in his appearance. Though his clothes were perfect, there was something tired and rumpled about his person: his eyes were tinged with blood, his skin pale and marred with light bruising underneath the eyes. If she were a few steps closer, she imagined she'd smell alcohol lingering on his breath.

He looked so like Alain, but here was proof of their difference: Alain would never have appeared in public like this.

"You persist in making this an adversarial relationship,"

Alfred said, his voice smooth and low. "You shouldn't, you know. You wouldn't like me as an adversary."

"I am not the one committing a felony," Alva said. "You *are* my adversary. I don't see the need to clothe the fact in fancy dress."

He made a tutting sound. "You're forgetting murder *is* a felony, dearest. Pot, kettle, and all that."

"I didn't kill your brother."

He shrugged. "I hope we're not going to rehearse this whole tiresome business every time I call on you, Alva. It's tedious. You used to be a better hostess."

"What do you want, Alfred?"

He sighed, as though such boorish behavior was painful to him. "I'm afraid I have to require an additional installment," he said. "Circumstances have changed. Another six hundred will suffice."

Alva stared at him, her back pressed hard against the cold marble of the mantel. Iciness spread from the stone through her back, down her arms, up into her shoulders. With it came clarity.

"You don't have any intention of sticking with our agreement," she said. "What you really intend is I should simply be your banker, at any time you so desire. I imagine you lost quite a lot of money at the gambling tables last night, and what could be easier than hopping a train to get some more? Tedious journey aside, of course."

"I wish you wouldn't speak of our relationship as though it were merely financial," Alfred said, his mouth tilting upwards in a mockery of a smile. "We're family. Family support each other."

"We're *not* family," Alva said. "You're nothing but a leech, a disgusting, violent-minded leech, just like your brother."

"A leech, am I?" Alfred stood, his slim frame still several inches taller than Alva's, and took a step towards her. His breath huffed out rank with last night's drink. "Are you going to try to squash me like you squashed him? I wouldn't try it, *Sister dearest*."

The sitting room door slammed open, making both Alfred and Alva jump.

"What!" Alfred exclaimed before he was picked up by the collar.

"Time for you to go," Sam said, his jaw set.

"Sam, don't—" But it was already too late: he was striding out of the room, half-dragging, half-marching Alfred out with him. She hurried behind them, coming into the hallway to see him throw Alfred—actually *throw him*—out onto the street.

"I'd better be seeing you walking away in the next three seconds," Sam growled. "Or there'll be worse coming to you than a crumpled collar."

"Sam!"

"Alva, stay out of this."

Alfred stood slowly, dusting his trousers and straightening his coat. "I'd advise you to keep your dog on a leash," he said to Alva, keeping well back from Sam. "When you're prepared to be rational, I'll be staying at the Bell and Whistle."

"Alfred," she said, and when he looked at her she simply stared into those beautiful blue eyes, so like his brother's. Trying, one last time, to understand. "What was your mother's first name?"

"What?"

"You heard me."

The expression to cross his face was so familiar it was as though she'd seen another ghost.

"Have you finally gone insane? What does that have to do with anything?"

"Her given name, Alfred. Do you know it or not?" Sam stood

tensely next to her, and though she knew what lay ahead, she took comfort in his nearness.

"Who cares?" Alfred said, and his voice wasn't malicious, merely puzzled, as if he honestly couldn't imagine why it was important. "She was a Baker, from the Philadelphia Bakers. That's what's important. I'm sure her first name is on any number of documents."

"Her name was Helen," Alva said quietly. "It's on her grave, too. Go. Now."

Sam started forward, and Alfred turned and hurried down the street as fast as he could without looking inelegant. She watched him leave, as alien to her as his brother had always been. When he disappeared around the corner, she nodded and turned to Sam. "I thought we were meeting at Liefdehuis," she said.

"I took your hatbox with me," he said. "I was dropping it off when I heard him."

"I see," she said. "How much did you hear?"

"Enough to know you're being blackmailed," he said. "Enough to hear him threaten you."

"Come inside," she said, the cold clinging to her bones. "We're not going to do this on the street."

She led him back into the sitting room, the servants who'd come out to watch the fight hurrying away ahead of her. This time, when she closed the door she made certain it was fully shut.

"Do you understand what he's blackmailing me with?"

"He thinks you murdered your husband. His brother?"

"Yes. And no, I didn't."

"I don't care whether you did or not," Sam said, running one hand through his shaggy hair. "Damn it, though, Alva, you should have told me."

She sat down heavily. She'd never seriously considered telling Sam about Alfred. This was what her life was, violent and complicated. Even if she was able to make something real with Sam—and for the first time in many, many years she thought it possible—the texture of her life would be the same. One way or another she'd never be rid of Alfred: either he'd slowly bleed her dry, year after year, reminding her that she'd never truly be free; or she'd stand up for herself, he'd go to the press, and she'd be haunted by murder accusations for the rest of her life.

The funny thing was that Sam was the one who'd given her the strength to choose between the two options. She'd been about to tell Alfred to go to hell when Sam had stormed in, to go public if he dared. Sam had reminded her—or maybe she'd never even known it before—she was worth standing up and fighting for.

She let her eyes run over him, dwelling on the dear laugh lines at the corners of his eyes, his silly rumpled hair, and his clothes in need of ironing and mending. Samuel Moore was a Good Man, a true-blue, kindhearted, genuine love of a man, and if she let him stay he'd never leave. He'd be at her back at every turn, he'd fight her battles for her if he could, and he'd be dragged through the muck and mire along with her.

Over time, it would take its toll. Maybe he'd get tired of fighting or his kindness and righteous anger would fade. Maybe he'd stay strong, but the public would turn against him and his work would go unseen. She wasn't going to be responsible for that.

"You should care, Sam," she said, hugging her arms to her chest. "That's not you, someone who doesn't care about murder."

"I trust you," he said simply. "And I know you. If you killed him, it was self-defense, and I'm not going to judge you for it."

Alva shook her head without meeting his gaze. He deserved to know the truth. She steeled herself to speak it aloud.

"I didn't," she said. "Which is different from I wouldn't, because there were times when I thought about it. I fantasized about it, planned it a million different ways, knowing I'd never have the courage. God help me, I considered using robbers. When I heard the news, I worried maybe I had done it. Done it and blanked it out afterwards. I had to ask the hotel clerk if I'd left my room the night before."

"What does he have on you?" Sam asked softly.

"I told you I was thinking of divorcing Alain before he died. If I'd had time to go through with it, if I'd divorced him, I would have been left with little more than the money I'd put aside from my columns. He would have retained control of my entire fortune. When he died . . ."

"You benefitted financially," Sam said. "Hardly proof, Alva."

"Not on its own," she said. "But it was suspicious enough timing that before I left I made sure the lawyer wouldn't mention I'd been to see him. I bribed him to stay quiet, but I forgot the clerks, and somehow the information got back to Alfred."

"So you were thinking of divorcing him," Sam said. "Shocking, perhaps, in some circles at least, but a pretty long ways from murder."

"I was in Monte Carlo the night he died," Alva said. "I . . . I'd gone there to see if we could work something out. I thought if we could negotiate a financial settlement that was hugely favorable to him, maybe he'd let me go. Maybe he was tired of all the ugliness."

"That took a lot of courage," Sam said, but Alva shook her head.

"I wasn't brave," she said. "I slunk into town. I was terrified the press would find out I was there, so I stayed under my maiden name. Now it looks like I did it so no one would connect me to his murder. I cornered him at the casino he was gambling at, and we fought. It seems Alfred has found witnesses. Alain was killed later the same night, flush with his winnings from the table. He didn't usually have very good luck, gambling, but I guess that night was different."

She paused, hugging herself tighter. "One of the robbers was probably in the casino, watching him, watching us." She looked away, surprised at the emotion welling in her throat. She'd hated the man, so why did she still feel emotion at his death? "That was the last time I saw him, sitting in the dining room of the casino, dressed in formal wear and backed by an enormous and truly terrible painting of Leda and the Swan. I read the rest from the papers. He left the casino late in the evening. His body was found the next morning, about a block away, a few feet from a refuse pile, with no money and no valuables on it."

"I'm sorry," Sam said.

She shrugged. "He wasn't a good person. I don't mourn him."

"I'm sorry it happened to you. I'm sorry he still hurts you, even after his death."

She stayed silent, looking at the fabric of her skirts.

"But it doesn't add up to murder, Alva."

"I was there," she said. "I was seen with him a few hours before the murder. Our separation was sensational when it happened, and I featured prominently as a sort of voracious, passionate vampire. No one would have trouble believing I killed him, if they were able to place me near the crime, and the money was more than enough motive. I doubt there'd be any formal charges, but the rumor would be enough to finish off my reputation. Book contract, gone. Last contacts in society, gone. Chance for redemption, gone."

"But you didn't do it!"

His outrage made her smile. "I didn't entertain four different men at a time in my Paris apartment, either," she said. "The truth doesn't always matter."

"We'll fight it," he said. "We'll make those liars eat their words. We'll sue them for libel—Henry will love it."

"*We're* not going to do anything," she said. "*I* probably am going to sue for libel, after he goes to the press. It's going to be a horrible, ugly mess, and the only thing it'll accomplish at the end is that I'll know I finally fought back. You aren't going to be involved."

"Like hell," he said. "Damn it, Alva, look at me."

He crouched on the floor in front of her, tilting her jaw forward with his hand so they were eye to eye. "I'm not going to let you bear the brunt of this," he said. "If there's a scandal, we'll deal with it together. And maybe we can forestall one."

"You're not listening to me," she said. "This is my business, not yours."

"That's not—"

"No. You need to hear me. I told you this because I trust you, because you deserved to know. That's where it ends. You've helped me see I'm worth fighting for, and I'm going to do just that, but I need to do it myself. Alone."

Sam sat back on his heels, his eyebrows coming together. "You're right," he said, his words coming slowly. "I haven't been listening."

"I was wrong to think I could offer you anything," Alva said, and the words sank into him like so many icy pins. "I'm sorry."

"You're ending this," he said. "I thought we were talking about blackmail, and you were talking about us."

She shrugged tightly, her eyes glued to her hands, knitted together in her lap. "It's the same thing," she said.

"It's really not."

"My life is like this, Sam. Scandal and blackmail and dirty fights. There's no room in that for another person."

He stood, moving away from her so he wouldn't give in to the temptation to grab her and hold her so tightly she wouldn't ever leave him. "You've been talking a lot about trust lately, Alva, but I don't think you really know what trust means."

"It isn't about not trusting you," she said, standing and taking a step forward. Her gaze finally lifting to meet his. "Please don't think that. I couldn't—I couldn't think higher of you if I tried. But this kind of life isn't for you."

"You mean you aren't willing to share it."

"No," she said, sitting down again suddenly. "I'm not willing to share my problems with you, if that's what you call dragging you into the middle of a national scandal. They're my problems to deal with."

"So you'll let me in on the good times, but not the bad."

She sighed, deflating slightly in her chair. "These last few days—they were wonderful, Sam. I couldn't have dreamed them better. But it wasn't real life—it was a hotel room and a snow-covered city and a magical restaurant on a block I've never seen. But we're back."

"And you've discovered that what worked for you in a snowy little bubble doesn't work for you outside of it," he replied, his words like acid on his tongue. "This isn't about *real life.* Real life is people leaning on each other when things are hard. It's loving each other so much there's no question about facing things together. It's fighting for each other and with each other and being damned grateful for every morning you wake up together. I've seen *real life*, and it's not what you're choosing. You're choosing fear, and control, because you don't want to get hurt again."

"That's not true," she said, sounding like she was fighting to keep her voice even. "There's a difference between not wanting to be hurt and not wanting to hurt someone else."

"Sure," he said. "Just not in this case."

"You may be right," she said. "Regardless, it's *my* decision."

Sam nodded, all his anger and grief balling up into a chunk of lead in the center of his chest. "Yes. It's your decision." He closed his eyes, struggling to find some place of calm, some wellspring of rationality he could pull from. "I told you once I wasn't going to be angry at you for things you couldn't help. I don't know if this is one of those things, but I do know that I'm angry. I think it's best if I go."

"Be angry," she whispered. "I—I haven't behaved well. For that I'm sorry."

He looked at her, drinking her in even through the anger. "Last time we fought you thought I'd left the project at Liefdehuis. You should know that won't happen this time, either."

Alva's lips compressed like she might be ill, but she nodded. "Thank you for telling me."

After a long gaze, he said, "Good-bye, Alva," and turned to the door. He heard her whisper good-bye right before it shut behind him.

CHAPTER TWENTY-SIX

She didn't know how long she sat after he left. Long enough for twilight to seep into the sky and the chair cushions to become extensions of her body. She stared at the wall opposite, memorizing it. One mantel, local stone. Two vases, one Chinese, one silver. One mirror, framed in gold, tarnishing at the edges. She watched as the light faded from the room entirely, replaced by a palette of charcoal and pewter and black.

It was over, then, whatever *it* had been, over before it had really begun. She'd been lying to herself in New York—and worse, by lying to herself, she'd lied to him.

Was he right, about her sacrificing love for safety, for control? Perhaps, she decided, but what he didn't understand was sometimes a person couldn't bear even one more risk. She could fight Alfred, but she'd rather lose Sam now than risk seeing him changed or hurt later.

The decision had been made. The only thing to do was go on.

Still she sat a while longer, remembering and not crying. There weren't any tears inside of her: only hollowness and cold and the kind of exhaustion that refused sleep.

She'd see him again, she realized, which provoked longing and surprise in equal measure. How could she grieve someone so much and still see him?

How could she grieve someone she'd barely had the chance to love?

"Enough," she whispered, shaking her head and standing. "It's time to end it."

Liefdehuis, the ghost, Sam—they were all tied together. She needed to cut through the knot once and for all, which meant only one thing. She needed to talk to Rose.

She called for Liza and asked for the carriage to be brought around.

In the faded light Liefdehuis was little more than a black hulk rearing high above Alva's head. The air was sharp around her as she walked up the front steps, stabbing little daggers everywhere her coat didn't quite cover.

Inside, the dark pressed close around her. She left the front door open so a sliver of light could leak through, using the mild illumination to spark the oil lamp she'd brought with her. If she came to injury out here, there would be no one coming to her rescue.

Rose had lived here for the first decade of her life, Alva mused as she looked around the dusty wreckage of the interior. She'd talked here, eaten here, slept here. What part of the house would her ghost be drawn to?

A memory, hazy around the edges, drifted through Alva's mind: a beautiful May day when she was nine or ten, seen only through the windows of her room because she'd spoken at dinner, violating her parents' strict rule against child-speech at mealtimes.

The afternoons she'd spent imprisoned in her room, because she'd failed somehow to meet standards she didn't even understand until much later.

If her development had been cruelly arrested at the age of eleven and she were to pick a room to haunt at her parents' house, it would have been that room, the place she'd been sent to so very often, decorated in pink and white ruffles, with a dollhouse she wasn't allowed to play with in the corner.

In her vision for Liefdehuis, there would be two staircases sweeping up from each side of the large elliptical entry room, curling around until they let out a few feet from the upper hallway that looked down on the ground floor through a large central opening. She comforted herself with the image as she slowly made her way through the warren of dark, closed-off rooms towards the one that held the shaky, barely-holding-together current staircase.

Holding her breath, she began to carefully climb, checking each stair for holes and weak wood before putting her weight on it. Even with precautions her boot went through two boards, the second causing her to fall painfully on her left knee. She swore and pulled herself back up, clenching her fists until the worst of the pain had passed, and continued to climb.

She'd only been on the second floor twice, both times in broad daylight. In her memory it was a touch worse than the ground floor: leaks from the roof had slowly eaten away at the ceilings and likely the flooring in several places, and there were distinct signs a family of squirrels had taken up residence in one of the larger bedrooms.

Presently, with the only light coming from her lamp, it seemed much, much worse. Possessions left by previous occupants were scattered around—dusty papers documenting a thirty-year-old trust carpeted the floor, and what had once been a fancy French doll sat in a corner with no arms, no clothes, and one eye, making Alva squeak in horror before she realized what it was.

"Stop it," she reprimanded herself, staring back at the horrible, mangled thing. "You're being ridiculous."

She walked back to the hallway and considered her options. There were six bedrooms on this floor: two large rooms, adjoining, intended for the master and mistress of the house, located on the far west end of the house, and here on the far east side a cluster of four. Rose's room would certainly have been one of them.

There were no closed doors in the hallway: years of neglect and weather had slowly worn away at them, so they either hung drunkenly on their hinges or weren't hung at all, propped up sideways against a wall, perhaps, or missing altogether. Nothing differentiated the rooms from the outside.

She walked into the closest one, and nothing happened. Well, she chided, what was she expecting to happen? There would be a shower of lights, or a ghostly specter floating in the corner of the room? Nothing this ghost had done had been obvious; why on earth would she start making it easy?

Alva stood uncertainly in the empty room, wondering what to do. Her mind flitted from Rose to Helen and it came to her. She needed to use Rose's name.

"Rose?" she called out. "Mary Rose de Boer? I'm not here to hurt you. I only want to talk."

Still nothing. Without any better plan, she walked into the next one and repeated herself. The only answer she received was the sound of the wind curling around the outside of the house.

Two more rooms to go. She walked across the hall into the

next one, tucked at the far end of the passage. It was the smallest of the four, with only one small window, even though it had two outside walls.

"Rose de Boer?" she said, her voice shaky and uneven. "My name is Alva Webster, and I want to talk with you. If you could make yourself known in some way—"

"What are you doing?" The voice came from behind her, and she screamed as she whirled around, clutching the oil lamp like a weapon.

"Calm down," Alfred said, standing in the doorway. "You'd think you'd seen a ghost."

In the scarce light cast by her lamp, it was as though she had. Alfred's blond hair shone like gold, his handsome features made stronger and rougher by the casting of shadows. Her skin twitched, as if it wanted to crawl off her bones and escape.

"Alfred," she said. "What are you doing here? Did you follow me?"

"Your . . . paramour . . . made it difficult to conduct our business," he said, smiling. The light reflected off the smooth enamel of his teeth. "I thought we would benefit from some privacy."

"I'm busy," she said.

"So I see. Going a little mad, are we? I can't say it's a huge surprise."

"What I'm doing is none of your business," she said, gripping the handle of the lamp tightly. "Please leave. I'll call upon you at your hotel later."

"I'm afraid I really can't wait upon your convenience, Sister mine. I must insist we settle matters immediately."

"You must have resorted to one of the less reputable establishments, to be this desperate," Alva said, not bothering to disguise her disgust.

"Now, now," Alfred chided, "speaking of none of your business. It really doesn't matter, does it? What matters is I have all the control in this situation and you have none. I don't know why you persist in playing this childish game when nothing different can come of it."

"Fine," she said, resigning herself. "I suppose now is as good a time as any. You won't be getting any more funds from me, Alfred. Do what you must."

"Alva, dearest, I don't think you've thought this through at all. What in heaven has gotten into your head?"

She shrugged. "I have a new policy against supporting blackmailers."

"I expect you'll find that policy quite hazardous to your health," he said. "I'm not bluffing, you know. I'm quite prepared to go to the press with everything, even if it's only revenge."

"I know," she said. "It's not that I don't believe you. I just don't care enough to do anything about it."

"I see," he said. "I have obviously underestimated your determination to self-destruct. I admit, I'm a little disappointed, Alva dear. I had thought we could conduct this like people of breeding."

"Yes," she said. "The men in your family were always quite interested in breeding, weren't they? But not very much in actual good behavior."

"There's absolutely no need to resort to insults," he said, and Alva could see the cracks appearing in his falsified good humor. "Don't you have any respect for the memory of your dead husband?"

She shrugged. "I hold his memory in precisely the respect it deserves," she said. "We're done here."

"Oh, I'm afraid we're not," he said. "I may prefer to conduct my affairs with a little subtlety, a little sophistication, but it doesn't mean I'm not perfectly capable of trying it the other way, too. I had thought my brother simply lacked finesse in his dealing with you, but I see that for once I've underestimated him. Clearly the only thing you understand is force."

"Take one step closer," Alva said, "and I'll hit you so hard with this lamp you'll be out for a week."

"Ah, the kitten flexes her claws and tries to hiss," Alfred said, and lunged for her, grabbing at her wrist. Alva swung the lamp towards his head, connecting powerfully with his temple. He stumbled to the side, letting go of her as he fell to the floor, and she didn't stop to see if he was still conscious before she ran for the door.

Something pulled at her skirts, yanking her to a halt. As she turned she saw Alfred, still on the floor, blood coming down the side of his face.

"You bitch," he said, pulling so hard on the back of her dress that she stumbled. She grabbed the fabric, jerked it out of his hands, and ran through the door without looking where she was going.

It was dark in the hallway—she'd left her lamp in the room with Alfred—and she could hear him knocking about behind her. He was getting up—she swung around what remained of the top banister—he was leaving the room—she hurried down the stairs—he was right behind her—she turned at the landing—his hand digging into her shoulder—she gasped in pain as *you bitch* slithered into her ear.

She fell, landing painfully on her side, and for a moment she couldn't move. Her vision, barely useful in the dark, blurred completely.

The snow was wet and cold underneath her, and the wind swirled around her body, cutting through her thin dress like it didn't exist. He was behind her, and she had to run, even though she knew for sure she'd never escape him.

She was in the woods, and this time she knew exactly how it would end—with a silver knife glinting in the moonlight.

Still, she ran.

CHAPTER TWENTY-SEVEN

It was over.

The thought kept repeating in his head: *It's over, it's over, it's over, it's over.* As he walked through the front door: *It's over.* As he checked on his experiments: *It's over.* As he continued the modifications on a piece of equipment: *It's over.*

When the knife he was using slipped and skinned his thumb, adding another cut to the scabbing one on his palm, he winced and thought: *It's over.*

He was hollowed out; tired and hollowed out. In the weeks he'd pursued her, he'd never really allowed for the possibility that they wouldn't have a happy ending. Buoyed by what he now recognized as cheerful arrogance, he'd seen their future together stretching forward decades. He'd seen them together as old people, cuddling on a sofa in front of a fire.

He'd been a fool. Their future had an end date, written in bright red letters, standing twenty yards high. He'd see her until his work at Liefdehuis was over, and that would be it.

A poem he'd memorized in school came back to him with

sudden force. *Since there's no help, come let us kiss and part,* it had gone, *Nay, I have done, you get no more of me.*

He heard the door open behind him, clattering as it banged against the sheets of metal sitting next to it. His body jerked around before he was even conscious of what he was hoping to see, but disappointment flooded him when it was only Henry, adding a layer of disgust to his mood.

"I'm working," he said.

"I can see that," Henry said. "I thought you might like to know Maggie was arrested this morning."

Sam dropped the knife and turned to look at Henry properly. The man looked exhausted, his face pale and his clothes lacking their usual crisp perfection. "What?"

"At one of those suffrage marches. The sooner your parents get her out of the city the better, in my opinion."

"But—why did they arrest her, if she was just marching?"

"Marching for suffrage is often more than enough to get a woman arrested." Henry rubbed his face, as if he was trying to increase his energy through friction. "But in this case she chained herself to the railing in front of City Hall. They had to cut the chains with a bolt cutter to drag her off."

"Is she all right? Do we need to—" Sam subsided at Henry's tired waving motion.

"She's out. Fortunately, I was already in town to meet with the city planners, who were gratifyingly concerned about your family's continued willingness to do business with them should there be any difficulty with Maggie's release."

"You pressured them," Sam said, sinking back onto his stool and mustering a weak smile.

Henry shrugged. "They chose to interpret events in a certain way—the correct way, I might add—and I did nothing to dissuade them. Still, it took all damned night, and when I finally managed to get the brat out all she wanted to do was tell me about the *truly fascinating* women she'd met inside."

"Other suffragettes?"

"Prostitutes."

Sam digested this. "It's not like our parents have sheltered her," he finally said. "She knew of their existence."

"They told her, and I quote, 'the funniest stories.'"

"Oh lord."

"Indeed."

The chime of the hallway clock was loud in the silence that fell.

Henry walked across the room to a dusty wooden cabinet; his arm reached inside and emerged with an almost full bottle of whiskey. "So," he said, unscrewing the top as he crossed back to Sam. "I'm guessing it's time for this."

"You warned me," Sam said, taking a long gulp. "You said, even if she wanted to try, she might not be able to trust me enough. Ever. You were right."

Henry nodded, taking a smaller swig of the golden liquid. "I did, yes. Did she try?"

Sam let his mind drift. "Maybe. Yes. She tried. It . . . wasn't enough. For a minute I thought—I thought maybe it would be. But we came back to reality, and—well." He shrugged.

"Reality," Henry said, "is an absolute bitch." He slid the bottle back.

"The worst part is I didn't listen," Sam said. "To her. To you. I could only think—we're so right together. How can that mean nothing? I assumed it would make everything all right. That all the other stuff—if I loved her enough and was patient enough I could make her better, I guess. Stupid. Stupid and arrogant. Even now, listen to me, talking about 'all the other stuff.' That was her *life*, her whole history. You told me. She told me. Everybody in my goddamn life was telling me and all I did was follow her around like a goddamn *puppy*, waiting for her to love me enough in return."

"Sam," Henry said, voice soft. "You know it's not about her loving you enough."

"It has to be. Because if it's not . . . if people can love each other that much and still not be together because of things from before they even met, well, it would be too goddamn tragic." His mouth twisted. "Alva said if people thought the dead could keep tormenting the living, even after they were gone, no one would be able to go on. Well, she was right."

"Is it definitely over?"

"She says it is. And I need to start listening to what she says, instead of thinking I know all the answers." He took another long swig, relishing the angry burn as the liquid ran down his throat.

"I always knew I was lucky," he said quietly. "My parents, my family, you. The money. The intellect. I didn't take it for granted, or at least I thought I didn't. These last few weeks, though, I've realized exactly how lucky I am. Everything's pretty much always worked out for me, and I guess I'm going to have to get used to the idea that this time it might not. It's just . . . I'm not quite sure how to . . . how to stop loving her."

"I don't know that you can. I'm not even sure you should. It's never a bad thing, love. It's just hard when it's not enough."

Sam nodded and took another drink.

"You said it would be worth it," Henry said. "Was it?"

"Yes," Sam said without hesitation. But before he could continue, he was interrupted by a loud knock on the door.

Sam's breath caught wildly, but he ruthlessly dampened his enthusiasm. It was probably only a neighbor, come to peek at the laboratory as they apparently liked to do.

Seconds later, Sally May appeared in the doorway, with a red-faced Liza behind her. "Begging your pardon, sirs"—here Sally May stopped to look appreciatively at Henry—"but here's Liza Mackey from Mrs. Webster's house, come to see you urgently."

"Liza?" Sam stood, frowning. "What's wrong? Is Mrs. Webster all right?"

"Oh, Professor Moore, I tried to talk her out of it, really I did, I reminded her of the last time, and it's not like I haven't told her time and again there's something wrong at that house, although this time you'd think she'd listen, since she's seen it for her own self, but no, she wouldn't hear me, and nothing would do but to head off to the house by herself—"

"Liefdehuis?" The icy clutch of fear squeezed his heart. "She's gone to Liefdehuis, alone?"

"And she looked ever so strange, when she went, and all she would say was that it was time she finished things—"

Sam swore roundly and pushed past the two girls to head for the stables. He already had the saddle on the horse by the time Henry caught up with him.

"What's going on?"

"What's going on is that damn fool woman is so intent on running away from what's between us she's risking her own life to end it," he said, buckling the girth. "She's got some stupid idea about confronting the ghost herself."

"I'm coming, too," Henry said, already leading Sam's second horse out of its stall.

"Fine," Sam said, swinging up onto his mount. "But I'm not waiting."

He urged the horse forward and headed towards Liefdehuis without looking back, memories of Alva's pale, unconscious face flashing before him.

There was a house on the other side of the woods. She'd been there before. As she ran, she could see a flash of golden light through the dark trees, but she never seemed to get any closer to it.

She knew, deep in her bones, that she was never going to see it. Already her breath came in ragged, painful gasps. She was going to die here, surrounded by darkness and damp and cold, and the merrymakers in the golden light would never even hear her scream.

Two more turns of the path, before the tree, the knife, and the closing night.

She knew how this ended.

He was closing in. She could hear his heavy breathing, branches breaking in his pursuit.

"Why are you running?" he called, his voice too smooth for a man who'd been running. "We both know what happens here. Why not stop?"

She wanted to. He was right, after all. There was no point in running—he was going to catch her, like he always did, like he was always going to.

Another shard of light from the house glinted through the twisted branches. If she strained, she could almost make out the warm sound of happy conversation echoing over the snow.

Maybe she could make it this time. The thought pierced her chest painfully as sudden tears streamed down her face, freezing cold in the brutal night air.

Hope was so much worse than acceptance, she thought helplessly. And, after the next turn of the path, she'd have to feel that die, too.

Riding down the drive towards Liefdehuis, Sam searched anxiously for some sign of life from the house, some sign Alva was all right. None met his eyes. The only light came from the moon overhead, casting a weak silver light on the road. The house was nothing but a black monolith in front of him.

What would happen if she was caught in Rose's world for too long? His mind worked frantically through possibilities. There was no way of telling what effect prolonged exposure to this kind of mental disturbance could have on the human mind—even her short experience earlier had left Alva weak and exhausted.

He reined in his horse in front of the house and slid out of the saddle. Alva's carriage sat a few feet away under a tree, barely visible in the deeper shadows. There would be a coachman, he remembered. He'd probably accompanied her inside. At least she wouldn't be alone—

The wave of relief evaporated when he saw the coachman slumped unconscious next to one of the wheels, his face pale in the moonlight, his breathing shallow.

"Damn it," Sam whispered, checking the man's racing pulse. Quickly positioning him so he wouldn't suffocate while unconscious, Sam took off at a run towards the house. The door stood ajar, revealing nothing but darkness and shadows. He paused to light the lantern he'd brought.

"Alva!" he shouted, his heart in his throat. "Alva!"

Only silence met him, soft, dense silence that seemed to suck his own voice into it, muffling his shouts.

Where would she have gone if she was looking for a confrontation with the ghost? She would have gone where she thought Rose would have spent most of her time during the decade she'd lived here, Sam decided, his thoughts racing. Where did little girls spend their time? Maggie had spent hers outside and in their parents' lab, but he didn't think this was standard for upper-class families. When Alva had described her own childhood, most of her time seemed to have been spent with her governess, in a world totally segregated from her parents.

He looked to the right, where the stairs were. The moonlight barely permeated into the house; he could only barely make out the first step. She would have gone upstairs, to find Rose's room. Up those dark, dangerous stairs, into the unknown . . . oh, when he found her they were going to have words.

He hurried up the stairs, dodging the weak spots and holes that appeared in his dim circle of lamplight. He saw where she'd caught her foot and fallen, cursing savagely as he leapt over it. He was so absorbed in avoiding bad spots that he almost missed the pale hand when the light caught it.

"Alva," he said, falling to his knees beside her. She lay twisted on the large landing, as if she'd fallen heavily, her left foot turned awkwardly out in a way that promised a sprain at the very least.

He fumbled with her wrist, his fingers stiff with fear as he searched for a pulse. When he found one he released his breath in a great gust of relief. It was fast and erratic, but she was alive. They'd been here before, he reminded himself. She'd be okay.

"Alva," he said, cupping her face in his hands. Her cheeks were ice-cold. "Honey, I don't know if you can hear me, but I need you to come back. Wherever you are, it isn't real."

He released her, shrugging out of his coat, placing it on top of her, and following it with his jacket, before he drew her into his arms, so she was cocooned by wool on one side and his body on the other. The clinical side of his brain knew that she was too cold and the cold might be more of an immediate risk than whatever was happening inside her head. He looked at the ankle and grimaced. It looked more like a break than a sprain.

"Well, you're not going to be dancing for a few weeks," he said, running his hand over her hair. "Which is a bit of a problem, because as soon as you wake up I'm going to dance you all over this entire house. I guess I'll have to hold you off the floor. We might have to stop for a cast first, but I swear there's going to be dancing, whether your feet can touch the floor or not."

He glanced back down the dark stairs, towards where he knew the door was. The haunting was at least partially contained by location, although the coachman's condition indicated Rose's influence stretched out of the house, maybe even to the property line, about a half mile down the drive. If he could carry Alva down the stairs and off the property, there was a chance Rose's hold would be broken.

There was also a chance the sudden break would do something much worse to Alva's mind. Even more immediately, he had no idea how badly the fall had hurt her, and until he could move her safely he couldn't risk it. Henry had been right behind him, he reminded himself. He'd think to bring a wagon, and they could find a board or something to carry her out on.

Until then, all he could do was keep her warm, and talk to her, and hope she would come back to him.

"Come back to me," he said fiercely. "Come back to me. What you're seeing isn't real; it's only a nightmare. Come on, honey."

The path wavered in front of her, and she stumbled in the snow, confused. This had happened before, she remembered, but it hadn't been real. Alain had never done this.

Alain. The name was something concrete to hold on to in the middle of the confusion. She had a name, too, though it danced just outside her reach. And whatever her name was, it didn't match with what was happening here.

She heard him—who was *him*?—behind her, closing in.

"That's right," he said, his hand landing on her shoulder and spinning her around. The moon glinted off his golden hair. "You can't outrun me. Best get it over with."

"Who are you?" she whispered, her voice rusty and hard to use.

The scene flickered around her, and suddenly she wasn't standing in the middle of a cold wood anymore; she was in her bedroom in the house she and Alain had owned in Paris. *That's right*, she thought. *We're in Paris.* The confused pressure lifted.

A fire crackled behind her, but the heat didn't even touch the cold sitting in her bones.

"I told you not to try me," he said, pushing her against the tastefully papered wall. Despite the light in the room, she had trouble seeing his face—he was Alain, but mushy around the edges. Sometimes he looked like someone else.

"Stop," she said, her voice far away in her own ears.

"No," he said, smiling, and the smile seemed to stretch across his whole face, revealing rows and rows of perfect white teeth. "And do you know what, you stupid bitch? You can't make me."

Slowly, as though he was making sure she could see what he was doing to be afraid of it, he raised his hand to her throat, fitting it carefully against her skin, and applied gentle pressure. She tried to struggle, to move her limbs, but she was frozen in place. It was as though someone had poured lead through her blood.

Gradually the pressure around her throat tightened, until she could barely breathe. Panic crashed through her, her whole world narrowed to the point where his hand met her windpipe.

"You think you're so strong," he said, leaning in so his lips almost touched her cheek. "But look at you. All you can do is cry."

She hadn't realized she was crying but at his words felt the tears running down her cheeks. She scratched at his hands, her air cut off entirely, and once more death was rushing at her. Sobbing and helpless was how she would die, and the shame that enveloped her was the last thing she felt before her vision started to go gray at the edges.

The bedroom door burst open, slamming against the wall, and suddenly the pressure around her throat released. She collapsed, gasping, aware of a scuffle going on around her but barely able to lift her head. When she finally pulled herself up, leaning against the wall behind her, she saw two men savagely wrestling.

He'd come for her, she realized, a small cry coming out of her damaged throat. Sam had come for her.

Sam.

Something caught in the light, a silver glint she remembered. She tried to yell out, to warn Sam, but the only thing her voice could manage was a croak.

Alain brought the knife down, plunging it deep into Sam's chest. Sam staggered back, one step, another. Blood seeped out, staining his white shirt in seconds, and the scream meant to warn him rang out too late as he fell to the floor.

CHAPTER TWENTY-EIGHT

Alva cried out, this time the long, panicked sound of a frightened animal. Sam's own fear took him by the throat, and he held her tighter.

"It's not real," he said, looking anxiously down the stairs as he willed Henry to hurry. "Alva, listen to me. Nothing you're seeing is real."

She'd already been under twice as long as before, maybe more. He'd never felt so helpless before, unable to do anything but wait while the woman he loved battled horrors he couldn't even imagine.

"You're strong," he told her, his voice thick. "It's the first thing I noticed about you. You looked like you were expecting a punch on the jaw and whoever swung first should be damn sure they could swing last, too. Everything about you is strong, Alva. Your beauty, your mind, your spirit. Your heart. Damn it, this is nothing to a woman like you. A little ghost. Throw her off and *get back here to me.*"

She was crying, he realized, tracing the path of her tears with a finger. His own throat clutched when he saw it.

“I love you,” he said, hunched over her as though to protect her with his body. “Come back to me. I love you. Come back to me. . . .”

He repeated the words until they blended together, chant-like. There was nothing he could do but hope.

She rocked back and forth, staring at the body on the floor. It was nothing but a shell. The man she’d loved wasn’t in there anymore.

“No,” she whispered. “No, no, no, no.”

“Oh dear,” Alain said, his face flickering. “Did you like him? You really should have known better, silly cow. Now he’s dead, and it’s all because of you.”

He squatted down next to her, running his bloody hand up her throat, leaving a red smear in his wake.

“There,” he said, giggling. “After all, there’s no need to be subtle, not when it’s just the two of us.”

She stared at him, taking in his smudged edges, and abruptly clarity flooded through her. The fear lifted from her senses, leaving only cold anger behind.

“You’re a puppet,” she said, the words coming more easily. She stood, still looking at him. His face was wrong because it couldn’t decide between Alain and Alfred, she realized. It was as if their faces were layered, one on top of the other. Almost, but not completely, matching.

“You’re not real,” she said.

“So you’ve finally lost your senses,” Alain-Alfred said, rising. “I suppose it was only a matter of time, but I assure you this is very real. Look at your lover’s body. How his eyes stay open in death, staring at you with nothing left behind them.”

She looked at Sam's bloodied body, and the distance she'd gained threatened to collapse. He was dead because of her, she thought. She'd done this.

I love you. Come back to me. I love you. Come back to me.

No.

It wasn't real. Sam wasn't dead, he was waiting for her, and all she had to do was go back to him.

Sam was alive.

The hope slammed into her, and her surroundings wavered, flickering in and out. She was in Liefdehuis, not Paris.

I love you. Come back to me. I love you. Come back to me.

She could hear him, a faint echo at the edge of her senses. He was with her, and if she concentrated hard enough, she could nearly feel his hand on her face.

"Stop," she said. "We're done here. Rose, stop hiding. I know you're here."

"You're raving," Alain-Alfred said, but his faces were shifting so quickly they looked like one congealed beige mass.

"Rose, I'm done talking to your proxies," Alva said, raising her voice. The damage to her throat was gone. "Get out here and speak to me."

It was as if she blinked and suddenly was standing in the frilly bedroom of a little girl. The bed was canopied in white ruffles, a beautiful dollhouse stood aloof in the corner, and sunshine streamed through the large windows. When she looked out of them, she could see an expanse of perfectly green lawn stretching down to riverbanks she recognized. They were back at Liefdehuis, and this was Rose's room.

She heard rustling behind her and turned. In the darkest corner of the room sat an old woman, her white hair cut short around her face, her blue eyes wide and full of fear. The chair she sat in was out of place in the room, plain industrial metal, and behind her the walls changed from the light pink wallpaper of the rest of the room to a stark white paint.

"You can't be here," the woman said, but when she spoke her voice had the high smoothness of a young girl. Alva flinched.

"You're Rose," she said, swallowing her surprise. "I'm Alva Webster."

"I've seen you before," Rose said, rocking back and forth in her chair. "In my dreams."

The woman was trembling, her lashes wet with tears. Alva's anger vanished. Whoever was responsible for what she had experienced, it wasn't this poor creature, the terrified remnants of a terrified life.

Alva pulled another chair over and sat in front of her, leaning forward slightly. "I've come to visit you," she said. "Is that all right?"

Rose bit her lip, hesitating, and nodded. "I guess so. If you have permission. They get mad if you do things without permission."

Alva was surprised to find she had any tears left, but at Rose's simple statement they pressed against her throat. Resolutely she pushed them back down and pinned a cheerful smile on her face. She could feel the sunshine through the window, the first bit of warmth she'd experienced since entering the haunting.

"Do you want to go outside?" Alva didn't know why she asked, except there were no walls outside.

"I'm not allowed," Rose said, looking longingly at the window. "Mother and Father said they'd take me outside, when they brought me here, but nobody ever does."

As she spoke, the rest of the walls flickered to white paint and Alva heard the bangs and painful screams she associated with the Bloomingdale Insane Asylum.

She kept the smile on her face. "There's been a change of rules," Alva said. "You're allowed to go outside now, whenever you want. You don't even have to wait for someone to go with you."

Rose's trembling became more pronounced, until it seemed as though her entire chair was shaking. "Not allowed," she said. "Not allowed, not allowed." Her voice rose in volume with each word so that by the end she was almost screaming. The light from the window faded.

Alva told herself to be calm.

"Rose, it is allowed," she said, attempting to blend compassion and firmness in her voice. "We're going to go outside."

The woman was sobbing, hunched over in her chair, and Alva saw her hands were tied behind her with thin twine that had cut into her skin. Rage burst in her chest.

"I'm going to untie you," she said briskly, "and then we're going outside."

She looked around the room for something to cut with and found a pair of small manicure scissors on the vanity. They would have to do. She crossed the room and touched Rose's shoulder to let her know she was there. The woman gasped at the contact and looked up, her eyes wild and vivid.

"Hold still," Alva said, and hoping desperately Rose would go along with her plan, she leaned over and cut through the twine.

Rose moved her arms in front of her, holding her wrists up in wonder. The deep wounds from the twine healed immediately, so there was nothing but smooth skin.

"It doesn't hurt anymore," she said, looking at Alva. "You made it not hurt anymore."

"It's never going to hurt again," Alva said. "Come on then; the sun's not going to wait for us."

As if on cue, sunlight flooded the room. They were fully back at Liefdehuis once more. Alva crossed to the door and opened it on to a hallway she barely recognized. The walls were painted a light gold, and an intricately patterned rug covered the smooth wooden floor. This was Rose's Liefdehuis, Alva realized.

She stood in the doorway and looked back at Rose, smiling. The woman stood slowly from her chair, looking at it cautiously, as though it might reach up and drag her down. When it didn't, she jumped away from it, out of whatever reach it might have.

"Ready?"

Rose nodded tentatively and followed her into the hall. Alva led the way to the stairs, remembering her own recent flight down a very different version of them. When she crossed the landing, an ornate, perfectly polished iteration of it, she heard Sam's voice.

I love you, he said. *Come back to me.*

I will, she promised, and kept walking.

They crossed through the dining room and two small sitting rooms before they reached the entrance. Three steps from the front door it changed, into a heavy metal door with a small barred window at the top.

"I'm not allowed to leave," Rose said weakly, and when Alva glanced at her she saw tears rolling down her cheeks. "They won't let me."

"Of course they will," Alva said, closing her eyes and sending one quick prayer to whoever might be listening. "I have the key."

Keeping her eyes closed, she reached into the pocket of her skirts. A *key,* she thought, *a key that will open this door.*

Her hands closed around metal, and she had to choke down the shout of triumph that threatened to erupt from her throat. Rose wanted to leave, too, and desperately wanted to believe she could. Enough that this key had appeared when it was wished for.

Alva took the key out as if it wasn't miraculous at all and fitted it in the lock. When she turned it there was an enormous groaning sound, like an entire factory of machines had come to a stop all at once, and the door swung open.

Sunlight beamed through the opening, bathing the two women in its warm, loving light, and Alva reached back, took Rose's hand, and stepped outside.

It was a perfect summer day. The smell of grass and dried dirt hit Alva first, followed by the sight of the lazy river, rolling along under the sun as though it hadn't anywhere better to be. There were birds singing in the trees, and some children in the distance launching model boats onto the water. Rose clung to Alva's hand, and when Alva turned to look at her she saw Rose's gaze locked on the building behind her rather than the perfect scene in front.

Alva followed her gaze, looking up at a huge stone building that flickered between Liefdehuis and Bloomingdale. "You don't have to go back there," she said. "Ever."

Rose jerked around, staring at Alva. "Mother and Father released me?" she breathed, as though she didn't dare to hope.

"I don't know where your parents are," Alva admitted, hoping the news wouldn't trigger anything. Somehow she knew, on this point, it was important to be honest. "You released yourself."

"I can do that?" Rose asked, her voice barely louder than a whisper.

"Yes," Alva said, nodding hard and unable to stop her tears now. "Yes, you can."

Rose looked up at the enormous building, and before their eyes it vanished.

"Come on," she said to Alva, smiling tentatively. "Do you want to fly a kite?"

"More than anything," Alva answered, and they ran across

the grass together, feeling the sun on their backs and summertime freedom in the air.

After that, events seemed to blend together. They flew a kite, raced model boats on the river, lay on the grass, and traced shapes out of the clouds, but everything seemed to happen all at once, so Alva was hardly aware of time passing. Soon the sun was dipping below the low hills on the horizon.

"I'm tired," Rose said. Over the course of the afternoon she'd grown younger and younger, and her voice had grown older and older, until the woman lying on the grass next to Alva looked and sounded about thirty years old. Alva suspected Rose was emulating her, adjusting her own behaviors until they seemed to fit. "This has been the best day I have ever had."

"I'm so glad," Alva said, giving a genuine smile.

"I'm going to rest," Rose said. "Thank you, Alva."

"You're welcome, Rose. Sleep well."

"I will."

CHAPTER TWENTY-NINE

When Alva came back to him, Sam had been sitting on the landing for a little over an hour. Twenty minutes before, when he had told Alva to come back to him she had murmured, "I will." Henry had arrived shortly thereafter, but after Sam heard Alva talk to him she had warmed up considerably, and he decided to let her stay where she was. Strength and vitality ran though her, and that was enough. He had to trust her.

It was the hardest decision he'd ever made, and when she finally blinked her eyes and shifted the relief that crashed through him was so violent he couldn't do anything except stare at her.

"Hello," she said, her voice soft.

He made some choking noise in response, and she shook her head and sat up. He had enough presence of mind to help, steering her so she was leaning against his chest.

"Alva," he managed, but she shook her head once more.

"No, don't talk," she said. "I have a few things I need to tell you, and it'll be easier if I get them out of the way at once."

Her slightly imperious tone sounded so much like the Alva he loved that still more relief coursed through his blood, and he laughed with gladness.

"Oh, sure, laugh all you want," she said, but she smiled back at him. "All right. First, Rose is gone. I don't fully understand it, but I . . . I think she's at rest now." When he opened his mouth to respond she put her finger up to it, silencing him.

"Second," she said, clearing her throat, "I . . . I was wrong, Sam. I was so damnably wrong about us." She looked down, as if collecting her thoughts, and the beginnings of hope stirred inside his chest. "You were right. I was terrified, of you, of us, of losing you. Of hurting you somehow, like Alain hurt me." She paused, her straight, dark eyebrows compressed in thought.

"I don't fully understand that, either," she said carefully. "But it wasn't about not trusting you. It was about not trusting myself."

"Alva—"

"You'll have plenty of time to talk in a minute," she said. "I'm trying to apologize here. The point is, I'm sorry. And I hope you'll have me back, but if you don't—" She swallowed, taking a deep, steadying breath. "If you don't, I'll understand."

She rushed on before he could interject. "Third, and this is a sort of branching third, you understand, an if/then third, if you *will* take me back, we should get married. But we might have to wait a few weeks, because *fourth*, good lord my ankle hurts, which leads me to believe I've broken or sprained it or something, which means I won't very well be able to walk up an aisle."

There was a silence while Sam stared down at her and tried to understand exactly how much his life had just changed. It was only when she grew tense in his arms that he remembered to speak.

"Nonsense," he said. "I'll carry you."

She jerked her head up to look at him, and time hung between them for several heartbeats as he waited for her to understand. Finally, she smiled, a beautiful, perfect, happy smile, and he knew, in that moment, he'd be able to see her smile at him for the rest of his life.

"That's settled, then," she said, her tone businesslike but her eyes beaming through tears. "Although you really are mad if you think I'm going to be hauled up a wedding aisle like a sack of flour. You'll simply have to wait a few weeks. It's not as though I'm going to deny you my bedchamber, and the servants will overlook the scandal so long as we're engaged . . . or once they hear the man in my bed is the *famous Professor Samuel Moore*."

Before Sam could laugh, there was a mild throat-clearing noise, and Sam remembered Henry was sitting only a few feet away. Alva looked over in surprise and, much to Sam's delight, blushed.

"I'm so sorry, Mr. Van de Berg, I didn't see you there," she said, attempting to squirm out of Sam's grasp and failing.

"Please don't think anything of it," Henry said, looking distinctly smug, as though he had somehow brought about this favorable result all on his own. Sam would remember to take him down a peg or two later. "It's very dark in here; I'm sure you're hardly able to see me. But on that point, if I might ask, who does that hand belong to?"

Sam and Alva both followed Henry's gaze. A hand barely fell into the circle of light emanating from the lantern, and when Sam squinted he could make out the body attached. In his concern for Alva, he hadn't even noticed. "What the—"

"Oh," Alva said, and pushed away from Sam so she might look properly. "It's Alfred Webster. He followed me here to renew his blackmail demands and, when I refused, became rather rough with me."

"He did what?" Sam said slowly, standing up and walking over to the unconscious man.

"He attacked me, and I hit him on the head with my lantern," Alva said, as calmly as though she were relating the events of a rather dull tennis match. "Then he chased me down the stairs, and I think he grabbed me, but I fell into the haunting. He must have, too."

Sam reached down and unceremoniously dragged the man into the circle of light. His head hit the floor a little roughly, and his eyes blinked open.

"Not again," he said, staring at the three people standing above him and curling in on himself. "Not again, please, no more, I can't take any more."

He burst into tears, and Sam looked at Alva, bemused.

"Rose drew people into their own fears," she said, staring down at the writhing man with a blank expression on her face. "Mine were bad enough. Imagine how full of fear a man like Alfred must be."

They continued to look down at him as he sobbed, screaming for invisible people to stop whatever it was they were doing to him.

"He doesn't seem quite right," Henry said.

"He never was," Alva said. "But somehow I don't think he'll be a problem ever again."

"I imagine Rose didn't like bullies very much," Sam said, glancing at Alva for confirmation.

"No," she said, slowly. "I don't think she did."

"Well, I can't very well beat him bloody in the condition he's in," Sam said, coming to a quick conclusion. "But just in case—Henry, this man was blackmailing Alva with a pack of dirty inferences and lies he was threatening to take to the press. Pressure him, please."

"My pleasure," Henry said, stepping smartly forward and

leaning down so that he was only a few feet above Alfred's head. "Mr. Webster, my name is Henry Van de Berg, Mrs. Alva Webster's attorney. I've been authorized to acquaint you with the New York State statutes relating to blackmail, as well as the penalties and damages relating to them. As you may be aware, extorting property from a person by accusing them of a crime is illegal under New York Penal Code section One-fifty-five. . . ."

"Sam," Alva said, looking away from Alfred as if he were nothing but a bit of spilled water on the floor. "Will you carry me out?"

"Of course," he said, reaching down and carefully lifting her into his arms. "You don't need to—er—witness this? For your own peace of mind?"

"No," she said, touching his cheek with her finger and smiling at him. "My mind doesn't need to have anything to do with him. Take me outside, won't you?"

Carefully he picked his way down the rest of the stairs and through the rooms by the light of a moon that suddenly seemed to permeate the house a little better. When they got outside, she told him to stop and tilted her head up so she could see the stars. "Rest in peace, Mary Rose de Boer," she whispered, before looking back at Sam.

"Fifth," she said, "I love you."

It turned out it was actually very awkward to kiss someone when you're holding her and trying not to jostle an injured ankle, but Sam managed it, with great enthusiasm, and continued to manage it until he heard a window slam open several feet above them and Henry shout out that he could drag Alfred (actually, he used a much ruder word) down the stairs, but it would be easier if Sam came and helped him, if only Sam could be bothered to stop kissing Alva for a minute. Sam wasn't at all sure he could be bothered, but Alva laughed and pulled away.

"Go," she said. "I'll be right here."

So he put her down on the seat of the wagon Henry had very thoughtfully brought, and since she was so pretty, and since she was going to marry him, he just looked at her until she laughed again and rapped him gently on the forehead.

"I love you, too," he said, and kissed her one more time, and the kiss lasted so long Henry had to put his head out the window and shout.

EPILOGUE

A year later . . .

It was dark outside Liefdehuis, pitch black, without a moon in sight. Alva stood looking at the house, shivering inside her coat, with her arms crossed.

"If you don't hurry up you're going to turn your wife into an icicle!" she shouted.

"Almost there," Sam's voice returned. "And it's barely below freezing."

She rolled her eyes and smiled to herself, pulling her coat more tightly. "Are you sure you did it right? I've heard electricity is complicated."

As her words echoed across the snow, the windows of Liefdehuis lit up, as if thousands of candles had been set aflame all at once. She gasped.

Clear, clean light reflected off the snow, as though the sun had gotten bored with night and had decided to make a surprise appearance. She couldn't tear her eyes away, simply staring at the sight in front of her until she heard Sam walking across the snow towards her.

"It's beautiful," she whispered. "It's the most beautiful thing I've ever seen."

"Not me," he said, winding an arm around her waist and looking down at her before turning his attention to the house. "But it's not bad."

The house was done, and as soon as she wrote the final section on electrical lighting the book would be done, too. Unsurprisingly, the marriage of the recently scandalous Mrs. Alva Webster and the famous inventor Mr. Samuel Moore had resulted in an enormous amount of press. What was surprising, Alva thought, was how positive it had all been—it seemed as though Sam's innate goodness really was infectious. The publisher was thrilled, with the publicity and the early drafts, and was already urging her to sign a deal for several more books focusing on interior design. She had Henry reading over the contracts.

She let her eyes run over the front of the house, enjoying the ability to see so clearly in the night. The light reflected off the metallic letters they had hung over the entrance.

"Rose House," she said to herself, and grinned when Sam squeezed her waist. "When I bought it I thought I was buying it to live in. This is better."

With Rose House finished, Alva would be turning the keys over to the manager of the trust she and Sam had created, dedicated to the compassionate care of people suffering from mental disturbances. The town of Hyde Park had been surprisingly accepting of the idea when Alva had first brought it to them, and adapting the house so it could welcome more inhabitants than originally intended had also been a smooth process. Rose House would be a beacon of care in a medical field too little understood and too often dominated by violence and ignorance.

"Of course, with this project complete, I'll finally have time to start the design work on our own house," she said.

Sam pretended to groan, but it was barely out before he spoke. "Actually, about my laboratory building . . ."

"Nothing will be done to your lab without your express permission," she said, laughing and pulling his head down to kiss him. It had been a year and still her whole body sang when she touched him.

When they broke apart, she turned and he wrapped both arms around her waist, drawing her close. She leaned back against him, suddenly feeling warm and cozy. "I hope she's happy, wherever she went," she said.

"I believe she is," he said.

Alva nodded and looked up at the sky, before she turned her head up and kissed Sam again.

"Fifth," she murmured against his mouth, "I love you."

"Fifth," he agreed, "I love you, too."

ABOUT THE AUTHOR

Lantz Simpson

DIANA BILLER lives in Los Angeles with her husband and their very good dog. *The Widow of Rose House* is her debut novel.